THE
SECOND KOREAN
WAR

BY TED HALSTEAD

To my son Adam, for his love and the highest compliment an author can receive - "You wrote this?"

To my father Frank, for his love and for repeatedly prodding me to finally finish this book.

To my mother Shirley, for her love and support.

To my daughter Mariam, for her continued love and encouragement.

To my wife Saadia, for her love and support over more than thirty years.

CHAPTER ONE

Tunnel No. 1, North Korea

Lee Ho Suk had been working in the tunnels for so long that he had a hard time remembering life before his arrest. It was all a blur - the arrest in the middle of the night, the trial where he had read the confession he was handed by the prosecutor, and the sentence of life at hard labor handed down by the judge. Lee had no idea what he had done to provoke the authorities, not that it mattered now. He could have been denounced by anyone in his village, for no other reason than the denouncer's desire to ingratiate himself with Party officials. His only certainty was that he would never see his wife and two children again.

As far as he knew, Lee was unique in surviving more than a matter of months serving a hard labor sentence digging infiltration tunnels from North Korea to the South Korean enemy. He had always been lean and wiry, and was able to get by on less than what most countries would call an average diet. In North Korea's constant state of famine or near famine, that helped explain how he had stayed alive long enough to reach adulthood and get arrested. More than that, though, he had always been able to endure more than most of the other villagers. Maybe it was envy of that ability that had led to his denunciation.

However, Lee's toughness was not enough to explain his survival, and he knew it. Instead, it was his skill at sensing dangers in the tunnels long before his comrades had any hint. Lee had not been able to see or smell the methane gas that accumulated in one tunnel, but had yelled for everyone to get out just before an idiot guard lit his cigarette with spectacular results. He saw no cracks or falling dirt, but again screamed a warning just before another tunnel's collapse. These were the first of many times that Lee had given enough warning for most guards and prisoners to escape tunnel disasters that would have otherwise killed all inside.

As a result, the guards gave Lee enough food and clothing to survive even the brutal North Korean winters, and he was spared the beatings that were often fatal to the other weakened prisoners. The guards did so because they were required to spend time in the tunnels with the prisoners, not because there was a real chance that the exhausted and malnourished men would suddenly tunnel their way to freedom, but because that is what the guards' regulations required. No guard would ever dream of acting against regulations, because they knew better than anyone the penalty for disobedience – becoming one of the prisoners they guarded.

Digging tunnels was almost always done with hand tools, both because construction equipment was scarce and expensive and because it was noisy. So, Lee had been surprised when he was moved to what the guards called in hushed whispers "Tunnel No. 1" that it had equipment that worked well, had muffled engine components, and even some specialist workers who were not prisoners. It was much deeper than the other tunnels where Lee had worked, and had a camouflaged entrance. Travel time from the entrance to the work site was so long that each work shift was two days long, with a seven hour break midway for sleep, and a twelve hour exit from the tunnel allowed only after three shifts.

None of these changes worried Lee, but another one did. The guards were anxious, and conversations Lee overheard confirmed his guess that they had been told to speed up work. Working prisoners to death in the tunnels was routine, but this time that was not the goal. Instead, Lee realized that this tunnel's progress was important to whoever gave the guards their orders. He did not know what the impact of the tunnel's high priority would be on him, but suspected it would not be good. Lee's predictions were usually grim, and unfortunately usually right.

The North Pacific

Captain Jim Cartwright frowned as he looked at the sonar display showing the North Korean *Romeo* class submarine they had been shadowing for the past week. Not because there was any chance they had been spotted. Cartwright was a firm believer in the proposition that the best fight was one that was as unfair as possible. There could hardly be a more lopsided contest than the one between the *USS Oregon* and a *Romeo* class sub built in North Korea from Chinese parts based on 1950s Russian technology. As the first Block IV *Virginia* class attack submarine to be completed, *Oregon* incorporated numerous upgrades to both passive sonar and propulsion that made its detection by the North Korean sub close to impossible, unless Cartwright or his crew made a mistake.

The US Navy was not in the habit of assigning personnel to its latest and greatest submarines who routinely made mistakes. In fact, one of the reasons Cartwright had been given command of the *Oregon* was that he had the distinction of being the only US naval officer to never miss a torpedo shot in any exercise over his entire career.

One exercise commander, determined to puncture Cartwright's reputation, even set one target outside the Mk-48 torpedo's rated range. Instead of complaining, Cartwright manually reset the torpedo's speed below its normal minimum to conserve fuel, and adjusted its proximity fuse to detonate when there was any chance of damaging the target. Post exercise analysis showed the torpedo ran out of fuel and coasted the last fifteen feet needed to reach the target's new proximity limit. Cartwright was awarded a hit by the exercise judges, and the exercise commander was later given a written reprimand that effectively ended his career.

In spite of this record Cartwright was frowning because, like nearly every serving US naval officer, he had never fired at another vessel. ISIS and the Taliban didn't have navies. Countries like Russia and China that did hadn't fought naval battles with the U.S.

Still, Cartwright's instructions were clear. Unless he got new orders in the next twenty-four hours, he was to sink the sub he had just been looking at on sonar, using sufficient force to ensure there could be no survivors.

Vladivostok, Russia

Vladimir Timoshenko hated the Russian winter. Bad enough at the best of times, the wind howling in from Vladivostok's harbor made this midnight meeting at a railroad switching yard truly miserable.

At least, Timoshenko thought, the money he'd make from tonight's sale would guarantee a warm future. He had sold a lot of Russian arms since the collapse of the old USSR, but this item was worth more than all the rest put together.

There had been much talk of "loose nukes" since the end of the Soviet empire, but few understood just how misleading the term was in practice. Certainly security was not what it was during the Cold War, but that did not mean it had disappeared. There were still plenty of Russian officers who took their responsibilities seriously, and even more who feared the price of getting caught stealing a nuclear weapon – a bullet in the back of the head, after a very short trial.

Even more critical was that without arming codes, nuclear weapons were much less valuable. Of course, the highly enriched uranium the weapon contained would still fetch a fair price, but extracting it took more technical skill and equipment than terrorists possessed, or even most states. Timoshenko chuckled dryly as he thought about Chechen and Palestinian attempts to do just that which had cost them some of their most talented operatives. Radiation sickness was not a pretty way to die.

Timoshenko stood a bit straighter as he thought about his greatest accomplishment. That was ensuring Russian military records did not show the tactical nuclear weapon in the back of the van was missing, or indeed had ever existed. It had been a stroke of genius to pick as his target the small and nearly forgotten inventory of weapons marked for use against Japan, ones that were from the first generation of these devices. They had never been updated or replaced, because Soviet doctrine came to regard Japan's military as a comparatively negligible threat once China both obtained nuclear weapons and ceased being a Soviet ally. Best of all, since they were low-yield weapons nobody expected to use, the arming codes had not been changed for years and were available to any officer at the storage facility near Vladivostok who took the time to find them.

It had been necessary to first bribe and then eliminate several Russian officers to erase all records of the weapon from the storage facility, and to obtain the arming codes. Timoshenko's last task after tonight's delivery would be to locate and kill the sole officer who had realized that the "accidents" suffered by the other officers were good reason to disappear. Then, Timoshenko thought, he could finally enjoy a well-earned retirement in one of the many warm countries ready to welcome anyone with money to spend.

A third of his payment had previously been wired into Timoshenko's Swiss account, and with tonight's delivery of the weapon and the arming codes he would become a very wealthy man. Russia was finally catching up with the times, and Timoshenko had already used his laptop to confirm that Vladivostok's wireless Internet cell signal penetrated even into this switching yard, so he could use his laptop to access his account and confirm that the fund transfer had taken place.

The North Koreans could be counted on to pay. Timoshenko knew they could also be relied on to tie up loose ends like him the same way he had done with the accident-prone Russian officers, so he had taken out an insurance policy. Lying prone on a container within easy range of his scope was an excellent sniper who Timoshenko had known since they were posted together in the old East Germany. If anyone can keep me safe, Timoshenko thought, Victor can.

Headlights moving towards him signaled that the North Koreans were, as usual, nothing if not punctual.

The man Timoshenko knew only as "Mr. Kim" got out of the dark sedan, quickly flanked by two much larger Korean guards with bulges in their jackets that said "We're armed" as clearly as dual revolvers worn on the hip.

"Good evening, Mr. Timoshenko," Kim said. "I trust all is in order?"

"The weapon is in the van and the codes will be e-mailed immediately following payment, just as we agreed," Timoshenko replied. "You are welcome to examine the weapon."

Kim nodded. "I shall do just that."

Timoshenko watched as Kim entered the van, took out several small instruments and began his inspection. It took no more than fifteen minutes before Kim reemerged, smiling.

"Well, it is old, but appears to be in perfect working order," Kim said.

"I am glad you are pleased, but you know what I need more than your approval," Timoshenko replied.

"Of course, of course!" Kim laughed, as he took out a small laptop, balanced it on the hood of the van and began to type rapidly.

Timoshenko's heart started racing as the balance displayed on his laptop screen suddenly jumped upward. Over two years of work, but the payoff had certainly been worth it.

"Now, you will please e-mail me the access codes," said Kim, still smiling.

"Yes, just a moment," Timoshenko responded, as he pulled up the already drafted e-mail and hit send.

A soft chime from Kim's laptop a few moments later announced the e-mail's arrival. Kim read the e-mail intently, and compared it to a paper he pulled from his coat pocket.

"Very well," Kim said, "It appears that these codes are at a minimum correctly formatted. With a weapon this old, I prefer not to arm and disarm it for a more conclusive test."

Timoshenko drew himself up indignantly and replied, "I went to a great deal of trouble to get these codes, and I guarantee they are absolutely authentic."

Kim looked at the Russian arms dealer thoughtfully and said, "I believe you, not least because we have heard about several deaths of Russian officers over the past few months in this area. All accidents of course," he said smiling.

Timoshenko's thoughts went from his bank account to his health in an instant, as he could see in Kim's smile that an accident has been planned for him too.

"You may kill me, but my man has been instructed to shoot the smallest Korean first," Timoshenko said in a low, firm voice.

Kim nodded back over his shoulder at one of his guards who reached into their sedan and, to Timoshenko's horror, pulled out a sniper rifle with blood on the stock.

"It appears that you should have kept in closer touch with your friend," Kim said. "Mr. Oh here has seen to it that he will not be interfering with our discussion."

"Now, I will give you instructions for returning the funds we have just sent you, and in return I promise that Mr. Oh will be...gentle, and quick."

It only took one look at Oh for Timoshenko to realize that he had no options left – none at all.

CHAPTER TWO

Vladivostok, Russia

Anatoly Grishkov sighed as he looked at the folders overflowing his battered wooden desk. When he was growing up he always knew he wanted to be a policeman, just like his father. He had many colorful stories about what it was like to be on the street keeping the country safe for good Soviet citizens. He even looked like his father, with his thick black hair, dark eyes and a face his wife said had "character." Also like his father, Anatoly was just a bit shorter than the average Russian, which his father had joked made him a harder target.

Well, his father's USSR was now Russia. While it may have been glorious to be a policeman in a police state, being a detective in a quasi-capitalist country run jointly by current and former KGB (now FSB), organized crime, and the oligarchs who controlled the oil and gas industry was something else again.

When he was promoted from being an ordinary policeman to detective he thought it was simply a great honor, and in some ways it was. Becoming the lead homicide detective for the entire Vladivostok region at the tender age of forty, even more so.

What Grishkov did not understand until it was too late, though, was how little time he would get to spend away from his desk as his responsibilities increased. It became more about managing the detectives who reported to him, and making sense of the mass of paper that flowed across his desk daily.

Managing meant training his detectives, setting them on the right path in their investigations, brainstorming with them when every trail came up dry, praising them when they succeeded, and giving them constructive criticism when they failed. The paper was reports to Grishkov of investigations both interim and complete, from Grishkov to his boss Captain Boris Ivansik of their progress, and a blizzard of forms requiring his signature that accounted for all the resources consumed by his division.

Today, though, all that paled in the face of Grishkov's biggest problem, dealing with Boris when he was angry and would not listen to reason. As always, that meant a trip to Ivansik's office, which while not luxurious was at least carpeted and furnished with a desk set made in this decade.

"Anatoly, I need you to listen to me while I say this slowly, so you can finally understand. There are no murders to investigate, and you need to stop wasting time and detectives so we can move on to real cases!" Ivansik fumed.

"Well, Captain, I think three officers from the same unit having "accidents" at the rate of one every few weeks are more than just a coincidence, and if you would approve the forensic tests I requested we could prove it. Plus, don't forget that a fourth officer went missing a few days after the last so-called accidental death, and may be dead too," replied Grishkov.

"Enough maybes! I have a real murder for you to focus on, and it is now your top priority. This man's head and torso were picked up by a fishing trawler a few miles offshore. The autopsy shows the body had been weighted, but a combination of decomposition and hungry fish separated the parts that ended up in the net from the weights," Ivansik said.

Grishkov quickly skimmed through the file, which gave time of death at about a week ago, and cause of death a single gunshot to the head.

"Why did this file come to you directly rather than through me, Captain? That is not procedure," Grishkov asked.

"That is why I am discussing this case with you in person. There is another file on this Vladimir Timoshenko, one classified well over your clearance level. Even for me, parts have been redacted," Ivansik said, as he took out a page from another file and waved it at Grishkov so he could see it contained large blacked-out sections.

"So, I will give you the key points. Timoshenko was one of the most successful arms dealers to emerge from the old USSR. He was able to operate successfully for so long because he usually worked alone, and was careful about his customers. We never considered him a high priority for prosecution because he never sold to Russia's enemies, and in fact spent most of his time outside Russia. It is not in the file, but I have heard that he also made certain friends in Moscow," Ivansik said, as he arched one eyebrow.

"And one of those friends gave you that file," Grishkov stated rather than asked.

"Anatoly, I knew there was a reason I promoted you to head of detectives," Ivansik smiled.

"Captain, surely there is a connection between the death of this Timoshenko and the three officers at the munitions depot! We must ask for an inventory at once!" exclaimed Grishkov.

"Now you will see why I am a captain," Ivansik said, still smiling. "At my request an inventory has just been completed, conducted under General Vasyukov, who arrived at the depot only last month and so has every incentive to find missing weapons that can be blamed on his predecessor. I have just spoken with him, and can tell you he was very disappointed to find all is as it should be. I think he was already polishing that second star," Ivansik said with a laugh.

"Captain, it is a great relief to hear that. I have heard that even nuclear weapons are stored there," Grishkov said, his voice lowered.

"Anatoly, sometimes you hear too much," Ivansik scowled, but then relented. "Yes, I have heard this too. It is why I was so quick to contact General Vasyukov. However, now that this depot with the dead officers has been ruled out, we need to investigate further. There are tons of munitions on Russian Navy ships berthed in Vladivostok harbor. There are other, smaller depots within a short distance of Vladivostok. We also cannot rule out the possibility that the weapons were shipped to Vladivostok as a transit point, either by sea or more likely by rail. Air is much less likely, due to tighter security, but should also be investigated as a last resort. Bottom line- I want to know what Timoshenko was doing in Vladivostok, and with an arms dealer that almost certainly means what was he either selling or buying. Find out who Timoshenko was dealing with, and you will have found his killer."

The North Pacific

Cartwright started awake as he felt a hand shake his arm.

"Captain, the *Romeo* has moved to periscope depth, and has extended its antenna," Lieutenant Fischer told him. Short and thin with sandy hair, Cartwright thought for maybe the hundredth time that Fischer looked like a much better fit for submarines than an officer like him who stood 6'2" without shoes. As he sat up and ran his hand through his closely cut, prematurely graying hair Cartwright gave thanks once again to modern Navy design, which had ended the height limitation that a generation ago would have prevented his service on submarines.

Now he just had to remember every now and then to duck. As an ensign he had encountered a high pressure air conditioning vent at eye level that switched on at the precise time needed to freeze one of his contact lenses to his eyeball. A corpsman had finally been able to get the lens loose with the help of nearly an entire bottle of saline solution.

Cartwright had Lasik surgery as soon as that deployment ended.

"How sure are you that they've deployed their antenna?," Cartwright asked.

Fischer grinned. "Really sure, Captain. I don't think they've lubricated that hunk of metal since they put the sub together. You should really hear the recording - at low volume, of course."

Cartwright shook his head, smiling. "I'll take your word for it. No new orders for us?"

Fischer's grin disappeared immediately. "No, sir. Do you think we're likely to get some, sir?"

Cartwright shook his head again. "No, Fischer, I don't. I'll stop by sonar in a moment."

Correctly taking this as his cue to depart, Fischer nodded and left.

Cartwright chewed at his lower lip. He knew why he would have to sink the North Korean sub. He understood there could be no survivors. His orders explained this.

They also explained why he would then have to do the last thing a submarine captain wanted to do after sinking an enemy sub.

He would have to surface.

Vladivostok, Russia

Grishkov pulled up to Timoshenko's hotel in his official GAZ Volga Siber, a black sedan assembled in Russia from American, Mexican and Russian parts. A British redesign of the Chrysler Sebring, the best Grishkov could say for it was that at least it had wipers for its headlights, which made driving in Vladivostok's endless winter a bit less dangerous. And, of course, it was a huge step up from the ancient Lada that Grishkov had been driving before his last promotion.

Grishkov marched up to the front desk and displayed his credentials to the clerk, whose name tag said "Mike". Grishkov would have bet a month's pay "Mike" was the Western name closest to his Russian one, used in a bid to improve rapport with the hotel's mostly European, American and Australian guests.

"So, Mike, did you get the call from my secretary to keep the cleaning staff away from Timoshenko's room?" asked Grishkov in English.

"My name is Mikhail, and Mr. Timoshenko's room was cleaned days ago. His belongings are still there because his credit is good, and he had told us he would likely stay for another week. Nobody has set foot in the room since your office called." the clerk replied in Russian.

"Ah, a spine. Good. Too many Russians working for foreign businesses seem to have had them surgically removed." said Grishkov.

"Do you wish me to accompany you to the room, or do you just want a keycard?" the clerk asked.

"I'll take the card." said Grishkov.

Grishkov's head swiveled around as he looked for anything out of the ordinary in Timoshenko's room, but he could see nothing. Sighing, he pulled out a pair of tin snips to remove the surprisingly weak locks from Timoshenko's suitcases. It probably meant there was little inside them worth stealing.

Ten minutes later, Grishkov had confirmed his guess. Aside from clothing, there was nothing but a one line "Wish you were here" postcard with no return address. No laptop, no address book, no map- nothing that would give him a lead, or any idea of where to go next. Of course, so many days had passed since Timoshenko's body washed up on the beach that any such item could have been removed from the room by his killer.

Bribing a maid for a keycard would have made entry undetectable, and the only security cameras were in the hotel's entrance and elevator.

Grishkov tossed Timoshenko's belongings onto the luggage cart he had brought from the lobby, except for the postcard, which he put in his jacket pocket. Something about it bothered him, but he wasn't sure what. Grishkov had learned from experience that when something nagged at him, it was usually best to put it aside for a while and let his subconscious worry at it, like a dog trying to get the marrow from a bone. Eventually, the answer would come – he hoped.

The North Pacific

"Captain, *Romeo* is blowing tanks. Assess she's preparing to surface," Lieutenant Fischer said calmly.

Cartwright nodded in acknowledgement, outwardly appearing to be just as calm. He suspected Fischer's calm was just as much an act as his, but in any case approved. Especially at a time like this, the crew needed to see that the boat was in steady hands.

Cartwright had been hoping it wouldn't come to this. The only circumstance under which he would have been allowed to avoid sinking the *Romeo* would have been if it had failed to surface. That would have meant the analysis the National Security Agency had made of the intercepted North Korean navy communication had been wrong. His orders had been based on the belief that a sub from what was normally a brown water navy that hugged the North Korean coastline came to the middle of the North Pacific for one specific reason.

To monitor the performance of a North Korean intercontinental ballistic missile (ICBM) during its terminal reentry phase, including impact. The ICBM would be broadcasting encoded telemetry giving the information North Korean scientists needed to see what had gone well and what had not, but the limited power available to transmit the signal meant the data had to be collected no more than ten miles from the point of impact.

This was data the North Koreans could not be allowed to have.

Cartwright looked around the control room at the pilot and copilot, the officer of the deck and the other crew members about to join him in making history.

"Designate *Romeo* as target *Sierra One*. Prepare tubes one and two for firing. This is not a drill."

Cartwright watched and listened silently as acknowledgements and reports confirmed what he already knew from dozens of drills - it would take only a few minutes to prepare the *Oregon* to fire.

As the last "Ready, Captain," came in, Cartwright unconsciously braced himself against a railing and said, "Fire tubes one and two, target *Sierra One.*"

CHAPTER THREE

Yongbyon, North Korea

Manfred Werzel peered through his binoculars at the distant Yongbyon nuclear complex. During the years he had been working for the International Atomic Energy Agency, or IAEA as everyone called it, he had visited Yongbyon several times, starting in 1994. It was the heart of North Korea's nuclear program both for power production and, as it officially admitted in 2002, for weapons development. On those visits he had walked around the complex, rather than looking at it from a distant bunker.

Today, though, they were going to see something special. Werzel and the other observers had been promised a front row seat as the entire Yongbyon complex was destroyed. After so many negotiations and so many broken promises from the North Koreans, it was hard to believe that Yongbyon was finally going to be demolished. Werzel was particularly puzzled by their bunker's distance from the facility, and suspected another trick by the North Koreans. At least they had not objected when he requested the use of his personal Zeiss Conquest binoculars. Waterproof and fogproof, they were evidence that his native Germany still manufactured some of the world's best quality goods.

As he focused in on the facility, Werzel had to admit that nothing appeared out of the ordinary. Yongbyon looked exactly as he remembered it, though that was due to change radically in less than a minute, according to the countdown being blared through a nearby loudspeaker.

Four, three, two, one, zero…nothing. No sooner had Werzel started to form the thought that this was a North Korean trick after all, when the bunker lurched like a ship at sea hitting a rogue wave. At the same moment, a deep rumbling coincided with Yongbyon's disappearance. It was simply gone!

A steady clicking from the personal radiation monitor Werzel carried with him at all times made his heart lurch. This far from the complex, and inside the concrete bunker, Yongbyon's destruction should not have spread nuclear materials triggering his monitor unless something had gone seriously wrong. A quick check confirmed that, at least, he and the others inside the bunker were in no immediate danger. Still, the readings made no sense unless…Werzel could not believe even the North Koreans capable of such an outrage.

The head of the North Korean government delegation, introduced earlier simply as "Mr. Kim" might have been reading Werzel's mind. After calling for the attention of "all our international guests" he read from a prepared text that "the Democratic People's Republic of Korea announces the complete destruction of the Yongbyon nuclear complex, as well as the elimination of all the DPRK's weapons as well as its weapons grade nuclear materials, through a nuclear device detonated underground below Yongbyon approximately five minutes ago. The DPRK has no other nuclear devices or materials, and you have all witnessed the destruction of the only nuclear facility in our country capable of producing more. We call on all right-thinking nations to abandon sanctions against the peace loving Korean people, and will be repeating this call soon at the United Nations." Kim looked up from his text and added, "I will not be taking any questions. We count on each of you to give a full and honest accounting of what you have seen here today to the rest of the world."

Stunned silence greeted Kim's statement. Werzel had trouble imagining even the North Koreans' capable of such gall. To bring international observers to North Korea's latest atomic test, and bill it as proof that their nuclear program no longer existed took the "big lie" concept to a whole new level. Of course, there was no proof that North Korea had no additional nuclear weapons or the materials to create them, and both were far easier to hide than the production complex the North Koreans had just demolished. Surely, the rest of the world would see through this charade for what it was – more evidence that the North Koreans had nuclear weapons, and were trying desperately to evade the sanctions designed to change their belligerent behavior.

Or would they?

The North Pacific

The *Oregon* carried the latest version of the Mk-48 torpedo, with the Advanced Capability (ADCAP) Mod 7 Common Broadband Advanced Sonar System (CBASS). This version's improvements made the torpedo far quieter and more capable of defeating counter measures than earlier models.

There was a reason every country but North Korea had retired the *Romeo* class, Cartwright thought as he watched the display of the track of the two torpedoes heading towards the sub that was slowly rising towards the surface.

It had no chance of surviving against a modern attacker.

Cartwright shook his head as the display showed the Mk-48s draw closer and closer, while the *Romeo* made no attempt to evade. His orders hadn't named the *Romeo*, even though Cartwright was sure the intercepted message must have included that detail. He guessed (years later he would find out, correctly) that there were two reasons for that omission. The first was that there was no chance of encountering a different *Romeo* by mistake, either in the North Pacific or anywhere else besides the North Korean coastline. The second was that it was better to avoid personalizing a sub Cartwright and his crew would have to sink.

As the two torpedoes reached the final leg of their attack run and switched on their active sonar, Cartwright finally saw the sub react. By then even the world's fastest and most agile sub would have had no hope of evading the Mk-48s.

The best term Cartwright could think of to describe the *Romeo's* attempts at evasion was - arthritic. They didn't last long.

"That's a hit for torpedo one...and a hit for torpedo two. Target movement has ceased. Multiple bulkhead collapse. Target failed to reach the surface. Structural integrity has been compromised. Target is taking on water rapidly. Passing one hundred meter depth...two hundred...three hundred. Target is breaking up. Target has been destroyed."

Lieutenant Fischer's calm voice recounted the *Romeo's* last few minutes with the same lack of emotion he would have used for a drill, which Cartwright appreciated. He had looked up the crew complement of a

Romeo class sub when they received the order to destroy her, and seen that it normally carried a crew of 54. If anything it had probably carried more personnel for this mission, just as Cartwright did.

Along with the order to destroy the *Romeo* had come instructions for an extremely rare at sea rendezvous with a Marine tilt rotor Osprey, which had delivered several unhappy looking technicians and their equipment. They were now going to carry out the second part of Cartwright's orders.

"Surface! Technicians and your equipment to the bridge."

Cartwright nodded to himself as he heard acknowledgements and reports confirming that his orders were being carried out as smoothly as in any drill. Well, he thought, that was the point of doing drills.

Now they would get to see whether the North Korean's ICBM test was a success.

And if it carried a live warhead.

CHAPTER FOUR

Pyongyang, North Korea

Park Won Hee's career in the ruling Workers' Party of Korea (WPK) had been little short of spectacular. A third generation WPK member, his grandfather had fought as a guerilla against the Japanese occupiers as a Party member. His recently deceased father had preceded him as one of the ten members of North Korea's National Defense Commission (NDC), which was responsible for management and oversight of all branches of North Korea's formidable military. As NDC chairman President Ko Ji Hun was of course far more than first among equals, but even he had to consider carefully any move opposed by a majority of NDC members. Not, Park thought with disgust, that there were many on the NDC with the spine to risk opposing Ko.

And if there were ever a time to risk opposing the all-powerful President, this was it. The plan to attack the South based on "Tunnel No. 1" was suicide, plain and simple. The problem was, Park had no way to effectively oppose it, and voting against it alone on the NDC would only guarantee that an unfortunate "accident" or "death by natural causes" resulted in his replacement with a more compliant committee member. Park's father had seen it happen several times, and warned his son of the danger of voting alone against the chairman before he joined the NDC.

Today, President Ko had called the NDC together at the Personal Secretariat building to give the committee "important news" on the invasion plan's progress. As the other committee members filed in, Park looked at their expressions for a clue as to how they viewed Ko's plan. Totally blank – what a surprise, Park thought to himself. Park sighed, chiding himself for failing to remember that you did not make it to the NDC without such skills.

As the highest ranking military officer then Marshal Ko had succeeded President Kim Jong Un after Kim's death in a plane accident that happened to have included his closest civilian advisors. Very soon after the announcement of the accident, Ko's appointment as President had been announced. On top of that, Ko still kept his rank of Marshal and all the power that went with it. At the same time, the North Korean people were assured that the Kim dynasty would live on, as soon as Kim Jong Un's children had completed their education. Since that would take over a decade, it was an easy promise to make.

Park had known several people who had questioned the circumstances of President Kim's plane crash. "Known," as in "I used to know him, but haven't seen him in some time." Curiosity was not recommended in North Korea, particularly in the upper reaches of its government.

Ko entered last, as always. He called the meeting to order, and then favored the committee with one of his rare smiles.

"I have good news to report, comrades. My agents have been successful in obtaining a device that will be satisfactory for our reunification plan to succeed." Ko said.

Park viewed the other committee members as they struggled, with varying degrees of success, to maintain their impassive expressions. Park was sure that he was not the only NDC member who had hoped that the invasion plan would fail when it proved impossible to obtain a portable nuclear device.

"With this success, I think it is time for a brief recap of my reunification plan," Ko said.

It's time for Ko to bask in his agents' success, Park thought sourly.

"You all know about the great success of our nuclear weapons and ballistic missile programs. However, deployment in the South of what the Americans call the "Terminal High Altitude Area Defense" program has meant we could not count on our nuclear tipped missiles reaching their targets."

Very true, Park thought. Of course, every test had also suggested the accuracy of the missiles was so poor that one aimed at Seoul could have ended up hitting their own forces crossing the DMZ instead.

"How, then, to be sure we can use a nuclear weapon against the South? Tunnel No. 1 has been under construction since the 1960s, and it is the only one to have made significant progress past the DMZ. It was started much deeper than the infiltration tunnels designed merely to bypass the DMZ's minefields, and we were able to take advantage of the rock formations in its area to dig deeper and farther than anyone in the South might suspect," Ko said.

"Our plan is only possible thanks to the extension north of Seoul's subway line No. 7 – that's "Lucky 7" for us," Ko chuckled, then waited for the dutiful echoes of the other committee members to die down.

"Tunnel No. 1 is now approaching the latest construction point of subway line No. 7, and the Southerners continue to dig straight towards us," Ko said with visible satisfaction.

Park could scarcely breathe. He had issued the orders himself to speed up construction at Tunnel No. 1, but had no idea that picking up speed on their side would be matched by the South's rapid construction pace on Line No. 7.

"As you all know, the Southerners have not discovered a significant tunnel since the one northeast of Yanggu in 1990, about 200 kilometers from Seoul. We deliberately allowed this one to be found after their previous discovery of a tunnel in 1978 just 44 kilometers from Seoul, capable of moving 30,000 troops an hour as well as field artillery. As we expected, the Yanggu tunnel, even larger than the one discovered in 1978, convinced the Southerners that we were focused on opening a second front in the East. Now that more than thirty years has elapsed since the discovery of a significant tunnel, we can be confident of complete surprise," Ko said.

Park looked around the circular table at the other NDC members, being careful not to move his head as he studied each of their expressions. If any of the others were alarmed by Ko's summation of his insane plan, they were hiding it well. He also noticed that they all had a shot of a traditional Korean rice wine, soju, in a glass in front of them. Apparently, a toast was coming.

"Soon, we expect to make the linkup between Tunnel No. 1 and Line No. 7, which will be timed for when the subway is closed. Our commandos will eliminate any Southern construction workers who survive the explosion creating the link, and then move our subway train containing a nuclear device we have built onto the Line No. 7 track. Of course, to prevent any attempt to stop it through a power cut to the rails, the train will be self-propelled. The commandos will transfer to Line No. 1 at the Dobongsan station, which will take them to the heart of Seoul at City Hall. There they will arm the device," Ko said.

Park felt the room starting to spin around him. He fiercely willed himself to calm, knowing that to project anything other than placid agreement would be his death sentence.

"We will then issue our demand for the South to immediately disband its military forces, and the departure of all Americans including both soldiers and civilians from Korean soil. The People's Republic of China will guarantee a peaceful transition to reunification, as well as helping to oversee a "two system" solution modeled on Hong Kong. Naturally, we do not want to kill the golden goose!" Ko laughed, and all the others at the table laughed with him.

"No, we want the factories to keep producing, and we want to avoid a mass exodus of skilled workers from the South. We will need all their resources if we are to succeed in our next great venture – revenge for Japan's treatment of Korea during its occupation."

It took all Park had to restrain himself, and he had to conceal a twitch by nodding his head in agreement, which Park could see immediately repeated by the other NDC members, much to his disgust. Incredible, Park thought, we have not yet succeeded with the first maniacal scheme and already Ko is thinking of another one?

"I expect the South's craven political leadership to surrender quickly, like the weak-willed women they are. However, if their American puppet masters do not allow surrender, we must be ready to act decisively after the device's detonation. We have timed the linkup to coincide with our largest military exercise of the year. Since we have been holding the exercise at this time for the past decade, the South's alert level will be only moderately increased," Ko said.

Park swallowed his laughter, which Ko's words made all too easy. The South would not surrender to a nuclear threat, and would instead only be more determined to defeat an enemy that would resort to the mass slaughter of innocent civilians to get its way. Also, though it was true that decades of repetition would have dulled the South's alarm at the North Korean military's latest exercise, it would not have erased it entirely.

"The nuclear explosion in Seoul will strike a deadly blow to the heart of the South's transport, communication, and governmental center. Since forty percent of all Southerners live in Seoul and its suburbs, rescue efforts, treatment of survivors and a mass exodus of millions will paralyze the entire country. The public will demand the puppet government accept our offer of a two-system solution, as our forces pour across the border," Ko said.

Here Park was forced to reluctantly agree. Detonation of even a small nuclear device in the heart of Seoul would indeed plunge the South into chaos. Only elderly Southerners knew true hardship, and few alive were more than children during the Korean War. With thousands dead and radioactivity permeating Seoul and its suburbs, even the toughest would have trouble avoiding panic. The most recent generation or two, who had known only plenty and luxury, might indeed grasp at any straw offered, even one as weak as the two-system solution.

"Of course, it is always possible that the Americans might prove...inflexible. So, we will transport the man-portable nuclear device we have just acquired to a large population center on their west coast. There it will serve as a gun pointed at the head of the American enemy. If anything goes wrong with the device in Tunnel No. 1, or if the Americans and their puppet Southern allies continue to resist after the first device's successful detonation in Seoul, then this additional threat will end all resistance."

Everyone present, including Park, knew that this was their cue to smile and clap furiously. As he did so, all Park could think about was the terrible destruction that would be visited on the North by the Americans if they carried through with this insane plan.

"One word of caution to all of you. We have found our Chinese brothers to be steadfast in their support of our revolution and its goals. However, they may see the use of a nuclear device within the U.S. as risking a wider conflict that could involve nuclear war between them and the Americans. We all know it would never come to that. Our Chinese brothers may not agree. So, in any contacts we have with the Chinese, this part of our plan must remain unspoken."

A universal murmur of agreement and nodding heads gave Ko the reaction he expected. Beaming, he raised his glass in front of him and cried, "To victory!" Everyone present echoed his cry, and downed their ritual shot of soju.

The North Pacific

"Captain, Mr. Spencer says the weapon is on its expected course," Lieutenant Fischer said, nodding toward one of the civilian technicians hunched over the tangle of cables, satellite dishes and equipment that now occupied nearly every square inch of the *Oregon's* deck.

"So, we can hope it won't land on top of us," Cartwright said lightly, knowing that the odds of that happening were incredibly small. Landing close enough that the shock wave and water displacement could damage the *Oregon* was a much more real concern.

Fischer shook his head. "No, sir. Impact is estimated at approximately five miles from our location. Mr. Spencer says we shouldn't move away further or it could affect their ability to intercept the weapon's telemetry."

Cartwright nodded. His orders were explicit about the importance of collecting data from the weapon. It made sense that the Pentagon wanted to know the capabilities of the latest North Korean missile. He was curious himself.

Cartwright thought back to the conversation he'd had with Spencer as soon as he and the two technicians he supervised had squared away their equipment when they first came on board. His orders had promised that Spencer would provide "additional details" about this phase of their mission.

Spencer had wasted no time explaining why he and his men appeared less than thrilled to be aboard the *Oregon.*

"There's a good chance that the North Koreans put a live nuke on that missile, and to intercept its telemetry we'll need to be close enough to have zero chance of survival if it does."

Cartwright shook his head. "My orders say Naval Intelligence rates the chance of a live weapon as extremely low. If they didn't believe it, I think they'd have sent a cheaper sub," he said, gesturing at the *Oregon* all around them.

Spencer grunted. "Captain, when I saw this was the sub the Navy sent, I was convinced that they don't think the missile is live. I'm even pretty sure I know why. I just think they're wrong."

Cartwright's eyebrows rose. "Now you've piqued my curiosity, Mr. Spencer. My orders just said the probability of a live missile was low, not why. So, let's hear it."

Spencer shrugged. "OK. First, they've never tested a live weapon on a missile before. Next, the trajectory of this missile overflies Japan, so if it falls short and detonates they start a war ready or not. Most importantly, adding an equipment package to monitor flight performance and broadcast telemetry wouldn't leave room for a warhead."

Cartwright nodded. "Sounds pretty convincing. Why do you think they're wrong?"

Spencer rubbed his forehead tiredly. "The North Koreans have run risks before. Hundreds of North Koreans have been killed by their nuclear program already. I don't think they'd care about thousands of dead Japanese, in fact I think they'd see it as a good start. Sanctions have started to bite since the Chinese started taking them at least semi-seriously, and I think they may see war as the only option left."

"But none of that is why I tried to turn down this assignment, and would have if the Navy hadn't threatened to terminate our contract. I think the next logical step in their testing program is to put a small fission warhead in the missile along with a small monitoring and telemetry package."

Cartwright frowned. "But you said there wouldn't be room for both."

Spencer shook his head. "Not necessarily. Their goal has to be putting the thermonuclear device they've already tested inside a missile. That's a fusion device, that needs a fission trigger. So, the logical next step is to test the fission trigger inside a missile. Remember, the missile design has to have room for the fusion device. That's the room they'd use for the monitoring and telemetry package."

Cartwright nodded. "And you shared these concerns with the Navy?"

Spencer looked at Cartwright sourly. "At what I'm sure they considered tiresome length. None of them believe the North Koreans could pull it off."

Cartwright nodded, more thoughtfully this time. "Nobody thought they could pull off a hydrogen bomb test, either, until they did. I'm starting to see why you're worried."

Spencer shrugged. "I obviously hope I'm wrong. Maybe they couldn't fit all that inside a missile yet, though I know they'd want to. Maybe they have, and the fission device will fail due to the stress of exposure to space and ballistic reentry. Maybe the device will be so small that we can survive a detonation a few miles away. Maybe they just want to test the missile's range, since this one is going farther than any of their previous launches."

Cartwright nodded. "But you don't really believe any of that."

Spencer shook his head. "No, Captain, I don't."

CHAPTER FIVE

Beijing, China

Li Weimin was one of the few who had sympathized with the Tiananmen Square protesters who still worked in the Chinese government, but he had been smart enough to keep his mouth shut, and over three decades later his hard work had been rewarded. At the Ministry of Foreign Affairs he was now Deputy Director-General at the Department of North American and Oceanian Affairs, a position that had served as a stepping stone for previous Foreign Ministers. What he had heard at today's meeting, though, made him wonder if that would still be true. If the plan under discussion worked, it would surely be a coup for his counterpart at the Department of Asian Affairs.

It was hard to grasp that a two-system solution for Korea was even thinkable. Everyone Li knew at MFA had thought it was just a matter of time, and not much time at that, before North Korea went the way of East Germany. Nobody at the meeting had said why South Korea would even consider accepting North Korean political and economic control, even if it was able to keep its economic system intact.

And yet, he and the other department heads who had just met with the Foreign Minister had been told in no uncertain terms to prepare to deal with the consequences of China "guaranteeing" a two-system for Korea. For Li, that meant attempting to predict the reaction of the United States. He had been posted twice to the US, once to the Consulate General in San Francisco and once to the Embassy in Washington DC, but all he knew for sure was that anyone who believed he could predict what the Americans would do was a fool.

Obviously, the Americans would strongly object to South Korea's takeover by the North, but it was not certain they would go to war to prevent it. If the South agreed to a two-system solution that would make them the North's Hong Kong, and if the US feared war with China could follow an attack on the North, it might well hesitate. With most of its combat ready troops already committed elsewhere, it would be neither easy nor cheap for the US to intervene to maintain South Korea's independence.

Much would depend on how the crisis began. If the South agreed to takeover by the North with few or no casualties, Li believed the US would probably bluster but do nothing. However, if more than a handful of the 30,000 US troops and large US civilian population in Korea were killed, then the US would intervene, no matter the cost or risk. And if Li was sure of anything, it was that China was not ready for war with the US. Though China's nuclear arsenal could inflict a heavy blow on the US, it was no match for the U.S.' ability to retaliate even after a Chinese first strike.

So, Li had to find out more about how the North Koreans planned to force the South's surrender. Unless it was sure the surrender would be bloodless, Li also had to figure out a way to stop the North's ambitions from drawing China into a war that could see the last generation's amazing progress wiped out, or even reversed. Of course, Li mused gloomily, he had no idea how to accomplish either goal.

Vladivostok, Russia

Grishkov nursed his third vodka at his favorite bar, the Black Crow, a dump near the docks that had a sole redeeming feature- it was close enough to his apartment to let him walk home. Driving drunk on Vladivostok winter roads was a good way to get either killed or arrested. Either way, he mused sourly, would be unlikely to help his career.

Grishkov pulled out the postcard he had found in Timoshenko's hotel room. Looking at it again told him no more than it had the first time. Scowling, he was about to put it back in his jacket when something stopped him. Something Captain Ivansik had said about how long Timoshenko had been operating as an arms dealer....and the friends he had made in Moscow....

Grishkov rubbed his right hand over his thick dark hair, a mannerism that he first learned helped him to think when he played in chess tournaments as a boy. So, Timoshenko's career went back many years, and friends in Moscow who would know a Vladivostok captain would be either law enforcement or intelligence. Intelligence....

Grishkov stared harder at the postcard. Could it be that simple? A microdot? He had only one contact in the Federal'naya sluzhba bezopasnosti, or FSB, who went back to the bad old KGB days and might have some idea of how to read a microdot. If there was anything Grishkov was sure of, it was that going through channels to have it read would be too risky. God knows what it would reveal, he thought, tossing back the last of the vodka. As he stood up to leave, Grishkov was also nagged by the feeling that whatever was on the microdot needed to be read right now, before time ran out.

The North Pacific

Cartwright looked in the direction the weapon was expected to traverse, even though he knew it would be traveling so fast it would barely register as an image before impact.

"Captain, Mr. Spencer advises the weapon will impact within the next two minutes. Still on course for impact about five miles away. I have made sure that Mr. Spencer and his team know that if you give the order to dive they are to head below immediately without making any attempt to secure their equipment."

Cartwright nodded. "Any objections?"

Fischer grinned, shaking his head. "I think one of the technicians summed up their reaction by promising to beat me to the hatch. Mr. Spencer said something about adding it to the Navy's bill."

Cartwright grunted. "And I couldn't really argue with him."

During the exchange both officers had been staring in the direction where the weapon was expected to land. They didn't have long to wait.

A brilliant streak of light came down at a rate that Cartwright would later describe as "one of God's fingers." It was immediately followed by a plume of steam that rose in the air first dozens, and then hundreds of feet high.

Spencer spoke without moving from the folding table holding his equipment, or looking away from its displays. "Obviously, the weapon was not armed. Also obviously, transmission of telemetry has ceased. We'll start breaking down this equipment and getting it below in just a few minutes."

Cartwright nodded. "Good. I'd like to clear the area as soon as possible. We'll stay close enough to the surface after we dive that you can still transmit data and analysis."

Spencer nodded absently as he continued to type, and then looked up. "Thank you, Captain. And let me say, I've never been happier to be wrong."

Cartwright smiled and turned towards the hatch. As his hands gripped the rungs leading to the tasks waiting for him below, he couldn't help turning one thought over in his head. Had the warhead been live, but failed?

Pyongyang, North Korea

Chung Hee Moon had accepted the doctor's report stoically, as he had such news throughout his life. Being told he had less than a year to live made him a more reliable choice for this mission in the eyes of his superiors. The truth was he would have had no objection to going on this one-way trip even if he had been in perfect health. He had to admit, though, that the end foreseen for this particular mission was far more appealing than the prospect of a long, lingering death from cancer. Cancer had claimed the lives of both of his parents, and so he had seen how unpleasant such a fate was first hand.

As a Sangjwa, or Colonel, in the North Korean Special Operations Force Chung had served in a long and illustrious career. Lean and muscular, he had long ago started having all the hair on his head shaved, though as the years had passed he noted wryly that the barber had less and less to do.

Chung was known in particular for one daring mission where he had led a three-man team that infiltrated into South Korea using an Antonov AN-2 retrofitted with wooden components to give it a primitive stealth capability. The AN-2 flew low offshore, and then landed the team on a deserted coastal highway in the dead of night relying on nothing more than instruments and the plane's landing lights. After carrying out the reconnaissance mission and making their way to the coast, they were picked up by a Yono class midget submarine.

By contrast, this mission appeared quite easy. Sit in a shipping container with a trunk containing a nuclear device for about ten days. Go to a residence that had already been rented. Wait to be told to detonate the device.

Chung was looking forward to his first trip to the United States.

CHAPTER SIX

Pyongyang, North Korea

Marshal Ko looked up from the report he had been reading as his chief of staff, Gye Tae Hyun, entered his office. To be honest, Ko welcomed the interruption, though nothing in his stern expression would have given that away. He had insisted that any documents prepared for him contain nothing but the truth, no matter how unpleasant the details might be. To drive home the point, in his first month as Supreme Leader he had three Party officials of varying ranks executed for trying to sugarcoat unpleasant North Korean realities. After that, the quality and accuracy of the reports he received improved considerably.

The downside was that reports on subjects such as the North Korean economy could be counted on to both dismay and depress. Like everyone in North Korea's elite, Ko had long known the truth about its economy. After all, its weak state was directly reflected in the resources available to the North Korean military. An outsider might have thought that such an understanding would result in a course change, perhaps allowing capitalism with one-party control, as in China.

Ko had considered and rejected that course, as the Kims had before him. Such a change would take too long to produce any real benefits, especially with the constraints imposed by Western sanctions. Even if successful, capitalism always created powerful people who owed nothing to the Party for their success. Ko had talked to several Chinese officials over the years who were very worried about this, and was determined not to repeat their mistake in his country.

As Gye approached his desk, Ko thought as he often did about the contrast between North and South Korea. Any objective comparison showed that the South's economy was far superior, and its standard of living higher. Rather than making him mindlessly ape the South, though, that knowledge only fueled Ko's anger. The U.S. had poured billions of dollars in aid to the South for over three decades after the Korean War, at the same time as it led international sanctions against the North. Over 30,000 American troops with billions of dollars worth of equipment continued to stand in the way of reunification.

Though dislike of the Japanese was one of the few things uniting all Koreans, they had played a critical role in the South's industrial development. Japanese technicians and engineers by the thousands worked for Southern companies, even if many of them flew back to Japan every weekend. Many of them joked that the only reason Korean cars ran were the Japanese parts they contained, even if that had became less and less true over time.

But, Ko mused, in the end all that mattered was that the North's system was the one that put him in power, and he wasn't about to give it up. With the South's resources at his command, he would finally be able to pay the U.S. and Japan back for the decades of humiliation the North had endured. The fact that he and everyone he cared about would keep the power and privilege they had struggled for all their lives? Well, he thought to himself, that would just be a bonus.

The collapse at the Punggye-ri test site in 2017 had not just killed 200 or so construction workers, as reported in the Western press. It had also resulted in the death of a dozen of North Korea's best nuclear scientists and technicians. It had made even maintaining their limited stockpile of nuclear weapons a challenge, and effectively ended progress toward more powerful and longer range missiles. Ko was looking forward to Gye's news on the latest missile test, which would finally mark the resumption of progress towards a credible nuclear capability.

"So, Gye, who is here to report on the latest missile test?" Ko asked.

"No one, sir," Gye answered. Even through his annoyance, Ko had to admire Gye's impassive delivery of news he had to know would enrage his leader.

"No one," Ko repeated, shaking his head. How many more would he have to execute before the rest of the elite got the message that he would never shoot the messenger - but would ruthlessly eliminate anyone who kept him from getting the information he needed to secure Korea's destiny?

"A Navy captain called to say that the report from the submarine assigned to collect the data transmitted from the missile test is overdue. Since it had been checking in as scheduled as recently as this morning, they do not think radio failure is a likely explanation," Gye said carefully.

Ko looked up sharply. "And what is a likely explanation?"

Gye shrugged. "The captain did not say. He promised to keep us updated if any further information is received."

Ko grunted. "I won't hold my breath." Absently tapping his pen against the papers on his desk, Ko said, "Find out how the sub received its orders. If it was by radio, get the name of the officer who made that decision. Also, get me the name of the officer in overall charge of this mission, the one who should have been making this report. With luck it will be the same officer, so I only have to order one execution."

Gye nodded as he made rapid notes. "You are not interested in the name of the captain who made this report?"

Ko smiled sourly. "Don't think I missed your failure to mention it. You were right not to. Underlings don't interest me."

Gye nodded again. "You think the sub was sunk, after its orders had been intercepted. By the Americans?"

Ko grimaced. "We'll never be able to prove it, but I'm as sure as you're sitting there that the Americans did it. Others could have done it, and might even have wanted to do it, like the Japanese. They haven't cared for our firing missiles over their precious homeland. But they just don't have the nerve. The Americans have proven many times that they are bandits who fear nothing."

Gye looked up from his notes. "How do you plan to respond?"

Ko grit his teeth. "I will have to give that some thought. I'd been hoping to have a credible nuclear threat to hit the U.S. mainland. Without these test results, the scientists tell me they can't be sure even a single one of our missiles would make it across the Pacific. They were able to fit a warhead inside the missile, but weren't sure it would stand up to reentry. They were hoping the equipment monitoring the performance of both the missile and the warhead would tell them what went wrong in the event of failure."

Gye nodded. "But I understand we have other options."

Ko smiled. "Yes, Gye. Yes, we do."

Tunnel No. 1, North Korea

Lee Ho Suk had never seen so much food since he started working in the tunnels. No, he had to correct himself. Since his village like all the others in North Korea had been hit by famine years before his arrest, he had not seen so much to eat in one place since childhood.

Lee knew in his bones that this was not cause for celebration. Hard experience had taught him that nothing out of the ordinary was reason to rejoice.

Even stranger, prisoners were no longer being rotated out of the tunnel. Moving prisoners between projects was a routine precaution against their becoming too familiar with the others working in the tunnel, which could lead to mass riots or escape attempts. Lee smiled wryly to himself at the guards' thinking – as though prisoners at hard labor had the energy left over for such heroic efforts!

Had the guards and their masters finally realized how foolish it was to waste time and effort by shifting prisoners between projects? No, Lee thought, in fact the improved food had given him and his fellow workers more energy than he had felt moving through his body in years.

Lee realized as he thought further that prisoners were not the only ones staying put. So were the guards and the specialized equipment operators. In fact, he could not think of a single person he had seen leave since starting work at Tunnel No. 1.

As his pickax moved rhythmically up and down, Lee kept chewing on the problem. More food, no rotations.

In a flash the answer came to him with such force that he nearly fell down. Extra food was to let the workers finish a high priority project faster. No rotations ensured that nobody outside the tunnel knew of its rapid progress.

And after the project was completed? Lee didn't have to think about that at all. The guards and the specialized equipment operators might or might not have enough value to keep. He and his fellow prisoners were already dead, they just didn't know it yet.

Well, Lee amended, the others don't know.

That left just one question – what could Lee do about it?

Lee could think of only one answer, which was to watch and wait for even the slimmest opportunity to escape. It would probably never come, but now Lee knew that even the most desperate attempt was worth trying, since every day the tunnel moved forward his death drew nearer as well.

Vladivostok, Russia

Grishkov raised his glass to Colonel Alexei Vasilyev, who was sitting across from him at the Black Crow. They were at a table in the far inside corner, from which they could see whoever entered, and were still far enough from the bar to make overhearing their conversation impossible. He had persuaded Vasilyev to meet him there by promising to pay for his drinks, and by pointing out that nobody in his right mind walked into an FSB building voluntarily.

Grishkov guessed that Vasilyev was about a decade older than he was, though he never talked about himself. Vasilyev was average in every way except one. When he chose, you could see a sharp intelligence in his eyes that was normally hidden. Grishkov had seen it when he stayed behind to ask questions after briefings Vasilyev had given to him and other soldiers in Chechnya. Grishkov had been surprised and pleased to find him in Vladivostok.

"So, Alexei, I have something that might be of interest to you," Grishkov began.

"Of interest to me, or the FSB?" Vasilyev asked, with eyebrows raised.

"Maybe both," Grishkov answered, handing Vasilyev the postcard.

"It belonged to an arms dealer named Timoshenko. Perhaps you have heard of him?" Grishkov added.

Vasilyev studied the postcard, then slowly nodded.

"Yes, I have heard of him. I heard that his body was fished out of the sea not too far from here. I heard that Timoshenko's murder was connected to the deaths of several Russian Army officers at the Vladivostok Armory by an overzealous detective, who had also secured all of his belongings. Finally, I heard that General Vasyukov has conducted a thorough inventory of the Armory, and found nothing missing," Vasilyev said.

"Your hearing is excellent, but then I would expect nothing less of such a capable FSB agent," Grishkov smiled.

"So, do you have any leads?" asked Vasilyev.

"As to the identity of Timoshenko's killers, no. However, there may be some information available about what he was doing in Vladivostok. To get it, though, I will need some help," explained Grishkov.

"From me, I suppose. What can I do to help the Vladivostok police?" asked Vasilyev.

"Examine the postcard in your hand to see if contains a microdot, and if so read what it contains," replied Grishkov.

"A microdot? The digital age has made them a bit passé," observed Vasilyev.

"No argument here. However, Timoshenko had been in the game since the 1980s, and had a background that could have given him the skills and the materials. Plus, you have to admit that hardly anyone would think to look for a microdot these days," Grishkov replied.

"Good points. Fine, I will check the postcard personally. And I will do so unofficially, without creating a record. One thing I need to know, though. What are you expecting to find? In other words, just how hot is this?" asked Vasilyev.

Grishkov took a pull at his vodka before answering.

"The truth is, I'm not sure. What worries me, though, is that the Vladivostok Armory contains…special weapons. I already knew about the inventory and its results. However, one of the officers there who had a so-called accident kept those records. He should not have been able to tamper with them, at least not well enough to fool a capable and determined inspector. I just don't know enough about the Armory and its personnel to be sure one way or the other," replied Grishkov.

"So, this isn't just hot, it's radioactive," said Vasilyev, frowning at his own bad joke.

"Well, maybe. We're still not even sure the postcard contains a microdot, let alone what it may contain," Grishkov pointed out.

"True. Very well. As it happens, the office should be thinly manned this evening, and I know just where to find the archaic equipment I'll need to examine this postcard. I should be able to tell you something by this time tomorrow. Same place?" Vasilyev asked.

"That will be fine. Whatever you find, I owe you," said Grishkov.

"Yes. But who knows? Whatever I discover may bring enough credit for the both of us to share. Imagine, the FSB cooperating with local police to thwart arms dealing in the Russian Far East. Could make for a nice headline!" Vasilyev said, laughing.

Grishkov nearly choked on his vodka.

CHAPTER SEVEN

Pyongyang, North Korea

Park Won Hee woke, as he always did, at 5:00AM sharp. The propaganda that had just started to blare from the massive speakers mounted near the Pyongyang Central Station guaranteed that for him, though he knew many people who managed to tune it out and sleep peacefully through the relentlessly cheerful reports of the government's latest triumphs. Like nearly everything else, the original Japanese-built structure had been destroyed in the Korean War, but the train station had been rebuilt in the 1950s. If only, Park thought with a groan as he forced himself out of bed, they could have picked a place to put the speakers a few more blocks away.

Ironically, the early hour Park woke and the proximity of the apartment he had first shared with his father and now lived in alone to his office helped to give him a reputation as an eager and dedicated servant of the state. If only they knew, Park thought, that he was determined to stop Marshal Ko's insane plan to take over the South by any means necessary. But how?

Park went mechanically though the five checkpoints necessary to reach his office, required due to its proximity to one of Ko's many offices. Once he finally entered, he was surprised to find a visitor. At his rank nearly anyone who came to see him did so by appointment, and the only exceptions were officials of similar rank who had important and unexpected business. Defense Minister Jung Min Soon certainly qualified as equal in importance, but he had never seen Park one on one for any reason.

"Defense Minister, an unexpected pleasure. May I offer you some tea?" asked Park.

"Thank you. That would be most welcome," replied Jung.

After Park's aide had withdrawn and the required inquiries about Jung and Park's families were complete, Jung went straight to business.

"Park, as you know I am completely in favor of our leader's plan to re-unify our glorious country. I know you share my heartfelt belief that he will be completely successful" said Jung, appearing in both tone and expression to be nothing but completely sincere.

"Of course, Defense Minister. You have captured my beliefs exactly," Park replied.

"We do not know each other well, Park, but I was a close friend of your father. Please call me Jung while we are speaking privately," Jung said with a smile.

"Certainly, Jung. I am honored, and am pleased to learn that you were a friend of my father. Not a day goes by that I do not miss his wise counsel," Park said, meaning every word.

"Park, with our leader's approval I have arranged a trip for you to visit our Chinese allies. They will play a key role in the success of Marshal Ko's glorious reunification plan, and we must be certain that they understand the importance of following his plan exactly," Jung said, slapping his knee for emphasis.

"You honor me with your confidence. May I ask why you selected me for this mission, rather than someone from your own ministry, or the Ministry of Foreign Affairs?" asked Park.

"A fair question, Park, and one I would have asked myself in your position. First, your position as one of the members of the National Defense Commission will give more weight to your mission than the other alternatives you mentioned. Also, you followed your father's advice and completed your university studies in China, for which you learned Chinese. No other NDC member speaks Chinese fluently. I think it is an elementary security precaution to have these discussions conducted without a translator present. Do you agree?" asked Jung.

"Your logic is unassailable. When do I leave?" asked Park.

"This afternoon. Your flight should arrive in Beijing, via Tokyo, late this evening," replied Jung.

"I will do my utmost to justify your faith in me, and to honor the friendship you had with my father," said Park.

"Fine words, and well spoken," Jung said, nodding approvingly. "I am sure your father would be proud of you."

Park shook Jung's hand as he led him to his office door, his mind racing. Here was an opportunity – but how could he take advantage of it?

Pyongyang, North Korea

Kim Gun Jun frowned as he reviewed the latest report from his agent in Vladivostok. Since his success in obtaining the nuclear device from Timoshenko, eliminating him and recovering the funds offered for the device's purchase he had been promoted to Deputy Director of the Research Department for External Intelligence (RDEI), North Korea's equivalent to the Russian FSB. Anything that cast doubt on that accomplishment was a mortal threat to his career, that must be dealt with at once.

Kim got up from his desk and walked over to the map on his office wall. About 425 miles from RDEI headquarters in Pyongyang to Vladivostok. Kim grimaced as he realized operational security would never allow a direct routing, no matter how urgent the mission. Once again, it would be a flight to Beijing, and from there to either Hong Kong or Tokyo before flying on to Vladivostok under either a Chinese or Japanese passport. Kim, of course, spoke both Chinese and Japanese fluently.

His agent had reported that Russian police had discovered Timoshenko's body, and that was bad enough. He also reported that the FSB was interested in the case, and that was much worse. The only good news was that interest in the case appeared to be limited to one detective, and one FSB agent. If both were eliminated, the damage should be contained. It would be preferable for the FSB agent's death to appear to be an accident, but the detective could simply be shot, since Russian police met violent ends quite routinely.

Kim wished that he had enough faith in his agent to trust him to carry out the killings, but with his career at stake the risks were simply too great. He had little time for things Western, but there was one American saying Kim had always liked. If you want a thing done right, do it yourself. There was just one detail he had to take care of before he could go.

En Route from North Korea to Japan

The flight to Tokyo would be the first time Chung Hee Moon had been outside his country. At least, Chung thought to himself wryly, as long as you agreed with his government that the line dividing North from South Korea was illegitimate. It was also the first time he had been allowed access to the Internet without the heavy restrictions placed on site access even for intelligence agents. Obeying the instinctive caution that had kept him moving up through the ranks of the North Korean military, Chung played it safe when he accessed his laptop using the airport wireless network.

Since there was no regular air service between Pyongyang and Tokyo and he was travelling under a counterfeit South Korean passport, Chung was at Shenyang airport, the closest major link between North Korea and the outside world. From there only two nonstop choices existed to Tokyo, Korean Air and China Southern. Korean Air was out of the question, since the chances of either he or his passport being spotted for what they were would be higher than with any other airline.

This made Chung's choice for his first real Internet use easy, both because his training encouraged him to learn everything about the tools he needed to accomplish his mission, and because of genuine curiosity. Why was he flying on an airline named China Southern from one of the northernmost cities in China? And why did China, a country where the government had once controlled all air travel, now have multiple competing airlines?

The first question was answered easily enough. China Southern had bought China Northern in 2003, after China Northern had one plane crash due to pilot error, an attempted hijacking, and in 2002 a crash killing all 112 on board when a suicidal passenger started a fire on the plane. Chung frowned at this history of incompetence, but then read on to discover that by contrast China Southern was Asia's largest airline measured by both fleet size and passengers carried. Following a wave of mergers, China Southern was now one of China's "Big Three" airlines, along with Air China and China Eastern.

The second question was harder. Chung knew that China had moved towards a capitalist economy, even though the Communist Party still had control over the government every bit as tight as the Party in his own country. He had never understood why, though, and nothing he read explained it.

Chung then slowly looked around him, at the interior of the gleaming Terminal Three building, like the other two bigger than Pyongyang airport's sole terminal. And Shenyang wasn't even one of the half-dozen most important Chinese cities. From where he was sitting he could see duty-free shops stuffed with luxury goods unavailable in any North Korean store. Nearly all the shoppers were Chinese.

An entire lifetime of indoctrination gave him reasons why he should ignore the success of the capitalist model. Ironically, it was his training as an intelligence officer that forced him finally to admit the obvious. The Chinese Communist Party had chosen to embrace capitalism because it worked.

Pyongyang, North Korea

Shin Yon Young had been a janitor living and working in Pyongyang for a year. He had worked for South Korea's National Intelligence Service (NIS) rather longer, but at twenty-seven years old was young for such an important assignment. It had helped that by South Korean standards he was thin and short, so he fit in well as a manual worker in North Korea.

The NIS had several agents in North Korea, but none had matched Shin's singular achievement. He had managed to obtain access to the most priceless information of all – the intentions of the North Korean leadership.

Shin had to admit to himself that much of his success was dumb luck. Yes, he had worked hard when many of his fellow janitors were doing as little as they could get away with. Yes, he had avoided the drunkenness and bar fights that marred the police records of many others. And yes, since he had no wife the police had never been called to his home to settle a "domestic disturbance".

None of that, though, guaranteed that Shin would be transferred to a job at an important government office. Let alone the building containing the National Defense Commission's conference room! Where Shin did deserve credit, though, was in quickly seizing this opportunity.

When he pushed his mop and bucket into the conference room, he saw immediately that the massive table dominating the room was the only reasonable target for a listening device. Any of the chairs could easily be moved or replaced, but the table was obviously custom designed for the room. With the target decided, the next step was to recommend a suitable bug.

Shin's training told him that any important meeting room would be swept to detect electronic eavesdropping. In any case, he had seen technicians enter the room with such equipment during his first week on the job. So, the device would have to be a passive collector, incapable of transmitting outside the room.

Shin's report to his handler also included another key detail, the table's precise color. Not just "black" but a detailed description of the precise shade and glossiness of the table's paint that allowed an exact match between the bug and the table.

The NIS had a close relationship with the American CIA that went back all the way to the founding of the Korean Central Intelligence Agency in 1961. Neither the American CIA nor the KCIA ever forgot who they worked for, but the common North Korean enemy and the threat they posed to U.S. as well as South Korean troops did much to help them see eye to eye.

When Shin's handler reported on the unprecedented opportunity Shin's new job presented, his superior at NIS headquarters in Naegokdong in southern Seoul was determined to seize it. He recommended that they seek the CIA's help in obtaining the most sophisticated bug possible to take full advantage of this intelligence windfall.

Shin's handler delivered the results of this request to Shin three weeks later. Custom made, it was a one-inch square thin plastic film embedded with micro sensors that recorded sound passively, emitting no electronic signal that could be detected by the CIA's finest equipment. The device's surface matched the table's color precisely, and was chemically treated so that when it came into contact with the type of paint used on high-end North Korean furniture the device would meld with it at the molecular level. A hand that touched the device after installation would find no telltale bump or roughness.

Collection of the bug's take was achieved through another device, disguised as one of the buttons on Shin's coveralls. Once it came within three feet of the bug, Shin could activate the transmit feature, which was done at a highly accelerated rate. Each recorded hour took only five seconds to transmit, and the device would only record if triggered by conversation, not merely noise.

Far and away the most dangerous time for Shin would be actually planting the device in the conference room. Concealing the tiny bug from the routine search he went through every time he entered the building was not difficult. However, the guard who accompanied Shin any time he went in the conference room was annoyingly observant, and had gruffly rebuffed every attempt Shin had made to engage him in conversation. Shin had no idea what his name was, and so had privately dubbed the stocky, round faced guard "Sunshine."

Shin was sure, though, that he would soon have his chance.

Pyongyang, North Korea

Kim Gun Jun looked up from his desk with a scowl, annoyed at the interruption, a scowl which only deepened when he saw how nervous the technician was who had entered. It didn't matter that this was the only matter he had to take care of before leaving to kill the two Russian troublemakers.

Nervous people never had good news.

"Report," Kim barked, not caring that the technician's reaction now made it appear he might have a stroke on the spot.

After a moment, the technician visibly collected himself. "Comrade, we have been successful in rigging the device to detonate remotely by radio command."

Kim nodded. "But..."

The technician swallowed, and then said in a rush, "We cannot make the device detonate immediately by remote command in the very short time we were given." Seeing Kim's scowl deepen, he started speaking even faster. "However, a close examination of the device revealed an important difference from its documentation that may make this less important."

Kim grimaced. "The documentation is not genuine?" He thought, maybe I should have had Oh spend more time with that toad Timoshenko before tossing him in the bay.

The technician shook his head vigorously, now clearly on firmer ground. "No, sir. It says that arming the device starts a two hour countdown. That makes a lot of sense for the Special Forces soldiers that were expected to arm it, since they would need at least that long to get outside the blast radius. But close examination of the device shows that is not correct."

Kim cocked his head, as curiosity overcame annoyance. "How can you be so sure?".

The technician frowned, as he obviously struggled to find the right words to explain a highly complex matter to a non-expert.

"It has to do with the device's design, which had to make many compromises to achieve such a small size. Once the device was armed, detonation could never be delayed for two hours. I estimate no more than twenty minutes, no matter what the detonation clock on the device says."

Kim tapped his pen on his desk, lost in thought. It made sense. You would have to train the soldiers who would use the device, so there had to be a way to disarm it and enough time to do so. And even though Russian soldiers were not suicidal fanatics ready for certain death, their leaders were absolutely capable of sacrificing them without a second thought, particularly in a war gone nuclear.

"And could you disable the disarm circuit?," Kim asked.

The technician shook his head. "As you would expect, the device has safeguards against tampering. Adding a capability like remote detonation was not only safe, it looked as though the designers had thought about adding it themselves and then were told to stop. Trying to remove a component that is already there though..." The technician's voice trailed off as he shook his head.

Kim nodded. He could hardly fault the man for wishing to avoid a nuclear explosion.

"And the disarming code?," Kim asked.

The technician shrugged. "It is the right number of digits for the display on the device. The only way to test it would be to arm the device, which would clearly be too risky. I can only add that the length of the code means millions of possible combinations, that could never possibly be guessed in twenty minutes."

Kim grunted. The technician had a point. He certainly wasn't going to include the disarming code with the device. That meant whoever they sent to ensure the device remained safe and undiscovered could, at most, enter a few dozen random number combinations out of millions of possibilities once the device was armed remotely.

The technician shuffled his feet nervously, and Kim tensed. It was a certain sign of more bad news to come.

"What else?," Kim asked quietly.

"You know that once the device is armed, a countdown clock is activated. Since the device predates digital electronics, the clock is of course mechanical. That means it will make a small amount of noise as it operates. Since you indicated to us the device will be in a container, our examination of the device suggests the clock's operation should not be audible to its operator."

Kim glared at the technician. "But?"

The technician clearly wished for nothing more than to be anywhere else at that moment.

"Once the device is armed, either on site or remotely, it triggers an audible alarm."

Kim stared at the technician in disbelief. "That is absurd. This was a weapon designed to be placed in secret by special forces troops. Such an alarm would have given them away. Have you confirmed it is present in the device, not just the documentation?"

The technician nodded, once again on firm ground. "Yes, and there is some good news. The alarm is very small, with a metal striking surface the size of a coin. The striker is metal, but the end that hits the surface is covered with a bit of leather. We had to use a magnifying glass to see the stitching," he said admiringly.

Warned by Kim's glare to get back to the point, the technician added hastily "So, though it will sound off when armed, we think you would have to be right on top of it to hear the alarm. If the device is inside a container, it may be inaudible. As to why the alarm is there at all, I would go back to the many design compromises made to achieve such a small size. Nuclear weapons normally have multiple safeguards against accidental arming for obvious reasons. This design allows only one. Maybe it's not so surprising that if the device armed, they wanted a chance that someone nearby might notice."

Kim sat still for a moment thinking over his options, before quickly realizing he had none. If a quick fix had been possible the technician would have already done it, and he had to get the device moving to meet the plan's timetable.

"Dismissed," Kim said to the technician, who quickly scurried off. He thought briefly about liquidating him for his failure, but almost immediately rejected the idea. The risk of detonating the device inside North Korea did warrant caution, and he still had what he needed to accomplish the mission. Besides, though he hadn't even bothered to learn the nuclear technician's name, Kim knew they didn't have enough of them to waste. Now, Kim thought, a couple of flights and just two more Russian loose ends to tie up.

CHAPTER EIGHT

Beijing, China

The US Embassy in Beijing was probably the end of the road for Jim Martinovsky. There were a lot of ways to be forced out of the Foreign Service, but so far Martinovsky had avoided all of them, because he was in fact a pretty good political officer. The first pitfall was taken from the academic world, tenure. You had to pass a tenure review board after your first two tours, nearly always both overseas. As part of that review, you had to get off language probation, with fixed classroom time allotted for each language based on difficulty. The U.S. was unique in not requiring entering Foreign Service officers (FSOs) to have foreign language skills, because the courts had ruled the requirement discriminatory.

Once you were tenured you had ten years to be promoted to each higher grade, and twenty-two years total after tenure to make it to the Senior Foreign Service. This "up or out" concept was borrowed from the military, which was fair enough since FSOs were commissioned by the President and confirmed by the Senate, just like military officers.

The tradeoff for "up or out" used to be that FSOs were not subject to the blanket "Reduction in Force" or RIF that could be used to remove federal Civil Service workers. FSOs were made subject to RIFs in 1995, and 100 were immediately fired.

Every year, the Promotion Boards referred what their review determined were the bottom five percent of tenured FSOs to a Performance Standards Board (PSB), which had the authority to fire them if they decided the FSOs did not meet Service standards, and used it every year on some of that five percent. There was no appeal to a PSB decision.

None of these ways, though, had affected Martinovsky. He had been promoted quite rapidly to FS-1, on the official Federal conversion table equal in rank to a full colonel. Martinovsky had been caught by "opening his window," a process where he requested consideration for promotion to the first rank of the Senior Foreign Service, which would make him the equivalent of a brigadier general. Once he made the request, he had six years to make the cut, or mandatory retirement would follow with a pension that would be about a third of his working salary.

It was now the sixth year, and Martinovsky was starting to panic. He had three children, two who would start college in the next two years. When he opened his window he had been sure he would be promoted, but then heart problems had been discovered during his overseas clearance physical. They came as a surprise, since unlike many of his mostly desk bound colleagues Martinovsky was in excellent shape, thanks to a career-long habit of working out with the Marines who guarded the Embassy. His heart issues were not serious enough to keep him in the US, but they did prevent him from volunteering for service in countries like Iraq, Afghanistan, and Libya, which had become a near requirement for promotion. No matter how much he wanted to go, MED's veto was absolute, since the purpose of the overseas clearance physical was to prevent the government having to pay for a medical evacuation.

Martinovsky's heart problems also prevented him from serving in a small post in China where he could have been in charge as Principal Officer, since the poor medical care available in those cities made the risk of medical evacuation too great. Instead, he was number two in US Embassy Beijing's political section, with a Senior Foreign Service boss. As in any office, number two got most of the work, and very little of the glory.

One of the few bright spots in Martinovsky's tour in Beijing had been the development of his relationship with Li Weimin, Deputy Director-General at the Ministry of Foreign Affairs (MFA). Normally his boss would have dealt with someone of Li's rank, but Martinovsky's superior command of Chinese had helped him develop a close rapport with Li over the past four years. It also helped that Martinovsky had met Li during each of his previous two tours in China.

All of Martinovsky's previous contacts with Li had been in either an office or reception setting, as was standard for interaction with MFA officials. Today, though, Li had asked to meet him for lunch at a restaurant near the Embassy. Martinovsky had two, very different reactions. The first was annoyance, since any contact with a Chinese official outside a "normal" setting had to be reported in tiresome written detail to the State Department's Bureau of Diplomatic Security, which rightly regarded the People's Republic of China as one of the world's leading security threats to the US.

However, the second was both curiosity and anticipation. Li would not have asked for a meeting outside MFA offices unless he had something important to say. Also, Martinovsky believed that Li was running a much greater risk with his own security services, which if they found out about the meeting were likely to ask for more than a written report.

"Minister Li, a pleasure to see you. I hope your family is doing well?" Martinovsky asked in Chinese.

"Indeed yes. And yours as well, I trust?" Li responded.

"Yes, very well," Martinovsky said, completing the required courtesies.

"Though I usually enjoy speaking with you in your excellent Chinese, for today I would like to practice my English, if that is acceptable," Li said.

"Of course," Martinovsky replied, while thinking to himself that this made another first for Li.

"Now, I have never been to this restaurant, and since it is new I am guessing that you have not either. If it is acceptable, I suggest we put ourselves in the hands of the chef," Li said.

"Certainly. I am also curious to see what new ideas this chef may have," Martinovsky replied.

Li went on to speak to the waiter in rapid-fire Mandarin, who smiled and bowed several times before beating a hasty retreat to the kitchen.

"There, that will give us a few minutes of peace," Li said, as he shook out his napkin.

"We have had conversations on many topics in the past, but never yet on the Democratic People's Republic of Korea," Li said, carefully using North Korea's official name in English.

Martinovsky nodded, but said nothing.

"Perhaps you could tell me what you think of my country's policy towards the DPRK," Li said with a smile.

Martinovsky smiled in turn. This was an old game, where he did most of the talking, and Li did most of the learning. It also minimized the chance that Li would say anything that could come back later to haunt him. As he had come to know him over the years, though, Martinovsky believed he was learning more from Li's reactions to what he said than Li probably realized.

"Well, I will start with the obvious. We have never understood why China has supported North Korea without question in recent years, even as it acquired nuclear weapons and ballistic missile technology. It is an outlaw regime that has been involved in counterfeiting US currency, drug smuggling, and kidnapping of Japanese nationals. We would expect the Chinese government to do its utmost to restrain the destructive tendencies of the DPRK regime before it destabilizes the entire region, or its actions even provoke a second Korean War," Martinovsky said.

"Yes, we have heard this from representatives of the US government many times, at many levels. Why do you think we have acted so?" Li asked.

Martinovsky paused, realizing that Li was now posing a serious test of his own personal understanding, not asking for the US government's official line.

"I think the roots of Chinese policy go back to the Korean War, when US troops reached the Chinese border at the Yalu River, and Chinese troops fought alongside North Korean troops until the end of the war. It is the only time since the Communist Party took power in China that foreign troops from a country China considered an enemy were so close, and it has never happened again since," Martinovsky said.

The waiter appeared with their meal, steamed duck and vegetables over rice, from which a delicious smell arose. Both Martinovsky and Li paused to eat, and pour more tea.

Martinovsky put his fork down, and continued.

"The next event to inform Chinese policy was the collapse of the Warsaw Pact, particularly East Germany. Once Gorbachev withdrew his support from the Communist states of Eastern Europe, and in particular once he made it clear the USSR would not use force to maintain them as it had in Hungary and Czechoslovakia, the Pact's collapse took place practically overnight. China's leadership decided that North Korea's collapse followed by absorption into South Korea, along the lines of East Germany's reunification with West Germany, could never be tolerated," Martinovsky said.

"And why would that be so bad?" Li asked, with one eyebrow arched.

"A reunified Korea would present severe challenges to China's position in Asia, and to the current Chinese system. First, there is the likelihood it would remain a US ally, mostly out of fear of China. That might once again mean US troops near China's border. Second, there would be the unwelcome spectacle of a democratic and capitalist country on China's border, providing unique inspiration to China's rising generation, which already yearns for greater freedom," Martinovsky said.

"Come now, don't Japan and the province you call Taiwan already provide such salutary examples?" Li asked with a smile.

"Not quite. For much of its history since Chiang Kai-Shek Taiwan has been a far from perfect example of democracy. And nobody in China takes Japan seriously as a model for a long list of reasons, starting with its actions during its occupation of China. Korea though has moved ahead rapidly in its industry and technology, while at the same time its people forced the military to give up power by street demonstrations that captured the attention of the entire world. It holds the same Confucian values as most Chinese, even most Party members. In short, I believe there is every reason to think a united, democratic and capitalist Korea is the last thing China's current leadership would want," Martinovsky concluded.

"I will not disagree with anything you have said," Li said, nodding. "However, is there not a possibility for reunification you have overlooked?" he asked.

Martinovsky was at first puzzled, and then smiled.

"Of course, China would favor reunification on the North's terms, but that is hardly likely," Martinovsky said.

"Really? Please explain," asked Li.

"The stalemate on the Korean peninsula has lasted for more than fifty years. Over that time, the South's military has become better armed, trained, and led. It is now a professional force, with no involvement in politics. It continues to be supported by thirty thousand US forces stationed in Korea, with a full complement of armor, aircraft, and access to satellite reconnaissance assets. Immediate reinforcement is available from US forces in Japan."

"By contrast, the North's soldiers are drawn from a population plagued by famine. Their aging armor and aircraft are poorly maintained. The fuel and other supplies needed for an offensive are not available to their bankrupt government. All their nuclear weapons and ballistic missiles have succeeded in doing is uniting all its neighbors but China against them. Not even Russia would support another Korean War. And even North Korea's leaders have to see their use of nuclear weapons would guarantee both a South not worth having, and a devastating retaliation to ensure such a criminal act would never be repeated," Martinovsky said.

"Well, let us leave aside for the moment the likelihood of the event, and instead think about its reality: A Korean peninsula united under the DPRK. How would the US government react to such an event?" asked Li.

Here it is, thought Martinovsky. Nobody with Li's rank and experience in the Chinese government would ask such a question out of idle curiosity. But how could he possibly be serious?

"Now, I am afraid that my imagination fails me," Martinovsky said with a smile. "May I have time to think about such an unexpected turn of events?" he asked.

"Naturally. I would have been surprised if you had an answer ready to hand. Of course, we have wandered some distance into the theoretical. I am sure you are right that a change soon in the Korean status quo is most unlikely," Li said.

As he smiled and nodded, Martinovsky thought that he had never heard a more insincere statement in his twenty-five years as a diplomat – and that took some doing.

CHAPTER NINE

Tokyo, Japan

As the taxi drove him away from Narita Airport, Chung Hee Moon looked out the window as the driver chattered about the Naritasan Shinshoji Temple, which he claimed had ten million visitors a year. Sighing, Chung realized he had only himself to blame for failing to pretend he didn't understand Japanese. Still, it was a more interesting drive than the one from the North Korean border to Shenyang, which had been done entirely at night. All he learned from that ride was that the Chinese had more lights on at night on that route than burned throughout all of North Korea, which chronic power shortages kept pitch dark throughout the year.

As with the Chinese at Shenyang airport, it was hard to miss how much richer the Japanese were than North Koreans, even the ones who lived like him in the relatively pampered capital of Pyongyang. Cars, satellite dishes, high-end cell phones, restaurants, shops — everywhere he looked the objects said "wealth." But the people were an even more convincing testimonial. They all looked healthy, were well dressed, and moved about without the air of quiet paranoia Chung had taken for granted his entire life.

After paying the cab driver, Chung looked around him at the dock where he had asked to be dropped. The smell of the sea was the same here as at home, though the ships and the cranes that serviced them were many times the size of the vessels and equipment at any North Korean port. Perhaps most striking was the lack of security. He could see no troops or even security guards, but did notice several cameras. Still, he could have climbed the wire mesh door and dropped to the other side in about ten seconds.

However, his instructions were clear. Wait outside the gate until admitted. After just a few minutes, through the gathering gloom of twilight Chung saw a dour, ascetically thin young Korean with slicked back hair approaching, dressed in a dark suit that had certainly been made outside Korea. The man opened the gate, and gestured for Chung to come inside.

With a flat, unblinking stare the man asked, "Your name?"

Chung gave him the name he had been assigned for this mission. The man nodded and said "You may call me Mr. Lee." Chung nodded expressionlessly, though he knew the name was no more the one the man had been born with than his own.

"You may be wondering at the lack of security. It is true that far fewer men watch many more ships than would ever be true at home. However, be aware until your departure that the cameras you see are manned, and armed security guards will react to any activity they consider suspicious. I have reported you as a business contact to our shipping concern, and so had no difficulty obtaining you a dock pass. Attach this to your shirt," Lee said, handing him a laminated pass with Japanese characters.

"It will only be valid for two days, but since you leave tomorrow, that will be no problem," Lee said with a thin smile. "Let us take a look at your new home," Lee said, as he swung open the door to a standard forty foot shipping container.

Inside, Chung saw a white van of an unfamiliar model, with no windows in the back. There was nothing else in the container.

"You will be inside for at least ten days, possibly eleven. In this envelope is enough Japanese currency to buy whatever you will need to subsist for that time. I suggest you eat as little as possible for obvious reasons. Operating instructions for the device as well as details on arrangements after your arrival in the U.S. are inside the van. The device itself will be loaded just before the ship's departure."

Lee looked Chung up and down. "I have been briefed on your medical condition. Are you still well enough to carry out the mission?"

Chung nodded. "I would not even know I had cancer if it had not been detected during a routine physical. The doctors say it will be at least another month before I even start to have symptoms."

"Good. You are unlikely to wait that long. Now, the closest store with the supplies you need will be one block to your right as you exit the dock. You have a reservation made under your cover name at the hostel across the street. This is not being done out of kindness, but for security. It is not practical to put you in the container immediately because as you can see activity at the dock now is light, and there is a good chance your entrance and failure to exit would be noticed. Tomorrow, you will enter at midday during a period of peak activity, with dozens of people coming and going through that gate. Do you have any questions?"

Chung shook his head.

"Good. Then I will see you here tomorrow at noon." Lee walked away, and Chung turned towards the gate and the next phase of his mission.

Beijing, China

Martin L. Fitzwilliam was Political Counselor at Embassy Beijing, and Jim Martinovsky's boss. Fitzwilliam was also a Senior Foreign Service (SFS) Officer who had already been promoted once within the SFS, and so was the equivalent of a two-star general. Though the customs of the Foreign Service required them to use first names when speaking with each other, both were just as conscious of their ranks as if they had been military officers. Fitzwilliam's bow tie and generous paunch were what Martinovsky thought of as proof positive that he was part of the "dinosaur generation" of FSOs. He was dreading discussing the cable he had drafted about his meeting with Li Weimin with Martin, but there was no avoiding it.

"Good morning, Martin," Martinovsky said.

"Good morning, Jim. So, an interesting conversation with Li Weimin?" Fitzwilliam replied.

"Yes, quite interesting. First, a couple of points on background. Both this meeting and its location at a restaurant near MFA were at Li's request," Martinovsky said.

"Unusual. I haven't had a lunch meeting with a Foreign Ministry official in over a year," Fitzwilliam noted.

"Li quickly steered the conversation to USG policy towards North Korea, which I explained per our standard talking points. I don't have to tell you that it's highly unusual for an official of Li's rank to discuss policy towards a country outside his area of responsibility with a foreign diplomat," Martinovsky said.

"Right. Normally I would get a call from the Asian division of MFA. Very peculiar," Fitzwilliam said, nodding.

"Li concluded by asking me how the USG would react to a Korean peninsula united under the DPRK, after asking me to leave aside the likelihood of the event. I asked for time to consider my response, to which Li had no objection, saying he would have been surprised if I had a ready answer. Li then tried to make light of his question, saying he was sure a change soon in Korea was unlikely. As you know, an official of Li's rank is not likely to engage in idle speculation with a foreign diplomat. Li had a concrete purpose for asking how the USG would react to a Korean peninsula united under the DPRK. Asking the question also suggests that either Li or other officials in the Chinese government believe Korean unification under the DPRK is a real possibility," Martinovsky said.

"I'm not sure that makes sense. After all, it could have just been an off-hand remark," Fitzwilliam objected.

"Well, I can't see any other purpose to our meeting, and it certainly wasn't lunch. I think we need to ask Main State how to respond to Li's question. I also believe US military and intelligence agencies should be made aware of an apparent shift in Chinese government intentions towards Korea, so they can take appropriate action," Martinovsky said.

"I agree that the conversation should be reported. However, I see no need for an action request. If anyone at Main State decides to take Li seriously, they can tell us to relay any response they choose," Fitzwilliam replied.

Martinovsky knew that this was the wrong call. He also knew his chances of convincing Fitzwilliam it was wrong were zero.

"OK, I'll get you the draft later today," Martinovsky said.

CHAPTER TEN

Vladivostok, Russia

Grishkov was more than a little surprised to hear from Alexei Vasilyev so soon, and even more concerned by the tone of his summons. Whatever he had found on the microdot, it was not good news.

As Grishkov walked into the Black Crow, he mechanically scanned the few patrons and the bartender. All were familiar faces, and none presented any threat. He bought a bottle of Stoly at the bar, and took it and two glasses to his usual table at the back, facing the sole door. Grishkov was sure they would want no interruptions, and if the news was as bad as he feared, they might need the whole bottle to help decide what to do next.

Vasilyev walked into the bar looking grim, and his sloping shoulders, set jaw line and furrowed brow even caught the bartender's attention, a first in Grishkov's experience. A glare from Vasilyev sent him back to polishing his glasses.

"So, I'll take the good news first," Grishkov said, in an attempt to lighten the mood.

It didn't work.

"I suppose you could call my success in accessing the information on the microdot good news, except for the information itself," Vasilyev said with an even deeper scowl.

"It had details on Timoshenko's theft?" Grishkov asked.

"Yes, full details. As a professional I should give him credit for coming up with such an elaborate scheme, which worked perfectly until it came time to sell what he had stolen," Vasilyev said.

"And what did he steal, exactly?" asked Grishkov.

Vasilyev looked around the room, which contained only the bartender.

"A man-portable nuclear device," answered Vasilyev in a near whisper.

Grishkov could feel all the color draining from his face.

"But there was a complete inventory done at the Vladivostok armory, and there was nothing found missing! Plus, it was supervised by a general who had just assumed command, who had every reason to find such a theft!" exclaimed Grishkov.

"I have no doubt that they conducted a complete inspection. However, the theft would have been impossible to detect," said Vasilyev.

"And how did Timoshenko manage that?" asked Grishkov.

"Through bribes to the officers responsible for managing both the records and their backups. And then eliminating the officers through so-called accidents," replied Vasilyev.

"Damn it! I told Captain Ivansik there were too many accidents at that armory for it to be a coincidence, but he wouldn't listen!" fumed Grishkov.

"Yes, well, it would not have mattered much if he had. With the records and their backups destroyed, no inventory or any other action could have revealed Timoshenko's treachery," Vasilyev said gloomily.

"But this is incredible. How could such important records be left vulnerable to destruction?" asked Grishkov.

"Ah, an important question, and perhaps the master stroke of Timoshenko's plan. He selected a weapon to target from ones intended for use against Japan. They were among the earliest man portable nuclear devices, and the ones in the Vladivostok armory were never replaced. The Soviet High Command never bothered because after China became a nuclear power and broke its alliance with the USSR, it became a far greater threat than Japan," replied Vasilyev.

"And that meant these records were just forgotten?" asked Grishkov.

"Not forgotten, but never made part of the classified central database of nuclear weapons maintained in Moscow. They should have been, but were simply overlooked. Ordinarily a theft would have been detected by a local manual inventory, but Timoshenko's bribes and killings erased all records and backups at the Vladivostok armory, as well as the officers who knew that those records were missing," replied Vasilyev.

"But it is not enough to have just the weapon. Isn't a code needed to arm them?" asked Grishkov.

"Yes, indeed. Unfortunately, I have discovered that an officer who was reported recently as absent without leave from the Vladivostok armory was responsible for these codes. Ordinarily such codes would not be maintained locally, but these early devices were not capable of receiving an arming code sent by radio. So, there was a local codebook," replied Vasilyev.

"So, this officer is the only person who can confirm that both the weapon and its arming code have been stolen?" asked Grishkov.

"Correct. Unless we can find him, everything I have just told you can be dismissed as speculation, and the microdot as a fabrication intended to fool Timoshenko's arms buyers," replied Vasilyev.

"Fortunately, I was already aware of this missing officer. And I have an idea where we can start looking," Grishkov said.

CHAPTER ELEVEN

Vladivostok, Russia

Kim Gun Jun's trip to Vladivostok from Pyongyang had been just as long and tiring as he had feared. Not that he cared about personal comfort, quite the reverse. However, it would make it more difficult to make effective use of the Mosin-Nagant 1891/30 sniper rifle his local agent had obtained for him. His hands needed to be rock steady, which his fatigue would make more difficult.

The rifle was a mixed blessing. It was of Russian manufacture, an absolute necessity since an expensive U.S. or West European sniper rifle would have been evidence that a foreign intelligence agent might be in Vladivostok. It was arguably the best sniper rifle produced during World War II, as shown by the fact that German snipers often used captured ones in preference to their own Mauser 98Ks. Since over 300,000 were produced, it was readily available and would not point investigators in any particular direction, which was important since Kim planned to abandon the rifle after tonight.

However, it had some real drawbacks. It was long and heavy, which made setup awkward. The wooden stock had warped over the years, as was typical of these old rifles. Most important, the trigger was not adjustable, as one on any rifle produced in the past thirty years would be, though it had been lightened to a shade over two kilograms.

Still, it would have to do. Kim was an excellent shot, and as he lined up the Mosin-Nagant's 3.5x scope on the Black Crow's front door, he was confident that Grishkov and Vasilyev would be meeting there tonight for the last time.

Grishkov had done his obligatory two-year tour in the Russian Army, even though he could have easily used one of the over two dozen exemption grounds to avoid service. Back then, he naively believed that service was a patriotic duty. Well, the truth was that he joined the police for similar reasons, so he hadn't changed much in his motivations. However, he did know that he didn't trust or respect most of the officers who had commanded him during his Army tour, and that meant he couldn't make it a career.

Nine months of service in Chechnya had taught him quite a bit, besides the certainty that he was not cut out for a career in the Russian Army. It taught him that many of Russia's ethnic and religious minorities had very little love for the Russians who ruled them. It taught him that overwhelming military force, indiscriminately and brutally applied, could be effective in overcoming local objections to rule by outsiders.

Perhaps the most important lesson, though, had been to listen to his instincts. Several of the soldiers in his unit, including ones Grishkov genuinely considered smarter than him, had failed to do so and died quick and violent deaths. One poor fellow had been captured by the Chechens and....Grishkov was grateful the nightmares that followed the discovery of his body had faded with the passing years.

Right now, as he passed through the Black Crow's front door, those instincts told him to drop flat and pull Vasilyev down with him.

An instant later, the top half of the door exploded in a shower of glass that covered them both, and Grishkov heard the shot. It sounded like it was coming from the roof of a building one street over.

Grishkov and Vasilyev both cursed as they scrambled to get away from the lit front door, and cut their hands with glass shards in the process. Another shot punched a hole in Grishkov's coat as it blew in the wind, but failed to strike the man inside.

Both of them would still have died, though, if not for a stroke of good luck. The Black Crow's garbage dumpster dated back to the Stalin era, when such items were made with no regard to profit and loss by men who regarded thick and heavy as marks of quality. Even so, the dumpster would not have helped them if it had been properly placed inside the alley where it belonged. Happily, Vladivostok's waste disposal service was not inclined to wheel it back and forth, precisely because it weighed a ton. So, it remained a few steps from the Black Crow's front door, mostly blocking the sidewalk, with the building housing the Black Crow on one side and a warehouse on the other.

Grishkov and Vasilyev moved behind the dumpster so quickly the sniper's next shot hit the dumpster's front. Though it pierced it, the round's momentum was not enough to punch through the other side.

"I know that sound from Chechnya! That's a Mosin-Nagant!" exclaimed Grishkov.

"Agreed," grunted Vasilyev. "Someone wants us very dead."

Two more rounds blasted through the dumpster's front, and then clattered off its back interior. Grishkov and Vasilyev both hunched even lower.

"Remind me to write a thank you letter to the manufacturer," Vasilyev said, knocking his knuckles against the back of the dumpster.

"I have other priorities," Grishkov said, as he pulled out his police radio.

Grishkov called police headquarters, and less than a minute later they could hear approaching sirens.

"What do you suppose the chances are that our friend will stick around for us to talk to him?" asked Vasilyev.

Grishkov's expression answered the question, with no words needed.

Fifteen minutes later, the area had been secured and Grishkov and Vasilyev were standing on the rooftop where the sniper had nearly killed them both.

"I want roadblocks and a house to house search over a ten block radius from this spot," Grishkov ordered. His men chorused "Yes sir!" and scrambled to carry out their orders.

"Do you really think they'll catch him?" asked Vasilyev.

"No. This was a professional, and he will have an escape plan that anticipates our response, both in terms of timing and resources. But, we have to try. And besides, we may get lucky," Grishkov responded, his lips drawing back in a feral smile.

"Yes. Now, take a look at this Mosin-Nagant. Notice anything interesting?" asked Vasilyev.

The rifle had already been dusted for prints and none found, so Grishkov picked it up and examined it closely. After several minutes of close inspection, including dry-firing the weapon, he shrugged and put it down.

"I see nothing remarkable," said Grishkov.

"Exactly. And that is what's wrong here," said Vasilyev.

Grishkov made a "come on" gesture with his hands.

"Look, whoever did this had to know that killing a senior police detective and a ranking FSB officer would amount to prodding the proverbial Russian bear with a very sharp stick. If you're going to risk that sort of response, then you make sure you get the target. But what do we have here? A World War II vintage rifle, with no enhancements to the scope or anything else. Why not a more modern rifle, with a better scope and a higher rate of fire?" asked Vasilyev.

Grishkov slowly nodded.

"And why a sniper? If someone really wanted us dead, we would have had little chance against several thugs with automatic weapons. Of course, we might have managed to take out one or more of the attackers before dying ourselves. I think that is the lesson to be learned from the type of weapon, and style of attack. The priority was not making sure we were dead, but rather ensuring we would not know who attacked us. There is only one type of organization with that priority," Vasilyev concluded.

"That would be?" prompted Grishkov.

"A foreign intelligence agency," Vasilyev said flatly.

"Which one?" asked Grishkov.

"Simple," said Vasilyev. "Whichever one obtained the missing nuclear device from Timoshenko."

Grishkov grunted his assent. "And they'll probably try again."

Vasilyev nodded. "I think we can count on it. Unless we can figure out who is behind all this first."

Grishkov frowned. "In the meantime, what other options does the assassin have?"

Vasilyev thought for a moment and then looked up at Grishkov. "He could kidnap someone the target cares about to use as leverage."

All the blood drained from Grishkov's face. "And since I have a wife and two children and you don't even have a dog…"

Vasilyev shook his head. "I think we have time. If it weren't for that dumpster and your combat instincts we'd both be dead right now, and I'm certain that's what the assassin expected – success. He didn't plan for failure. Still, call your wife."

Grishkov had already pressed the speed dial number on his cell phone. Vasilyev stood nearby and listened, his expression saying more clearly than words, "This is why I never married."

"Arisha, hi. How is everything there? Good, good. Now listen, I need you to pack a suitcase for you and the children. You will be going to see your mother for a few days while I take care of some business. I will explain why when I get home within the hour. I have to stop by the office first. Love you too."

Vasilyev cocked one eyebrow. "And the stop at the office is for…?"

Grishkov started running for his car, with Vasilyev having to scramble to keep pace. "I have to get Captain Ivansik's approval to have two of my men watch over my family while I am in Khabarovsk."

Vasilyev nodded. "Which is where you think the sole survivor of Timoshenko's nuclear weapons acquisition has been hiding."

Grishkov smiled grimly. "Precisely. He has family in Khabarovsk, and since a check of hotel registry records nationwide found nothing, he either has excellent fake papers or is staying with relatives. I'm betting on the latter."

Vasilyev nodded again as they both entered Grishkov's car. "Agreed. Whatever Timoshenko paid him would not have been enough to buy fake papers, especially since a military officer would have had no idea where to safely obtain them. What do you need from me?"

Grishkov punched hard on the accelerator. "I want you to find out where there could be a record of the missing nuclear device. It was sent to the Vladivostok armory from somewhere, and whichever office sent it must have a record. I'm positive that record still exists somewhere. The question is where."

Vasilyev's head snapped to the right as they took a turn on two wheels. "Very well. Assuming I survive the ride to your police station, I will question my contacts in Moscow. I agree that there must be a record somewhere, and such a record would never be discarded. The question is, after a half century can it be found in time?"

CHAPTER TWELVE

En Route from Tokyo to Long Beach, CA

Military discipline came to Chung Hee Moon as naturally as breathing. And that was fortunate, because without that discipline coping with conditions inside the forty-foot metal container would have been far more difficult. He wasn't sure whether incompetence by the mission planners had resulted in the container's placement out on the ship's open deck rather than the hold, or if attempting to direct the container's location on the ship had been too risky. He could imagine "Mr. Lee" avoiding anything that might make the crew more inclined to look inside the container, and insisting on the container's placement in the ship's hold might have done that.

Direct exposure to sunlight on deck, though, heated the inside of the metal container to over 40 degrees Celsius, or as the Americans would call it over 100 degrees Fahrenheit. It was fortunate that Chung had brought sufficient water to remain hydrated, or his part in this mission could have been quite brief.

Night brought temperatures down to near-freezing. This posed less of a problem, since adding additional layers of clothing was not difficult. There was only so much, though, that he could take off.

Chung read and reread his mission instructions until he had committed them to memory. Then, as was standard for any such operation, he ate the rice paper on which the instructions had been written. Not as dramatic, he thought with a smile, as movies he had seen with directives on tapes and disks that had disappeared in a puff of smoke after they had been played. But just as effective.

After the ship docked at Long Beach, the container would be off-loaded to a customs bonded warehouse. Chung shook his head as he read a U.S. government publication explaining the types and purposes of such warehouses. There were no fewer than eleven types of customs bonded warehouse specified under American law, including "Bonded warehouses established for smelting and refining imported metal-bearing materials for exportation or domestic consumption" and his personal favorite, "Bonded warehouses established for the manufacture for domestic consumption or exportation of cigars made in whole of tobacco imported from one country."

The one Chung would go to, though, was one of the most common types, an "Importer's private warehouse used exclusively for the storage of merchandise belonging to or consigned to the proprietor." This particular warehouse had been used successfully for years by North Korean government agents to move the drugs and weapons that constituted their country's sole exports to the US market. Bribes paid to Customs and Border Patrol (CBP) and Drug Enforcement Agency (DEA) agents had so far been successful in helping them avoid detection. The much greater flood of drugs and weapons through Mexico also helped by focusing attention elsewhere that in most countries would have seen the North Korean operation discovered within months. Put simply, CBP and the DEA had much bigger fish to fry.

The only tricky part had been making sure that the CBP and DEA agents bribed did not learn that they were being paid by North Koreans. Being brought to court on bribery charges was one thing, but post 9/11 terrorism charges for working with a charter member of the "Axis of Evil" were another matter. There was also the possibility that an agent might have a relative actually serving in the U.S. military in South Korea. Such an agent might refuse a bribe, no matter how generous.

The solution was simple – they had told all of the agents involved that they were working for the Chinese triads. Though it was tempting to rely on the "all Asians look alike" belief of many Americans, the North Koreans did not leave this detail to chance. Thousands of years of a shared border with China and frequent intermarriage had left many children with Chinese features who had grown up to work for North Korean intelligence. The well deserved reputation of the triads for the brutal execution of those who betrayed them served the North Koreans well, and so far no agent they had bribed had breathed a word to any law enforcement organization about their operations.

Only one detail was missing from his mission instructions, the location where he would wait for orders to detonate the device. Nodding approvingly, Chung agreed that this was basic security in case he was somehow discovered and captured before arrival in the US. He would learn this detail from the agent who unlocked the container after the ship had docked at Long Beach.

Once he had committed his mission instructions to memory and read all of the background briefing details, Chung was surprised to find that the greatest challenge was being left alone with his thoughts. As a member of an elite North Korean military unit training, drilling, exercises and indoctrination sessions occupied any time not occupied by actual missions.

The only "free time" anyone had went to the few who had spouses and children before they were transferred to his unit. Surprisingly, this did not cause resentment. The majority who, like Chung, had no family lived vicariously through these lucky few. They admired their photos, told and retold the stories of their children's accomplishments, and on a few rare occasions such as a graduation even had the chance to share in their joy.

Now, though, Chung had days of total quiet and isolation to reflect on his life, which now was drawing to a close. As his ship steamed across the Pacific towards Long Beach, he realized he had a lot to think about.

Pyongyang, North Korea

Shin Yon Young stood in line with all of the cleaners, cooks, and assorted others who had been granted nothing more than a plain white badge with their name, photo and position to get through security to enter the Personal Secretariat building. The conference room that was his target was in the Main Office of Secretaries, in effect the North Korean Foreign Ministry. Marshal Ko had moved the NDC's meetings here last year, so that he could have quick access to the latest reports from overseas before each meeting.

Every day Shin was required at a minimum to empty his pockets and walk through a metal detector, and most days that was all. Some days they also patted him down. Only once had they forced him to a side room to strip, so they could thoroughly search his clothing.

They would have to literally tear his clothes to shreds to find the bug. His jacket was made in China, like those of most North Koreans, but had been modified before his mission. The polyester lining sewn firmly to the cheap rubbery jacket exterior was not the original. Instead, it was a fabric specially treated in one small area to be removable with a sharp horizontal tug. Normal wear, or even a rough search, would not betray the bug's resting place. Searches upon departing the building were less frequent, but the guards would not find a tear in a maintenance worker's jacket lining any cause for concern even if they did.

Shin shuffled slowly as the line inched forward. Many parts of this as- signment, he thought sourly, required no acting skills at all. Maintaining an air of sullen but silent resentment as they were treated with harsh indif- ference by the guards carrying out the searches was part of blending in, and Shin found it came quite naturally. He was careful to smile only to himself as he thought that he was certainly the only one in line who de- served the guards' callous treatment.

CHAPTER THIRTEEN

Tunnel No. 1, North Korea

Lee Ho Suk knew what the fine pattern of cracks in the earthen ceiling of the tunnel meant. It said, in fact shouted, "Run if you want to live!" But he commanded his feet to remain still, even though they positively twitched with the desire to propel him towards light and safety. He continued to mechanically move his arms back and forth, swinging his pickax against the wall of the tunnel as he had for hours, as he had done every day for years uncounted.

Lee knew that calling the alarm too soon carried an even greater risk than a collapse of the tunnel so complete it buried all of them under tons of rock and earth. That was the tunnel's successful completion, followed by the elimination of every prisoner who knew it existed. Lee had to time his warning so that he and the others could escape the oncoming collapse, but the collapse itself could not be avoided.

In fact, Lee was amazed that it had taken this long for a disastrous tunnel collapse to threaten him again. The radical increase in the tunnel's rate of construction would have normally led to catastrophe in short order. However, Lee had to give grudging respect to the civilian workers who had been brought in to supplement the regular prison labor force. They knew their business, and he had overheard several conversations that explained why- they were miners. Real miners, who normally dug mines for the strategic minerals used to produce North Korea's weapons, and one of the few areas where exports made the government hard currency.

However, though the civilian miners were far more experienced and capable than the malnourished and exhausted prisoners, they were simply being pushed too hard and too fast by the officers in charge of the tunnel's construction. Lee had no idea what could be so urgent about the tunnel's completion, but every barked order and worried expression made it clear to him that if the tunnel was not finished on time, the responsible officers would pay a terrible price.

Lee just hoped that the tunnel's impending collapse would give him the opportunity to escape in the confusion. He doubted he would get another chance.

En Route from Pyongyang to Beijing

Park Won Hee had wondered idly why he was being sent to Beijing via a charter flight to Tokyo, rather than simply flying straight to Beijing. The jet provided for his trip had more than adequate range to make the trip direct, so refueling was not the answer.

The answer was sitting in the seat next to him. It was occupied by a dour, ascetically thin young Korean with slicked back hair who had boarded in Tokyo. He was dressed in a conservative dark suit that he had certainly bought in Japan. Though he had been introduced as "Mr. Lee" Park was quite sure that was not his actual name. Park was just as certain that Lee was his minder, assigned to make sure that Park did not defect during his trip to China, as many other North Koreans had over the years. In a single incident in 2008, for instance, eleven North Koreans had made it from China to South Korea via the Philippines.

North Korea had no Embassy in Japan, but of course it had a robust unofficial presence that the Japanese government tolerated, as long as it did not generate enough trouble to make action and headlines necessary. Lee was part of that operation, which meant that he was part of the elite in North Korea's security and espionage program. Park had no interest in knowing which of the many different agencies included in that program Lee worked for, but he did want to determine his capabilities and interest level. In particular, whether this was just a routine assignment for Lee, or whether Park would have him attached like a magnet dogging his each and every step. So far, the obvious approach of conversation had been a complete nonstarter.

Park looked out the aircraft window as the plane idled on the runway, awaiting clearance for takeoff to Beijing on a typically gloomy and overcast Tokyo day. Not far away was the 579 acre US naval base at Yokosuka. From there they could provide ready reinforcements to their forces in South Korea.

Park's thoughts then turned to the damaged reactors at Fukushima, less than two hundred miles away. He could not help sighing at the irony of the name, since Fukushima literally meant "good fortune island."

Maybe Marshal Ko was right that the time had come to strike a blow for reunification.

If only his plan didn't start with a nuclear detonation that would make the disaster at Fukushima look like a balmy spring day.

Vladivostok, Russia

Captain Ivansik chewed on the end of his pen as Grishkov finished his report. "So, having failed to kill you and this FSB officer what do you think their next move will be?"

"I think they will target my family," replied Grishkov, doing his best to make his expression as impassive as possible.

"Yes, I agree. However, you know there is no way I can authorize the use of our resources to guard the family of my lead homicide detective. That would suggest our city was a not altogether safe place, correct?" asked Ivansik, arching one eyebrow.

"Yes, sir," Grishkov said carefully.

"Yes. Well, I have another idea. Who are your two best men?" Ivansik asked.

"Petrov and Nikitin, sir," Grishkov responded without hesitation.

"They would have been my choices as well," Ivansik grunted with approval. "Get them in here."

In less than a minute both of them were standing in Ivansik's office, and Grishkov turned to go. Ivansik shook his head and pointed to a chair, while his glare at Petrov and Nikitin told them they were to remain standing.

"I have a dangerous assignment, for which I need two volunteers. By dangerous I mean there is an excellent chance one or both of the volunteers may be killed. You will be on unpaid leave for the duration of this assignment." Ivansik said evenly.

"I'm in," said Petrov.

"Me too," said Nikitin.

Ivansik nodded at Grishkov. "Your boss will brief you on the details. He told me you were the best he had – I'm glad to see he was right. Dismissed."

Grishkov led Petrov and Nikitin out of Ivansik's office, and said "Both of you get your gear, including vests, and meet me in the parking lot in five minutes."

With a chorus of "Yessirs" both scrambled towards their desks.

CHAPTER FOURTEEN

Vladivostok, Russia

Grishkov had met Arisha right after he had finished his tour in Chechnya, as he was starting his training at the police academy in Moscow. Though he had no intention of making his career in Moscow, Grishkov knew that the experience and resources available there could not be matched anywhere else in Russia. Once he had learned the trade, then he would move on to a smaller police department where he could hope to advance to a responsible position without "connections" that he simply did not have.

Grishkov had told Arisha right from the start that a police officer's life was dangerous, and that danger extended to the officer's family. He also told her that he would understand if she decided not to marry him, and pointed out that many officers never married because of the hazards their wife and children would face.

Arisha told him in no uncertain terms that he was being a fool. She poked him in the chest as she described the heart attack that had killed her father, a lawyer, when he was forty-eight. She cried as she told Grishkov about her anger and frustration at the death of her sister, a librarian, at twenty-seven because of a drunk driver. Nobody knew better than her, she said, that everyone who lives risks death every day.

Arisha's voice rose highest, though, when she told Grishkov that if everyone thought like him then Russia was doomed. "The people with the courage to defend the nation against the thugs and barbarians who would prey on decent people should be the first to have a family! Are criminals the ones who should feel safe enough to raise children? Do you expect to make it through the rest of your life alone without the love and support of a family to help you deal with the stress and challenges of a life fighting crime? I know you are smarter than that!"

Grishkov smiled when he thought about how passionate Arisha had been in their discussions, and how quickly she had erased his doubts about marrying her. Now, though, their fourteen years of marriage would face their first test. His family had never been threatened before today.

As Grishkov opened the door to his apartment his two sons Sasha and Misha boiled out, nearly knocking him over. Sasha was twelve and Misha ten, both dark haired and growing like weeds. "Are you coming with us?" they asked in near unison. "No, I have to go on a business trip. But I know you'll like seeing your grandmamma."

As he gathered Sasha and Misha in his arms and dragged them into the apartment, he saw that Arisha had already packed and was ready to go.

"My mother is expecting us. Are the two men waiting in the car downstairs coming with us?" Arisha asked.

Grishkov breathed an internal sigh of relief at not having to raise the topic of his men accompanying his family himself. He should have known that Arisha would notice them.

"Yes. Their names are Petrov and Nikitin. You don't have to worry about them, though. They will either be on patrol outside your mother's house or in their car."

"Nonsense. Are they going to pee in the bushes? What are they going to eat and drink? I have explained to mother what is going on, and she is like me. We will do whatever is necessary."

Grishkov looked Arisha in the eye and said, "I regret that this is happening. I am doing everything I can to end it as quickly as possible."

Arisha nodded and replied, "Don't think I have forgotten our discussions before we were married. I meant every word I said then, and still mean them now. You can tell me what this is about after it's over. For now, we need to get the children to safety."

Grishkov hugged her quickly, and told the children to turn off the TV. In under a minute, they were all heading for the car.

En Route from Vladivostok to Khabarovsk, Russia

Less than twenty miles from the Chinese border, Khabarovsk had in fact been under Chinese rule until Russia seized it in 1858. A city of over half a million, Khabarovsk's role as a trading hub with China was underlined by over one million Chinese visitors a year.

Right now, though, Grishkov's mind was on another statistic – it was 400 miles from Vladivostok to Khabarovsk over not great roads. Vladivostok Air did operate flights, but the last one had already left for the day, and he had missed the overnight train's departure as well. So, it was wait until tomorrow, or drive.

Grishkov drove.

After several hours driving at speeds that were not only in excess of the posted speed limit but arguably of his official GAZ Volga Siber's safe driving capabilities, he was not surprised to see flashing lights in his rear view mirror. Grinning, he turned on his own lights, and was rewarded by the pursuing car's lights being extinguished. The other car pulled up alongside him, and Grishkov held up his badge in the window. Nodding, the policeman turned and spoke to his partner. Thanks to an engine with at least double the horsepower his GAZ could claim, the highway patrol car sped off.

He was not so lucky with his next encounter three hours later, a highway patrol car manned by a single officer, who waved him to the side of the road.

"So, you are a detective from Vladivostok," the officer said, as he dubiously examined Grishkov's badge.

"I am the lead homicide detective for the Vladivostok region," Grishkov said, annoyed at the time he was wasting.

"And you are on official business?" asked the officer.

"Yes," Grishkov snapped.

"And who can confirm this?" asked the officer.

"Captain Boris Ivansik. You may use my radio," Grishkov said with a smile that finally told the officer just how dangerous his conduct had become.

"Unnecessary. You may proceed," the officer said, doing a quick about face and nearly running for his cruiser.

Grishkov shook his head. No wonder the idiot was patrolling this desolate highway by himself.

Long Beach, CA

At last the ship had come to a stop. Chung Hee Moon's stomach lurched as the container was picked up from the deck of the ship and loaded onto the back of the truck that would take it to the customs bonded warehouse. As a counterpoint to his flip-flopping stomach, the impact of the container hitting the truck bed closed his teeth shut with a resounding clack that Chung hoped could not be heard outside by dock workers. In fact, though, the din of normal port operations was so loud that even if Chung had been shouting at the top of his voice, it was doubtful he could have been heard outside the sealed metal container.

After a drive in the tractor trailer lasting no more than five minutes, Chung was jerked to a halt. The vehicle had halted inside the warehouse, and its driver quickly emerged. After a look around to make sure they were alone, he opened the container.

"Welcome to America, Sangjwa Chung," the man said, with a raised eyebrow and ironic tilt to his greeting that told Chung he appreciated the unusual circumstances of his arrival.

"Thank you. And your name?" Chung asked.

"You may call me Mr. Lee," the man said, smiling.

"Ah, another one," Chung said, smiling in turn.

Lee laughed, and said "I'm sure you appreciate the need for security. Here, help me get this ramp in place, and we can be on our way."

Chung worked with Lee to wrestle a portable ramp into place outside the container to allow the van's exit. Once it was in place, he slowly backed the van out until it was safely on the warehouse floor.

Lee nodded. "Good. Now, through that door you will find a shower, toiletries, and fresh clothes that should fit you. This nose has smelled worse, but we need to make sure that you attract no attention when you enter your apartment. It is not exactly a luxury building, but we do not want you mistaken for one of the street people who live outside it," he said, pointing towards a plain metal door nearby.

Shaved, showered and changed Chung felt better than he had in a long time. He hadn't realized just how smelly and exhausted he had become until the water hit him.

"Excellent!" said Lee with a smile. "Let us waste no time getting you to your new home."

"And where is that?" Chung asked, as they both climbed into the van.

Starting its engine, Lee replied by handing him a map. A neat black X marked a location in Los Angeles.

Looking at the map, Chung could see why this apartment building had been picked. It was on the edge of Koreatown, so he would have no trouble blending in. It was also between two stops on the Los Angeles metro, so he had that option for transport. Most important, its location guaranteed the destruction of many LA landmarks, even if the device was lower yield than they thought. Historic downtown LA, the Civic Center, Union Station, Dodger Stadium, Los Angeles City College and Paramount Studios were well within even the most conservative blast radius.

Frowning, Chung also saw that the Chinese Consulate General was only a few blocks away from his apartment. Well, he supposed that could not be helped.

CHAPTER FIFTEEN

Vladivostok, Russia

Kim Gun Jun could not believe how his luck had turned. An operation that had gone like clockwork, delivering exactly the nuclear device required for his country's final reunification in complete secrecy, now threatened to become unraveled at precisely the wrong time. The invasion plan demanded complete surprise, and now these Russian pests were threatening to ruin both the plan and his career. Well, the truth was, more than his career. Failure at his level usually ended more than that.

Kim now had to choose between two obvious options. Kill the Russian investigators, or seek leverage over them by kidnapping their family members. After mulling it over, he decided to do both. If killing the investigators was successful, he could always kill the relatives too. The only problem was, he couldn't do both at once.

Here at least the answer was clear. In planning to kill Grishkov and Vasilyev his file review showed that only Grishkov had living family members. By now Grishkov would surely have relocated his wife and children, and the file made the location simple to deduce, since Grishkov's parents were both dead as well as his wife's father. That left only Grishkov's mother-in-law, and her address in a dacha well outside Vladivostok was in the file. Finally, Kim nodded to himself, his luck was starting to turn the right way again. With the help of a few local contractors, he was sure he could dispose of whoever Grishkov might have guarding his family, and then get him to surrender in the hope of an exchange.

Kim frowned, as he thought about the more direct option of simply killing the Russian investigators. First he had to locate them, and so far his agents had only been able to report that Vasilyev was so far sticking to his well guarded FSB office, while Grishkov appeared to have left Vladivostok. But to go where?

Captain Ivansik chewed on his pencil as he eyed his deputy sitting at his desk just outside his office, visible through the glass upper half he had installed immediately after becoming captain five years previously. Ivansik didn't trust Lieutenant Anton Fedorov as far as he could throw him, but political connections had made resisting Fedorov's appointment as his deputy impossible.

Ivansik sighed, thinking that Fedorov was a problem for another day. Keeping Grishkov, his best detective, alive was the immediate issue. As he mulled over Grishkov's situation, he realized he could do something constructive. He knew the police captain in Khabarovsk personally, and while he was no genius he could be trusted to support a fellow officer. Ivansik grunted to himself in approval as he thought that if Moscow picked a man like Bogdan Tarasov for a sensitive post like Khabarovsk, there might be hope for Russia yet. As he picked up the phone he kept an eye on Fedorov, but he made no move to pick up his own phone and listen in. Ivansik thought with some satisfaction, at least I will have done all I can to help my lead homicide detective get back to clearing cases.

Dacha 30 Kilometers From Vladivostok

After getting Arisha, her mother and the children settled inside the dacha, Petrov and Nikitin started pulling out the gear for their protective detail from the car. Petrov frowned at a large rucksack Nikitin had just extracted, his expression saying as clearly as words "What the devil is that?"

Nikitin laughed and said, "Why, this is a M16A1 Claymore mine, packed in an M7 bandoleer. The Claymore contains a pound and a half of C4, as well as lots of nasty ball bearings that will shoot out over a radius of up to 250 meters, though the optimum kill zone is more like 50 meters. By the way, did you see the movie Braveheart? Remember the sword he used? That was called a Claymore, and that's the weapon which gave the mine its name. The Claymore mine was actually designed by the Germans in World War II, though they never had a chance to produce and deploy it. The Americans took over its development and started using it in the Korean War, and have used it ever since."

Petrov stared at Nikitin and said "I'm not sure where to even start with questions. OK, here are two: How do you know all this, and how did you get your hands on a Claymore mine?"

Nikitin grinned and said "The first one's easy. I just did a search on Google. The only thing missing from the bandoleer was the instruction sheet, but the first page of search results had one, plus all the details I've mentioned and more. You can even get handy diagrams of fragmentation dispersal patterns, plus details on the M40 circuit tester, the M6 electric blasting cap, and the M57 firing device used to detonate the Claymore remotely."

"The second one you should have been able to guess, since you know I did a tour in Chechnya. I got it off a Chechen who no longer had any use for it." Nikitin's grin was wider now, and even less pleasant. "The instruction sheet was probably on his body, but after our ambush caught him and a dozen of his comrades there wasn't much left of it. Fortunately, the bandoleer was undamaged."

Petrov shook his head. "How did Chechens come to have an American weapon?"

Nikitin shrugged. "They seldom did. Most of their weapons were captured from us, or were old Chinese and East European models. I suppose some arms dealer included it in a shipment. I never heard of another American weapon being captured or used against us, though I suppose it may have happened and I didn't know about it. I don't think the Americans have any particular love for the Chechens, especially after 9/11 made Moslem freedom fighters less attractive than in the old Afghans versus Soviet days."

Petrov nodded. "That all makes sense. But how did you get to keep it?"

Nikitin's laugh was a short, sharp bark. "I set up and commanded the ambush after our squad's officer was killed earlier in our patrol. We didn't lose another man that day, and wiped out the animals who killed our officer. When I picked up the bandoleer, nobody said a word. I knew it would come in handy someday. If Grishkov is right about the people who will be coming to visit – and Grishkov is usually right about such things – then this little jewel just might keep us alive."

CHAPTER SIXTEEN

Los Angeles

The Los Angeles apartment building was not particularly impressive, but neither was it notably run down, Chung Hee Moon saw with approval. Lee smiled as he saw his reaction.

"Yes, we spent quite a bit of time finding a location that was as inconspicuous as possible. Not too upscale, where building security might be a bit nosy. Not a dump, where your van might be a target for thieves your first week. Also, where some Koreans live, but not so many that everyone feels obliged to find out who the new Korean is in the building."

"That is good," Chung said nodding, "I saw in my briefing papers that I have a very detailed identity as an unemployed former soldier from Uijeongbu. That makes sense, because I know much about the South Korean military from my studies both before and after joining special forces, and since Uijeongbu is close to the demilitarized zone nobody will question my accent. It has also grown so large as a de facto suburb of Seoul that nobody will insist we had to know each other, as might have happened if I claimed to come from a particular small village."

Lee frowned, and said "Yes, but you must guard against over confidence. I will show you to your apartment, and our first task will be a drill where I question you on your identity as someone from Uijeongbu. It is no coincidence that I lived there as an agent in place for over a decade before starting this assignment. That is why I selected Uijeongbu as your cover location before you came to the U.S. Of course, it will always be best to avoid contact with others whenever possible."

Chung shrugged. "That is obvious. However, I will have to emerge from my apartment on occasion, if only to buy food."

Lee scowled and said, "Yes, that is just as obvious. Still, you have much to learn to avoid arousing suspicion. Americans may be naïve, but they are not all stupid."

Chung nodded, and said nothing further. He knew that underestimating an enemy usually had just one result.

Vladivostok, Russia

Lieutenant Anton Fedorov knew that Captain Ivansik didn't trust him, which proved he was not a total idiot. However, like many of his generation Ivansik trusted and understood new technology even less, a weakness Fedorov was now pleased to use against him. Fedorov had jumped on Ivansik's complaint about his old phone's unreliability to replace it as well as his own with a new model. Unknown to Ivansik, along with digital call quality it also included Bluetooth conference call capability, a feature Fedorov had set to "always on." He had also paired it to his Bluetooth earpiece, which he made sure to wear constantly, and just to be sure on the side of his head out of view of Ivansik's office window. Since many other officers wore Bluetooth earpieces paired to their cell phones, Ivansik had never remarked on Fedorov's.

Ivansik had his office swept for electronic listening devices frequently, and always looked out his office window to see whether Fedorov picked up his phone to listen in on calls. Fedorov never did, except on the rare occasions when Ivansik specifically invited him to do so.

Nevertheless, thanks to Bluetooth Fedorov heard every conversation Ivansik made. Most were of no value, but a precious few contained information that Fedorov could either save for use against Ivansik when he made his move to replace him or were immediately salable. As he listened, Fedorov realized that this conversation fell into the latter category.

So, Grishkov was going into a potentially dangerous meeting in Khabarovsk, and needed backup. Fedorov knew that Grishkov was both a potential succession rival and loyal to Ivansik, so anything that happened to him would be good for Fedorov. Plus, since Ivansik already knew that Grishkov's assignment was dangerous, if he was hurt or killed no suspicion should fall on Fedorov. Yes, this information could be quite valuable, and Fedorov had a good idea who would be willing to pay for it.

Well, it was only fair, Kim Gun Jun thought. After his run of bad luck, it was about time to have some good. The odds of Grishkov going to Khabarovsk, one of only three cities in Russia where North Korea had a diplomatic post, were long indeed. But, thanks to a traitor in Grishkov's office, that information had been sold to the Russian mafiya. Kim's good luck had not stopped there. The RDEI agent at Khabarovsk was one of Kim's protégés and at his direction had made a point of cultivating the mafiya as a source of information. So, when the information surfaced that Grishkov was bound for Khabarovsk, it was a matter of minutes before it reached Kim.

Now, what to do with the information? Go to Khabarovsk to make sure personally that Grishkov and whoever he was there to see were dealt with? Drop the plan to kidnap Grishkov's wife and sons?

No, Kim thought reluctantly, shaking his head. Grishkov had too long a head start. There was no way Kim could be sure of reaching Khabarovsk before Grishkov had his meeting there and started the return trip to Vladivostok. He would have to order the RDEI agent at Khabarovsk to hire local contractors to ensure Grishkov and his source were killed at their meeting. The location of that meeting was the only detail not included in the information sold by the traitor in Grishkov's office.

Kim paused at that thought. The traitor had been careful to conceal his identity when he sold his information. Such a source could be very useful. Once this mission was done, he would have to make sure that traitor did not stay anonymous, at least to him.

It would be nice to think that he could count on his agent in Khabarovsk to dispose of Grishkov and his contact. But, he thought as he grinned to himself wryly, he could hardly do so when he had failed to kill Grishkov himself after having him literally in his sights. No, I will have to proceed with kidnapping Grishkov's family, in case he escapes again.

Not that Kim truly believed that likely. After all, as Kim had experienced himself, all lucky streaks good or bad had to end sometime.

CHAPTER SEVENTEEN

Tunnel No. 1, North Korea

Lee Ho Suk knew in his bones that the tunnel's ceiling could collapse at any second. All that had kept him from sounding the alarm hours ago was the certainty that the tunnel's completion would spell the end for him and all the other prisoners who had worked on it. The trained miners and heavy equipment that had been added to the usual prison labor force meant that this was no ordinary tunnel. Now, though, the time had come to act. He just hoped he had not waited too long.

"Comrade Lieutenant, may I please speak?" Lee asked, as he bowed low with his eyes downcast in respect.

The soldier Lee knew only as Lieutenant Hong scowled and nodded. Lee never spoke frivolously, and his reputation for predicting tunnel collapses was well known to all the guards.

"Comrade Lieutenant, there is a fine pattern of cracks in the tunnel ceiling that is difficult to see, but I know what it means. In spite of the valiant efforts of the brave miners who have helped us come so far and so fast, the ceiling is about to collapse. If we leave this section of the tunnel now, we can save the men and equipment so important to completing our glorious mission, and quickly dig through the collapsed section with only a short delay," Lee said.

Lieutenant Hong scowled again and instead of answering Lee, called for the man Lee guessed was the senior miner in charge. A heated exchange followed, which Lee could not overhear after he was dismissed with an impatient gesture from Hong. It was clear, though, that neither Hong nor the miner were happy at the prospect of reporting delay. Lee hoped his record for accurately predicting tunnel collapses would be enough to help overcome the fear of punishment from their superiors.

A rising buzz of low conversation around Lee among the guards and miners told him they had picked up on the discussion between Hong and the senior miner. The prisoners, of course, kept their mouths shut. Ones who did not usually had no chance to repeat the mistake.

With a series of gestures and rapid-fire commands, the senior miner sent several of the civilian miners back through the tunnel. When Lee saw them moving backwards, he had a brief moment of hope that they would only be the first to leave. When no one else followed, Lee realized that they had just been sent on an errand, probably to bring back materials to reinforce the ceiling. Lee knew they would never make it back in time. Well, he thought glumly, at least a few of us made it out of this tunnel alive.

Beijing, China

Park Won Hee's head was throbbing after three grueling days of negotiations with his fraternal Chinese "comrades." His hotel bed was nicer than any he had ever laid on, but it could have been full of rocks for all the luck Park was having in finding sleep.

Park had never had any illusions about the reality of North Korea's relationship with China. China was far richer and more powerful than North Korea by any rational measure, and as China had proved through its intervention during the Korean War, North Korea owed its very existence to China's military. When he had attended university in Beijing, Park had also been subjected daily to Chinese university students' attitude towards Koreans, which were similar to those for all non-Chinese. This attitude could be summed up this way: China was the historic center of world civilization, and all other countries had done little but copy from its accomplishments. With more people than any other country, China's voice should naturally count for more than that of any other nation. Though China had no interest in world geopolitical conquest, commercial domination was taken for granted as "Made in China" became what people expected to see whenever they looked at a product label whether they lived in Omaha, Buenos Aires, Manila, Johannesburg, Cairo or Naples.

The truth was, Park had no problem with these views. China's accomplishments, past and present, were undeniable. It was the corollary that China was entitled to view the rest of the world as created to serve China's interests which troubled Park. The last three days had brought home to Park just how ingrained that attitude really was.

There were three basic scenarios that Park had been discussing with Chinese negotiators over the past three days. In the first and most hopeful, South Korea bowed to the threatened detonation of a nuclear device in its capital, and agreed to reunification on the North's terms. China would need to do little more in that case than provide diplomatic support bilaterally with the US and with the United Nations. As expected, China was perfectly willing to provide such support.

In the second scenario, which Park thought far more likely, the South refused to surrender and was supported by the US. The war, however, remained limited with only air strikes launched against the North, and no additional nuclear strikes. Here discussions centered on whether and when China's air force would become involved in helping to protect the North's installations. Park had been unable to obtain a firm commitment from the Chinese, only vague promises that China "would not abandon its fraternal socialist allies in a time of true need."

The third scenario was the one that would not let Park sleep, and kept his stomach churning no matter how many antacid pills he swallowed. The US response was not limited to conventional air and cruise missile attacks, but instead included tactical nuclear strikes at suspected North Korean ballistic missile sites. US special forces teams were inserted deep inside the North to kill its political leaders and destroy key installations, a capability the US had demonstrated when it eliminated Osama bin Laden. US forces in Japan were rapidly redeployed to the South in preparation for a counter-offensive that would extinguish the North Korean regime.

Strangely this was the scenario that the Chinese were almost exclusively focused on, though nobody in the North except Park, as far as he knew, thought it possible. Even stranger, they almost seemed to look forward to this scenario. While in a limited war scenario the Chinese negotiators were unwilling to make any firm promises of military support, in an all-out conflict they were emphatic in saying that "imperialist aggression would never be allowed to succeed." It was almost as though they were hoping for all-out war, though that of course made no sense. China's economic interest in maintaining trade relations with the US was far more important than its desire to see Korean reunification on the North's terms. There had to be some element Park was missing, but he was too tired to even try to think about what that might be.

Instead, Park thought about a fourth scenario that had not been discussed, and that he would never raise with the Chinese. That was that the North Korean device, once placed at the detonation site in Seoul's subway system, failed to detonate. Of course, North Korean scientists had promised their device was in perfect working order. Park was not convinced, and thought it was ridiculous not to plan for the possibility of its failure. But, once the device had been declared "certain to detonate" it became far too risky for Park or anyone else to raise the issue, without incurring the dread charge of defeatism. In North Korea there was no more certain way to end up in a camp at a minimum, or even being stood against a wall and summarily shot.

The device's failure would bring the worst of all possible scenarios. Without the disruption caused by a nuclear detonation in the South's capital, a coordinated counterattack by US and South Korean forces would be both swift and devastating. A failed detonation would give the US and the South the support of world public opinion, and China might well abandon such an inept ally.

Park rubbed his temples and longed for a sleep that would not come.

Chapter Eighteen

Pyongyang, North Korea

Pushing a mop and scrubbing restrooms was not the sort of work Shin Yon Young had imagined when he went to work for the NIS. No baccarat tables or exotic beauties here, as he thought back to the Bond movies he had loved as a teenager. *I knew that wasn't reality, but this is a bit too much,* wrinkling his nose at the smell emanating from the toilet he was cleaning.

A guard jerked open the restroom door and gestured at Shin to follow him. Shin straightened and pointed to his bucket and other cleaning supplies. With an impatient nod the guard indicated he was to bring them. One of the first things Shin had learned was that maintenance personnel were expected to speak as little as possible, and avoid making noise. From what he had seen the guards and other staff had similar instructions.

Shin's heart beat quicker as he realized they were headed for the NDC conference room. Even better, this was not the regular guard for this floor, but one who appeared in spite of his best efforts at concealment to be nursing a hangover. As the guard used a key to open the door to the conference room, Shin was surprised to see the table littered with cups and dishes filled with half-eaten snacks. Shin strove to keep his face impassive as he thought of how many starving North Koreans would gladly wolf down the trash that would be thrown away from this table.

Gesturing at the table, the guard rightly thought no more needed to be said. Then he did something the regular guard never did – he left! As his hands moved mechanically to clean the dishes and debris from the table, Shin was elated to finally have the chance to place the bug he had been carrying for weeks. As the guard's footsteps retreated, he slid off his jacket and started to tear the inner lining. He only needed a moment....

Beijing, China

Li Weimin was walking through the Ministry of Foreign Affair's "flower bed" as he often did at the end of a long day. The "New Ministry Building" as old-timers like Li still thought of it started construction in June 1993, and was completed in July 1997. Covering an area of 61,000 square meters and with a floor space of 128,600 square meters, the grey convex building was easily the most impressive structure on the East Second Ring Road in Beijing. The "flower bed" consisted of flowers and bushes shaped like a dove of peace. Li was savoring the irony of that design as he inhaled the fresh growing smells around him. It usually had a calming effect on him, but not tonight.

Li was surprised to see Song Hailong striding towards him. The Vice Minister was a rare sight outside his office, a conference or high-level meeting. To be fair, the activities in those settings probably took about all the time Li imagined Song had in a day, leaving little for idle strolls in a garden. Unusually tall for a Chinese official, Song's hair was still dark and thick, unlike Li's graying strands.

"Li, it is a pleasure to see you. I hope you and your family are well?" Song asked.

Li smiled and nodded. "And I hope yours as well, Mr. Vice Minister."

Song laughed and said, "Li, we have known each other too long for titles. When we are alone like this, it must be Song, as it was before my time ceased to be my own."

Li continued to smile and nod, while his mind was racing. Song would not waste his time on idle chitchat. Whatever he had to discuss was critically important.

"Come, let us walk. I would like the advice of an old friend," Song said. Li fell into step beside him.

"So, Li, if I asked you our most important foreign policy goal, how would you answer?"

"Peace, security, and the prosperity of the Chinese people," Li answered automatically.

Song smiled and shook his head. "You have been at this game too long, Li, and our public answers come to your lips without conscious thought. No, I have something more concrete in mind."

Li nodded and pursed his lips. Finally he looked up, blinked, and said "Reunification."

"Yes, just so. I knew you would understand. Just as I am sure you now understand why I have raised this topic with you." Song arched an eyebrow as he waited for Li's response.

Comprehension came flooding into Li's mind like water rushing through a shattered dike. "Our support of North Korea's plans is merely a diversion. We are finally going to reunite Taiwan province!"

Only Li's decades of experience at hiding his true thoughts allowed him to insert the key words "finally" and "province" to his reaction, which was actually horrified disbelief. Taiwan had evolved into a prosperous democracy, with a standard of living and degree of personal freedom far higher than on the mainland. Nobody in his right mind would trade that for reunification without a fight, and Taiwan had spent billions on American military hardware to make taking it by force an expensive and risky proposition. Like most Chinese, Li had come to regard the status quo as destined to endure indefinitely.

"Yes, Li, finally indeed. I am glad to see that we are like-minded in this regard," Song said, his eyes glinting. Li shuddered inwardly as he thought of what the wrong answer would have cost him. Either a quickly arranged "accident," or his hasty retirement for "personal reasons" followed by a heart attack. Probably the latter, considering his age.

"So, you see why your task of sounding out the Americans on their reaction to possible North Korean reunification is so important. We want their attention focused on the Korean peninsula, while we make our preparations to reunite Taiwan as our twenty-third province," Song said.

"I understand. So far I have learned little from my US Embassy contact, because I have been careful to take no risks in gauging their reaction," Li responded.

Song nodded. "Your prudence was understandable. However, risks are now warranted. You must speak more plainly to your Embassy contact, so that we may decide whether this plan is worth the dangers we undertake. And you must do it soon."

Li twisted his lips into a grimace. "This is an awkward question, but I must ask it. How high does our support go for this project?"

Song smiled grimly. "I would have been surprised if you had not asked. The Politburo Standing Committee, the Central Military Commission, and the State Council have not yet been officially briefed. However, key members of all three have been informed, and have authorized us to proceed up to this point. Whether we move from planning to action will depend largely on our report on a likely American response. Of course, I have other sources I will use to help me make my decision on this matter. However, yours will be the most important. You see, Li, I have faith in your experience and judgment."

Li inwardly translated this to mean that if he failed to accurately predict the Americans' reaction, he would be the one held responsible for the project's failure. And there could be only one punishment for failure of a project this important.

"I will arrange to see my contact immediately, and report on his reaction at once," Li said, straightening to attention as though he were reporting to his platoon leader forty years ago.

Song noticed, and nodded with appreciation. "Excellent, Li. I am glad to see you are approaching this job with the appropriate degree of enthusiasm. Together, you and I are going to help bring forward a new and glorious chapter in our country's history."

Li smiled and felt his head bob up and down while inside it was churning. How could he stop this madness before a war started that would erase the progress of the last two generations?

CHAPTER NINETEEN

Dacha 30 Kilometers From Vladivostok

Sweat popped out on Nikitin's forehead as he twisted the last strands of wire connecting the Claymore to the gate leading to the dacha. He knew enough about explosives to have some idea of the risk he was running by using ones picked up off a battlefield from an untrained enemy. Plus, there was no way to know how old and potentially unstable these explosives were, or on the other hand whether the firing mechanism still worked. Oh well, Nikitin thought to himself with a grin, only one way to find out for sure.

Petrov poked his head outside the back door to check on Nikitin's progress. "How's it going?" he asked.

Nikitin nodded, brushed off his gloved hands and responded, "Done. Anyone opening that gate, or tripping the wire connecting the Claymore to it, is in for a very unpleasant surprise."

Petrov grunted his approval. "Good. Animals who come to attack women and children deserve everything we can give them."

Nikitin smiled and clapped Petrov on the back. "I knew there was a reason I liked you. Nothing on your last perimeter sweep?"

Petrov shook his head. "No movement except the usual birds and small animals. When those go still, that's when we'll know we have company. Anything from the boss?"

Nikitin frowned and pulled out his cell phone. He had been so focused on planting the Claymore without setting it off that he could have easily missed the phone's vibration in his pocket.

Nikitin peered at the phone's display, and then shook his head. "Nothing. I'm sure we'll hear from him soon. How's the family?"

Petrov grinned and shook his head. "The boss's mother-in-law is a tough old bird. Did you see the size of that shotgun she has? It's almost as tall as her, but she handles it like a woodsman half her age. Told me it belonged to her late husband, who was a prison guard. And here's the best part – it's a KS-23!"

Nikitin frowned. "What's so special about that model?"

Petrov laughed. "Well, it's no surprise you haven't heard of it, since it was designed in the 1970s for one special purpose – suppressing prison riots. It must have been an unofficial retirement gift for her husband. The KS-23 was made from 23 mm anti-aircraft gun barrels rejected due to manufacturing flaws. Though unable to handle high-explosive rounds safely, these barrels were considered acceptable for the lower stress of firing slugs and buckshot, and so were cut down for use as shotgun barrels. You can tell that it's an original KS-23 rather than a later model like the KS-23M, because it has a fixed wooden buttstock. She says she uses buckshot so she doesn't have to worry so much about aiming, and that she keeps it all cleaned and polished as protection against bears. Like anyone has seen a bear here in the past fifty years!"

Nikitin nodded solemnly. "All the way out here she's right to worry about the two-legged variety. I'm glad to hear we'll have some backup. And Mrs. Grishkov?"

"She has the boss's backup piece, a 9mm pistol with all serial numbers and other identifiers very illegally removed. Just like ours!" Petrov laughed.

"Excellent. And the children?" asked Nikitin.

"Mrs. Grishkov had the foresight to pack a video game console with two controllers, which Sasha and Misha have now been using for the past three hours straight. She tells me they normally get very limited time with such distractions from their schoolwork, so we can count on them to stay put in front of the TV, and not wander off," Petrov replied.

"Good. She and her mother know that they and the children must not leave the house under any circumstances?" asked Nikitin.

"Yes. I think we've done our best to be as prepared as we can," Petrov said. His expression echoed Nikitin's doubts that their best would be good enough.

Los Angeles

After hours of drilling Chung Hee Moon's admiration for "Mr. Lee" had grown considerably. He always respected professionalism, and it was clear that Lee was going to do everything in his power to prepare Chung for his assignment.

That did not mean, though, that Chung would necessarily enjoy the experience.

"What is budae jjigae?", asked Lee.

"Literally it means army base stew, and is made with hot dogs and spam. The city government didn't like the association the dish had with the war and Americans, so it tried to order the name changed to Uijeongbu jjigae, though the few restaurants that paid attention called it instead Uijeongbu budae jjigae. The best versions are supposed to be served at restaurants on what locals refer to as "buddaejjigae street".

Lee nodded. "Good. What is the U line?"

"Also called the Uijeongbu LRT, it is a completely driverless, rapid transit line going from Uijeongbu to the north of Seoul. The "U" stands for the city Uijeongbu and the U shape of the line itself. The line opened in June 2012, going from eastern Uijeongbu through its center and ending by connecting to Seoul Metropolitan Subway's Line 1. The line is about ten kilometers long on elevated track and has fifteen stations. During rush hour trains come every few minutes, and every six to ten minutes during other hours. Trains are in service from 5 am until half past midnight. Travel on the line is about half again as fast as driving a car, and twice as fast as a bus."

Lee smiled. "Very thorough. And how much does a transfer cost from the U line to the Seoul Metro?"

Now it was Chung's turn to smile. "Trick questions? Really? They are different systems with different tickets, so even though they connect there is no such thing as a transfer, in the sense of a discounted or combined ticket."

Lee frowned. "Yes, you should expect trick questions from me – and from suspicious neighbors too. One advantage of living in a socialist paradise such as ours is that people keep to themselves. Though that is sometimes the case here, you will find generally that people are much nosier in

Los Angeles than in Pyongyang. That goes double for strangers, and triple for foreign strangers."

Chung laughed. "But both my briefings and my eyes tell me that there are more foreigners here than there are Americans. Do they suspect everyone?"

Lee shook his head. "You do not understand. This is not just a simple matter of Americans versus non-Americans. There are people here from nearly every country on the planet, and if you are not from their country, you are a foreigner. Even being from a nearby country doesn't help. Do you automatically trust all Japanese, who are from a country a two-hour boat ride away?"

Chung snorted at the thought. "Certainly not, or rather the reverse of trust. Very well, you have made your point. I will do my very best to avoid contact with my neighbors, and to keep any unavoidable conversations brief."

Lee nodded approvingly. "If you stick to that approach, your chances of completing your mission without incident will improve significantly. Now, let us continue..."

CHAPTER TWENTY

Khabarovsk, Russia

The officer responsible for the missing weapon's code at the Vladivostok armory that Grishkov was coming to see was Podpolkóvnik, or Lieutenant Colonel, Aleksandr Buryshkin. Buryshkin's career had been long, but not particularly distinguished. He had performed well at the end of the war in Afghanistan, making him one of the few remaining officers with combat experience in that conflict, the loss of which had as much to do as anything else with ending the old Soviet empire. After that, though, he had shuttled from one post to another without any chance to do especially well or badly. Training he had received after service in Afghanistan in the care and use of nuclear weapons had put him in a skill category that made him one of the rare combat veterans not assigned to service in Chechnya, and the conflict in Georgia had ended so quickly there was never any chance of being transferred there. Without recent combat service or any other opportunity to shine, Buryshkin had actually done well even to make it to Podpolkóvnik, and he knew it. When Timoshenko had approached him in a Vladivostok bar he had at first threatened to report him to the police, but a subsequent review of his finances made him reconsider.

Timoshenko promised that the device would not be used inside Russia, and Buryshkin believed him. Only the Chechens would wish to do so, and they did not have the money to hire someone like Timoshenko. Besides, a nuclear device was not their style. Chechens preferred their killing up close and personal; unlike the recent wars in Iraq and Afghanistan an unseen enemy planting IEDs was not the main source of casualties in Chechnya.

Buryshkin's upcoming military pension would not even cover his food and lodging, and he was too old to seek a second career in the Mafiya. After the initial rush of anger over Timoshenko's offer had subsided, Buryshkin realized that he in fact had no choice but to accept it unless he was ready to join the many pensioners living rough on the street, or to seek charity from his sole remaining relative.

Buryshkin laughed bitterly as he looked around his sister's house. Or more precisely, his brother in law's house. Avoiding that idiot was one of the main reasons he had finally accepted Timoshenko's offer, rather than reporting him. And now he had to be grateful that he was in his house after all. It was a stroke of luck that "the idiot," as Buryshkin thought of him, had taken his sister and their daughter with him on a business trip to St. Petersburg that was followed by a long vacation. He had actually welcomed Buryshkin's offer to housesit, not having any idea that he was absent without leave and trying to avoid the fate of Timoshenko's other accomplices.

Buryshkin scratched his thinning hair as he thought about the same topic that had occupied his every waking moment since his arrival at the house in Khabarovsk- what would he do when his sister's family returned? Staying would mean providing an explanation for his earlier than expected retirement, which could be blown by a single phone call to his old office. Besides, Buryshkin knew staying with "the idiot" for more than a day or so would end with an argument that would see him out of the house as surely as night followed day.

Timoshenko had almost certainly left Vladivostok by now, though there was no telling whether he had agents there who might still try to kill him. Buryshkin knew, though, that even if he were safe from Timoshenko his status as absent without leave left him with nowhere to go. Any policeman who stopped him would find the arrest order. So would any hotel where he tried to register. Buryshkin had spent the first few days at the house in Khabarovsk thinking he would be arrested any minute, only to realize that the military had no need to look for him. Sooner or later, Buryshkin would turn up.

Buryshkin's salary of course had been stopped, and he would never see his pension. At his age he doubted he would survive his upcoming stay in a military prison. Buryshkin's mind raced every day he spent in the house as he tried to think of a way out, but so far nothing had come to him. He was thinking through his situation yet again, but nothing would come.

Grishkov's right foot ached from pressing down on the accelerator all the way to Khabarovsk. While he was still an hour outside the city, Captain Ivansik had called to tell him that Captain Tarasov would make an officer available to him as backup for Buryshkin's arrest. Though Grishkov could do nothing but thank Ivansik for the assistance, which he knew was sincerely given, Grishkov couldn't fight off a sinking feeling in the pit of his stomach. Whoever was trying to cover up what had happened at the Vladivostok armory had been one step ahead so far, and now that his family was threatened Grishkov was determined to end that. He was certain Buryshkin was the key.

The delay required to report to Captain Tarasov made Grishkov grind his teeth in frustration, but he did see Ivansik's point. If he had to call on Khabarovsk's police force for help, it would come a lot faster with Tarasov on board from the outset. At least Tarasov had the good sense not to demand a chapter and verse account of what brought Grishkov to Khabarovsk, and assigned him an officer who appeared to be competent and alert. Officer Dotsenko did, though, appear a bit puzzled by the presence of Vladivostok's lead homicide detective for the arrest of a military deserter.

As soon as they made it back to Grishkov's car, he pulled out two sets of body armor from the trunk and handed one to Dotsenko. Dotsenko eyebrows flew up as he hefted the vest and started strapping it on.

"A bit heavier than what we're used to using in Khabarovsk. Unless it's not police issue at all?" asked Dotsenko.

"We've had a bit of trouble with this matter already. It's just better to be prepared, that's all," Grishkov replied, as he slammed the trunk closed.

"Uh huh. Anything else I should know about this deserter, detective? Like he has friends, or you happen to know he plans to go out in a blaze of glory?"

Grishkov shrugged as the opened the car door. "I'm not worried about Podpolkóvnik Buryshkin's friends. I am concerned by his enemies."

Dotsenko nodded slowly as he climbed into the car. "Well, that's all clear then. So, wear the vest and keep my eyes open and mouth shut."

Grishkov's laugh was a short, sharp involuntary bark that emerged while he was in the middle of wheeling the car out of the parking lot. "Exactly right. Do just that, and you may make it through today alive."

His foot tingling as he pressed hard on the accelerator, Grishkov prayed he wasn't already too late.

Arseny Konchin had no idea that Kim Gun Jun of the RDEI was responsible for this job, and his payment. Of course, that's exactly how Kim had planned it. Using the Khabarovsk mafiya as his cutout meant that if anything went wrong it would be discounted as just ordinary criminal activity, of the sort Russia was awash with throughout the country.

Killing an army deserter and a policeman would add two more notches to Konchin's tally of over three dozen, though admittedly few of them had either guns or warning. Most had been people stupid enough to report mafiya activities to the police, or pushers who had attempted to withhold more than the authorized cut from drug sales. Street level pushers rarely carried anything more dangerous than a knife, since the penalty for being caught with a gun far exceeded that for possessing a small quantity of drugs.

His boss had told him emphatically that he had to hire help for this hit, and Konchin agreed that he couldn't go it alone. On the other hand, everyone else he brought on reduced his take from the job. After wavering back and forth and negotiating as hard as he could, he settled on two extra men. Three to two of whom only one would be armed plus the element of surprise should do it, he thought, as he snapped a clip into his pride and joy, an AKS-74. The "S" stood for skladnoy, or "folding," and was a variant of the AK-74 equipped with a side-folding metal shoulder stock. Designed for airborne infantry, the AKS-74's sturdy stock was made from stamped sheet metal struts, pressed into a "U" shape and assembled by punch fit and welding. With a rate of fire of 650 rounds per minute, it could make short work of this job, he thought with satisfaction.

CHAPTER TWENTY ONE

Khabarovsk, Russia

Grishkov parked a block away from the apartment where he believed Buryshkin was staying, and out of sight of the building's windows. He pulled a PP-2000 and PP-19 from the trunk, handing the PP-2000 to Dotsenko. Both were submachine guns designed for police use, firing 9mm rounds much less likely to go through a wall and kill innocent civilians than rounds from typical military weapons.

Dotsenko took the PP-2000 with what Grishkov saw was less than enthusiasm.

"So, this deserter took some souvenirs with him when he left, and perhaps some ammunition as well?" asked Dotsenko.

"Maybe," Grishkov shrugged. "But again, it's not Buryshkin, his family or his friends I'm worried about. I'm concerned by the people Buryshkin is hiding from. They nearly killed me once, and I'm not going to make it easy for them this time."

"Nearly killed you? Then, there's a lot more to this than just picking up a deserter," Dotsenko said, flatly.

"Did the body armor or the PP-2000 give it away?" Grishkov said, smiling without humor.

"If this arrest is so dangerous, why is it just the two of us?" asked Dotsenko.

"A fair question," Grishkov replied with a nod. "I don't know who to trust in Khabarovsk, and I wouldn't even have you with me if my captain hadn't called Captain Tarasov. There are no police departments without mafiya informants, who will sell information to anyone with the cash to pay. The fewer people involved in this, the better."

"If you are right, might these people already have made it to this deserter's place before us? If they are willing to attempt to kill a homicide detective, they are obviously highly motivated," Dotsenko observed.

"Possible, but I doubt it," Grishkov replied, as he added a clip to his PP-19. "I found the address for Buryshkin's family in Khabarovsk in a Vladivostok military paper file that had information not available in any computer system. I was the only person to check out the file since Buryshkin's last performance review, so I think I'm the only one who knows he has family here."

"Yes, but anyone following you would be led straight to Buryshkin. Are you certain you weren't tailed when you left Vladivostok?" asked Dotsenko.

"As certain as I can be of anything," Grishkov replied, shaking his head doubtfully. "Maybe a better question is whether we were tailed from the police station here."

"Yes, I was checking as we came here. I saw nothing obvious. However, spotting a tail in city traffic isn't so easy, especially if they're using more than one car. We should assume that the people who tried to kill you are right behind us," said Dotsenko, pulling back the slide on his PP-2000.

Grishkov grunted acknowledgment. "I'm glad to see Captain Tarasov has not seen fit to use this opportunity to rid himself of an expendable officer." Pulling off his jacket and draping it over his PP-19, Grishkov added, "Let's go pay our respects to Podpolkóvnik Buryshkin."

Pyongyang, North Korea

Shin Yon Young had given a great deal of thought about the best place to plant the bug. It obviously had to be on the underside of the table, but not so far inside that sound quality was compromised. Fortunately, the NIS had been able to obtain furniture produced by the same company that had custom-made the NDC conference table. The underside of each piece was finished to the same glossy sheen as the top about eighteen inches in, as far as the hands of anyone sitting at the table would touch. Past that, though, the underside's surface was simply smooth and painted the same color. This was critical, because the bug's ability to bond to the table without being detected depended on its sinking into the porous structure of the wood itself. It could do this through paint, but not both paint and the shellac used to give the table's top its permanent shine.

Willing himself to calm, Shin took the bug he had extracted from his jacket lining and placed it on the table's underside about two feet in, and swiftly resumed cleaning. As soon as he straightened up, though, he could hear familiar boot steps clacking down the hall towards him. As the door jerked open, he saw it was his regular guard, Sunshine. The guard glared at him, and then gestured Shin to leave the room. As they both entered the hallway, Shin saw the hung-over guard rounding the corner. In spite of the distance Shin could see the guard's skin turn even paler as he saw him standing with Sunshine.

The guard nearly ran the rest of the way, saluted, and stood mutely at attention.

In a low and furious voice Sunshine asked, "Did you fail to understand my order that *you* clean this room, corporal?"

Shaking his head, the miserable corporal said, "No sir! I thought, though, that since it was this man's job to clean…"

Shaking with barely controlled fury, the Sergeant said through clenched teeth, "You are not paid to think, *private*. You are paid to follow orders. Since you have been proven unable to do so, I will find you new duties. Return to your post!"

With a quick salute the newly demoted private left to stand his post, and to wonder just how unpleasant his new duties would be.

Scowling, the sergeant then turned to Shin. "You I cannot fault for following a guard's orders. However, know that under no circumstances can you ever be in this room without a guard's supervision. Now, finish cleaning this room, and be quick about it!"

His head bobbing, Shin rushed to complete his task as the sergeant continued to glare. It was obvious he was suspicious of Shin, though he had given him no reason. Shin just hoped he would get a chance to come back and collect some of the information it had taken so long to secure.

CHAPTER TWENTY TWO

Los Angeles

Kang Ji Yeong's day had been long already, and was far from over. Being a registered nurse didn't pay very well and guaranteed an exhausting shift, especially at a big public hospital. And she still had to buy groceries and fix dinner for her son. Sighing, she opened the door of the neighborhood market closest to her apartment building. On top of everything else, her beat up old hatchback wouldn't start, and was with the only mechanic she could afford to get it fixed – by next week, maybe.

So until then, she had to drag groceries two blocks. Since her son ate like a horse, she had to buy all the milk, bread and other groceries she could carry daily. At least she no longer had to feed the good for nothing husband who had walked out two years ago and never come back, and good riddance too, she thought savagely.

While she had been preoccupied with her thoughts, her hands had worked without her, stocking her cart with all her usual purchases. Before she knew it she was at the cash register. Exchanging the usual pleasantries in her native language with the market's owner was probably the high point of her day, she thought wryly. As she handed over the cash for her purchases she thought sadly, at least one of my countrymen has made good here. Gathering up her grocery-stuffed plastic bags for the trek to the apartment, she did her best to balance the load between both hands.

Gritting her teeth, she set off. It took no more than ten minutes, but by the time she got to the apartment building her hands were on fire. She was lucky enough to have someone exiting the building's lobby at the same time she entered, and so was spared having to put down the bags, open the door and then try to get them through while holding the door open with her body. But as she looked towards the elevator down the hall, she saw its door was closing! It was the only elevator for the entire building, and just missing it meant an epic wait while it stopped at every floor in both directions. "Please hold the door!," she yelled, as she did her best to rush forward.

Chung Hee Moon had just completed a brief walk around the block, or as he thought of it, essential reconnaissance. In particular, he was focused on routes of escape, and spots most likely to be used by police snipers. He was just congratulating himself on completing this task without incident, when he heard a voice loudly asking for him to hold the door. He was the only person on the elevator, which he had seen earlier as good luck. Now, though, it meant that he was the only one available to operate the controls of an unfamiliar piece of equipment. He briefly considered letting the door close, but then rejected that option as he realized that annoying the building's occupants was the most likely way to attract their attention. He saw a symbol that almost certainly meant "open door" and pressed it, and was rewarded by the doors stopping and then reversing their motion towards each other. This was followed by the near explosion of a Korean woman and a dozen plastic bags through the opening doors. He could hear a muttered "Thank you" as the bags carried in one hand hit the elevator floor, just as the doors slid closed again.

Chung noticed that while not young, the woman was still about ten years younger than him. Though he would not call her beautiful, there was an intelligence in her dark eyes that he found attractive. The woman started to press a button and then stopped as she saw it was already illuminated. Apparently they lived on the same floor, a realization that the woman appeared to reach at the same moment. She rubbed her free hand against her pants, and he could see the red mark where the weight of the bags had pressed into her skin. The doors opened, and the woman grabbed up her bags again.

The bottom of one of the bags burst, and groceries flew out on the elevator floor just as Chung stepped out. He was about to continue to his apartment when he heard sobbing behind him and saw the woman sitting on the elevator floor, cans and bottles strewn around her. He knew as he did it that it was a mistake, but he stepped back into the elevator and hit the door open button again. Quickly and methodically, he moved the intact bags out of the elevator, and picked up the additional items rolling on the floor. Then he offered his hand to the woman, who was still sniffling on the elevator floor. She took it, and let him pull her up. Without saying a word, he helped her move her groceries to her apartment.

She opened the door, her hands still shaking, and Chung placed the groceries on the counter of an apartment that he saw with approval was kept both spotlessly clean and well organized. He then moved to leave, but with a sharp command the woman told him to sit on the apartment's only couch. Bemused, he considered leaving anyway, but found himself sitting down instead. He shortly heard the sounds of tea being made. A few minutes later a tray containing tea and cookies appeared on the coffee table in front of him, and a hand with a red mark across it was thrust towards him. "My name is Kang Ji Yeong," the woman said. "Welcome to my home, and thank you for your help."

Dacha 30 Kilometers From Vladivostok

Arisha scowled at Nikitin and said "I don't care what you say, you must eat! Even soldiers in combat must do so," she added triumphantly.

Rather than answer her directly, Nikitin pressed the button on his Bluetooth earpiece, and asked Petrov to check in. After Petrov confirmed his latest sweep around the house had found nothing amiss, Nikitin raised his eyes to meet Arisha's glare.

"Very well. I thank you for your concern, and appreciate your effort to assist us," Nikitin said as he sat down and started to eat. His stomach's rumbling as he took his first bite reminded him that it had indeed been nearly twenty-four hours since his last meal.

Arisha snorted. "It is I and my family that thank you. You are risking your lives for us, and I know the danger must be very real for you to be here with us in this dacha."

Nikitin nodded soberly. "Yes, it is. But you must not worry. Petrov and I have a surprise in store for any uninvited visitors."

Arisha laughed. "And that's why we can't leave the house? What did you do, plant a mine by the gate?"

Nikitin squirmed uncomfortably in his seat, and said "Why no, of course not," while he tried to remember if there was any time she could have observed his work as he planted the Claymore.

Arisha stared at him. "My God, you did plant a mine by the gate, didn't you? Just how much trouble is Anatoly in?"

Nikitin squirmed even more uncomfortably. "Mrs. Grishkov, your husband is the most capable detective I know. The criminals are the ones who have something to worry about, not him and not your family."

Arisha chewed her lip and nodded. "Enjoy your meal. Please tell Petrov the food in the dish in the oven is for him. All the rest of us have already eaten." Before Nikitin could thank her again, Arisha had disappeared into the cellar where her mother and children were already gathered.

A few seconds later, Nikitin heard the sound of a shotgun being loaded.

CHAPTER TWENTY THREE

Tunnel No. 1, North Korea

Lee Ho Suk felt the rumbling in his bones a split second before he heard it. Even before that, without conscious thought his feet had propelled him towards the tunnel entrance, now who knew how many thousands of feet away. The last thing Lee saw as a curtain of earth closed off everything around him was a soldier raising his rifle to fire at him from behind, only to drop it as panic replaced the anger that had been on his face a split second before. Then a roaring filled his ears, followed by silence as he seemed to fall into a deep well, in which there was nothing but blackness.

Los Angeles

Chung Hee Moon was grateful for every detail that Lee had put in his head about his fictional life in South Korea. It helped that Kang Ji Yeong's family came from Pusan, a port city in the southern region across from Japan, so she was unfamiliar with the region bordering North Korea he claimed to come from. Kang had also accepted his accent as from that region, which came as a relief. Of course, his Special Forces infiltration training had included a focus on moderating his North Korean accent, but he knew it had not been completely successful.

Chung knew, though, that his luck could not last forever. It was time to turn the conversation away from him.

"But, please, enough about me. Please tell me something about yourself. You said that you are a nurse?"

"Yes," Kang nodded. "I am what they call here a registered nurse. I work at a hospital near here, where I sincerely hope you will never be a patient."

Seeing Chung's raised eyebrows, Kang laughed. "No, it is not that the care is so bad. Generally, medical care is better here than in Korea, and as you know the quality of Korean medicine has gone up tremendously over the past generation." Chung nodded, though all he actually knew of medicine came from his encounters with North Korean military doctors. The news they had recently given him that he had cancer they could not cure had done little to raise his already low opinion of their abilities.

"There are three areas where medical care here excels. The first is emergency care. From the work done by paramedics at the scene and in the ambulance, to treatment upon arrival at the hospital, nobody does it better than Americans. The second is equipment. The best machines to image and monitor patients, to support surgery, to record patient records – it's all here. The last is the reason kings and presidents come to the US for medical care. They have the finest specialists in both diagnosing illness and performing surgery in the world."

Chung laughed. "Well, that all sounds perfect. What else is left?"

Kang frowned. "Why don't I want to see you as a patient in my hospital? Well, first, do you have medical insurance?"

Chung shook his head.

"Well, many of the advantages I talked about just went away. You will never see those outstanding specialists, because you can't afford to pay them. In fact, you will only get access to care at all through the emergency room."

"But I thought you said that the emergency care was outstanding?"

"Yes, it is. But the emergency room is not just about emergency care. In fact, most of the people in the emergency room do not have a life threatening condition. They come because it is the only way they can get medical treatment, unless they go through the paperwork needed to get medical insurance for the poor. And many can't cope with that paperwork, or are afraid of being discovered as illegal residents."

Chung shook his head. "I'm sorry, but what you are saying makes no sense to me."

Kang smiled. "That means you are starting to understand the problem. Only a hospital emergency room is required to take patients who cannot afford to pay for treatment, and have no insurance. Even then, that means doing the minimum to treat the immediate issue that brought them in, not to address their overall health. To get that minimal care, the average wait for a no-insurance patient at my hospital is seven hours."

Chung stared. "Seven hours?"

Kang nodded. "A few years ago, a man died in another hospital's emergency room after waiting for nineteen hours. But such extreme cases are rare, and not the main problem. The biggest one is that the waits are so long, many people try to live with whatever their problem is until it is impossible to ignore. Not only is their condition then harder and more expensive to cure, sometimes it is simply too late to treat successfully."

Chung nodded his understanding. "But surely once a person is admitted for treatment, you do your best for them."

Kang scowled. "Yes and no. All that great equipment is there, as well as a capable staff. But that's what you can see. Lurking behind it is an enemy you cannot perceive –disease." Seeing Chung's confusion, Kang hurried to add, "Of course, people often come to get treatment because they have a disease inside them. But the hospital itself is a source of infection, often with antibiotic resistant bacteria that is extremely difficult to cure. I have seen dozens of patients come back to our hospital after they were released with illnesses more serious than the ones they came to us with originally. The government estimates that about 100,000 people die of infections contracted in a hospital every year."

"But surely someone is doing something to fix this problem, yes?"

"Well, yes. The government's insurance programs, called Medicare and Medicaid, reduce payments by two percent if a hospital does not report on measures it takes to reduce post operative infection. But all the hospital has to do is report. It does not have to meet any particular standard. But even this is not the most serious problem."

Chung stared again. "There is more?"

"Yes. The greatest danger is simple human error. Surgeons operate on the wrong body part. The wrong medicine is administered. One patient is confused with another. At my hospital, such mistakes happen almost daily. The results range from the patient getting sicker, to death."

"And is no one doing anything to fix these problems?"

Kang shrugged. "We have started routinely asking patients to confirm their names when we give them medicine or take them from their rooms for surgery. Some of us even listen to their answer," she said, smiling. Chung smiled back.

"As you know, in Korea we have compulsory national health care that covers everyone regardless of nationality. Recent changes in American law have extended insurance coverage to more people, but millions still have no insurance."

Chung in fact knew nothing about South Korean national medical insurance, and so just nodded.

"Anyway, I have unloaded enough on my frustrations. Tell me more about what you did in Korea, and what you plan to do here."

"Well, I have just retired from my twenty-five year career with the Army, where I was a noncommissioned officer," Chung said.

Kang nodded thoughtfully. "I thought you probably had a military background, just from your posture. You also have an air of command about you, like some of the sailors I have met in the Navy. I am afraid that though I knew several Navy sailors in Pusan because it is such a large port, I am not familiar at all with the Army."

Chung nodded, thankful for this bit of good fortune. "Well, all that is now behind me. I have a small pension to live on as well as some savings, and I have not really decided what I want to do in the US, or even if I want to stay here yet. First I need to learn more about this city, and this country, and then I will decide what to do next."

Chung held his breath for her response, because that was as far as his prepared story went.

To his relief, Kang appeared satisfied.

"Well, that makes sense. Keep in mind, though, that if you do decide to stay you'll need to get your immigration papers in order and get a job. That's the only way most people can get medical insurance, and that becomes important as you get older."

Kang regretted the words as soon as they left her mouth. She liked this man, and now she was calling him old, and continuing to harp on issues related to her job. He must think I am obsessed!

Fortunately, he did not seem offended.

"Thank you. That seems like good advice," was all he said, to her relief.

"Please stay for dinner. It is the least I can do to thank you for helping me get our groceries here."

Chung shook his head. "I am sure your husband will be home from work soon, and do not wish to impose."

Kang could feel the color rising in her cheeks. "My husband is no longer with us."

Chung was just as embarrassed. "I'm sorry, but when you said our groceries I just assumed…"

Kang nodded. "I understand. It is just me and my son. He plays sports after school, but should be home in time for dinner. I would like him to meet a military man. Positive role models are important for growing boys."

Chung could see no polite way to decline. "Well, in that case I would be pleased to join you for dinner, but only on condition that you let me help."

Kang smiled. "And what can a soldier do in the kitchen?"

Chung pointed at the vegetables she had left out on the counter. "Well, the first thing the military teaches new privates is how to peel these."

CHAPTER TWENTY FOUR

Khabarovsk, Russia

Buryshkin started when he heard a knock on his door. Nobody as far as he knew was aware he was here, and his few friends were all in Vladivostok. For a split second he thought about running, and then he heard the voice at the door say they were police. For another second he considered the possibility that it was an assassin sent by Timoshenko, and then realized that a killer would have just kicked in the flimsy front door. Sighing, Buryshkin got up from the sofa and went to answer the voice.

Grishkov tensed as the door opened, and then relaxed as he examined the drawn and frightened features of the man before him.

"Podpolkóvnik Buryshkin?" Grishkov asked.

Buryshkin simply nodded.

"I am senior homicide detective Grishkov from the Vladivostok police. With me is Officer Dotsenko of the Khabarovsk police force. May we speak with you?" Grishkov asked, in a tone that made it clear it was not a request.

Buryshkin nodded again, and mutely led the way to the apartment's tiny living room, where he took his old place on the sofa. Grishkov jerked his head towards the living room's window to Dotsenko, who without a word took up watch.

"I am here investigating the death of Vladimir Timoshenko," Grishkov said, examining Buryshkin's face closely for his reaction.

Buryshkin made no effort to conceal his relief at the news, but again did no more than nod.

"You knew Timoshenko, correct?" Grishkov asked.

"Yes, but not well," Buryshkin responded slowly.

"How exactly did you become acquainted?" Grishkov asked.

"Why does it matter? I certainly didn't kill him," Buryshkin replied defiantly.

"We know that. You had deserted your unit several days before Timoshenko was murdered. However, do not forget that your desertion was a crime punishable by a lengthy stay in a military prison. Whether or not you cooperate today will make a significant difference in whether that stay is long or short, and whether it is bearable or...not," Grishkov said, his eyes glittering as they focused on Buryshkin.

Buryshkin visibly quailed at the threat, and it was obvious that he knew well how deserters normally fared in military prisons. It was the main reason desertions in the Russian military were rare, no matter how bad the pay and treatment.

"Very well. Timoshenko needed information about one of the weapons at the Vladivostok armory. I suppose you know he was an arms dealer," Buryshkin said.

Grishkov nodded, making a "come on" gesture with his hands.

"First, I want to make it very clear that I did not sell any military weapon to Timoshenko. The weapon he was asking about, he got from someone else. What he needed from me were the codes required to arm it," Buryshkin said, licking his lips nervously.

"And what exactly was 'it'?" Grishkov asked.

"A very old, very small device. It hasn't been tested or maintained in ages, and may not even work," Buryshkin said, his voice rising defensively.

"What kind of device, Podpolkóvnik Buryshkin?" Grishkov asked.

Buryshkin sagged back into the sofa, despair etched in his face as he finally had to admit to someone else what he had done. "A nuclear device," he whispered.

Grishkov nodded calmly, though his stomach was roiling. It was exactly what he had feared most.

"Describe the device," Grishkov said, his tone making it clear it was an order.

Buryshkin rubbed his face, obviously collecting his thoughts. "First, it was so old we had no manuals or procedures for its use or maintenance. It was one of several devices that had been in storage at least since the 1960s, or maybe even earlier. It was stored in a large trunk, the size people used to use for a long sea voyage. The device used an arming code that was never changed, at least while I was stationed at the Vladivostok armory."

Grishkov stared at Buryshkin in disbelief. "So, with the codes you gave them, the device should work?"

Buryshkin shook his head. "No, I did not say that at all. It is so old that nobody could know whether it will work. Also, I did not see the device that was delivered to Timoshenko, so I have no idea of its condition. Corroded contacts, fouled wiring, any of a number of problems might make the device unusable. And I doubt that there is anyone after all this time with the knowledge needed to make repairs."

Grishkov glared at Buryshkin with open hostility. "So, this is how you justified to yourself taking that jackal's money? Do you really think an arms dealer like Timoshenko would have spent his money on a device that he didn't think would work? Or that he could hope to sell it if he did? Do you have any idea what you have done?" he asked.

From the way Buryshkin buried his head in his hands and sobbed, it was obvious that he did.

"All right, you can start to make amends by answering my questions honestly and completely. What is the weapon's yield? Can it be disarmed remotely? How many men does it take to transport it?" Grishkov asked.

Buryshkin wiped his eyes and answered slowly. "I don't think it can be disarmed remotely. There was a simple keypad for entering the arming code, and I saw no evidence that the device had a radio or any other type of communications capability. A single person with a dolly could easily move the device. Or they could even drag it a short distance. As for its yield, I don't know. With a device that small, though, I doubt it would be much more than twenty kilotons."

Grishkov looked at Buryshkin with growing horror. "Not much more than twenty kilotons. Give me a comparison that will make sense to me, say, the bomb the Americans dropped on Hiroshima."

Buryshkin, now on more familiar ground, quickly became more composed. "That is an interesting question. As you may imagine, it is one we have researched thoroughly. It turns out the pilots who dropped the bomb on Hiroshima were much more concerned with clearing the blast zone than giving their crewmen time to make careful measurements. So, even the Americans have little good data on the precise yield of the first combat use of a nuclear weapon. Their guess was between twelve and eighteen kilotons, based largely on the blast damage they were able to observe following Japan's surrender."

Grishkov could not believe his ears. "How could such an old device, capable of being moved by a single person, still be more powerful than the weapon that destroyed an entire Japanese city?"

Buryshkin nodded, now clearly in his element. "I understand your surprise. However, consider that an atomic weapon, even by the 1950s, was merely the trigger for a hydrogen bomb. For us to make a thermonuclear device transportable by an intercontinental bomber, let alone a missile, radically shrinking the device's atomic trigger was an absolute necessity. From there it was a very short step to making the device man-portable."

Grishkov ground his teeth in frustration. "Can you tell us anything that will help us locate the device? Did they have a homing signal? Did they leak enough radiation to be detected remotely?"

Buryshkin shook his head. "These devices were intended for Spetsnaz use. The last thing Special Forces troops wanted was a location device that could be triggered inadvertently and give away their position. Even more modern devices have no locator beacon. As for radiation, as long as the trunk used to transport the device is intact, it should not leak enough radiation to be detected until you are practically on top of it. Again, Spetsnaz troops would hardly want to be responsible for deploying an easily detected device."

Grishkov's head jerked up as he saw Dotsenko's "movement to front" hand gesture. Grishkov smiled grimly as he thought how many times he had doubted that what he had learned in Chechnya would ever matter again. This time, at least, he was glad to be proved wrong. His mouth had just opened to tell Buryshkin to take cover, when the living room window was shattered by a spray of bullets.

Chapter Twenty Five

Khabarovsk, Russia

Arseny Konchin looked over the two men he had hired doubtfully. Both had killed before, but never anyone who had the opportunity to resist, let alone an armed policeman. Neither had more than a pistol. Two pistols would have been fine along with his trusty AKS-74, except that it turned out Grishkov had company. He had no idea who the other man was, except that his dress and bearing said "police" to anyone with Arseny's many years of criminal experience.

Arseny had a decision to make. Carry out the contract with the two men he had hired, postpone until he could hire additional men, or walk away from the contract altogether. That last possibility Arseny considered and rejected almost instantly, knowing what would happen to anyone in the mafiya who failed to perform as promised.

Postponing was very tempting, since three to two armed men gave him far less attractive odds than three to one. Unfortunately, Arseny could not be sure of catching both the army deserter and the policeman together again, and his contract was very specific about killing them both.

Arseny shrugged as he came to his decision. He still had surprise, and his AKS-74. That should be enough.

As simply and clearly as he could, Arseny explained to the two hired guns their plan of attack. They would move to the house's back door and text Arseny once they were in position. Arseny would then spray the living room window with his AKS-74. As soon as Arseny did so, they would kick the door in and kill any survivors. Arseny would then join them via the front window.

Arseny left out one part of his plan. That was, after confirming the death of the army deserter and the two policemen, killing the two hired guns as well. Arseny would have no trouble explaining their death to his boss considering the unexpected extra policeman, and so the entire contract payment would go to him. Yes, he thought with satisfaction, that would make the extra risk of carrying out this contract quite worthwhile.

The same combat instincts that had saved Grishkov outside the Black Crow had him hugging the carpet before he was conscious of what was happening. He heard the crash as the back door was kicked in, and shouted a warning to Dotsenko. A quick glance at him, crouched behind a heavy table with his PP-2000 leveled, convinced Grishkov he knew what was coming.

Grishkov emptied half of his PP-19's magazine at the first movement he saw down the short hallway connecting the living room to the kitchen, and was rewarded with a high pitched scream followed immediately by two rapid pistol shots. Dotsenko answered those with a burst from his PP-2000, which was followed by the dull thud of a body hitting the kitchen floor. Grishkov just had time to think to himself that the gunman out front was still out there and twist towards the living room window when a dark shape came hurtling through the shattered frame.

Arseny knew in his gut that things had gone badly wrong when he heard two different automatic weapons being fired at the gunmen he had sent through the back. Still, he knew abandoning the contract was not a survivable option. Pulling back the slide on his AKS-74, Arseny's legs churned as they propelled him through the shattered living room window.

Grishkov emptied the other half of his PP-19's magazine at the intruder at a range of less than ten feet while he was still in mid-air. The figure dropped flat on the floor, twitched, and then was completely still. His ears still ringing from the gunfire, Grishkov used combat hand gestures to ask Dotsenko whether he was injured, and whether he could see any movement. Dotsenko shook his head no to both, though Grishkov could see Dotsenko's face and hands had been badly cut by flying glass.

There was no need to check on Buryshkin since he had been hit by at least five bullets, and his face had the open-eyed stare Grishkov had seen far too many times in Chechnya.

Grishkov kicked the weapon out of the hand of the dead man near the window, and then frowned as he recognized the AKS-74. With a jerk of his head towards the kitchen, he had Dotsenko accompany him. Both gunmen there were dead, with their pistols lying on the floor nearby.

"Do you recognize them?" Grishkov asked, nodding towards the two bodies.

Dotsenko shook his head, and then walked to the crumpled body near the window.

"This man, though, I do know. Even if I didn't recognize him, no other criminal in Khabarovsk has an AKS-74. This is Arseny Konchin, a killer we have known about for some time. He is well connected, and doesn't come cheap. Do you think it was you or Buryshkin who was the target?"

Grishkov shrugged. "I don't know. My guess is both of us."

Dotsenko nodded, and then gestured towards Buryshkin's body. "I hope you had no more questions for him. He obviously won't be able to give you more answers."

Grishkov shrugged again. "I don't think he had anything else useful to tell us. And I think a quick death is the best Buryshkin could have hoped for after the way he betrayed his duty."

Dotsenko gingerly touched the largest of the many cuts on his face, and winced as he extracted a shard of glass. "I think I need to get these stitched up. What next?"

Grishkov bent down to pick up the gunmen's weapons, and then gestured towards the door. "We call this in, and get you to a hospital. Then I'm heading back to Vladivostok, to make sure my family is safe."

Dotsenko looked at Grishkov soberly, and then at the four bodies strewn around them. "I think we should hurry."

CHAPTER TWENTY SIX

Kaesong, North Korea

Lee Ho Suk slowly regained consciousness in completely unfamiliar surroundings. As he lifted his pounding head from his pillow and looked at the plastic tube in his arm, he realized he was in a hospital. The harsh buzzing light of overhead fluorescent lights made him squint to see. A doctor wearing a white coat with a stethoscope draped around his neck immediately entered the room.

"I am Doctor Moon," he said, peering at Lee intently through gold wire rimmed glasses. "How are you feeling?"

"Surprised to be alive," Lee said, with deep sincerity.

Dr. Moon nodded. "You are right to be surprised. You were the only survivor who was still in the mine when the mine's supports gave way."

Lee nodded gravely, while his mind was racing. Obviously, this doctor had not been told the truth about the tunnel, and the reason for the deception was obviously security. The real question was, why had he been placed in a civilian hospital with the evident intent of keeping him alive?

After examining him for an uncomfortable fifteen minutes, the doctor said "You will soon have a visitor. Rest now while you can. You will have many questions to answer." With that, Dr. Moon marched out of the room as though he had been on parade. Watching him, Lee was sure he had seen military service, probably the reason he had been chosen as his doctor.

Just as predicted, less than ten minutes later an unusually tall Korean officer came striding into Lee's hospital room, holding a slim manila folder. Lee had no idea of his rank, just that he knew he had never seen such a uniform or insignia during his many years in the tunnels.

"I am Colonel Park, and you are prisoner Lee Ho Suk," the officer announced.

Lee nodded and quickly said, "Yes, Colonel."

Park leaned over Lee, examining his bandaged face and pulling back the bedcovers to look at the rest of his body.

"It is remarkable that aside from a mild concussion and some bruising, you appear to have survived the tunnel's collapse unscathed," Park said, with an inflection that turned the statement into a pointed question.

"Colonel, I did my best to warn the guards that the tunnel was nearing collapse. I did that well before I started to run for the tunnel entrance," Lee said, knowing that the truth was unlikely to save him.

But to his amazement, this time it did.

"Yes, two men had been sent out to bring back reinforcing materials based on your warning, and they reported your action. The blame is not yours, but belongs to men who are now beyond the reach of punishment," Park said, with a gleam in his eye that expressed how much he wished for more survivors.

Park opened the folder and looked at its contents, and then down at the bandaged figure on the bed in front of him, his face clouded with doubt.

"How long have you been serving your sentence?" Park asked.

"I do not know, Colonel. I only know that it has been many years." Lee replied, wondering what the point was of all these questions.

"I took the trouble to answer that riddle. It turns out you have a nickname. It is "Lost Bet," which at first confused me when I heard it," Park said with a thin smile.

"Lost Bet, Colonel? I do not understand," Lee said, bewildered.

"The clerks who maintain prisoner files had a betting pool for the date of death of the longest serving prisoner. That prisoner is you, and has been for some time. Of course, once I found out about the pool, I ended it and made sure that the money in it was put to good use. Naturally, the clerks who participated will now get a chance to break your record. I wished them luck personally," Park said, his eyes glittering.

"I still do not understand, Colonel," Lee said, his head pounding.

Park nodded. "You see, for years clerks bet on your date of death- but you never died. The money just rolled over in the pool, and everyone who played lost their money. So, you became known as "Lost Bet." Year after year, clerks – especially new ones – would place wagers in the pool, sure that you would not survive much longer. In a way I don't blame them for their greed. You certainly have managed to beat the odds," Park said, chuckling.

"How long have I been a prisoner?" Lee asked, his pain and exhaustion having worn away all caution.

Park opened the file and visibly calculated the dates in his head, as Lee watched his fingers and lips twitch slightly.

"Twelve years, three months, and sixteen days. The next longest serving prisoner has been serving his sentence for five and a half years, so you see you are rather special. Which brings us to the next question – what to do with you next," Park said, still looking at Lee's file.

Lee's heart sank, knowing that his status as the longest surviving prisoner in North Korea would not be seen as an accomplishment by anyone in power. So why, then, was he still alive?

Park looked up and smiled at Lee's expression. "Your concern is understandable, but in this case unfounded. No, we have use for you, and no soldier succeeds by throwing away a weapon that has proved its worth. The doctor tells me that by tomorrow you will be ready for discharge, and will be able to return to Tunnel No. 1 in a new role," Park said.

"Yes, Colonel," Lee said dully, not really caring what new punishment awaited him.

"Ah, you should react with more enthusiasm than that! Your status will be much improved, with better food and drink, sleeping quarters, and continued medical care. You will be in charge of tunnel safety, and though you will of course still be a prisoner, only the site commander will be able to overrule you on safety issues. And I have made it clear to him personally the risk he will take in failing to follow your instructions," Park said, smiling at Lee's obvious confusion.

"But Colonel, nobody will take orders from a prisoner!" Lee exclaimed.

"Ordinarily, you would be right. In this case, however, I have assembled all of the staff and guards working at Tunnel No. 1, and ordered that you speak with my authority on matters of safety. I have also told them that if you are able to see the tunnel through to completion without further incident, you will be declared rehabilitated, and will be released," Park said, slapping his knee for emphasis.

"Colonel, this has never been done," Lee said, unable to believe his ears.

"That is true. However, we have also never had a project of this importance before. Believe me when I say, success will change your family's future," Park said, examining Lee closely for his reaction.

"My family," Lee repeated carefully, in part because he still did not dare to hope.

Park pulled a photo out of Lee's file. "I had one of my lieutenants track down your family. Your wife never remarried, and has been working since your arrest in a factory producing military uniforms. Your two sons are in high school, one about to graduate and the other a year behind. The lieutenant took this picture to illustrate his report," Park said, handing the photo to Lee.

Tears welled in Lee's eyes as he examined the photo. There were streaks of grey in his wife's hair, though he knew she could not have yet reached forty. His sons had grown to be taller than their mother, so much so that he could hardly recognize them, but all three were painfully thin.

"They have been told nothing about the reason for my interest, and were instead informed that a spot check was being made of workers and their families in industrial jobs supporting the military. You may be interested to hear that they asked about you, in spite of the risk involved in showing any concern for a prisoner such as yourself. The lieutenant told them the truth, which was that he knew nothing about you," Park said, as Lee's tears finally spilled from his eyes in spite of his best efforts to control them.

"Success in this project will mean both your release and your being reunited with your family. Are you ready for this challenge?" Park asked, though he was certain of Lee's answer.

He was not disappointed. Lee sat up straight in his bed, his throbbing head forgotten. "I will do everything in my power to make this tunnel a success, or die trying!" Lee said, with tears still streaming down his cheeks.

"Good, good," Park beamed. "That is all I needed to hear. Remember, if you see a danger to the tunnel's completion you are to tell the officer in charge to notify me personally. Heavy equipment is clearing the tunnel as we speak, and we will be ready to resume excavation tomorrow. We will see you then." With that, Park turned on his heel and left.

Lee blinked, drawing his sleeve across his face to remove the tears. He did not trust a word he had just heard, but did believe that the photo was genuine. If nothing else, he was now confident that at least his family was still alive, which he had doubted for years now.

There was only one way to explain these efforts to motivate him. This tunnel had to be more vital than he had imagined, and he had already believed it to be the most important one he had seen in his many years of digging. Its importance, though, only guaranteed his death at its completion. Icy fingers clutched at his heart as he realized that now that his family had been located, they would be eliminated as well. Not because there was any real chance Lee could have passed them a message including the tunnel's location, but just to be thorough. It was the way a man like Colonel Park worked, Lee thought bitterly.

So, nothing has really changed. I have to watch and wait for any chance to escape – no matter how small that chance may be.

CHAPTER TWENTY SEVEN

Los Angeles

Chung Hee Moon had no idea that the small market where he shopped was the same as the one Kang Ji Yeong had used the day before. He just knew that it was the only one within walking distance of his apartment building, and so the only realistic choice for someone like him without a car. If he had thought about it, he would have probably realized that was the main reason most people shopped at this market, in spite of its limited selection and high prices compared to national chain supermarkets.

At first Chung paid no attention when the small bell attached to the market's front door rang, as it had done every minute or so since he started shopping to announce the arrival or departure of a customer. When he next saw the two who had entered out of the corner of his eye, though, all of his combat instincts immediately came into play. He used the reflection of a glass display case to study them more closely, and quickly confirmed his initial impression.

Chung first noticed that both men, unshaven and in their twenties, were dressed in clothes that were far too hot for the sunny California weather. The dark-haired man, who Chung guessed might be Mexican, had on a brown leather jacket which did little to conceal a bulge that to Chung's trained eye said "pistol" as clearly as embroidering the word on the garment's lapel. The blond man was taller, but his dark wool coat still went down almost to his knees. That gave more room to hide a weapon, but Chung still had no trouble seeing the stock of a shotgun peeking out next to his left shirt pocket.

Due to the heavy presence of security forces everywhere and a completely unarmed citizenry, store robbery was practically unknown in North Korea. Chung knew, though, that this is exactly what was about to happen in this small LA market. And he had no chance to leave before it did. Chung quickly decided that he would stay quiet and uninvolved, since the worst that could happen was that he would be robbed of the thirty dollars he had brought to do his grocery shopping. He crouched down in the aisle, confident that neither man had seen him.

There was just one customer at the only open cash register, a very obviously pregnant woman in her thirties, with stringy brown hair and a full shopping cart. The cashier was a young Korean woman, who Chung thought was probably the owner's daughter. Chung had briefly met the Korean owner two days before on his first trip to the market. He guessed – correctly, as it happened – that the owner made a point of introducing himself to any Koreans who shopped at his market.

Chung next saw the dark-haired man go to the door and flip over the "open" sign on the door to "closed." He then twisted the lock at the top of the door.

Just as the cashier was about to ask the man what he was doing, the blond man swept aside his coat and with one fluid movement had the shotgun pointed directly at her head. Jerking his head towards the register, he snapped "Open it." Trembling, the cashier rushed to obey.

Without the man having to ask, the young woman emptied the register of its bills, even making a point of lifting the cash drawer to pull out the lone hundred dollar bill that had been collected that morning. She then thrust the wad of bills toward the blond man, saying "That's all there is." The man took the money, but then shook his head and said just one word – "Safe."

The cashier started shaking even harder. "I don't have the combination. Only my father does, and he's not here."

"Where is he?" the blond man asked, his eyes narrowing.

"I don't know," the cashier said.

The pregnant woman, who had been standing in stunned silence to that point, then started to cry. "Please, just leave us alone," she sobbed.

"Shut up," the blond man replied, without emotion.

"Hey, let's get out of here before the cops show up. We've already got a pretty good haul for a little bodega like this," the dark-haired man said, curling his lip at the small market.

"Naw, man, the Chinese don't trust banks. The real cash is gonna be in the safe. And this whore is going to get it for us!"

At that the cashier stopped trembling, and was clearly angry. "I am not a whore, and I am not Chinese! And I don't have the combination to the safe!"

The pregnant woman, who had never stopped crying, then sobbed again in a loud, whining voice, "Please, just leave us alone!"

So quickly that Chung was caught off guard, the blond man reversed the shotgun and struck the pregnant woman in the head with its butt. She dropped like a stone next to the register, blood flowing from the wound in her scalp. The cashier screamed.

"Now, open the safe!" the blond man shouted.

Without any conscious thought, Chung stood up.

The dark-haired man spotted him first. "Hey, get over here. Where did you come from?"

Chung walked slowly towards the cash register, keeping both his hands in plain sight and by his sides. Quietly, he answered, "I was at the back. I want to help the woman, if you will let me." He then gestured towards the woman lying on the floor.

For the first time, the dark-haired man pulled out his pistol and pointed it at Chung. "I don't like the look of this guy, and I don't think she's lying about not having the combination. Let's go, now."

His eyes glittering, the blond man shook his head, and pointed his shotgun at Chung. "I don't like him either. I say let's get rid of him, and then open that safe."

Chung didn't wait to hear the dark-haired man's answer.

Using the skills and instincts drilled into him by years of Special Forces training, Chung dove towards the blond man. Even as he saw the man's finger beginning to tighten on the trigger, he had grasped the barrel and pointed it towards the dark-haired man behind him, at the same moment that he dove towards the floor.

Chung had only guessed that the dark-haired man would also fire, a guess that turned out to be correct. Based on where he had been just a fraction of a second before, he had also guessed that the round would be likely to strike the blond man.

When he pushed off from the floor one-handed, he saw that guess was correct as well.

The shotgun round had struck the dark-haired man squarely in the chest. The round from the pistol had entered the blond man's head just below his right eye, and exited through the back of his skull. Both men were very clearly dead.

Chung turned to the cashier, whose neck was sprayed with blood from the blond man. "Are you injured?" he asked. She shook her head. "You should call for help," Chung said, as he tore off a strip of cloth from the blond man's shirt to lightly bandage the pregnant woman's scalp wound.

The cashier nodded, and reached into a drawer for her purse to remove her cell phone. Once she did so, Chung pointed towards the back of the store. "There is an exit that way?" The cashier mutely nodded. "I cannot be involved in this. Do you understand?" The cashier nodded again, and whispered, "Thank you." With a nod, Chung walked swiftly out the back of the store. As he exited, he could hear sirens coming closer.

Chapter Twenty Eight

Beijing, China

Li Weimin felt the call of nature more and more often with every passing year he spent at the Ministry of Foreign Affairs. His doctor shrugged and told him that this came naturally with age. Li wondered idly if a Western doctor could do better.

Li spotted a restroom just as an unfamiliar face dressed in a suit that was obviously not Chinese opened its door. A better dressed, but still obviously foreign man remained outside speaking with one of Li's colleagues from the Department of Asian Affairs. They were walking away from him toward a nearby tea cart, set up in corridors throughout the building. Li was surprised to hear that the man's Chinese was quite good, though he could not quite place the accent.

As Li entered the restroom, he saw that he and the man in the poor quality suit were its only occupants. More out of curiosity than any sincere interest, Li nodded and said, "Welcome, I hope that your visit here is going well. May I ask where you are from?"

Park Won Hee turned to look at the Chinese diplomat as he washed his hands, smiling as he said in flawless Mandarin, "I am from the Democratic People's Republic of Korea. My visit here is going quite well, thank you."

Li's automatic "Excellent, I am glad to hear it" came simultaneously with the thought that here was an opportunity not to be wasted. But the risk made him feel dizzy. Li now realized the man at the tea cart had to be Park's minder, and that he would not wait long before checking on his charge.

No! He would never forgive himself if he wasted such a chance.

"I am Li Weimin, Deputy Director-General at the Ministry of Foreign Affairs," Li said, bowing slightly.

Park returned the bow. "I am Park Won Hee, envoy of the Democratic People's Republic of Korea."

"Are you here to discuss the reunification plans?" Li asked, trying to gauge whether Park was willing to talk at all about them.

Park simply nodded, his face expressionless.

Li realized there was no chance that a North Korean official would make the first move in a discussion with a Chinese official, even one with Li's high rank, especially in a bathroom. But this was a chance he would never get again.

"Have you considered that there may be more to this plan for reunification than you have been told?" Li asked, knowing that his life hung in the balance depending on Park's reply.

"Please explain," Park said carefully, still deadpan.

"We do support Korean reunification on your terms. However, it is of only secondary importance for us. Its real use is as a distraction for the United States while we pursue reunification with Taiwan," Li explained, watching Park's face carefully for his reaction.

There was none. Instead, Park asked "Why are you telling me this?"

Li shrugged. "Because I think the plan will fail on both counts. The US will never allow South Korea to be taken over by the DPRK. Nor do I think they will be sufficiently distracted by your actions to allow our uncontested takeover of Taiwan. Instead, I fear a rapidly escalating conflict that could involve nuclear weapons. I will do whatever is necessary to stop that from happening," Li said emphatically.

Park slowly nodded. "I must consider this further. As we walk out, invite me to dinner tomorrow night. I will introduce you to my minder, and ask that he accompany me. Please agree, or I will never be allowed to go. You can then think about how we can speak further without the minder overhearing," Park said, reaching for the bathroom door handle.

Li felt a rush of relief, replaced quickly by concern. How was he going to occupy the minder long enough to let him have a meaningful conversation with Park?

Vladivostok, Russia

Kim Gun Jun ground his teeth in frustration. How could one Russian police officer be so hard to kill? He had eagerly answered the call from the RDEI agent at Khabarovsk, certain it would be good news. Hearing that an entire three person team had failed to kill Grishkov had sent him into a rage that left the RDEI agent on the other end of the call rightly fearing for both his career and his life. One bit of good news was that Timoshenko's contact had been killed, though there was no way to know how much he had told Grishkov before dying. At least he could not testify, or be interviewed at greater length.

Even better was that all three on the hit team had died in the attempt. The whole point of using local contractors had been to minimize the chances of the killing being traced back to the RDEI, which is why Kim had forbidden his agent to participate. Their deaths made discovery of North Korean involvement even less likely.

He had no idea Grishkov would have backup when he went to see Timoshenko's contact. It simply didn't track with what he knew of Grishkov. As Kim thought more about it, he realized that Grishkov's boss must have asked for the help.

Kim sighed. He had to stop underestimating the Russians. No matter how backward and inept they often were, Russians had still managed great feats in many fields.

Well, this time he was going to be prepared. He patted his PP-19 Bizon-2 submachine gun, the Makarov variant with an integral sound suppressor. Since it used a simple straight blowback operation method its operating cycle had a very short recoil stroke, so that 9x18mm ammunition would only drive the bolt partially to the rear of the receiver. As a result, it achieved a cyclic rate of 700 rounds/min, reducing recoil and increasing controllability and accuracy.

There were no fewer than seven men meeting him at the home of Grishkov's mother-in-law, all well armed combat veterans. He might lose one or two, but there was no way he would fail this time. And with Grishkov's family in hand, he would have no choice but to hand himself over to Kim. Kim smiled to himself in anticipation. He was going to enjoy getting the information he needed out of Grishkov, one bloody relative at a time.

CHAPTER TWENTY NINE

Beijing, China

Jim Martinovsky had certainly hoped he would hear from Li Weimin again at some point to continue their puzzling discussion on Chinese and US policy towards Korea unification. He never dreamed it would be later the same week.

Yet, here they were again at the same restaurant near the Chinese Ministry of Foreign Affairs.

After the usual pleasantries, which were even briefer than their previous lunch, Li came right to the point after their tea had been served and lunch order placed.

"I am sure you recall our recent discussion of our respective policies towards the Democratic People's Republic of Korea, and the possibility that it might someday be reunited with the regime to the South," Li said, as he lifted his teacup for a first sip.

"Of course," Martinovsky replied.

"Good," Li nodded. "Then, you have had a chance to think further about our discussion?" he asked.

"Well, yes," Martinovsky said, frowning. "But I must say I am still puzzled. Why spend so much time on such an unlikely scenario? Unless there is an element to consider I am unaware of, perhaps?" he asked in return.

Li took another sip of tea as he considered his response. As put his cup back down, he said slowly, "What I am about to tell you is likely to strike you as quite incredible, perhaps even delusional. However, I assure you that every word will be the truth. I will ask that everything I am about to say be held in the strictest confidence, though I am well aware that it is only a matter of time before what I say becomes known to my superiors. As the Wikileaks episode underlined, your security is truly very poor," Li said, smiling thinly.

Martinovsky's heart began racing almost as fast as his thoughts. Uppermost was please, Lord, don't let me have a heart attack just when I'm going to get the break that will save my career.

"Naturally anything you say to me will be given the highest security," Martinovsky replied. "We have made many changes to ensure that our reports are never again exposed as they were recently."

"Yes, I'm sure that is true," Li said, his tone making it clear it was anything but. "In any case, you will shortly understand why I am compelled to provide you with this information, regardless of the risk to me personally."

Li stopped speaking as waiters appeared carrying their lunch order. Once they departed, Li resumed.

"Elements within my government are supporting a DPRK plan to reunify Korea that will involve the use of a nuclear weapon. Though the conspirators hope the plan will be successful, Korean unification is not the plan's principle aim. Instead, it is to use the distraction the crisis will provide to allow us to take over Taiwan without US intervention. The conspirators believe that I support their plot, though obviously I do not. The reason they have asked me to speak with you previously and again today is to help gauge the US response to an attempt to reunify Korea by force. Naturally, your reaction will be only one of many sources that will help them decide whether to proceed with their plans."

Martinovsky stared blankly at Li as he struggled to take in what he had just heard. "I hardly know where to begin with questions. I suppose the first one is obvious – how sure are you of all this?"

"I have spoken directly with Song Hailong on this matter," Li said, simply.

Martinovsky started, and sat up straighter in his seat. "The Vice Minister? He is involved? Then this plan must have the support of the entire Chinese government," Martinovsky said.

"No, that is not the case," Li responded, shaking his head emphatically. "There are many others who are part of this conspiracy, including other senior officials. However, this plot has not been sanctioned by the Politburo Standing Committee, the State Council, or the Central Military Commission. I do not believe it would be approved if the full membership of each body knew about these plans, though I must admit I am not certain of this."

"I need as much detail as you can give me. We know that North Korea has several nuclear devices. How does it plan to use one to threaten South Korea? Surely they must know that we would respond to such a threat by destroying any site we suspected capable of launching such an attack," Martinovsky said.

"I do not know," Li responded, shaking his head. "I have heard, though, that the South will be unable to intercept the weapon, and that its target will be Seoul."

Martinovsky shook his head in disbelief. "How could North Korea be sure the weapon could not be destroyed or stopped? Both we and the South Koreans have anti-missile batteries, and they are capable of intercepting any missile the North has tested so far."

Li shrugged. "Again, I do not know. However, I must point out I did not hear that North Korea would fire a missile at Seoul, only that it would use a nuclear weapon to threaten the South. How such a weapon might be delivered goes well beyond my area of expertise. I will only caution you against making any assumptions, especially based on such limited knowledge."

"How soon will this plan be put into action?" Martinovsky asked.

"I do not know exactly, but soon. The Vice Minister himself asked me to see you as soon as possible. However, I am not sure how long will pass between my report back and the plan's implementation," Li responded.

Martinovsky chewed on his lower lip. "If you report back that we are likely to respond with overwhelming force to a threatened nuclear attack on Seoul, would that make the plotters cancel their plans?"

Li nodded. "Yes, I have given this question much thought. I do not believe it would. For the attack on the South to work as a diversion, it would in fact have to provoke a strong US response. Ironically, I think only the likelihood of your weak response to the North Korean threat would force the plotters to reconsider."

"Yes, I see your point. But surely a tepid reaction by my government won't be credible to the plotters, or else they would not have moved forward to this point, whatever that point may be. We have to think of some justification for a weak US response, or else anything I say to you will be discounted as the ramblings of an out of touch diplomat," Martinovsky said, smiling wryly.

Li removed his glasses and began to polish them. "Perhaps something like this. The US is rethinking its military deployments in Asia. With the recent increase in the number of Marines stationed in Australia, a strengthened US Navy presence in Singapore, and a renewed commitment from Japan to support a strong American military presence there, the US sees less need for a large force in Korea. Budget problems are forcing serious reconsideration of whether the US can afford to fight another major war so soon after the conclusion of the conflicts in Iraq and Afghanistan under any circumstances, other than a direct threat to the US itself. A US economy still suffering from the recent collapse of the euro and sharply reduced exports to Europe cannot afford the disruption that would be caused by war in Asia, especially if that war could involve China. Therefore, the US response to a direct nuclear threat by North Korea would be to negotiate, rather than attack."

Martinovsky shook his head dubiously. "That's probably the best you could do, but I'm not sure the Vice Minister will believe it. In any case, he'll know I would never give you a response like that without talking it over with my boss. And he's not likely to agree to my saying anything to you on the record without clearing it with DC."

Li smiled and nodded agreement. "All you say is true. However, your objections only apply to a formal, binding statement. We would have merely been discussing unlikely hypothetical scenarios. I think you call it 'blue sky thinking.' I believe I could convince the Vice Minister that you were willing to engage in such a conversation. Anyway, I see no choice, since I know he will not wait long for a response."

Li frowned and added, "I must also advise you that I have been in touch with a North Korean official named Park Won Hee who I believe may also have misgivings about this plan. I will have dinner with him tomorrow, and I hope to get further information from him then."

Martinovsky drained his tea cup. "Do you have any idea what other sources the Vice Minister will use to gauge our likely reaction to a North Korean nuclear threat? If so, we can try to influence them as well."

Li twisted his lips in frustration. "No. When I spoke with the Vice Minister I did not ask, because doing so would have invited suspicion that I cannot afford. Song Hailong has a very wide range of contacts, both official and unofficial. I also have no idea whether your statement will be given more or less weight than those from other sources. The bottom line is simple: I can only try to slow down this plot. I doubt anything I do will stop it."

Martinovsky frowned and said "Speaking of suspicion, once I report our conversation to my superiors there is an excellent chance that either here or in DC your government will be challenged regarding this plot, including its Taiwan component. Revelation that we know a North Korean nuclear threat is only to distract us from a Chinese invasion of Taiwan may lead straight back to you as a source. Has this occurred to you?"

Li smiled without humor. "I knew I was a dead man the moment I decided to share this information with you. I am only trying to divert suspicion long enough to at least postpone disaster, and perhaps to give you the time to find a solution that I could not."

Martinovsky looked at Li with frank admiration. "I don't know that your death should be taken for granted. You would not be the first defector we have relocated in the US. Far fewer Chinese have gone that route than Russians used to, but it has happened. Let me talk with others in the Embassy and see what I can arrange."

Li shook his head. "No. I am too old to start over in a new country. Besides, I am too closely watched. I also think that events will move too quickly to allow time for a plan that would have any chance of success."

Martinovsky leaned forward and put his hand on Li's shoulder, a gesture of such unexpected familiarity that Li jumped with surprise. "I understand your misgivings. However, there is another point to consider. Before deciding how to respond to the plotters, my superiors in Washington may very well want to speak in person with the source of my reports. Your defection is the only way that would be possible."

Li blinked and squirmed in his seat uncomfortably. "Yes, I can understand that they would. But do you believe a defection by someone of my rank is really possible?"

Martinovsky smiled. "I am not an expert on such matters. But we have succeeded many times in the past, and I think we can do so again. Maybe your North Korean friend would like to come along as well. Besides, what choice is there?"

Li cocked an eyebrow at that. "Well, put that way I must agree. For me to talk with your superiors, I see no choice at all. However, I have no idea whether Park would be interested in defecting. He is interested in hearing out my concerns, but that may be just to more thoroughly report on my treason."

Martinovsky laughed. "If you really believed that, I don't think you would have invited him to dinner. And as I'm sure you know, North Korean officials have defected before, including out of Beijing."

Li nodded. "That is true. And that's why Park will come to dinner with a companion, whose job it will be to make sure Park returns home. If you are serious about offering Park a chance to defect, you will have to account for his minder as well."

Martinovsky shrugged. "If Park wants to defect along with you, the two of you will be a pair that nobody in DC can ignore. A piece of paper reporting on events is one thing. Two people willing to risk their lives to stop a war is something very different. So, please tell your security detail to expect two Westerners at tomorrow's dinner."

Li took off his glasses and absently polished them with his napkin, then placed them back on his nose. He then nodded sharply. "Very well, I will let them know."

CHAPTER THIRTY

Beijing, China

Jim Martinovsky had been dreading the need to brief Martin Fitzwilliam on Li and Park's defection, but since he was his boss he had little choice. As he finished explaining why Li wanted to defect, and his assessment that aiding his immediate defection should be the Embassy's top priority, his heart sank as he saw Fitzwilliam's expression. No matter how he ended up saying it, Martinovsky knew he would not have his boss' support.

"First, Jim, you were absolutely right to bring this to me immediately. We need to report this up the chain right away. You have a draft message ready?"

"Yes, it's in your classified in-box. I sent it to you just before I walked in."

Fitzwilliam nodded and pulled up the draft telegram. He immediately frowned on seeing it was an action message, but said nothing until he had finished reading it. Once he did, he took out his handkerchief and started polishing his glasses, a habit that Martinovsky knew meant their meeting was over.

"Thanks, Jim. I'll work on this and get it sent out this afternoon."

Martinovsky knew that his message urgently recommending action would be watered down to one reporting Li's statements and leaving action, if any, to the foreign policy mill in DC. Wang Lijun, chief of police and vice mayor of Chonqing City had fled to the Consulate General in Chengdu a little over a decade ago. That had caused an armed confrontation between Chonqing police and military forces sent to capture him, and forces from Sichuan ordered to take Wang into custody and stop the Chonqing police from arresting him. That had led to an embarrassing standoff that had ended only when Wang finally gave himself up. The stakes this time would be even higher, and Chinese acceptance of Li's departure for the US even less likely.

So it was not a surprise that Fitzwilliam was not interested in dealing with two high ranking defectors. That left just one career-ending alternative.

Dacha 30 Kilometers From Vladivostok

Petrov oiled his KBI GM-94, as Nikitin looked on.

"So, you find my Claymore remarkable, and now have a pump-action grenade launcher?" Nikitin asked with an amused snort.

"Well, it was actually designed for use by police special response teams, and came into military use only a few years ago. You may notice that though much larger it is based on the RM-93 shotgun, and operates the same way," Petrov said, as he demonstrated.

"Pump the barrel forward to load a round into the chamber and to eject any fired shell, and back again to lock the barrel and cock the weapon. Pull the barrel halfway forward to load the magazine on top of the weapon. The barrel has two hand stops to help in working the action and gripping the weapon. You don't see too many of these because the ammunition is designed solely for the GM-94, and is not used by any other weapon. Though the magazine can normally hold four rounds, since I am using thermobaric rounds it can hold only three, since these grenades are longer than other types of ammunition," Petrov said, as he showed how the grenade launcher operated.

"And how do you happen to have one?" Nikitin asked with a grin.

"Well, I happen to have a good friend on a special response team, who was willing to loan it to me. Talking him out of his only thermobaric rounds was a bit harder," Petrov said, shaking his head ruefully.

"Are you sure you know how to use this elephant gun?" Nikitin asked.

"Well, since I only have a few rounds I didn't want to waste any on practice, which now that we're here would likely attract unwanted attention. Besides, the whole point of these is that I don't have to score an exact hit. Anyone within a three meter radius of impact is dead, and the radius for serious injury is more than double that, particularly since all the brush and debris out there will make for multiple blast-driven projectiles. My only concern is reload time. I'll be surprised if I manage to fire more than a couple of grenades before survivors are at the door," Petrov said with a worried air.

"Well, that's what our PP-2000s are for, right? We should be able to get off more than a couple of rounds with these!" Nikitin exclaimed, holding up his submachine gun with a grin.

"You have a point, yes indeed you do," Petrov said. Then he frowned. "Do you hear that?" he asked.

"No, I don't hear anything," Nikitin replied, frowning even more deeply.

"I think it's time. As we rehearsed, you back and me front. Good luck to all of us," Petrov said, as he balanced the grenade launcher on the window sill, peeking out through the window pane he had removed that afternoon. Where the hell is Grishkov, he thought as he peered out into the gloom, seeking movement.

Chapter Thirty One

Los Angeles

Paul Valone had been a detective for fifteen years, and had seen plenty of robberies, including ones that resulted in fatalities. When those dead included the thieves, it was usually because of quick reaction by the police, but on occasion a shopkeeper managed to fight back. He couldn't think of any case, though, where the robbers had managed to shoot each other. Something was not adding up here, and his experience told him that this cashier was hiding something.

"OK, ma'am. I know this has been a difficult experience for you. But I need you to tell me again how this happened."

The cashier glared at him. "Look, how many times do I have to tell you! They were idiots, and they shot each other. I had no gun. Nobody else here had a gun. What else do you think happened?"

And with that the cashier folded her arms triumphantly and lifted her chin, and Valone had to agree she had a point. The wounds in each body did appear to have come from the other's weapon. He had done a field gunshot residue test on the cashier, and she came up clean. The only other person in the store had been an unconscious pregnant woman now on her way to the hospital. Unless...maybe she hadn't been the only other person in the store?

"You said that there's no surveillance system in this store?"

"See for yourself," the cashier said, pointing to a 1970s vintage camera suspended from the wall, with a cable dangling limply behind it. "It's been like that since I started working here four years ago."

A bell jingling told Valone that someone had entered the store. He turned towards the sound, annoyed that the patrolman he had stationed outside had failed to follow his simple instruction to keep everyone out until he had finished this interview. Just as he had the thought, the patrolman stuck his head in the door. "I think you'll want to hear what this guy has to say," he said, and then withdrew back outside.

The young Korean man who walked in was wearing a ball cap, sunglasses, and T-shirt. He nodded to Valone, and began moving towards him.

The cashier frowned when she saw who had entered, and said something to the man in rapid-fire Korean. He simply shrugged.

"I hear you're looking for footage of the robbery that happened here. Any chance of a reward for that?" the man asked.

"First, who are you, and why should I believe that you can get that for me? You sure won't get it from that," Valone replied, gesturing at the ancient unplugged camera.

"I'm the owner's son, which gives me the access needed to get the footage. I go by Max. As for how, that piece of junk isn't the only camera in the store." Max then moved two stuffed animals aside on a shelf to reveal a webcam.

"It's hooked to an old laptop that was just gathering dust, like this webcam. I told the old man he should have visible security, but he doesn't like it. Says he hates the idea of a camera always watching, and it's a safe neighborhood. Guess he's not right about everything, huh?" he said, pointing to the two dead bodies.

"Right, you've answered my questions, now I'll answer yours. Yes, there is a reward for any video record of what happened here," Valone said.

A smile began to spread across Max's face.

"The reward is not being arrested for obstructing a homicide investigation," Valone continued. "I'm sure that's worth quite a bit to you."

Max frowned. "That's not fair. I go to the trouble to come down here and help you out, and all I get is threats? It's not even like you're going to use the footage to catch the guys who came here to rob our store. They're already dead."

Valone nodded. "True enough. So why did you think your video was interesting enough to sell?"

Max sighed, and shook his head. "OK. The video is amazing. But it won't help you much."

Now it was Valone's turn to frown. "That doesn't make any sense. Anyway, give me the tape, and I'll see for myself."

Max laughed. "Tape? What is this, the 80s? Give me your business card."

Valone handed him one. Max looked at it, then his fingers blurred over his smartphone. A few seconds later, Valone felt his phone buzz in his pocket.

Max grinned. "It's for you-hoo!"

Squinting, Valone poked at an icon that had appeared on his phone's surface. He was rewarded with a grainy video of the robbery, finishing with the death of the two thieves. Shaking his head, he turned to Max. "I see what you mean. It is amazing- I've never seen anyone move so fast. He's had either martial arts or combat training, or maybe both. I know how this ended, and I still couldn't help thinking that this guy was getting shot. But the picture quality is terrible. All I could tell is that he's Asian."

The cashier glowered at Max, and spoke to him even more rapidly in Korean than before. Valone arched one eyebrow, and asked Max for a translation. Embarrassed, Max said in a low voice, "She is angry because I have shown you the face of the man who saved her and the pregnant woman. All he asked was to be left alone."

Valone nodded. "Well, based on what I've seen I can't see how he's in any trouble. He didn't pull a trigger, and self defense covers this pretty neatly. No prosecutor will take this on as a homicide, or even man-slaughter. But we do need a statement from the guy. Either of you know where we can find him?"

Both Max and the cashier shook their heads. The cashier said, "I never saw him before he came in today." Max added, "I've never seen him at all, except in this video."

Valone's experience as a detective was especially helpful at letting him know when people were lying to him. These two weren't.

"All right." Turning to Max, he said pointedly, "This is the only copy of this video, right?" Max shifted uncomfortably, and did not answer. "Right?" Valone repeated, obviously annoyed.

"Look, this is the coolest thing I've ever seen, and it happened right here in our store! You couldn't expect me not to share!"

Valone glared at Max. "OK. Who did you send it to? Maybe we can limit the damage."

Max laughed. "Damage? What damage? This guy is gonna be famous! I put it online, and when I last looked it had over half a million hits!"

The cashier looked pale, and her hand flew to her mouth.

"What's the matter?" Max asked the cashier. "Why are you so upset?"

"Because, genius," Valone said, shaking his head, "maybe he has a good reason not to want his face all over the Internet."

CHAPTER THIRTY TWO

Tunnel No. 1, North Korea

Lee Ho Suk looked in amazement at the number of men and pieces of heavy construction equipment operating inside the re-excavated tunnel. The foreman had to practically yell in his ear to say that they were lucky only about a tenth of the tunnel had collapsed completely, though they were adding additional supports to the walls and ceilings throughout the tunnel's length. Lee nodded numbly as his heart sank. He had hoped that construction might be delayed by months. Now it looked like weeks, or at this pace maybe only days before they were past the tunnel's previous end point.

Still, Lee did his part. As he walked through the length of the tunnel, Lee pointed out areas that needed extra bracing, or where older supports need to be replaced. No sooner did Lee point out a problem than the foreman had workers on it. Though a bullet in the head might be waiting for me at the end of this tunnel, Lee thought, at least it will be a quicker and less painful death than being crushed in a tunnel collapse. Wincing, he rubbed his right arm, which still had some nerve damage that had not been fixed during his hospital stay. Some things, he had been told, just take time to heal. Or, he thought ruefully, not.

Beijing, China

Jim Martinovsky waited until Mark Bishop had finished reading his original draft telegram on Li Weimin and Park Won Hee before he started his pitch. As Jim had thought, his boss had watered down his action message and left out any mention of Li's interest in defecting and the chance that Park might be willing to come as well from the version sent on to DC.

Bishop was the deputy station chief at the U.S. Embassy in Beijing, which ordinarily meant he was the second-highest representative of the CIA in country. At the moment, since Bishop's boss was back in the US on leave, he was actually in charge. Martinovsky thought, as he had many times before, that Bishop looked nothing like spies did in movies. Middle aged, slim, medium height and brown hair, wearing silver wireframe glasses and clothes that would have made him at home in any office cubicle in America, there was absolutely nothing remarkable about him.

Probably what made him so effective.

Staff at the Embassy from different agencies talked to each other every day. However, there were strict rules for someone from one agency asking for another to take action. The most important was also the simplest – the highest ranking agency representative had to make an action request.

Martinovsky both understood and supported this rule, in principle. Now, though, he had to break it.

"So, quite different from the version I saw in the cable traffic this morning. This sounds like a great opportunity to acquire two valuable intelligence sources. But your boss isn't interested. Any idea why?"

Martinovsky shrugged. "Wang Lijun," he said, simply.

Bishop winced. "Well, yes, that was quite a mess. Not our finest hour. Of course, he showed up at our doorstep cold, and we had absolutely no planning or preparation in place."

"So, you think we could do better with Li and Park?"

Bishop snorted. "We could hardly do worse. Actually, precisely because of the Wang Lijun episode I've given a lot of thought to how we could get defectors out of China quietly. The first point is that they never come to the Embassy. Instead, we come to them."

"Makes sense. We know that everyone's entry to the Embassy is logged by Chinese security."

Bishop nodded. "Next, we get the defectors new identities. I've got facial recognition software set up to scan the US passport photos on record for every US citizen now in China. We find the closest matches in our database to the defectors, produce new US passports, and we have their exit documents."

Martinovsky frowned. "Don't we have to get them here to get photos to do the matches? And why not just create brand new identities?"

Bishop shook his head. "We have digital biographical files on all important foreign officials. I pulled up the ones for both Li and Park when I read and filed your original cable, and both have photos that will work to get us the matches we need."

"As for why we need to make those matches, remember that Chinese security will want to match their exit from China with their most recent entry. If they have no entry on record, they will certainly be discovered for who they really are. With entries on record and valid US passports, they will just be two among the hundreds of American citizens who pass through Beijing Airport every day."

Martinovsky looked incredulous as he asked what he thought was an obvious question. "And what happens when the real Americans who made those entries try to leave China, and the record says they've already left? Shouldn't we at least warn them?"

Bishop shrugged. "We thought about that. First, we've checked and confirmed that Chinese immigration records aren't perfect, any more than any computer system is flawless worldwide. Next, remember that the real Americans will be exactly that – the real deal. They have nothing to hide. And that's why we won't tell the real identity holders anything. Their best defense is they will be telling the absolute truth, that they have no idea why Chinese records show them having exited already."

"So, you don't think that the Chinese will connect the real holders of these identities with the two defectors we're smuggling out of China?"

Bishop shook his head emphatically. "No way. Exit records fail to match entry records every day, mostly because of mistakes in data entry, but also because of a range of other issues from database corruption to software glitches. Remember, we're talking about a database that tries to pull in data from not just airports but also seaports and land crossing points. Each port type, land, sea and air has a separate system that tracks different data. So, the seaport system has a data field for a seaman's book, which a crewman can use in place of a passport. The land crossings have a data field for license plate numbers that are cross-referenced to the driver, and so on. A match failure will raise questions, but as long as they have nothing to hide – and the real Americans don't – they'll be fine."

"For their sake, I hope you're right."

CHAPTER THIRTY THREE

Pyongyang, North Korea

Shin Yon Young had been starting to think that he would never be called in to clean the bugged conference room again, after the dour guard he had privately dubbed "Sunshine" had found him alone in the room. Even though Shin had been there cleaning the conference room at another guard's orders, he knew that Sunshine had his doubts about him.

Apparently, though, those doubts had not been communicated to the other guards. A different guard had ordered him to clean the conference room, and now months of hard work were about to finally pay off. All he had to do was lean under the table far enough to be within the two foot range of the button shaped receiver and activate it to have the bug perform its two second download.

Later, Shin could not have said why he did not bend down. He just had a sudden, sharp feeling right down to his bones that if he did he was a dead man.

He glanced at the bored guard who was there to supervise his cleaning. No, nothing about his behavior gave any hint that he suspected Shin. He thought back to his training, which drummed in many points repeatedly, none more than "Trust your instincts."

Shin thought about the months of misery that had led up this moment, both in the brutal covert missions training and in the daily grind of life as a North Korean janitor. He thought about the fact that he might never have the opportunity to collect this incredibly valuable intelligence again.

Then Shin remembered the words of one of his trainers, one of the very few who had spied on North Korea and lived to tell about it. He had said – in fact shouted – to the trainees that "Whenever your thoughts argue against your instincts, remember these words – My brain is trying to kill me. Listen to your instincts, ignore reason, and you may survive."

Shin stayed straight, finished cleaning, and nodded to the dull-eyed guard that he was done. As he walked out of the room, Shin wondered if he had just made the greatest mistake of his life.

"Are you sure you will be able to intercept a transmission?" the guard Shin had named "Sunshine" asked the technician.

The technician scowled at the guard before answering. "I am doing this check for you as a favor to a senior guard. Please do not question my competence!" Watching the storm clouds gather on the guard's face, he reluctantly added "This is the latest German equipment, and it was not easy to get. It will detect even a burst transmission. Furthermore, if it is within this building I will be able to tell you within a two-foot radius where the signal originated."

"Why don't you have this equipment turned on and monitored at all times?" the guard asked.

The technician gave the sigh reserved for the professional forced to tolerate the ignorance of those outside his craft. "Because this equipment requires precise calibration prior to each use, and the number of times it may be used and the duration of each use is finite. Thanks to Western sanctions, when this device breaks – and with such delicate equipment that is only a matter of time – parts to fix it will be just as hard to get as the device itself. And when I am asked to check for the use of a listening device, I do not wish to say that I can't because the equipment is broken!"

Reluctantly, the guard nodded. "Well, if he did plant a listening device as I suspect, I am sure he would activate it now. He seldom gets such an opportunity."

The technician scratched his head, and asked "If you suspect him, why not simply arrest him? Who would care about a janitor?"

Now the guard practically seethed. "You are right, that it is how it was in the past. But no more. Since our new leader came to power, we now understand that there must be proof behind accusations. Otherwise, the accuser risks being condemned himself."

The technician nodded. "Very well. If he does activate a recording device, you will have your proof. My testimony and a printout from this equipment will document his guilt completely."

The guard grunted his satisfaction. "Good. He should clean the room in under fifteen minutes. Let me know as soon as the proof is in hand, so I can radio the guard with the janitor to have him arrested."

The technician nodded again and settled in to examine his readouts, making small adjustments to the dials as the guard looked on impatiently. Time crawled forward for five minutes, then ten, and finally at fourteen his radio crackled to life. It was the guard with the janitor reporting that the janitor had finished cleaning the conference room, and that the guard was locking the room and escorting the janitor from the floor.

The technician thought the guard at his side might have a stroke, as his eyes bulged and face turned red. His concerns subsided as he saw the guard make a visible effort to regain his composure, and calmly acknowledge the report.

The guard sat down heavily, and the technician frowned. "So, it appears we have been wasting our time."

"No! I am sure that janitor is up to no good. If it's not a listening device, then it must be something else."

The technician shrugged. "Very well, for all I know you may be right. However, detecting such a device is all I can help you with. As I promised, I will keep the use of this equipment today between us. However, if you wish to do so again, you must make your request through proper channels."

The guard nodded unhappily. Maybe he had been wrong about what the janitor was doing in the conference room, but he knew something about him was off. Perhaps if he spent some time following him after work...

CHAPTER THIRTY FOUR

Los Angeles

Paul Valone had seen plenty of captains come and go while he had been a detective. Normally he reported to a lieutenant but on important cases he had been called in directly by captains before, usually to their office, just like this time. He'd even talked to this one, Captain Gonzalez, on two other cases. On both he'd measured up to his rep, which was that he was a straight arrow guy who wanted to do the job right, and didn't care about politics. That meant Valone respected him, and did his best to do what Gonzalez wanted. Until now.

"Look, Captain, I don't get this. We canvassed the neighborhood, and found no trace of the missing- well, let's call him a witness. We agree that whatever his role was in the death of these two scumbags, it's nothing that a prosecutor would touch. Since they're both dead, we can close this case without his statement. Why don't we?"

Gonzalez' lips pressed together, but that was the only sign that he was trying hard to keep his temper in check. "I don't like this any better than you do, but I have my orders from the top. They think letting this guy get away makes us look stupid, and as long as the video is on a constant loop on half a dozen channels, they won't drop it. The guy who uploaded the clip and titled it 'The Matrix is Real' sure didn't do us any favor."

"So how long am I supposed to waste time on this?"

Gonzalez shrugged and stood up, which Valone knew meant that the time the captain was going to spend on this with him had reached its limit. "There are two answers to that. The first is, however long it takes you to find this guy, get his statement, and hand him over to the reporters who know this interview footage will sell a lot of commercials. The second is, whenever there's a story that pushes this off the front page. Up to you, Paul."

All Valone could say to that was to nod, and avoid slamming Gonzalez' door as he left his office.

Now, how was he going to find this guy?

Beijing, China

Jim Martinovsky and Mark Bishop drove up to Li Weimin's residence exactly on time, as was expected for official events in China. The concept of "fashionably late" was one Martinovsky had never cared for, both because it always felt rude and because he hated guessing just how late he was supposed to be. It was one of the many little things he actually preferred about China. Just as he had the thought, he smiled wryly to himself. It would be hard to more exactly conform to the stereotype of a diplomat away from home too long.

Well, if anyone felt like questioning his willingness to upset the Chinese government, tonight's planned activities should satisfy them, especially if his role in them were ever discovered.

The guards outside Li's residence were not particularly alert, nor did they impress Martinovsky as being the best Chinese security had to offer. They noted the car's diplomatic license plates, and without either checking their IDs or even really looking at them opened the gate for the short drive to Li's door. Martinovsky saw that there were two cars already parked ahead of them in the driveway.

Li was at his home's open door even before Martinovsky and Bishop had finished exiting their vehicle, a large Chevy Suburban with heavily tinted glass. As they made their way up the sidewalk, Li called to them "I hope you had no trouble with the guards, my friends."

Both shook their heads as each in turn shook Li's outstretched hand. Li was making a point of doing that rather than an exchange of bows, which was his way of saying that they were truly welcome in his home. Martinovsky doubted that many other Chinese officials would do the same.

As they entered, Martinovsky and Bishop saw two men rise up from their seats in the living room. One looked at them neutrally, while the other was clearly having trouble controlling both his expression and his temper.

Li gestured towards the two men. "Please allow me to present Park Won Hee and his assistant, Mr. Lee. Jim Martinovsky and Mark Bishop are both with the US Embassy." Park bowed while a white-faced Lee spoke in a low voice very rapidly in Park's ear.

"My colleague is reminding me that our government has not authorized us to meet with American officials," Park said, shrugging apologetically.

Li spread his hands wide, taking in all four men with the gesture. "Of course. But this is not a meeting, simply a social gathering. I did not intend us to discuss policy. I hope that by this means, we can begin to improve understanding between our peoples. I am sure you will not wish me to report to the Vice Minister that you were unwilling to even share a meal with our American guests."

For the first time, Lee appeared uncertain. "You are saying that Song Hailong knows of this?"

Li smiled. "It was his idea. If you think about it for a moment, I'm sure you will understand why."

Lee's eyes widened as he took in the meaning that Li intended. This was another effort to find out how the US would react to North Korea's plans for the South.

"Yes, yes of course. I apologize for my initial reaction. I was simply… surprised." Lee's voice trailed off, as he started to more carefully examine the two American officials.

"Excellent," Li said with satisfaction. "Now, everyone please have a seat, while I see how the cook is progressing with dinner."

CHAPTER THIRTY FIVE

Enroute from Khabarovsk to Dacha 30 Kilometers From Vladivostok

Grishkov's right foot ached from the pressure he had been placing on the accelerator for the hundreds of kilometers back to the dacha outside Vladivostok where his family was in danger. He had left in such a hurry that he hadn't realized his cell phone battery had drained, and the radio in his car was good only for a limited range within Vladivostok city. Grishkov doubted it would work out in the forest where his family waited for him.

He had thought several times about stopping at a service station to make a call, and even started to turn off the highway once. At the last second, though, he had veered back onto the road, as he had to admit to himself that calling would do nothing to help his family, and would only make him feel better. No, only by getting to his mother-in-law's dacha would he be able to do anything real to help. He only prayed he wouldn't be too late.

Dacha 30 Kilometers From Vladivostok

In a low voice, Kim Gun Jun explained to the seven hired guns exactly what he expected from them. In a nutshell, that was to capture Grishkov's wife and two children alive, and kill everyone else. Kim expected two or at most three armed men to deal with inside the house.

Kim would go in the front with three men, while the other four would make a wide circle around the back of the house. Kim had all the men synchronize their watches, and told them he expected all of them to attack at precisely 6:05PM. They would still be able to make out the house and its doors clearly, but any defenders looking outside would have trouble spotting the attackers as they made their approach. All nodded as they checked their weapons, which Kim saw with satisfaction were all automatic. He frowned as he noticed none but he were wearing body armor. Kim then shrugged. With the numbers he had, it shouldn't matter.

Using a kitchen towel to muffle the noise, Petrov had already broken and removed the glass from the bottom of the two front windows to give his KBI GM-94 an unobstructed field of fire. He had also removed and twisted some of the vines that crawled up both the front and back of the dacha around the grenade launcher's barrel, so that it would be harder to spot by any intruders. As Petrov swiveled his head slowly back and forth, he had to resist the temptation to do the same with the barrel, since any movement would make his position much easier to spot.

There! It was only a brief trembling of a few low-hanging branches, but he was sure it was not an animal. Not, he thought to himself, the four-legged kind. Without conscious thought, he aimed at the point of movement and fired. The recoil and noise were not nearly as bad as he'd expected, though if he'd had the time to think he would have realized the police version would not be as demanding as one used by the military.

Petrov was rewarded almost immediately by a high-pitched scream, followed by silence. He wondered how Nikitin was doing.

Nikitin jerked as Petrov's grenade launcher hit its target. Almost simultaneously, a faint rustling outside the back gate preceded a loud explosion that took the gate off its hinges, along with a sizeable chunk of the fence. Nikitin peered out the window, but saw no movement. It was too much to hope for that the Claymore had taken out all of the attackers, though it had clearly slowed them down.

Nikitin moved over to another window with a better view of the undamaged fence. If he had run into something like a mine, he would try to enter the yard at the point as far away from the first explosion as possible.

Nikitin did not have to wait long. First a hand, then an arm, then a head followed by a body appeared over the fence, as Nikitin took careful aim with his PP-2000. A short burst, and the intruder fell heavily to the ground. The gunman twitched, and then lay still.

So far so good, Nikitin thought.

No answer from the four men he had sent to the back of the dacha, and one of the three with him dead. Kim Gun Jun simply could not believe it. What kind of police had mines and grenade launchers? A small, dark part of his brain answered almost immediately, "Apparently Russian homicide detectives in Vladivostok." The same part told him that the odds had shifted too far in the defenders' favor, and that it was time to retreat and regroup.

No. Kim no longer cared about the risk, or operational security. He was going to succeed, and prove he deserved the rank he had earned after his success in obtaining Timoshenko's nuclear device.

Besides, he had a surprise of his own.

Nikitin had not been surprised to hear Petrov's grenade launcher go off at almost the same moment the Claymore detonated. A simultaneous two-sided assault made sense, especially with the numbers their attackers had available. He was puzzled, though, by the several minutes that had passed since with no movement to either front or back. Repulsing the attack could not be so easy, surely?

Of course, he mused, perhaps they had not expected mere police to be so....well equipped!

Kim's RG-60SZ grenade was manufactured in Russia by the Scientific Research Institute of Applied Chemistry. With its ovoid shape, smooth exterior surface, two-piece body and fly-off lever fusing system it looked like most other flashbangs, though with a flash intensity of more than 60 million candles and a sound pressure wave exceeding 160 decibels it was more effective than most. Kim had already explained to the other members of his assault team that the women and children inside the house were not to be killed, or even injured if at all possible. Kim had learned from past operations that having to care for a wounded hostage made for unpleasant complications. Their goal was to kill or incapacitate the policemen inside as rapidly as possible, and then escape with the hostages. For all Kim knew, backup could have already been summoned and be minutes away.

The flashbang was their ticket inside. While Petrov's grenade launcher had taken care of one attacker, the noise and shower of debris created by the grenade's explosion had been more than enough cover for the other three to advance to positions near the front of the dacha.

Kim drew back his arm, and aimed for one of the dacha's windows.

Petrov saw a sudden movement out of the corner of his eye, and was swiveling his grenade launcher towards it when a small dark shape flew through the window next to him. Almost immediately, the wave of light and sound following the flashbang's explosion had him on the floor clutching his head, the grenade launcher forgotten. Petrov's last conscious thought as the front door flew open was that he had failed Grishkov's family.

Chapter Thirty Six

Beijing, China

Li Weimin smiled at Park Won Hee and his assistant, Mr. Lee, and then turned toward Jim Martinovsky and Mark Bishop.

"Gentlemen, I have failed to fulfill one of my most basic duties as a host."

Martinovsky smiled, and guessed correctly. "The tour."

"Indeed. I have already taken our Korean friends around my home. Now it is your turn."

Martinovsky and Bishop rose, and followed Li out of his living room. All three noticed that Park and Lee began whispering furiously as soon as they were out of sight.

"I am very proud of my collection of porcelain pieces. As you know, China excels at this means of artistic expression," Li said, pointing to each piece in turn as he moved through the hallway towards the stairs. "I have several more upstairs."

As soon as they reached the second floor, Bishop removed a small glass vial from his pocket and handed it to Li.

"This is how we'll persuade Mr. Lee to take a nap and let both you and Mr. Park begin your journey. Just put this in a cup and swish it around. It will quickly evaporate, coating the sides of the cup. Then add any liquid, hot or cold. It leaves no smell or taste. It will make him fall asleep, but has no lasting harmful effects."

Li nodded. "I had planned to serve tea next anyway. I presume that will serve?"

Bishop smiled. "That's the first drink we tested. It works perfectly."

The three men walked back downstairs, Martinovsky and Bishop to re-join Park and Lee, and their host to the kitchen. Li called to the others, "I'll be right back."

Park and Lee continued to whisper to each other. Martinovsky and Bishop looked at each other, both silently urging Li to hurry.

Dacha 30 Kilometers From Vladivostok

Nikitin's ears rang from the grenade's explosion, though the light had no impact on him from his position at the back of the dacha. He was sure, though, that Petrov needed help, if he was even still alive. Nikitin threw himself prone as soon as he had reached the end of the hallway connecting the back of the dacha to its front, just as a cloud of splinters erupted from waist to head high above him. His PP-2000 was already stretched out in front of him, and sliced sideways through the living room. Nikitin's luck held, as the burst connected with two gunmen who went down hard. He scrambled upright, and after a quick check found both of them dead.

Now where was Petrov? A hasty search quickly proved successful, though at first Nikitin feared the worst. Petrov was unconscious from the flashbang's detonation less than a meter away, but his pulse was still strong. Nikitin nodded with satisfaction. It was lucky for him that I did not dawdle on the way to the front of the dacha, or the men I just dispatched would have given him the same treatment.

Nikitin next saw that the door to the cellar had been kicked open, at the same moment he heard a female scream.

Arisha had done her best to prepare for unwelcome guests. The dacha's heat came from an ancient coal-fired iron furnace, which vented heat through equally ancient metal pipes throughout the dacha. The amount of smoke the furnace produced was directly proportional to the quality of the coal fed into it. Over the years, Arisha's mother had picked through the best nuggets of jet black, low smoke coal to feed into the furnace, letting the brown high smoke chunks accumulate at the bottom of the bin. Now they finally had a use. After tossing them in, Arisha next adjusted the fur-nace louvers so that the thick smoke belching from them blew towards the stairs leading down to the cellar. Anyone coming down those steps would have to lose precious seconds before having any chance of spotting his intended victims.

Next she had locked Sasha and Misha into the root cellar, over their strenuous protests. She was only able to quiet them by pointing out that they only had two weapons, and neither of them had yet been trained in their use. Arisha also had to promise that when this emergency was over, Sasha and Misha would both get the training needed to use weapons properly. If we get out of this, Arisha thought to herself grimly, I may just keep that promise no matter how young they are.

As Arisha checked her pistol, she saw her mother continuing to methodically polish her late husband's shotgun. It already gleamed, and looked better than new. It was hard to believe the two of them could be all that stood between these criminals and her children.

The reality of their situation was made unmistakable by the sound of the explosion upstairs. As she took the pistol off safety, Arisha vowed that her children would be taken only over her dead body. She glanced at her mother, who gave her a tight smile and a nod that said as clearly as words, "Me too."

CHAPTER THIRTY SEVEN

Dacha 30 Kilometers From Vladivostok

Kim Gun Jun had left the two men upstairs with a simple order. Find and kill the remaining defenders, while he secured the hostages. As he kicked in the door and started down the stairs, he was immediately greeted by thick, billowing smoke. At the same time, he heard the exchange of gunfire in the room he had just left. He knew what a PP-2000 sounded like, and knew that the men with him weren't carrying one. When it was the last one to speak, he knew he was the only surviving member of the assault team. Well, he hadn't come this far to leave empty handed.

As Kim walked down the stairs, an ear shattering boom registered at the same time that an impact against his flak jacket pushed him up hard against the cellar wall. Blood dripped down the side of his face near where several buckshot pellets had grazed his scalp. Still unable to see, he sprayed an entire clip from his Bizon-2 submachine gun into the cellar, and was rewarded with two thuds, one metallic and one not. Just as he was congratulating himself on taking out the shooter, the flat bark of a 9mm pistol was immediately followed by a sharp pain in his left arm, followed by numbness that told him of impending shock. He then heard the distinctive sound of Russian police sirens rising and falling as they came closer to the dacha.

Cursing, Kim realized he had no hope of accomplishing his mission, and would do well now to escape in one piece. Reversing course, he took the stairs back up two at a time, launching himself into the room headfirst as several PP-2000 rounds went directly above him. Aiming his Bizon center mass at the target in front of him, Kim squeezed the trigger and was horrified to realize he had failed to change magazines. Fortunately, there was one round remaining, and it hit home. As the man went down, Kim rushed past him towards the sedan he had hidden nearby. He had scouted the nearby roads thoroughly, and was sure he could escape as long as he had a head start over the police. Kim was more determined than ever to stop Grishkov, whatever it took.

After hearing the single shot upstairs, Arisha waited tensely for more. When she heard nothing but the slam of a door and the increasing sound of the nearing sirens, she went to her mother. Closer examination confirmed the sick feeling Arisha already had in the pit of her stomach. Her mother was dead, hit by at least three rounds. Along with sadness, though, she felt pride. Arisha knew that her mother had been ready to give her life for her daughter and grandchildren, and she had made a real difference. If that criminal had not been slowed down by her mother's shotgun, Arisha doubted she could have aimed accurately enough to hit him before he made it down the stairs. She had also seen the blood on his face before she shot him, and knew that her mother had hurt him. Good, she thought savagely. I wish we had killed the bastard.

Arisha next unlocked the door to the root cellar, and hugged Sasha and Misha close. She looked them directly in the eyes and told them about their grandmother's sacrifice. Then Arisha told them that there would be time later to grieve, but that for now they needed to be strong and silent until the police arrived. Tears were welling in both of the children's eyes, but they nodded somberly. Holding them close to her again, Arisha vowed to herself that she would do anything she could to help her husband stop the man who killed her mother.

CHAPTER THIRTY EIGHT

Los Angeles

Chung Hee Moon cursed his softness for intervening in the robbery. He should have stayed hidden and avoided involvement. Now, he was in the worst possible position for a soldier on a covert mission in enemy territory – he was being actively sought by the authorities. Of course, they didn't know why he was here. If they found him, though, a search of his apartment was certain. The device had to remain under his control, and there was no other place he was authorized to go. Under these circumstances, Chung was not even sure it made sense to contact the emergency number he had been given.

No, it would be better to move on his own. But where would he go?

A knock on the door made Chung's head snap up. Had the police found him so quickly? But no, the knock was soft and hesitant. No matter how different this country was, Chung knew that the knock of a policeman would be loud and authoritative.

Peering through the lens of his door, Chung was astonished to see that it was Kang Ji Yeong, the nurse he had helped with her groceries. He had never told her which apartment he lived in, but evidently she knew.

Chung opened the door, and Kang quickly pushed her way in.

"Close the door!" she hissed.

Puzzled, Chung shrugged and shut the door behind her.

Hands on her hips, Kang demanded "Have you seen?"

Chung cocked his head sideways in confusion, and asked the obvious question, "Seen what?"

Rather than answer, Kang marched to Chung's TV set, turned it on and began flipping channels with his remote. A few seconds later, she pointed to the screen and exclaimed "Seen that!"

Chung was horrified to see the scene at the market where he had "assisted" the two thieves in shooting each other. The voice accompanying the video was saying that authorities were seeking the Asian man in the scene for questioning. When the video stopped and the camera went back to the two reporters in the studio, one added "I think the question should be 'Would you like to join the LA police department?' They could sure use the help!" The other laughed and nodded in agreement.

Kang glared at Chung, her arms crossed. "Well? That was you, right?"

Chung had observed that the video's quality was poor, but she could see that he was wearing the same clothes, so there was no point in denying the obvious. He just shrugged agreement.

"So, you are here on a tourist visa hoping to find work, and this is how you start? There have been police throughout the neighborhood for hours searching for you. They will be here any minute."

"The woman they hit was pregnant. I could not just stand by."

Kang glowered at Chung for a moment, and then abruptly nodded. "Get your things, and come to my apartment."

Chung looked at her in confusion. "But I thought you believed my actions were mistaken."

Kang shook her head in frustration. "Idiot. I don't like that your actions put you in danger. But no mother would condemn what you did to save a woman and her unborn child. Now hurry up before the police get here."

Rounding up Chung's few possessions took less than five minutes. When Kang saw the large trunk holding the device, she frowned. "What's in there?"

Knowing she would ask, Chung had his answer ready. "It is full of mementos of my time in the military. Some are items I wish to keep for sentimental reasons. Most, though, I plan to sell if I can get a good price. I was told that there is a good market here for such things."

Kang nodded. "All right, if they can help you make money I will find a place for it. But we must hurry!"

Holding the door open for Chung, Kang held the plastic bags into which they had stuffed his few clothes and toiletries, while Chung dragged the trunk into the hallway. Since Kang's apartment was only a few doors away, it took less than a minute to complete the move.

It turned out to be not a moment too soon. A few minutes after Kang closed her apartment door, they heard multiple footsteps in the hallway, followed by a knock that sounded like it was on Chung's door even though it could be heard throughout the floor. Chung felt oddly pleased that his guess about police door knocking habits had turned out to be correct.

A few minutes of silence followed, shortly interrupted by a series of knocks that moved closer and closer to Kang's apartment. Once they reached her door, Kang answered. When they asked to come in, Kang said no and walked into the hallway, closing the door behind her while Chung hid in Kang's bedroom closet.

Ten minutes later, Kang stepped quietly back into her apartment. A full twenty minutes after that, once all noise outside had ceased, Kang came back to her bedroom closet.

"I told them that my son was sick and sleeping inside, and I did not want to disturb him. That nosy weasel of a landlord confirmed for them that I do have a son, who fortunately is spending tonight at a friend's house. I told them that I saw you heading for the elevator carrying a suitcase, but that you had said nothing about where you were going. I also said I had only seen you in the hallway, and had no reason to ask."

"Your door was hanging open and there were men inside. The door looked undamaged, so the landlord probably let them in. If you left anything back there, I don't think you'll be getting it back."

Chung shook his head. "I think we got everything, and any small item I left behind doesn't matter. Everything I own of value is in my trunk."

Kang nodded. "Good. You know it will be days before you can even think about leaving this apartment. I have no idea what I am going to tell my son tomorrow."

Chung shrugged. "I see no alternative to telling him the truth. Do you think he will accept your decision to let me stay?"

Kang looked at him thoughtfully. "Well, he did say he liked you. I know he will approve of what you did at the market. We may be all right, but I won't know for sure until I have a chance to talk to him. You need to be in another room while I do."

Chung nodded agreement. He then bowed deeply. "I must offer my deep and sincere thanks for helping me to avoid the police. Even if they did not put me on trial for what I did, they would certainly have sent me back to Korea. I used much of what money I had to make the trip here and rent that apartment. Being forced back home would have been very difficult for me." Especially once they saw what was in my trunk, he added to himself silently.

"I am doing what I think is right. It is what I have always tried to do, and I have raised my son to act the same way. All I ask is that you do all you can to avoid leading the police to our home. That means staying out of sight until I think it is safe."

Chung again nodded. "I will follow your lead. You know this country and its ways far better than I. It would be both foolish and ungrateful of me to argue."

Kang laughed. "Well said. No matter what happens, I will not regret helping the only man I have ever met who seems to have at least a little common sense."

Kang and Chung smiled at each other.

Chapter Thirty Nine

Beijing, China

Li Weimin turned to Jim Martinovsky and nodded. "I know you are familiar with our tea ceremony, but as a more recent arrival to our country, perhaps Mr. Bishop is not."

Bishop smiled, and said "First, please call me Mark. Second, I have of course heard of this ceremony, but welcome a chance to see it performed."

Li turned to the two Koreans. "Of course, I know you have your own version of this ceremony in your homeland. I hope you will find the differences and similarities interesting."

Park Won Hee briefly inclined his head. "I am certain of it."

Li kept up a running narrative as he carried out the ceremony. "The first stage of preparation is to lay cups and pot on the table. I then warm and sterilize them with hot water, and pour away the excess. Then, I invite you all to see and appreciate the tea's appearance and smell. This is Longjing tea, which to be authentic must come from villages and plantations in Hangzhou's West Lake area. The Ming Qian premium variety of Longjing tea has to be produced from the first spring shoots prior to the Qingming Festival, which this year was on April 5. Quantities are very limited because the production cycle is so short, no more than ten days before Qingming every year."

An appreciative murmur arose from all four guests. The tea's smell was indeed stronger and more fragrant than any in their experience, and it was easy to see that they were already impressed, even before tasting the tea.

Next Li filled the teapot with tea, and rinsed the leaves using hot water poured about a foot above the pot, which he had placed into a catching bowl. Li kept adding water into the pot until it overflowed, and then gently removed the debris and bubbles on the surface, and closed the lid. Li then poured this first brew into the cups. Smiling, Li said "This is simply an extended washing of the tea leaves, and will not be consumed."

Li then refilled the pot with fresh hot water until the water reached the mouth of the pot, followed by emptying the hot tea from the first brew over the outside of the teapot. Li let the tea steep for a minute, and then began to pour a cup for each guest.

As Li passed each guest a cup, he smiled and said, "I would like to propose a toast. To better understanding between our great nations."

All nodded and appreciatively drank from each cup. Soon each was empty. Just as Li was about to propose a refill, everyone turned toward Mr. Lee as his cup fell from nerveless hands, and his head fell sideways. Park in particular appeared alarmed.

Li bent towards Park and said in a low voice, "Now you have your opportunity to turn words into action. These men can get us to the United States so we can each save our countries from a terrible tragedy. However, you must decide now. Your minder is only asleep, and we must be well underway before he wakes up."

Park sat stock still, obviously shocked by what had happened and its suddenness. "How will we do this?" he finally asked.

Bishop quickly responded, "I have an American passport with your picture in it, as well as another for our host. I have packed suitcases for both of you with suitable clothing in the car. You each have electronic tickets on file under the names in your passport for this evening's last flight on Trans Pacific, thirteen and a half hours nonstop to Washington DC. If we leave right now, we'll be in time to get you to the airport and through immigration and security."

Park drew a deep breath, and then slowly nodded as he stood up. "Very well," he said. "I am ready."

Tunnel No. 1, North Korea

Lee Ho Suk thought he had seen every kind of tunnel bracing there was over the years, both wood and metal. The metal lengths being brought into the tunnel now, though, looked like nothing he had seen before. They were also not quite long enough to stretch from tunnel floor to ceiling. And they had an odd shape. In fact, they looked more like train tracks than bracing, though they were not quite as thick and heavy as he remembered from tracks he had seen near his village.

Lee started to move towards the soldier who was obviously in charge of the delivery to ask him its purpose, but then stopped himself before he had even made a complete turn in the man's direction. No matter what new responsibilities he had been given, he was still a prisoner. If the tracks related to the tunnel's construction, as they obviously did, he would be told whatever he needed to know. In the meantime, the less attention he attracted the better.

Tracks, Lee mused to himself. Tracks to where, and carrying what?

CHAPTER FORTY

Pyongyang, North Korea

Shin Yon Young had continued his cleaning duties without incident after that day when his instincts told him not to collect the take from the bug he had planted with such effort in the conference room. Since then, he hadn't even been assigned to clean on the same floor as the one containing the device, but on the bright side he hadn't seen the grim-faced guard he called "Sunshine" recently either. Shin had no way to know this, but that was because the senior guard had a bad case of the flu. Due to his refusal to take the disease seriously, he had been forced by his supervisor to check into a nearby military hospital after he had been seen vomiting on duty, after a stern lecture about the danger of infection he was exposing government members to by his "pig-headedness."

Enough time had passed since that the orders "Sunshine" had given to keep Shin off the conference room floor had not been heard by a newly-transferred guard. So, once again Shin had the opportunity to activate the bug and download its recordings.

This time, he heard no internal warning bells, and in less than fifteen minutes had cleaned the room and collected the recording. The bored guard escorted him off the floor, and since his work shift was now over Shin could leave for his apartment and get the information it had taken him months to collect back to NIS headquarters without delay. Finally, Shin thought to himself, this job was working the way it was supposed to.

Dacha 30 Kilometers From Vladivostok

Grishkov surveyed the scene with a fury that threatened to make him lose control. He had nearly lost his entire family! Nikitin spotted this, and pulled himself upright on the gurney. "Boss, your wife and children are safe. I'm sorry about your mother-in-law, but everyone else couldn't be safer if they were in the Kremlin. Captain Ivansik has eight men guarding them, and you know that anyone trying this again will be just as dead as these guys," Nikitin said, gesturing towards the seven bodies lined up in a row with sheets covering them.

The fury in Grishkov's eyes softened as he looked over the sheeted bodies. "You and Petrov did very well to fight back these animals. So, two versus eight. How did you do it?"

"Well, first I have to correct your math, boss. Your wife and mother-in-law both took a piece out of their leader, as the blood trail coming out of the house shows. But to get to your real question, here it is: I had a Claymore, and Petrov had a KBI GM-94 grenade launcher."

Grishkov stared at Nikitin in disbelief. "You had an American anti-personnel mine and a pump-action grenade launcher?"

"Yes, sir," Nikitin replied.

"Well," Grishkov said thoughtfully, surveying the bodies lined up in front of him, "I guess I can't argue with results. I just wish you'd been able to bag the bastard who hired them."

Rubbing his chest where the body armor had saved his life, Nikitin replied "Me too, sir."

Clapping Nikitin on the back, Grishkov said, "Don't misunderstand me. I don't think any other policemen in all Russia could have done what you two did here tonight. I'm just worried that with the leader still free, he'll keep trying to attack my family. Did you get a look at him?"

Nikitin shook his head. "I just heard a sound on the stairs, and as I was bringing my weapon to bear, I felt a hammer hit my chest and then blackness. Maybe your wife got a look at him."

Grishkov nodded. "Well, that's my next stop anyway. Rest up. I'll see you are both promoted for this."

Nikitin smiled. "Thank you, sir," he mumbled, and then his eyes closed as the pain medication fully kicked in.

Pyongyang, North Korea

The guard known to Shin Yon Young as "Sunshine" scowled at the guard who had just been transferred from Wonsan, one of North Korea's busiest ports. "I was not here when you began duty. Give me a detailed account of your activities."

"Yes, Sergeant. I began with a thorough review of all your written standing orders."

"Good. Go on."

"Most of the day, I stood my post. My only other activity was to escort a janitor to clean two conference rooms on the schedule for maintenance."

His scowl deepened. "And the name of the janitor you selected?"

The newly transferred guard had no idea why he had just become so nervous. "Let me check my shift notes…it was Shin Yon Young."

The reaction was everything he feared. The sergeant's eyes seemed to pop out of his face, which had turned a bright red.

"Did it never occur to you to check with any of the other guards? I have standing orders never to let that man near any of the conference rooms!"

"But sir, I checked your written standing orders! They say nothing about this!"

"Not all my standing orders are written!" Even as he said this, though, the sergeant had to admit to himself that he could not even formally discipline this guard, as he had done with the other who had failed to follow orders to clean a conference room himself. In fact, if he made this a matter of record he could be disciplined himself by his lieutenant for failing to put his order in writing, so that it could be followed even in his absence.

And of course he couldn't do that, because he had absolutely no reason other than gut instinct for believing that Shin Yon Young was a security risk. He had followed Shin from a discreet distance three times, and seen him do nothing more incriminating than buy rice.

It was time for more direct action.

CHAPTER FORTY ONE

Beijing, China

Li Weimin nervously adjusted his tie as he stood in the long line for exit control at Beijing Airport. Just as Mark Bishop had predicted, the guards had paid no attention to their departure in Jim Martinovsky's car, with Li and Park Won Hee both bent over in the back seat. How long it would take for Park's minder to wake up was unknown, but Bishop had assured them it would be long enough. And Li was sure that if their flight left as scheduled, he'd be right.

But Li knew as well as any other air traveler in China that the chances of an on time departure were slim. He had read a survey of the world's major international airports ranking Beijing dead last with only 18% of flights leaving on schedule. Underlining how poorly Beijing ranked was the fact that even Shanghai did better at 29%. Rounding out the bottom four were Istanbul at 38%, and Paris at 60%. Beijing was clearly in a league of its own.

There were official explanations, as well as quite a bit of online speculation on the subject. Government controlled newspapers reported that whenever they happened, military exercises could cause up to a quarter of all flights to be canceled. Blogs claimed that some were delayed to allow an official to make the flight. Li was worried most, though, by persistent unofficial claims that delays were caused to intercept Chinese citizens fleeing the country, usually to escape corruption charges.

Of course, deliberate delays to catch corrupt officials would work just as well to help catch traitors.

Yes, Li thought glumly, the staff at exit control could let the line stretch as long as they liked, secure in the knowledge that it was unlikely anyone would miss their flight as a result. Ironically, as a high ranking official in good standing Li had never had to stand in such a line. Now, though, as a supposed American citizen he got to wait with everyone else.

Li gritted his teeth and made a conscious effort to stop such negative thoughts. He had to avoid suspicious behavior, and appearing overly worried would cause a level of scrutiny his cover might not survive.

Finally, he reached the exit control counter, and slid over his American passport and departure control form. Without even looking up, the man behind the counter slid his passport through a reader, and asked, "Name?".

Li was ready for the question, and without hesitation gave the name on the passport. With his head still bent over his computer monitor, the man asked, "Date of birth?". Li was ready for this question as well, and quickly provided the correct date.

Now the man finally looked up, and visibly compared the person in front of him to the photo in the passport he was holding.

"How long have you been in China?"

"A month," Li responded, knowing that was the answer that would match the passport's record of use.

"How was your trip?"

This was not a question Li had expected, but he had no trouble answering.

"Too short. I was seeing family as well as taking care of my business interests."

"And what sort of business is that?"

Li had thought through this part of the interview.

"I am a software engineer with my own company. I have been looking for contacts with the government who might be interested in taking advantage of my expertise. I see you spend quite a bit of time with your computer. Are you happy with the quality of your software?"

As Li had hoped, the man's eyes visibly began to glaze over. There was a universal weariness in China with foreigners seeking to profit from China's booming economy, and a special contempt for outsiders with Chinese ancestors "returning home" for that purpose.

"Yes, quite happy," the man said, stamping Li's passport and departure form. He then handed the passport back to Li, and gestured for Li to move forward to the departure hall.

Li bit back his annoyance at the man's rudeness, and walked forward. Having passed this hurdle, Li wondered just how long his flight would be delayed, and whether Park had made it through his exit interview without incident.

Sighing, Li walked towards his gate, knowing that only time would give him the answer to both questions.

Tunnel No. 1, North Korea

Lee Ho Suk still had no answer to the mystery of the rails that had been dropped at the tunnel entrance. In fact, now there was another puzzling argument going on between the foreman and a military officer, who was gesturing towards the end of the tunnel and shouting, while the foreman shook his head and looked more glum with every passing second. Whatever he was being told to do, Lee knew it would not be easy.

Finally, the soldier stalked off towards the tunnel's exit, and the foreman walked over to Lee. Perhaps, Lee thought, I will get the answer to at least one mystery today.

"Well, Lee, I'm sure that you have been getting bored just going straight ahead, right?" the foreman said with a strained smile. Like everyone working in the tunnel who was not a prisoner, the foreman had never given Lee his name, and never would.

"I like boredom," Lee said with deep feeling. "Excitement nearly always goes along with pain, or most recently with a hospital stay I barely survived."

"Well, yes, I remember," the foreman said, clearly embarrassed. "But I'm afraid we have no choice. We will have to start building this tunnel on an upward slope."

Lee's eyebrows arched up with surprise. "How sharp a slope?" he asked, dreading the answer.

"Not too bad, not too bad," the foreman said, eager to reassure him. "Thankfully we still have some distance to go, so I think we can keep it to a few degrees."

Lee slowly exhaled. "That should be manageable. Why the change?"

The foreman shrugged. "I heard for the first time from the officer who just left that we are to join this tunnel with another. Whoever calculated the depth of the other tunnel did not include the difference in terrain between where we are now and that tunnel's end point. We're lucky that the difference was not too great, since we don't have far to go."

Lee did his best to appear casual. "And how far is that?"

The foreman smiled and shook his head. "You know I can't say. Even I have only a general idea, enough to think that the calculations made by the chief engineer look about right, given what we know now. But I don't have to tell you that we will need to be even more careful."

Lee nodded, but said nothing. More careful was quite an understatement. Going up at a slope would add to the stress on the tunnel's walls and ceilings, and put Lee in unfamiliar territory. He had plenty of experience with tunnels going down, and staying straight. He had even helped to dig a narrow access passage that went almost straight up, designed to let a single man at a time up from the main tunnel. None of that, though, would help him with the challenge they now faced.

Lee sighed, and decided all he could do was continue to trust in the instincts that had kept him alive this far. With luck, they would keep him going a little while longer.

CHAPTER FORTY TWO

Vladivostok, Russia

Grishkov pulled up outside the Vladivostok address Captain Ivansik had given him over his car's radio. He was surprised to see three soldiers in full combat gear carrying automatic weapons standing guard outside the building, which was ringed by a five meter high wall, topped with barbed wire. Floodlights blazed outside the entire building perimeter, turning night into day for at least twenty meters. After he presented his identification, their squad leader radioed inside, and received clearance for him to proceed.

Grishkov was stopped at the building's door by two more soldiers, who once again demanded his identification, and radioed for clearance before allowing his entry.

Grishkov was again surprised to find Captain Ivansik himself in the large conference room immediately to the right of the entrance, studying a display presented on one of a half-dozen LCD screens grouped around a central table.

Grishkov did what anyone with military training does when surprised by the appearance of a superior officer – he saluted. "Sir, I am pleased to see you here."

Ivansik grunted. "After your family was nearly murdered or kidnapped, it was the least I could do. I thought being guarded by two of our best detectives would be plenty to ensure their safety. That judgment got your mother-in-law killed, and both detectives wounded. It's nothing short of a miracle that they were able to fight off eight heavily armed men. Did you hear how they did it?"

Grishkov nodded. "Yes, Nikitin gave me the details."

Ivansik shook his head. "Resourceful doesn't quite seem to cover it. I presume you will put both Nikitin and Petrov in for promotions?"

"Of course. I have already told Nikitin this. Petrov had already been taken to the hospital by the time I arrived."

Ivansik smiled. "Excellent. A performance like that deserves reward. Now, let me explain how this came about," he said, swinging his arm to indicate the building. "This serves as an emergency command post for Russian Pacific forces. Ordinarily there is a single duty officer manning the post, with two security guards out front. When I explained the situation to my contact in the Russian Navy, he was kind enough to make the facility available to me, and increased security as you have seen. I also have eight police officers standing guard inside the building on rotating twelve-hour shifts, so that there are four here at all times. In the unlikely event that any attackers make it past the five soldiers out front, those police officers will ensure your family's safety."

Grishkov said with all the sincerity he could muster, "I deeply appreciate all you have done, Captain. Putting myself in harm's way is what I am paid to do. My family is another matter. The scale and ferocity of this attack, though, tells us something important. Whoever is behind it wants my investigation stopped at all costs, and has resources and intelligence behind him that suggest this is not simply a criminal enterprise."

Ivansik nodded thoughtfully. "Yes, I read your report on the traitor Buryshkin. However, at this point you have only the word of a dead man that the nuclear device he is supposed to have sold even existed. I have spoken again with the general who recently assumed command at the Vladivostok armory, General Vasyukov, who was so eager to conduct an inventory to prove his predecessor had allowed the disappearance of a nuclear device that he had subsequently detected was missing. Now that Vasyukov knows Buryshkin went absent without leave while he was in command, even though the device was removed before the general arrived, he knows he will be held responsible for failing to do more to locate Buryshkin. That's particularly true since a lowly Vladivostok police detective did so after being on the case for just a few days, while his military police had the case sitting inactive on their desks for weeks."

Grishkov stared at Ivansik in disbelief. "You mean that Vasyukov cares more about his career than what could be done with a man-portable nuclear weapon? What if it is exploded in Moscow? Even if it is used against another country, it might be one that would retaliate against us. I have done some research on this, and the kind of radioactive material used in a bomb's construction is like a fingerprint. Even if we deny responsibility, would that save us from attack?"

Ivansik threw up his hands defensively. "You are saying nothing I have not already. Chechens head a long list that might use such a weapon against us here at home. Islamists head an equally long list that might use such a device in either the United States or Europe. However, it is precisely these grim prospects that are encouraging General Vasyukov to plant his head firmly in the sand. Do you have any proof, other than Buryshkin's word, that these weapons were at the Vladivostok armory?"

Grishkov frowned, and then slowly nodded. "An FSB Colonel I know named Alexei Vasilyev was going to check on whether a record exists at the Defense Ministry office that sent the device to the Vladivostok Armory after its manufacture. I have not had a chance to talk to him yet, but will contact him as soon as I have seen my family."

Ivansik nodded. "Just one more question. How is it, do you think, that they found Buryshkin at exactly the same time you did?"

Grishkov shook his head, and said "Only one answer makes sense. Someone had to have tipped off the killers that I was coming, and followed me from the Khabarovsk police station. And it couldn't have been someone from that end, because they wouldn't have had enough time to organize a three-man hit squad. It had to be someone in Vladivostok."

Ivansik grunted agreement. "Your thoughts agree with mine. However, I told no one in Vladivostok you were coming and I trust the police captain in Khabarovsk, Bogdan Tarasov, to have kept his mouth shut until after you arrived."

"Very well," shrugged Ivansik. "Then we have to ask ourselves who we do not trust at our own station in Vladivostok."

Nearly simultaneously, both said "Lieutenant Anton Fedorov."

In spite of themselves, both Ivansik and Grishkov had to laugh.

"Perhaps we can use our suspicions to our advantage," Grishkov mused.

Grishkov then explained his plan to Ivansik, who nodded agreement.

Ivansik waved toward the door. "Do not let me keep you further. And don't worry – we will keep your family safe."

Grishkov stuck his head inside the break room door, where he saw four cots had been set up for his family. Sasha and Misha occupied two of them, and they were fast asleep. Arisha leapt from the third as soon as she saw him. Grishkov couldn't have said who squeezed who harder, but it was Arisha who finally pulled free.

"I am glad to see you are safe," she said, with a tear running down her cheek.

"Me! You and the children fared far worse. And words will never tell you how sorry I am that you lost your mother," Grishkov replied.

"Yes, well, I asked your Captain Ivansik if anything had happened while you were in Khabarovsk and told him I would compare his story with yours. I promised consequences if he held anything back. Did he?" she said, her eyes roaming over him in an obvious check for injuries.

Grishkov shook his head emphatically. "Just a few scratches from flying glass. Nothing to worry about."

"Humph. Maybe so. I understand the man you were questioning was not so lucky. And, neither were your attackers," she said, her eyes glittering.

"Yes, that is all true," Grishkov admitted.

"And the men who attacked you, they worked for the same man who led the attack against me and the children?"

"Yes, I think so. Did you get a look at him?"

"I did, but not a clear one. I had deliberately vented smoke from the furnace to obstruct his view and slow him down, but that worked both ways. He was definitely Asian, but I'm not sure from which country. If I had to guess, I would say he was Korean."

"What makes you think so? Just his features?"

"Well, you may think this is foolish, but even across a cellar full of smoke I thought I could smell that kimchee the Koreans like so much. You know, that dish with fermented cabbage, peppers and garlic. And what I could see of his features looked more Korean than Japanese or Chinese. Still, I can't say for certain. He said nothing, so there was no accent to help identify him."

Grishkov nodded. "Well, that's the first clue we have, and it gives us a place to start looking."

Arisha frowned. "This isn't over, is it? What will you do next?"

"I am going to speak to an FSB Colonel I know who may help me decide where we should go from here. I really shouldn't say more than that, and anyway I honestly don't know much more."

Arisha sighed and waved her arm around the room. "I'm not going to complain about these luxurious accommodations, because I know that no amount of money would keep us as safe as all these soldiers and police officers. But can you give me some idea how long I'm going to keep these two entertained?"

Grishkov smiled, and held her hands. "I hope not long. But the truth is I don't know. The surest way to make sure you and the children will be safe is to catch up to the man behind all this."

Arisha looked up at Grishkov, squeezed his hands tightly, and looked him straight in the eye. "I understand. Just do one thing for me."

"Yes, dear?"

"Don't arrest him."

CHAPTER FORTY THREE

Beijing, China

Park Won Hee betrayed no outward emotion as he handed over his American passport and departure control form to the man at the exit control counter. Having lived his entire life in a totalitarian state, being placid and unthreatening in the face of authority came to him as naturally as breathing.

The man at the counter had no particular interest in Park or his passport until he opened it. Park saw the man stiffen, though he said nothing as he ran the passport through a reader, and read the results on the screen intently.

Park had no way to know it, but his luck had just taken a sharp turn for the worse. Zhang Jie, the man behind the counter, had no interest at all in Park until he saw that the place of birth listed in his American passport was Korea. That interested Zhang a great deal, because of his experience when he went to university in Korea starting in 1993. Korea had just opened diplomatic relations with China the previous year, so Zhang was one of the first Chinese students to come to Korea from the People's Republic.

It had not been a happy experience for Zhang.

China and Korea had always been neighbors that had played important parts in each other's histories, and part of the prejudice Zhang encountered came from that shared past. On the Chinese side, Zhang was well aware that the Japanese colonial period in the generation prior to Japan's defeat in World War II had featured Korean troops in the Japanese Army participating in its many atrocities. Zhang also knew that South Koreans had not forgotten China's intervention on the side of North Korea during the Korean War.

However, Zhang had not expected the outright contempt he experienced from many of his fellow students. It turned out that this hostility had little to do with history, and instead was caused by the belief that China's government would soon collapse just as the Soviet Union's had a few years before, and that it would be what one Korean student called "good riddance to bad rubbish." Zhang later learned that this was an American saying, which was one of many factors making him almost as hostile to Americans as Koreans.

Koreans laughed at the China of the early 1990s, considering it poor and backward. One trade deal between Korea and China while Zhang was in Korea bartered Chinese coal for Korean electronic goods. It was a barter deal because China lacked the hard currency to buy Korean goods. And as Zhang knew, even now Korean TVs, cars and cell phones were superior to anything produced in China.

"How long have you been in China?," Zhang asked.

"Two weeks," Park replied, just as Mark Bishop had said he should to match the date the passport had been used to enter China.

"Where were you before arriving in China?"

"I came here directly from the United States."

"Who accompanied you on this trip?"

"No one. I arrived and am leaving by myself."

"Purpose of your visit?"

Bishop had briefed him on what to say to this question. "Business. I work for a semiconductor company, and much of the manufacturing of our designs is done here."

"So, was the quality of the product up to your expectations?," Zhang asked.

Park was surprised both by the question and by the hostility of Zhang's tone. Carefully keeping both his voice and expression neutral, Park nodded and replied, "As usual, our subcontractors are doing excellent work."

Glaring at Park with open dislike, Zhang asked, "And if that is usual, why did you have to come in person to check? I would like to hear more details from you about the type of semiconductors your company designs, and the company that makes them in China."

Park was sure this official knew nothing about semiconductors. The problem was, he did not know enough to even pretend. Before he had a chance to respond, though, Zhang's phone rang.

Zhang turned his face away from Park and gestured at him to remain there. "Yes, sir?" he said quietly into the phone. Only his supervisor could call either him or the other border security staff from the command center, where they were all under constant surveillance.

"Why are you spending so much time on this man? Has he done or said something suspicious? Are there any flags for him in the computer system?"

Zhang ground his teeth in annoyance. Beijing Airport's dead last ranking in on time departures had not escaped official attention, so the freedom he used to have to pay back Koreans for their insolence was more limited.

"No, sir. But my instincts tell me he is not who he claims to be."

"Where is he from?"

Zhang could feel a knot growing in his stomach. "He is American."

"I am looking at him on screen now. Where was he born?"

Zhang felt the knot tighten. "Korea."

The voice exploded in his ear. "I have warned you about this obsession! There have already been numerous complaints, and nobody you have stopped has been guilty of anything but being Korean!"

His supervisor's voice then lowered, which Zhang knew from experience was when he was truly angry. "If this man is a genuine threat to national security, then refer him to secondary inspection and get the line moving. You may remember, that's why we have secondary inspection."

Zhang winced at his supervisor's sarcasm. At every airport, any suspect traveler was pulled out of the regular line, and his luggage and person were searched at secondary inspection. That search plus extensive questioning guaranteed the unlucky traveler would be certain to miss his flight.

"But Zhang, this time you'd better be right."

Zhang immediately flashed on the image of his wife's face. It was not a smiling image, in fact most days it was yelling at him. His job paid well enough to get by, but they would never be rich like so many Chinese who had gone into business, or who worked in parts of the government that often received "rewards" from businessmen for decisions favoring their company.

If he lost his job, she'd probably leave him. And losing his job was what "you'd better be right" meant.

Zhang knew there was something wrong with this man. He had a funny accent Zhang didn't remember hearing when he'd been in Korea, and he doubted he was a businessman. He seemed like someone used to giving orders, and not just for his secretary to bring coffee.

But was it worth the risk? He had only an instant to decide.

"Sir, you are right. I will pass him through." The click of the phone in his ear as his supervisor hung up was the only response.

Zhang tossed the American passport back at Park and jerked his thumb towards the departure corridor. Park wasted no time in moving forward.

Zhang, his face impassive, was seething inside. But, following his instincts would have just been too big a risk.

It was a decision Zhang and his supervisor would both soon regret.

CHAPTER FORTY FOUR

Pyongyang, North Korea

Recent advances in technology had made working in places like North Korea much easier for spies like Shin Yon Young. Just a decade earlier, it would have been a real challenge to pass the information he had obtained from the conference room bug to NIS headquarters from a country with a vast range of listening posts that constantly monitored cell phone and radio transmissions, and allowed Internet access only to authorized government users. Of course, even that access was monitored.

Now though satellite phones made direct communication from nearly anywhere not only possible but practical, even for countries like South Korea without the resources needed to orbit a fleet of satellites. NIS first became aware of Thuraya, a company based in the United Arab Emirates, when it launched its first satellite in 2000. That satellite happened to be in geosynchronous orbit over Korea. Two other satellites were subsequently launched, each improving service and reliability.

Once their sales reached over half a million satphones, NIS decided Thuraya was worth a trial. Their latest model was able to operate both over a GSM cell phone network and when connected to their satellite network. Testing confirmed their claimed ability to support microSD cards, a built in Internet browser and data transmission via satellite. Data compression and encryption built into both the bug and the collection device meant that there was nothing for him to do but load the microSD card into the handset, press an icon and hit "send."

Of course, it helped that he planned to hit the send button from a near perfect location. In most cities, the top floor of an apartment building in the capital would have commanded high rents, afforded by only the rich and well-connected. Pyongyang was not most cities.

Though there were many high-rise apartment buildings in Pyongyang, they all had problems. Their electrical wiring was substandard to begin with, and repairs were only patchwork when they happened at all. Though better than anywhere else in North Korea, power in Pyongyang was subject to blackouts as well as surges that placed intolerable stress on these poor quality systems, leading to frequent electrical fires. Civilian fire departments had shoddy and infrequently maintained equipment, and ladders that only went up to the fourth floor, at best. As the result, upper stories in apartment buildings were informally known as "death floors" and shunned by anyone with the money and status to avoid them.

It didn't help that the elevators in high-rise apartment buildings usually stopped working within the first year, and were hardly ever repaired.

This was, though, all music to the ears of someone like Shin who was looking for an elevated location with a clear line of sight for his satphone transmission. It meant that a janitor could live on an upper floor, and nobody would think it unusual.

However, it was about the only good news for someone like Shin used to South Korean living standards. Water pressure was intermittent at best, and the hot water had never worked. The kitchen countertop and sink were made from poured concrete, which had the metal fixtures and piping jammed in before it finished hardening. Shin had spent days when he first moved in sweeping cement dust off the floors, walls and ceiling. More seemed to accumulate every day. It probably helped account for the hacking cough he woke up with every morning.

The apartment's furnishings were as basic as one would expect a janitor could afford. A threadbare sofa, a scuffed coffee table, and a TV on a stand were the total of the items in the living room. Shin had bought them all used. No pictures adorned the walls, other than the obligatory portraits of Kim Il Sung and Marshal Ko.

The single bedroom had a metal frame cot with a thin mat taking the place of the mattress and box spring Shin had grown up with in South Korea. Fortunately, after a typical day of janitorial labor Shin was so tired that he could have slept on practically any horizontal surface. Since he had no dresser or nightstand, his few clothes were stacked in a cardboard box in the corner near the bottom left side of his cot.

The apartment had its own toilet and a small shower. All included, it was no more than a few hundred square feet, and exactly what anyone would expect from a janitor's apartment in Pyongyang.

Shin was about to find out the apartment had one great disadvantage. It had a really flimsy front door.

He made this discovery when the front door burst open, quickly followed by the bulky figure of the guard Shin knew only from the name he had given him, "Sunshine." At the moment he came barreling in, Shin happened to still be holding the satphone, into which he had just finished loading the microSD card. He had not had time to press send.

In many other countries Shin could have bluffed his way out of this situation. The satphone did not look very different than an ordinary cell phone, unlike previous models that had been several times its size. Even in North Korea, there were civilians who had cell phones.

Sadly, none of those civilians were janitors.

The guard's "now I have you" expression matched up well with Shin's, which could hardly have looked more surprised and guilty. There was no hope of talking his way out of this.

However, Shin noticed immediately as "Sunshine" advanced on him that he was alone. Visits by North Korean police, either regular or secret, were always made by groups for obvious reasons. Shin also saw that the guard's only weapon was his baton. Though Sunshine was armed at work, Shin knew that security guards were required to turn in their weapons to have them secured after every shift. That told Shin this visit was not official, but instead the guard's idea.

Of course, in this case his superiors would applaud the guard's initiative, once he brought Shin in for questioning with his satphone. Shin's only chance was to prevent that from happening.

All this went through Shin's mind in an instant, and then the guard was on him. And he was just as strong as he looked.

The guard's first swing of his baton nearly took off Shin's head, but he ducked just in time. He wasn't so lucky with the guard's left arm, which caught him in the ribs hard enough to leave him gasping for air. Though Shin had been given intensive martial arts training as part of his preparation for this assignment, the complete surprise Sunshine had achieved had rattled Shin so much that all those abilities seemed to have evaporated. All he could manage was to keep moving. The only direction available was towards the kitchen.

With a bellow of rage the guard came at Shin again. This time Shin remembered his training, and timed his response so that Sunshine's momentum carried him to the concrete countertop. Without conscious thought, Shin brought his arm down on the guard's neck at an angle that put his forehead on a collision course with the edge of the countertop. With a sickening crack, the fight was over. Sunshine dropped like a stone.

Blood stained the countertop, and was beginning to pool around the guard's head. Shin pressed his hand against Sunshine's neck, and was unable to find a pulse. After another minute of checking and failing to find any sign of life, Shin walked to the door and closed it. Though now the door could not be locked and anyone could simply push it in, it would hopefully be a less obvious sign of trouble than a wide open door would be.

Fortunately, Shin knew that his neighbors on both sides were at work at this time of day, and there was a good chance that most of the other residents of this floor were as well. That meant there was at least a chance that no one else knew his door had been kicked in.

There was also a chance that anyone who did hear something would decide not to call the police. Living in North Korea taught you that avoiding the police was always a good idea, even if you were not the one who had committed a crime. Besides, there was always the chance that it was the police who had kicked in Shin's door. Ironically anyone who had seen the guard's uniform, which was very similar to a police uniform, could have easily reached that conclusion.

Still, Shin knew it was only a matter of time before the real police turned up at his apartment. He had to do something, and do it fast.

CHAPTER FORTY FIVE

Tunnel No. 1. North Korea

The question of the rails had been worrying Lee Ho Suk for days, while he struggled with the additional challenge posed by the addition of an upward slope to the tunnel. They didn't look big enough for train tracks, so maybe he was wrong and they were for some other purpose. But they weren't long enough for bracing material... His mind went around and around in circles on this, until he finally abandoned his habitual caution and asked the foreman.

"So, these don't look long enough to be very effective as braces," Lee said, gesturing towards the pile of rails near them, just like the first one that had been dumped at the tunnel entrance. Now there were many piles of rails, each a few hundred meters from the next.

The foreman looked at Lee thoughtfully, chewing his lower lip for several seconds before finally answering.

"Yes, I think it is time for you to know about these, because soon work will begin on the line's construction. You will need to think about its possible effect on the tunnel's stability."

Lee stared at the foreman, not believing his ears. "Do you mean to tell me that we are having a train line go through this tunnel?"

The foreman laughed. "No, no. I forget that you have never seen a subway tunnel. This train will be much smaller than the diesel locomotives you have seen above ground, and it will be electric, so no smoke."

Lee frowned. "OK, smaller and no smoke sound good. How heavy will this train be?"

"The news there is good too. This subway train was imported from Germany, was the lightest available because it is made from aluminum, and only has three cars."

Lee's frown deepened. "That all sounds great. How heavy is it?"

The foreman paused. "One hundred tons."

Lee stared at the foreman as though he'd just grown a second head that had started speaking Japanese.

"You know that is completely insane. We are barely coping with the extra stress to the walls from adding a grade to this tunnel. Now we are going to roll one hundred tons across this tunnel's floor? The only good news is that they won't have to pay to bury us, because this tunnel will become a tomb for everyone in it whenever this train moves forward."

The foreman shook his head. "You won't get any argument from me. I don't want to die down here any more than you do. The problem is that this train is the whole point of the tunnel. So, saying it can't be done isn't an option. If we insist, they'll just shoot us and replace us with someone else. We have to think of some way to get it done, and get it done fast."

Lee scowled, but finally nodded. "You are right. Once they've made up their minds, there is no changing it. The only answer I can see is more and heavier bracing, throughout the entire tunnel. And metal, not just wood."

The foreman shrugged. "I can argue for that, and may succeed. Where is the need for bracing most important?"

"Before I try to answer that, how frequently is this train going to travel down these tracks?"

The foreman smiled. "You will like this answer, at least. It will go just one way, and only once."

Lee stared at the foreman in disbelief. "We are doing all this so the train can make just one trip?"

"That's what I've been told."

"And what will it carry?" Lee asked.

"Troops and equipment. I've been told that their total weight won't be greater than between one and two tons."

Lee nodded. "OK, if we put extra bracing on the most critical spots, the tunnel's structure may survive a one-time trip. We'll need to start with reinforcing the areas we've already braced, since we know a failure at any of those points would definitely cause a collapse."

As Lee continued to walk the foreman through the next steps they needed to take, he couldn't help another part of his mind wandering off in a completely different direction. What purpose could a one-way trip have that would be worth all the years of effort that had gone into making this tunnel?

Vladivostok, Russia

Grishkov looked around at the tasteful furnishings and decorations, and inhaled the strong, pleasant fragrance of coffee that permeated the café. It was inside one of the high-end Western hotel chains that made Vladivostok's winter a bit more tolerable for visiting European, American and Japanese businessmen.

Alexei Vasilyev looked at him with amusement. "Quite a change from the Black Crow, isn't it?"

"Well, yes. But then I always knew that the FSB had refined tastes."

Vasilyev chuckled over his cappuccino. "Well, it's too early for vodka, anyway."

Grishkov smiled tightly. "I hope you have news for me?"

"I do. First, let me tell you how sorry I am to hear about your mother-in-law's death, and how glad I am to hear that the rest of your family is unharmed."

Grishkov nodded. "Anyone else, I would ask how you knew. For an FSB officer, that would be a stupid question."

Vasilyev smiled. "You are learning. Did you find out anything about the attackers, both the ones who attacked you in Khabarovsk and the ones who attacked your family?"

Grishkov frowned. "All of the bodies were Russian, all criminals for hire. However, my wife gave me one clue." He then went on to repeat what Arisha had told him about her belief that the leader in their attack was Korean, and added "I have told no one else that she saw the man, or her guess of his nationality, not even Captain Ivansik."

"A wise precaution, since your office obviously has a leak. Korean?" Vasilyev said, arching one eyebrow. "That is very interesting. If she is correct, that gives us two candidates. The South Koreans, as far as we know, have no nuclear weapons and therefore would appear to have a motive in acquiring one. The North Koreans have several, but none remotely as compact as the device we believe sold by Timoshenko. So, which is more likely?"

"My money is on the North Koreans. Their leaders have publicly threatened a preemptive nuclear strike against the United States. I say look to the country that would not just buy such a weapon, but would actually use it."

Vasilyev scratched his chin absently, then nodded agreement. "If you are correct, that is both good and bad news. The good news is that the North Koreans are very unlikely to use such a device against Russia, one of the few countries with which they maintain trade, military and diplomatic relations. The bad news is that their likely targets, South Korea and the U.S., will hold us responsible if a nuclear device we have made is used against them."

Grishkov scowled. "Damn Timoshenko, Buryshkin, and all the other traitors who put us in this mess."

Vasilyev nodded. "Well, damn them indeed. However, they are all dead, so we must deal with the living to get the proof we need to prevent the weapon from being used."

Grishkov brightened. "You found the office that has records for the device being sent to the Vladivostok Armory?"

"I believe so," Vasilyev said carefully, "but getting access to them will not be easy."

"Why not?" Grishkov said, jerking upright so fast that he nearly spilled their cups.

"Because these records are maintained by the Strategic Rocket Forces at their headquarters at the Kuntsevo district of Moscow, which fall under the jurisdiction of neither the FSB, nor the Vladivostok police."

"But surely you have contacts within the military who can get us access, correct?"

"Yes, perhaps. But my contacts have warned me that any documents they give me authorizing access can be countermanded by the commander of the records facility at Strategic Rocket Forces headquarters. We will have to be, well, diplomatic."

"Did you say we?"

Vasilyev nodded. "Yes, I justified this request as being both a national security as well as a criminal matter. That actually required having you accompany me to Moscow. However, there was another purpose in having you come."

"And that was?"

Vasilyev smiled. "Why, to serve as bait."

CHAPTER FORTY SIX

Beijing, China

Ordinarily Li Weimin had no use for science fiction. However, one of its ideas had always fascinated him - time moving at different speeds. That's because it was the only science fiction concept Li had personally encountered.

Right now in this airport waiting lounge, Li sincerely believed time had begun to travel even more slowly than it did at his doctor's office, which he would never have imagined possible.

Making matters worse was that normally Li would have killed some time by walking around the terminal, and looking through airport shops at goods he had no intention of buying. Now, though, he had to remain still and quiet in an effort to avoid attracting attention.

So far, it seemed to be working. Li had long since finished reading his copy of the People's Daily, a safe choice since it was the official newspaper of the Communist Party. Along with everyone else he had looked up at the overhead display as it showed first a one hour delay, and then two hours. Unlike most of the others, he'd neither groaned nor complained, but just kept reading his paper a second and third time.

He saw a flurry of movement among the Trans Pacific staff at the gate, and then saw one of them pick up a microphone.

"Attention, please, all passengers waiting at Gate E25 for Trans Pacific flight 898, with nonstop service to Washington Dulles Airport. We will shortly begin the boarding process. Please have your boarding pass and passport ready to present at the gate. We will be boarding by zone. Please take a moment to check the zone on your boarding pass."

Li tuned out the rest of the announcement, which was shortly repeated in Chinese. He had seen Park sit down at the other side of the lounge over an hour ago, and had carefully avoided any contact with him.

Li had trouble believing it. Was he really going to make it out?

En Route from Vladivostok to Moscow, Russia

Grishkov looked out the window of his flight to Moscow, but could see nothing below but clouds. According to the pilot, they had climbed to avoid weather below. Vasilyev snored on the seat next to him, much to the annoyance of nearby passengers. Well, he wasn't the only one on this red-eye flight to be doing so. It was practically a snoring symphony, and Vasilyev was far from the loudest instrument.

In fact he had Vasilyev to thank for being on this flight at all. Even with Captain Ivansik's help, it would have taken at least a couple of days to arrange authorization and payment for a flight to Moscow, but it had taken Vasilyev only hours. Grishkov was starting to think that Vasilyev was more than just a colonel in the FSB, important though such a person might be. Looking at the way he was dressed only added to the impression. A suit and tie was one thing. But cuff links?

He just hoped that the charade being played out in Captain Ivansik's office would work.

Vladivostok, Russia

Captain Ivansik had a good idea that Lieutenant Anton Fedorov was the man behind the leak that had almost led to Grishkov's death in Khabarovsk, even before talking that episode over with Grishkov.

He just had no idea how.

For what he had planned now, though, that didn't matter. In fact, this time he made sure that Fedorov was in place at his desk before making his call to his contact in Moscow.

Captain Yefim Kozlov was far better connected politically than Ivansik, which helped to explain why he was a rising star in Moscow while Ivansik was in Vladivostok. That was only part of why Ivansik did not trust the man, but in this case, that was all to the good.

This time he stared right at Fedorov while he made the call to Kozlov, but he saw not even a twitch. Once this was all over, he would have to figure out just how Fedorov was intercepting his calls.

"Yefim! How are you? A long time since our party days at the academy, no?"

Kozlov laughed. "Boris! It has indeed been many years. May I hope that you will soon be in Moscow to help us relive some of those good times?"

"No, I regret not. But one of my best detectives will be arriving to-morrow afternoon. I have his flight details, and I hope you can have him met. Both he and his family have been attacked by unknown criminals, and I want to make sure he survives this trip."

"Of course! We will do everything we can to help. Do you know who is behind the attacks?"

"Not yet, but that is what we are hoping to find out from this trip."

"Very well. I presume you will send us what you know so far?"

"Yes, I will send you all of my detective's reports on both the attacks and the criminal motivation we suspect is behind them. Unfortunately, I have to underline the word suspect, since the only testimony we have so far was given by a man who was killed within minutes of speaking to my detective."

Kozlov grunted. "Well, that seems to confirm that this is a serious busi-ness, in any case. Just how many men have been killed so far during your investigation? "

Ivansik laughed. "Well, let's see. Starting with the arms dealer whose death started this investigation, including the dead witness and finishing with the men who were killed attacking my detective and his family, the total would be twelve. If we count the deaths of the three men who we believe were killed by the arms dealer to keep them quiet, that would make it fifteen."

Ivansik heard a moment of silence over the phone.

"So, this is a serious matter, even by Moscow standards. Fifteen deaths in a single case is an unusually high number even for us. And you have made no arrests?"

"No, and it was not for lack of trying. But when your attackers are using automatic weapons and grenades, it is perhaps not surprising that the defenders were unable to use handcuffs."

"Fair enough. But you obviously think that some of these criminals are still at large."

"Yes. The man we believe paid for the attacks against my detective and his family escaped, and we think he will try again."

"Do you have a picture or a physical description of this man?"

"Unfortunately, no. There were no surveillance cameras at the scene of the attack, and nobody got a clear look at him."

"Well, that won't make it easy for my men, will it?"

"No, it won't. However, the usual rules apply. Whoever tries to follow my detective and his associate will either be working for the criminal's paymaster, or be the paymaster himself."

"The reports will have details on your detective's associate?"

"Yes. I will not say more about him over the phone."

"Understood. It seems life in the provinces is more exciting than I would have thought. I suppose for men in our line of work that's both good and bad news."

Ivansik laughed. "Well said, Yefim. Thanks for your help with this."

"Happy to help out an academy classmate. And Boris, I hope you will make it to Moscow at some point. The first round will be on me."

"With luck I'll be able to take you up on that someday, Yefim. Thanks again."

As Ivansik hung up the phone, he glanced over to Fedorov's desk, where the man appeared to be engrossed in whatever was on his computer screen. If he had been listening to Ivansik's conversation, he gave no sign.

Ivansik shrugged. There was no way he could think of to be sure, but his gut told him that news of Grishkov's arrival in Moscow would be reaching the man who wanted so much to kill him very soon. This time, though, they would have a one day head start. Maybe that would be enough to finally stop the killings, and find out what lay behind them.

CHAPTER FORTY SEVEN

Los Angeles

Chung Hee Moon blearily looked at the sleeping figure of Kang Ji Yeong lying in the bed beside him. All he could think through the pounding in his head was "Oh no!"

Wanted by the police? Bad enough. Taking up with his own ready made family, which he could not leave without walking into the arms of the police? Much, much worse.

How did it happen? Chung began thinking through the previous evening, and then realized that it didn't matter. All that counted was what he did next.

Considering that the success of his mission depended on his continuing to receive sanctuary from the woman in bed beside him, there seemed to be just one thing to do.

Chung quietly left the bed and dressed. He then began cleaning the apartment and making breakfast.

Tunnel No. 1, North Korea

Lee Ho Suk watched the foreman and a captain argue away from the rest of the men working on the tunnel with growing concern. They were careful to keep their voices low enough to avoid being overheard, but their expressions told Lee that whatever they were arguing about, it was serious.

Lee's respect for the foreman had grown as they worked together, and the only reason he could imagine for him arguing at such length was that he was being pushed to do something that was not safe. As he saw the argument end, the foreman stalked towards him. At least he might now find out why he had been arguing with the officer.

"Sir, I hope we are not going to face another change to the tunnel's construction," Lee said as cautiously and tentatively as he could.

The foreman scowled at Lee, and then relented. "I'm not going to take this out on a prisoner who doesn't even know my name. Yes, there is another change. But it's not construction. More like destruction," he said, his face darkening with anger.

Lee did not like the sound of this at all. "I don't understand, sir."

The foreman looked at Lee thoughtfully. "Your instincts have kept you alive a long time. I shouldn't tell you any of what I'm about to, but I'm going to trust you to keep your mouth shut."

Lee nodded, and both looked around them to make sure there were no guards or workers within earshot. The noise of construction all around them came close to guaranteeing the privacy of their conversation.

"That captain just told me we're going to link up with another tunnel. A tunnel being built by the enemy to the South."

Lee just stared, too shocked to respond.

"Since joining the tunnels is obviously not part of the Southern devils' plan, the captain told me his intention is to blast our way through the last meters, to 'guarantee surprise' for our side."

Lee's head bobbed up and down. "Yes, their surprise will be complete when they are covered by the dust coming from our side of the tunnel, which will have collapsed along most of its length due to the explosion."

The foreman smiled grimly. "That is what I told the captain. He says that is defeatist talk, and that there is no other way."

Lee thought furiously for a moment. "We must find a better way, one without explosives."

The foreman nodded, understanding that Lee was thinking out loud. Lee started by asking the obvious question.

"Is there a way to see what is ahead of us through the earth as we dig, so that we can achieve surprise without an explosion?"

The foreman frowned. "You mean, instead of relying on measurements of our tunnel's progress and what we know of the other tunnel's location, actually looking ahead through the earth itself?"

Lee nodded vigorously. "I broke my leg when I was a child. They put it in a machine that looked through my flesh at the bone underneath. Is there anything like that we can use?"

The foreman looked at Lee with new respect. "I have read about X-Ray equipment that could help us, but have never seen it myself. Two techniques are used. XRF, or X-Ray Fluorescence analysis, measures the intensity of x-rays fluoresced by individual elements. XRD, or X-Ray Diffraction analysis, measures the intensity of crystal diffraction peaks due to individual chemical compounds. One method is not necessarily better than the other. They are complementary techniques which, when combined, give the total picture."

Lee shook his head. "But how will such analysis help us? It's not as though we'll be looking through the earth, right?"

The foreman smiled. "Right. But I guarantee that to make such a tunnel the other side has been using explosives. In fact, the captain told me so, to justify his using them as well. That means the chemicals used in such explosives will permeate the earth for many meters, and should be easy to detect by equipment with XRF and XRD analysis capability."

Lee's eyes widened. "So, this could solve our problem. How do we get such equipment?"

The foreman lifted an eyebrow. "I'm sorry, but such equipment does not exist in our country as far as I know. It might have helped in theory, but in practice I'm afraid we're stuck with explosives."

Lee's shoulders slumped, and then straightened. "Well, when the charges go off, maybe we'll live long enough to see what's on the other side."

The foreman nodded. "Like you, I'm actually curious to see what a Southern devil's tunnel looks like."

Moscow, Russia

Grishkov shook Vasilyev awake as the flight to Moscow taxied to the gate. "So, we have transportation?" he asked Vasilyev in a low voice.

"Yes," Vasilyev said in an even quieter voice, stretching his arms as far as the cramped seats would allow. "I left instructions for a nondescript sedan to be left in the usual spot for this airport. Like all cars we use, it has been modified to open and start with a single key issued to authorized persons, such as myself."

"Impressive. No rental cars for you, then!" Grishkov said, shaking his head.

"It is not merely convenience. It is operational security. We take that very seriously."

"Of course. I suppose, then, we should wait to discuss our next steps until we are in that car."

"A good idea. And I don't know about you, but I'll take even an airport coffee."

Luck was with them, as it turned out a Western coffee chain had made it to airports in Moscow. Rolling their suitcases beside them with a cup of strong coffee in the other hand, they trudged to the parking garage exit. Both paid close attention to their surroundings, but saw no sign that anyone was particularly interested in them. Finally, they were at the sedan, which was just as plain and anonymous as Vasilyev had said it would be. They tossed their suitcases in the trunk, and settled in for the ride to Kuntsevo district.

"You know, after all that has happened over the past few days, it's unnerving to have this much quiet," observed Grishkov.

Vasilyev shrugged. "Enjoy it while it lasts. I think it means that our deception may have worked. If so, we may have enough time both to obtain the evidence needed to prove the theft of the device, and to set our trap for whoever has been trying to kill us."

CHAPTER FORTY EIGHT

Beijing, China

A Vice Minister for a Chinese department as important as Foreign Affairs rated two key perks. The first, which Song Hailong didn't care about, was a large office furnished with Chinese antiques beautiful enough to impress foreign visitors. The second, the freedom to choose his own staff, Song cared about a great deal. Having people around him he could trust was a matter of political and even personal survival.

Song had left strict instructions not to be disturbed, so when his deputy Liu Jie entered without even knocking he knew that the interruption was important. One look at his deputy's face told him that the news, whatever it was, was not good.

"Sir, you asked me to check on the whereabouts of Li Weimin, who did not appear at his office today. It took some time to establish that he is not home. The guards at his residence would not enter until I went in person to give the order," Liu said, his voice carefully neutral.

Song's heart sank. For Liu to be starting out this way, the news must be bad indeed.

"After entering the residence we found no trace of Li Weimin or any clue to his current location. However, we did find the unconscious body of Park Won Hee's minder, a Mr. Lee. You will recall that Park is representing North Korea in current discussions on the future of the peninsula," Liu said, as Song impatiently gestured for Liu to continue.

"I asked the guards whether anyone had been at the house, and they confirmed that Park and Lee had been there the previous evening. They said two Westerners had also been there for dinner, but that they had left about an hour after arrival. I had a photo array brought to the house of staff at the American Embassy. Fortunately, just as it arrived Mr. Lee regained consciousness. He was able to identify one of the men at Li Weimin's home last night as Mark Bishop."

Song had to grab the edge of his desk as a wave of nausea assaulted him. "CIA deputy chief of station Mark Bishop?" Liu nodded gravely, and continued.

"I can only guess, but I think it is likely that Li Weimin and Park Won Hee are either at the American Embassy now, or on their way out of the country. I have checked with our monitors outside the Embassy, and they have seen no one matching their description enter or leave. I also have men we can trust questioning exit control staff at Beijing Airport, and have sent an alert to all airports. I should add that questioning all exit control staff will take some time, since we have to reach some at home who were on shift last night." Liu shrugged, and added, "I stand ready to take any additional steps I have missed."

Song shook his head. "No, you have been quite thorough. Report once we know whether the traitors are still in China, or if they have left when and how. How long ago did they leave Li Weimin's residence?"

"About nine hours ago, sir," Liu answered.

Song nodded thoughtfully. "And where is Park Won Hee's minder, Mr. Lee?"

"In custody. He has insisted loudly that he be allowed to contact his Embassy, but I have refused to allow him to contact anyone."

Song felt a bit of relief. "Good. Make sure it stays that way. Lee is to see or speak to no one except you or me."

Liu bowed. "As you say, sir," and left.

Song chewed on his lower lip and thought over the implications of Li Weimin and Park Won Hee's treachery. If word of what he had planned was revealed before Song and his allies were ready to move it could be disastrous. Faint hearts on the Politburo could accuse him and his colleagues of exceeding their authority, or even treason. No, it was clear what had to be done. Li Weimin and Park Won Hee had to be stopped at all costs.

CHAPTER FORTY NINE

Pyongyang, North Korea

All spies like Shin Yon Young living in a hostile country had an emergency evacuation plan. In Shin's case, if he failed to check in via a text consisting of the single letter "S" sent over his sat phone once every three days, a South Korean Navy submarine would wait for him off the North Korean Yellow Sea coast. Upon seeing a prearranged series of light flashes, they would send a small inflatable to pick him up.

When Shin had been told about this arrangement he'd laughed and said, "Could this be more World War II?" His instructor had scowled and pointed out that all he had to bring to the pickup was himself and a flashlight. He added, "When it's you against the entire North Korean police and military, you won't think it's so funny."

As with almost everything his instructor had said, Shin was only now realizing just how right he was.

His first problem was getting out of Pyongyang. All travel within North Korea required authorization. Though he had papers to use in an emergency that would allow him to travel to the coast to visit a fictitious sick relative, those papers were in his name. An alert would go out as soon as he failed to report for his shift, and another one with a higher priority once Sunshine's body was discovered.

His next problem was that the stubby antenna on his satphone had broken off during the struggle. It appeared to be working otherwise, but the GSM cell phone function wouldn't work in North Korea. That had never been an issue, since the whole point of the phone had been to use it to communicate via satellite. Now, though, it meant that he couldn't send the recording he had worked so hard to obtain until he was able to use the sub's communication equipment after pickup, or...until he got close enough to the South Korean border to use its GSM cell phone network.

But how could he even get out of Pyongyang?

Looking at the guard's body, the answer came to him.

Shin quickly stripped the guard's uniform, which fortunately had not been stained by the blood pooling around his head. It was a little baggy on him, but the fit wasn't too bad. Shin looked over the guard's papers, and frowned when he saw that even at a glance he did not match the photo. Well, his training had taught him how to deal with that.

Going to the tiny bathroom, Shin propped the guard's ID next to the mirror, and began to carefully trim his hair until it matched the guard's haircut. Then he assumed the grim look he saw in the ID. Much closer. Fortunately, the ID had been issued several years before, so his thinner face could pass a cursory inspection as long as the viewer wasn't actively suspicious.

Here Shin finally caught a break. Among the guard's papers was an authorization to leave the capital, since his closest relatives lived in a village some distance outside the capital. This would get him through the checkpoints around Pyongyang, which had been his biggest worry. As he looked more closely at the papers he realized that he had caught an even bigger break. The village was near Haeju, a city only a few dozen kilometers away from his pickup point. Even if he was stopped after leaving Pyongyang, these papers would cover his travel in the direction he needed to go.

Now, he needed to delay discovery of the body. Wrapping it tightly in his bed sheets would help to delay the smell of decomposition from reaching the neighbors.

Next, transportation. Like any janitor, Shin had none other than his feet and public transport. After a bit of thought, Shin asked himself how the guard got to his village. And for that matter, how had he come here to make this unauthorized attempt to arrest Shin?

Stuffing the satphone, the guard's papers and a flashlight in the pockets of his new uniform, Shin decided to play a hunch.

Closing the door carefully behind him, Shin looked at it critically. Though close inspection would show marks around the door jamb and latch, the damage was much more visible on the inside. His neighbors were unlikely to see anything worth reporting.

Now came the most dangerous part of his escape. If anyone who knew him saw Shin as he was leaving wearing the guard's clothes, he was certain to be reported. Gritting his teeth, he opened the door to the stairwell leading to the ground floor.

Shin was halfway down when he heard what he had feared most, footsteps heading up. He did the first thing he thought of, which was to open the door to the next floor and duck into the hallway. As he did so, he could hear the steps that had been going up slow, and then stop.

Cursing to himself, Shin realized that whoever was on the stairway was wondering why someone would be going from an upper floor to a middle floor. The stairwell was used just about exclusively for tenants entering and exiting the building. Few of the tenants knew each other well enough to visit, and those were almost always their immediate neighbors.

No, there were two much more likely explanations. The first was that Shin was a mugger, lying in wait for his victim. Street crime was punished mercilessly and in North Korea's police state criminals were often caught, but many were desperate enough to try anyway. The second was the one that actually applied here – Shin did not want to encounter whoever was coming up the stairwell.

This left the person on the stairwell two options. Go back down and seek help from the police, who were present on nearly every street corner in the capital. Or, continue up and hope for the best.

Of course, bringing yourself to the attention of the police carried its own risks.

After about a minute, the footsteps slowly resumed their march up the stairs. As they came to Shin's floor, their pace picked up to a near run. Shin stood quietly until a slam from an upper floor stairwell door told him that the way was now clear.

As he opened the door at the bottom of the stairwell and came into the building's grimy lobby, Shin looked outside and saw that both his training and his hunch had paid off. The first rule he had been taught in his training was to carefully observe all aspects of his surroundings. In the case of his building, that meant all of the vehicles parked outside. Since the inhabitants of this complex were of middling status at best, there were only a few old cars parked here, and many more bikes and scooters. Most of these were gone during the day, being used to get their owners to work. There was just one unfamiliar scooter.

After two tries, one of the keys on the guard's key ring worked, and the scooter's engine came to put-putting life. Shin was on his way. But he had a long way to go.

CHAPTER FIFTY

Beijing, China

Harsh pounding on anyone's door is not the preferred way to wake up. In a police state like China, it was especially unwelcome.

Zhang Jie bolted upright, and still in his underwear staggered to his apartment door. He knew without having to have it explained that if he wasn't quick enough the door would be kicked in, and replacing a door wasn't cheap.

Two men in nondescript suits stood at the door, and without saying a word immediately entered. Both were entirely average in appearance, though one was several inches taller than the other. The short one pulled two photos from his jacket pocket and thrust them at Zhang.

"Have you seen either of these men?," he asked.

Zhang said the first thing that came into his head, with no idea he was sealing his fate.

"I knew it!," Zhang exclaimed, as soon as he saw Park Won Hee's face.

The men said nothing, and just looked at Zhang expectantly.

"Yes, I saw him just hours ago, during my last shift," Zhang said, nodding briskly.

"Why did you say 'you knew it' a moment ago?," the tall man asked.

Suddenly Zhang realized he might be in trouble, though it was far too late to save himself.

"Well, I had my suspicions about him, but I was overruled by my supervisor," Zhang said defiantly.

Both men nodded, as though they agreed.

"And where was he going?" they asked.

"That was the only thing about him I didn't question. He had an American passport, and was going back home to the US. I remember it was to Washington Dulles airport because I thought to myself that had to be one of the longest flights there was. Is that what you needed?," Zhang asked.

The tall man nodded and said softly, "You will need to come with us."

Zhang paled and shook his head. "But why? I have done nothing wrong!"

The tall man smiled and patted Zhang on the arm. "Don't worry. We just know that our boss will want to speak to you and your supervisor in person."

As the two agents walked Zhang to their waiting car, the short man had to admire his colleague's technique. The truth always sounded more convincing, and their boss would indeed want to see Zhang and his supervisor in person. Getting Zhang to their car without attracting attention was a key part of this assignment, and that truth had helped to avoid dragging him to the car in handcuffs.

Of course, he smiled to himself wryly, Zhang actually did have quite a bit to worry about.

Song Hailong looked up eagerly when Liu Jie walked into his office. He knew his assistant would not have returned unless he had progress to report. He was not disappointed.

"We know where both traitors went, sir. They left Beijing on the same flight for Washington DC over two hours ago," Liu said.

Song folded his hands upward in front of him and placed them in front of his chin, a gesture Liu knew from long experience meant Song was concentrating fiercely on the problem before him.

"Who else knows about this?," Song asked.

"Two agents I trust and the border control agent who cleared one of the traitors to depart. As a precaution I have also had the border control agent's supervisor detained. He appears to have intervened to allow the departure of at least one of the traitors, though it is not yet clear whether this was intentional or simple incompetence," Liu replied.

Song nodded. "Good. Find out which, and then have them both eliminated. We can't risk leaks at this stage."

Liu simply nodded.

"Obviously, that plane can never reach Washington," Song said intently.

"Yes, sir. I have already told Beijing Air Traffic Control to order it to return to Beijing at once. However, it is a Trans Pacific Airlines flight with an American crew, and has already left our airspace. It may refuse to return."

Song gritted his teeth in frustration. To have come so far...

"If they refuse to return, they must be forced."

Liu shook his head. "Sir, I regret that is not practical. I have checked with our colleagues in the Air Force, and none of our aircraft have the range to overtake a Boeing 787 and force it to change course through formation flying."

Song shrugged. "That's not what I meant. Surely it's not too late to shoot it down."

Liu paused, and said carefully, "Sir, have you considered the full implications of such an action? Wouldn't the Americans consider it an act of war?"

Song chuckled grimly. "The Russians did it twice, once with that Korean airliner in the 80s and then again over the Ukraine just a decade ago. The first airliner had dozens of Americans, and even one of their Congressmen! The second had hundreds of Europeans. War? Ha! Some half-hearted sanctions that no one took seriously. That was all. No, Liu, the stakes are too high. We can't let these traitors stop us now."

Liu nodded dubiously. "Very well, sir. If the plane fails to return, I will give the necessary orders."

"How long before we know?," Song asked.

Liu checked his watch. "I expect to hear from Beijing ATC within the next five minutes on the plane's response."

Song nodded. "Good. I hope their captain makes the right choice."

CHAPTER FIFTY ONE

En Route from Beijing to Washington, D.C.

Bert Fowler looked exactly like the former military pilot he was, right down to the almost crew cut dark hair, trim physique and piercing blue eyes. Nobody on the crew of this Trans Pacific flight to Washington wanted the glare from those eyes directed anywhere near them, though they had all had the experience. Fowler had handpicked everyone on his crew, a privilege given only to Trans Pacific captains who had been with the airline since its founding seven years before.

For years Fowler had divided his flying time between Trans Pacific and the Air Force Reserves, which he had joined after completing twenty years of active duty with the Air Force. While he was in the Reserves he'd continued doing what he had while on active duty, piloting an RC-135V/W Rivet Joint intelligence collection jet. The RC-135V/W was a large, four jet engine Boeing aircraft, so transitioning to the Boeing 787 he was flying now had not been difficult for Fowler.

All of the Rivet Joint missions Fowler had flown had been off the coast of China. His luck had been better than the captain of the US Navy EP-3E AIRES II forced down on China's Hainan Island on April 1, 2001. After that plane had collided with one of the two Chinese J-8 II fighter jets that had been harassing it, the Chinese pilot of the J-8 II was killed and the AIRES II had been forced to make an emergency landing. The crew was not released until eleven days later, and additional months passed before the Chinese government agreed to allow the AIRES II's removal, which required it to be disassembled.

It surprised neither Fowler nor anyone else that China responded to the incident by stepping up its harassment of US intelligence collection efforts even further. It didn't matter that these Rivet Joint flights were in international airspace according to the US and every other country but China. No, all that mattered was that China didn't like outsiders to know what it was doing. So, Fowler was used to being painted by surface to air missile radar, and Chinese fighters coming close enough to his plane to scrape paint.

Fowler never talked to the specialists he flew off the Chinese coast, and would not have expected them to tell him anything even if he asked. It didn't matter. Just like every other US military officer, Fowler knew that China was using its new wealth to arm itself to the teeth. He also knew that their priority target hadn't changed in the decades since the People's Republic of China was founded in 1949. It was Taiwan.

It had been a quiet flight so far, and Beijing Air Traffic Control (ATC) had handed them off to Korea's Incheon ATC ten minutes earlier. Suddenly, the voice of the Beijing ATC controller was back in the cockpit, this time on the International Air Distress frequency.

"Trans Pacific Flight 898, you must return to Beijing Airport immediately! This is a matter of national security, and you must comply at once! Trans Pacific Flight 898, respond!"

Fowler saw his first officer Tim Shields reach towards the microphone transmit switch, but it took no more than an icy blue stare to stop his hand's forward movement.

The 787 only needed a flight crew of two, but for a flight this long they had two complete crews, and one of the relief officers was also in the cockpit.

"So, do either of you feel like heading back to the People's Republic?," Fowler asked.

Both grinned, and shook their heads no.

"Right. I make our position as just crossing the coast to pass over Korea. Confirm?"

GPS was nearly always accurate and reliable, but it never hurt to be sure.

Shields checked the plane's backup inertial navigation system, and was nodding in less than a minute.

"Yes, sir. At our current speed we'll be across Korea and over the Sea of Japan in about half an hour."

"Excellent. Then, we stay on course for Washington Dulles," Fowler said.

"But, sir," Shields asked nervously, "shouldn't we find out why they want us to go back?"

Fowler grinned. "Think about it for a second. They haven't told us about any threat to the flight, or given us any reason to return besides "national security." I think that means there's a person or persons on this flight they want back."

Shields nodded. "OK, but couldn't they send planes after us?"

Fowler shook his head. "Even half an hour ago that might have worried me. But we're well inside Korean airspace, guarded by both the Korean Air Force and by US Air Force fighters out of Osan Air Base. Once we're out of Korean airspace we go directly to Japan's, where both the Japanese Air Force and our fighters out of Kadena Air Base would give any Chinese aircraft a warm welcome. By the time we pass Japanese airspace, we're over the Pacific and well out of range of anything in China's inventory."

Both of the other officers nodded. Shields said, "Sounds good, sir. So, ignore the transmission and carry on as normal?"

"Exactly. And if my guess is right, we can expect company as soon as we get to Dulles," Fowler said, smiling as he thought to himself, anything that annoys the Chinese is just fine with me.

CHAPTER FIFTY TWO

Tunnel No. 1, North Korea

Lee Ho Suk's day had been good so far. The foreman had just told Lee that the x-ray equipment they needed to see where to link up with the Southerners' tunnel was on its way. Progress forward was good, and bracing the tunnel to take the impact of the small train rolling down its length was nearly complete. In fact, Lee had come from the end of the tunnel where bracing had started all the way to near the tunnel entrance to inspect the bracing work done so far, and in spite of examining all of it had not found a single problem.

For someone with Lee's history, such a day could hardly avoid filling him with dread.

So, when Lee felt tremors through his feet, it gave him an odd mixture of concern and relief. Though definitely cause for worry, a tunnel collapse was a familiar danger he had faced and overcome before. What truly puzzled Lee was that he was sure he could hear laughter and applause from the tunnel entrance, hidden from his view by one of the tunnel's few bends, caused by a massive granite formation.

As he rushed towards the tunnel entrance, Lee saw with dismay a spiderweb of cracks in the tunnel walls heralding a serious problem, though he also saw that they became less visible as he ran. Finally, he rounded the bend and came to the tunnel's entrance, to be greeted by a sight that at first made no sense to Lee. A man Lee had never seen before had a piece of equipment nearly as tall as he was gripped by his hands on both sides. At his feet was a length of rail, and Lee could see that the man had just finished using the device to secure it to the tunnel floor with...three spikes. As he counted the spikes Lee could feel his fury rising, and he could see confusion on the faces of the onlookers, who were no longer laughing and clapping.

"You must stop what you are doing at once!" Lee shouted, bending double and gasping for breath from his breakneck run.

The man with the device sneered when he saw Lee's prisoner clothing. "How is it that you even speak to me, let alone give me orders?," he said, laughing as he reached for another spike.

The onlookers stirred uncomfortably while Lee was still struggling to regain his breath. One of them said carefully, "Kyung, Colonel Park has said that on matters of tunnel safety, prisoner Lee speaks with his authority."

Kyung drew his hand back from the bag of spikes, but still frowned and shook his head. "How does this demonstration have anything to do with tunnel safety? Pneumatic hammers like this have been used in many mines, with no problems of any kind."

Lee slowly straightened, and glared at Kyung. "This is not a mine. Most of this tunnel was dug by hand, and so far not all of it has been braced. We have been working from the end of the tunnel towards the entrance, because it's further away from the entrance where we have already had collapses. The pounding of this powered hammer is more than these walls can take."

Kyung carefully lowered the pneumatic hammer, and then made a show of examining the tunnel walls, while several of the onlookers snickered. "I see no sign that anything I have done has hurt your precious tunnel. Besides, I have been told that finishing this tunnel quickly is a top priority, and laying these rails is part of that. If we don't use power tools, getting these rails done will take at least twice as long." Kyung crossed his arms with a look of satisfaction, and a murmur from the crowd made it clear he had impressed the onlookers with his argument.

Rather than answer, Lee walked to Kyung's bag of spikes and pulled one out, placing it inside the one hole remaining in the first rail. Lee then walked to a nearby pile of tools and pulled out a sledgehammer. With a single fluid motion, Lee pounded the spike into the rail.

"I'm just a prisoner, and not nearly as strong as you and the other miners. I'm sure you could do better," Lee said blandly, being careful to keep his face free of expression.

Kyung looked like he was ready to bite through one of the remaining spikes in his bag. "That still says nothing about any danger caused by this tool."

Lee nodded. "Please follow me," he said, turning back the way he had come. It wasn't long until Kyung and the others saw the cracks in the tunnel walls. No one said anything. Several sharp intakes of breath was all Lee needed to hear.

Kyung was the first to speak. "This makes no sense. Why are the cracks getting worse farther away from where the hammer was used? Are you sure that's what caused these cracks?"

Lee kept his expression impassive, and asked "Are the walls of the tunnels where you have mined rock or earth?"

Kyung shrugged. "Rock, always. We mine for minerals, and those are to be found in rock."

Lee nodded. "There is your answer. Earth does not behave the same way as rock. If you impact rock, it is so dense that the effects usually take place on the spot. This earth is loose, porous and will transmit energy in ways no one can predict. That's why the impact of your device was not visible where you were, but mere meters away around the corner a disaster was about to happen. You could not have predicted that result simply because it was not within your experience mining rock."

Kyung grunted and rubbed his neck. "So, what were you, a professor?"

Lee shook his head. "A high school science teacher. But that was a long time ago."

Kyung smiled thinly. "Yes, I'm sure it was. Very well, we will drive the spikes manually. The earth here appears loose enough that we can do it quickly enough to stay on schedule."

Lee nodded mutely. One of the first things he had learned as a prisoner was to stop talking when things started going the right way.

Now, he could return to worrying about what would go the wrong way next.

CHAPTER FIFTY THREE

Moscow, Russia

Grishkov looked dubiously at the grey concrete edifice in front of them. "It looks like a Stalin-era prison."

Vasilyev laughed. "Well, its construction may have started before Stalin's death, though it was not completed until Khrushchev's time. The Strategic Rocket Forces dates back to 1959, but of course other units had carried out similar missions earlier in a more piecemeal fashion."

Grishkov frowned. "I don't understand why they have the records we seek. After all, the device that was stolen hardly qualifies as 'strategic', does it?"

"That's actually an excellent point. In this context, strategic means missiles with a range of over 1,000 kilometers, which obviously does not apply to our device. My source, however, tells me that the records of all early devices that were to be deployed by Spetsnaz forces are here."

Grishkov's frown deepened even further. "That makes no sense. I hope we are not wasting our time here."

Vasilyev cocked one eyebrow, and said, "Consider the history. The first commander of Strategic Rocket Forces was killed when an ICBM test ended with it blowing up on the launch pad. Hence the Nedelin catastrophe, which was covered up for decades starting with Khrushchev himself with the claim that Nedelin and others present at the test were killed in a plane crash. It was also Marshal Nedelin who insisted that records for all nuclear devices should be transferred to the care of the Strategic Rocket Forces, whether they were truly strategic or not. After his death this nonsense ceased, but the records placed here prior to Nedelin's death in 1960 were never moved."

Grishkov stared at Vasilyev in disbelief. "Their first commander died at a test launch? After we were the first country to put a satellite into orbit? How could that happen?"

"It was not just bad luck. An investigation later determined that Nedelin's insistence on performing the ICBM test before the November 7th anniversary of the Revolution in order to impress high-ranking Party members resulted in a rushed test schedule, with many safety procedures dropped to save time."

Grishkov shook his head. "Let's get to it, then," he said, as they both walked into the headquarters' entrance.

Vasilyev spoke quietly to Grishkov as they approached the lone receptionist, a burly man who sat behind bulletproof glass next to a heavy metal door, obviously the only one leading inside the building from this entrance. "Please let me do the talking, and just present your credentials. My rank and these papers are our only hope of getting what we need."

Without waiting for an answer from Grishkov, Vasilyev raised his voice and addressed the receptionist. "Colonel Vasilyev to see Comrade Pavel Golovkin, accompanied by Senior Detective Grishkov."

The receptionist raised both eyebrows, and sniffed as though he had stepped on a dog turd. "Colonel? And yet I see you are in plain clothes. Which branch of the service are you with?"

"FSB," Vasilyev said calmly.

"Humph," the receptionist said. Pulling a lever that slid a metal drawer towards them from below the glass, he added, "Papers, please."

Grishkov passed over his police ID and badge, while Vasilyev added over a slim leather folder with his FSB ID, and a thick sheaf of papers that for the first time caught the receptionist's interest. "So, you have authorization to conduct research at this headquarters? You should have said so from the start!"

Vasilyev nodded, and stayed silent.

Sniffing, the receptionist picked up the phone. "Comrade Golovkin, please. Yes, an FSB Colonel named Vasilyev here to see you, along with a policeman. Yes, they have authorization papers to conduct research. Very well, I will have them wait for you to escort them to the archives."

The receptionist pulled out two plastic cards with the word "Visitor" on them in large letters, each attached to a metal chain. Pulling on the lever, the metal drawer slid towards them again, and the receptionist said sharply, "All phones, cameras, weapons and metal objects of all types must be deposited with me until your departure from this building. You will pass through a metal detector before you are allowed entry past this lobby, and any metal objects detected will be confiscated permanently."

Once they had dropped everything they were carrying in the drawer, it went back and then returned with the visitor cards and Vasilyev's authorization papers, but not their IDs. "Wear these at all times while you are inside this headquarters. You must remain in the company of your escort at all times. Failure to do so is a breach of security regulations. You will retrieve your IDs and possessions when you return your visitor cards." Pointing to two hardcast plastic chairs that appeared to have been in place since the building opened, the receptionist added, "Sit, please, and await Comrade Golovkin."

As they sat down, Grishkov asked Vasilyev in a low voice, "Why are you both using Comrade as a title, as though this were the 1980s USSR?"

Vasilyev smiled, and spoke even more quietly. "I'm glad you noticed. As far as most of the people in this organization are concerned, nothing of importance has changed since the 1980s. It may be Russia now rather than the USSR. But they are still the main reason anyone pays attention to us, as far as they are concerned. Do you know what Russia's GDP was last year?"

Grishkov shook his head.

"A little under two trillion US dollars."

"Well, that sounds impressive, doesn't it?"

"Until you compare it with the US, which has a GDP of over fifteen trillion."

"Well, OK, but they have a greater population than we do."

"True, so let's take France. Its GDP is almost three trillion, and it has a population of only 65 million. Our population is more than twice as large, at 142 million. And France isn't even the biggest economy in the European Union. That's the Germans, with a GDP of over three and a half trillion."

"What's your point?"

"Simple. Only the Ukrainians and Syrians fear Russian conventional military forces anymore. After the disaster in Afghanistan, it was even a challenge to keep order in places like Chechnya, as you know well from personal experience. Former Warsaw Pact countries have joined the EU and NATO. We don't have the money anymore to buy friendship in places like Cuba. The oil and gas production that makes up most of our GDP and nearly all of our exports can be replaced from many other sources. No, as far as everyone in this building is concerned, there is just one reason Russia is still taken seriously. It's because we're the only ones besides the Americans to have enough nuclear weapons to send the human race back to the Stone Age. Just as it was when Russia was only a part of the glorious USSR."

With that, the metal door opened and the man on the other side gestured towards them to pass through the metal detector and enter.

CHAPTER FIFTY FOUR

Beijing, China

Ma Bingwen's entire extended family had been on hand for the ceremony where he had been promoted to Kong Jun Shao Xiao, or squadron commander, in the People's Liberation Army Air Force (PLAAF). Ma had actually been more proud of an accomplishment his family knew nothing about, being put in charge of a squadron of MiG-29Ks secretly acquired from Russia. After Russia had completed its piecemeal annexation of Ukraine the Europeans had finally used a combination of solar power, increased French nuclear energy production, and liquefied natural gas from North Africa to wean itself from its dependence on Russian natural gas. China had signed its first large contract for gas with the Russians in 2014, but the collapse of its European market left China in a much better bargaining position with Russia for the most recent deal.

The squadron of MiG-29Ks was one of the concessions China had gained from Russia as part of that gas contract. Both sides had an interest in keeping that part of the deal quiet. The Russians had already sold MiG-29Ks to the Indian Navy, and the Indians would not have been happy to learn that the same plane had been sold to one of its most bitter regional rivals. For its part the Chinese were eager to keep news of the MiG-29Ks and the addition of its capabilities to the PLAAF from both the Americans and their puppets in Taiwan.

Slender and just under five and a half feet tall with a thin, pinched face Ma was not an imposing presence. His unimpressive physique, though, concealed a sharp intellect Ma put to good use in advanced air combat training in Russia, where he had impressed his instructors as a natural combat aviator.

Since they had just been acquired and Major Ma and his squadron were still training on the MiG-29Ks with the help of Russian instructors, the aircraft had not yet seen operational use. That would change today.

"Major Ma! A word, please."

Major Ma looked up in surprise from the MiG-29K he had been inspecting at the figure of General Huang. He had so far seen Huang only twice, first at his promotion ceremony and next at the delivery of the MiG-29Ks to their current base at Beijing's Nanyuan Airport. In fact, Nanyuan was China's oldest airport, having opened in 1910. Previously a dual use civilian and military airport, it had become purely military after the opening of Beijing's Daxing International Airport.

"Yes, General. At your service, as always," Ma smiled.

Huang patted the side of the MiG-29K Ma had been inspecting inside the closed hanger where they were all kept to hide them from the prying eyes of American satellites. All of their training had to be conducted during gaps in satellite coverage, a schedule which Ma had consulted so often he now had it memorized.

"And how have our latest additions been performing?," Huang asked.

"Very well, General. All members of the squadron now have flight time on the aircraft, and I believe training will be complete by year-end. All aircraft are operational, and we will have these last few repainted later this month." Ma gestured to three MiG-29Ks that still bore Russian Air Force markings, since they had originally been slated for deployment on the Russian aircraft carrier *Admiral Kuznetsov*.

"I have an urgent mission for you, Major," Huang said. "Let's speak in your office."

Ma gestured towards his tiny office, only a few steps away on the outer wall of the hanger. Closing the door, he waited until Huang was seated before taking his place behind a desk covered with reports and requisition forms.

"I need you and another pilot you trust to undertake a long-range mission with two aircraft. Do you have drop tanks for these MiG-29Ks?," Huang asked.

"Yes, sir. We have a dozen," Ma replied.

"Good. With three drop tanks their range is increased to about 3,000 kilometers, correct?," Huang asked.

Ma nodded. "Correct, sir."

"Your mission will be secret. No one else may know of it besides you, me, and the other pilot you select. Is that clear, Major?," Huang asked, looking Ma directly in the eye.

Ma nodded again, this time emphatically. "Clear, sir."

Huang smiled. "Good. Now for the details. You are to intercept and destroy a Trans Pacific Airlines flight that departed Beijing International Airport a few hours ago that is now passing over Korea with two traitors on board headed for the United States. These traitors must not be allowed to reach their destination. We have already contacted the plane and ordered it to return, but they have refused to respond. You must not make any attempt to contact the plane's crew. Instead, you must destroy it. You will be vectored to the flight by a KJ-2000. Questions?"

Ma's mind raced as he thought through what would be needed for the success of the mission. It did not occur to him to question the deaths of the hundreds of others on the flight who were not traitors to China. It had been drummed into him throughout his training that orders were always to be obeyed rather than questioned, and that collateral damage was an inevitable part of warfare.

"Sir, the plane is a Boeing 787?," Ma asked.

Huang simply nodded.

"Assuming it is at normal cruising speed, the target will be past Japan by the time we can intercept it, but still within range of American and Japanese patrols. We can attempt to evade them by flying at extreme low altitude, but the impact on fuel consumption will make return to this base impossible, even with drop tanks. It would be regrettable to lose these aircraft," Ma said carefully.

Huang smiled. "Not to mention their pilots. Don't worry, we have thought of that. One of our submarines is in the area where we have calculated you will intercept the target. After you complete your mission you will need to eject, and will then be picked up by the sub. I regret the loss of the planes, but we can always buy more."

Ma nodded as though he agreed, but he was not a fool. Though Huang might have been telling the truth, he knew it was just as likely that he was making up the happy coincidence of one of their submarines happening to be in exactly the right place to pick them up to avoid telling him the truth, that this was a suicide mission.

Huang smiled even more broadly. "Good. One more detail. Use two of these planes," he said, gesturing towards the MiG-29Ks still bearing Russian Air Force insignia. "It's unlikely you will be seen in mid-Pacific or that any debris will survive after you eject, but if either happens it would be best for the Russians to take credit for this operation. After all, they have done this before," Huang said, arching one of his eyebrows.

Ma smiled in return, but in fact he was not amused. He would finally fly a combat mission, but it would be against a plane that couldn't defend itself, flying a plane with another country's colors.

Of course, Ma thought, the Americans and Japanese could be counted on to make the mission a challenge worthy of both his planes and his training.

CHAPTER FIFTY FIVE

Moscow, Russia

It was all Grishkov could do not to stare at the man outright as they walked down the corridor to the record archives. Golovkin looked like a mole in human form, right down to the blinking eyes and skittering walk. A crooked bow tie, gold wire-rim glasses and a perfectly bald head completed the picture.

Vasilyev spoke to him as though he was the Russian President. "It is a great pleasure to meet you, Comrade Golovkin. I appreciate your giving us so much of your valuable time."

Golovkin waved his hands absently. "Yes, yes. I have to admit when I saw the urgent request from your office I was curious. It has been a very long time since anyone asked to see records that pre-date the establishment of this headquarters. As you know, any strategic weapons dating to the 1950s have long since been destroyed and replaced with far more capable models. But then, the weapons you want records for aren't really strategic, are they?"

Vasilyev smiled broadly. "Ah, you are quite right, Comrade Golovkin. And it has indeed been many years since these records were transferred here. Still, I am sure that if anyone can locate them, it will be a senior researcher with your many years of dedication and experience."

Golovkin peered up at Vasilyev over his glasses, and for a moment Vasilyev feared he had laid it on a bit too thick. Then Golovkin said, with evident satisfaction, "Well, you may be right about that. We shall see."

With that, Golovkin settled to the task of unlocking the door to the record archives, which took several steps. First, Golovkin placed his hand on a scanner, and bent towards a lens that appeared to examine his eye, probably for a retinal scan. Finally, he typed a code onto a keypad, and gestured for the others to follow as the door slid open.

Rows of plain metal file cabinets marched in ranks that to Grishkov's eye appeared to number in the dozens. Seeing their expressions, Golovkin laughed. "Well, in a way you are in luck. Records pre-dating the establishment of this headquarters have been segregated from the beginning. We've also disposed of any records relating to weapons that were destroyed either due to replacement with more advanced models or due to strategic weapons agreements with the Americans. The remaining records should not take long to review."

With that Golovkin led them all the way across the room, and then turned left. Now they could see against the corner several filing cabinets that unlike all the others, were painted green. "I'm not sure why anyone would want to paint a filing cabinet. It doesn't make it do its job any better. But, that's how they were when we got them, so that's how they've stayed."

Vasilyev nodded. "My request was clear about the records we seek?"

Golovkin peered up through his glasses again. "Yes, yes. Man-portable nuclear devices shipped to the Vladivostok Armory in the 1950s. Intended for use against Japan. I've never seen these records, but if we have them, I'll find them."

Golovkin then pulled a large key ring from his pocket, and began fishing for the right ones.

Grishkov glanced over at Vasilyev, and was pleased to see that he had also been successful in keeping the obvious humor of this situation from his expression. After all of the modern security at the door to the archives, inside were Russia's nuclear secrets, secured with a filing cabinet lock that could be defeated by any teenager with a penknife!

After a bit more fumbling, Golovkin finally located the set he needed, and started opening the first cabinet. In less than ten minutes, he held a file aloft in triumph. "Exactly what you were looking for, I believe. Complete with device descriptions and instructions for use, shipping details, as well as arming and disarming codes."

Vasilyev positively beamed with pleasure. "Excellent work, Comrade Golovkin. May we go to your office to examine these documents?"

"Certainly," Golovkin replied. "My office is just two doors down."

Golovkin led the way to an office barely large enough to hold an ancient metal desk and two rickety wooden chairs. Sitting down behind his desk, he handed Vasilyev the file. "You understand that it will not be possible to make copies of these documents."

"Of course. I simply need to review them," Vasilyev assured him, as he went through each page of the file. Grishkov noted that he had an odd way of reading them, moving his hands carefully along the edges of each page, nodding to himself as he did so. Still, it did not take him long, and in less than five minutes he handed the file back to Golovkin. Vasilyev was just thanking him for his help and getting up to leave, when Golovkin's door flew open.

While Golovkin had reminded Grishkov of a mole, the corpulent figure at the door made him think of an angry bullfrog. The growth of fat under his chin would remind everyone of such an amphibian, and the redness of his eyes suggested that he had already been at a vodka bottle in spite of the early hour.

"Golovkin! Who are these people?" the man shouted.

"Comrade Director! These are FSB Colonel Vasilyev and Senior Detective Grishkov of the Vladivostok police," Golovkin replied, visibly wilting under the man's glare.

"And who authorized their entry to this facility?"

"Why, your deputy, sir. Their papers are completely in order. Colonel Vasilyev has them with him, if you would like to review them."

"My deputy, eh? Well, we'll see about that. Have you given them copies of any of our files?"

"Oh, no, sir. That would be strictly against security regulations."

"Well, I'm glad to see you managed to do at least one thing right." Turning his glare to Vasilyev and Grishkov, he snarled, "And what business does a KGB colonel and a policeman from the other end of the Russian Federation have in the headquarters of the Strategic Rocket Forces?" As Vasilyev opened his mouth to answer, the man shouted, "Enough of this! There can be no good reason!" Pointing to Golovkin, he hissed, "Give me that file. Then, march them out of this building."

Golovkin nodded miserably, handed over the file, and waved Vasilyev and Grishkov to his door. The Director was already stalking off, clutching the file they had come to Moscow to see. As they walked towards the exit, Golovkin whispered, "Sometimes he's just like that, you know." Vasilyev nodded sympathetically, but said nothing. Grishkov just shook his head in disgust.

CHAPTER FIFTY SIX

Tunnel No. 1, North Korea

It was big. Really big. And shiny. Lee Ho Suk had heard a commotion from over a hundred yards up the tunnel and come running, worried that yet another problem had appeared. And it had, though in a totally unexpected way.

There were only three cars joined to the engine of the subway train occupying the tracks in front of Lee. That was the good news. One of the cars, though, was nearly filled by a metal case. What little space was left in the car was packed with heavily armed soldiers, none of whom looked happy to be there.

More soldiers were outside the train, all of them busy with something. Cleaning their weapons seemed to be the most common occupation, while others appeared to be checking lists and equipment. They wore uniforms different than any Lee had seen before, and had a hard muscular edge and sense of purpose very different than the soldiers Lee had seen before as prison guards.

Lee didn't like what he was seeing one little bit. Yes, the Germans had done a beautiful job on the train. The aluminum skin was polished to a jewel-like sheen, and it even smelled good. Sadly for Lee, only the North Korean elite ever got to experience "new car smell," but now he at least had some idea.

Lee would have happily traded the opportunity for just one more ordinary day. He knew better than anyone what it would mean to have the train rolling through this earthen tunnel, even once on a one-way trip.

His walk started briskly and soon became a jog, as Lee moved to the brace point closest to the train. He hoped he would have enough time to check all of them before the train began to move.

En Route to Attack Trans Pacific Flight 898

Major Ma looked at his fuel gauge again dubiously, now that both he and his wingman had jettisoned their third drop tank. As he had expected, flying at extreme low altitude had significantly increased their fuel consumption. Still, based on the speed and bearing they had been given by the KJ-2000 airborne warning and control system tracking the Trans Pacific flight, they would have just enough time to intercept the target.

One good thing about targeting a commercial airliner was that they could generally be counted on to maintain the same course and speed. The KJ-2000 was under orders not to contact Major Ma unless the target made an unexpected change in speed or direction, since any communication might reveal the MiG-29Ks' presence in Japanese airspace.

Ma once again did the calculation, and fractionally relaxed. They would be able to destroy the target. Once their mission was complete, they could then see whether there really was a sub ready to pick them up, or if this was a strictly one way mission for both the MiG-29Ks and their pilots.

Los Angeles

Chung Hee Moon looked up from the frying pan to see Kang Ji Yeong emerging from her bedroom, wearing a dressing gown.

"Good morning!" he said. "I wasn't sure what you like for breakfast, so I guessed based on what you had in your cupboard. Toast, coffee, and this omelet is just about ready. It has tofu and spring onions."

Kang smiled. "Perfect. The cooking smells were what woke me up. The last time that happened was when I visited my mother. I still can't get over a Korean man who can cook."

Chung laughed. "For military men, it's a survival skill. If a soldier is not at a major base with a kitchen, what you can cook is what you can eat. Dining on nothing but cold rations gets old very quickly."

Kang began pulling out plates and utensils and setting the table. "We must eat and have the kitchen clean before my son gets home. I have to talk to him before he sees you here, and I must do it without you in the room."

"I understand," Chung said. "You have not yet mentioned his name."

Kang blushed. "Yes, I am not sure why. It is Chin Hae."

"Truth. Well, that reminds me that there is a truth I must share with you."

Kang shook her head. "Let's eat first. I can't take too much truth on an empty stomach."

Both fell to the food with a will, and a few minutes later both pushed back empty plates. They looked at each other, and each smiled. Kang spoke first.

"I didn't realize how hungry I was. I don't know what gave me such an appetite." As soon as she closed her mouth she blushed furiously.

"I was just as hungry. Now, for that truth I promised."

Kang looked glum, but nodded.

"I do not regret anything about the time we have spent together, but honor compels me to tell you that it is destined to be short. Doctors in Korea have told me that I have inoperable cancer, and that I only have a matter of months to live. So far I have few outward symptoms, but that will change before long. I will not inflict the care of a dying man on a woman who is already burdened with a demanding job and raising a child alone. After you judge that it is safe for me to leave, I will move to another apartment building, and you will not see me again."

Chung had given this short speech considerable thought, and was quite proud of it on two counts. First, it was in fact the truth. Second, it neatly avoided his either being trapped with a new family, or being forced into a messy breakup scene that could bring him to the attention of the authorities. He realized he was actually holding his breath waiting for Kang's response.

He was puzzled to realize from her expression that it was relief.

"I thought you were going to say that you had left a wife or fiancée behind in Korea, or that you had one here. Illness, I deal with every day. So, what have the American doctors you've seen had to say about your condition?"

Chung was at a complete loss for words. The security requirements of this assignment had made a visit to an American doctor unthinkable, and of course given the assignment itself quite beside the point.

"You mean that you haven't seen a doctor since you came here?"

"Well, no," Chung said in a weak voice that sounded lame, even to him.

"Idiot!" Kang said, her eyes blazing. Chung thought wryly that he seemed to have acquired a new pet name.

"It is true that medical care in Korea has advanced considerably in recent years. In fact, you could even say that the typical Korean doctor is as good as the average American doctor. But, American specialists are the best in the world. And for cancer, you need to see a specialist. Are your medical records in your trunk?"

"No," Chung said quickly. "I didn't bring them. I thought there would be no point."

Kang frowned. "I don't understand. Why are you so willing to give up? You look to me like a fighter. You certainly did on TV, anyway," she said, smiling.

"My mother died of colon cancer and my father of lung cancer, and the doctors explained that the genes they had passed on to me meant that there was no hope of successful treatment. So, I have focused instead on making the most of the time I have left. That's why I am here. I have always wanted to travel, and the US was always the country outside Korea that interested me the most. I thought that a little work, plus selling some of my mementos, would give me enough to see first California and then a few other states in the time I have left. Besides, as you said I know that medical care here is expensive. I didn't want to waste what money I have on treatment that will be useless anyway."

Kang shook her head. "That's not the right way to think. It won't be that expensive just to see a specialist to confirm the diagnosis and prognosis you received in Korea. And if a specialist says you do have a chance at recovery, we can worry about cost then."

"I'm sorry, but my mind is made up."

"So is mine. I know an excellent cancer specialist, and I will make the appointment and take you to see him myself. I will also pay for the visit. You either agree, or I will turn you over to the police right now!"

Chung cocked up an eyebrow, smiled and softly said, "Would you really?"

Kang blushed, and shook her head. "But you will go with me, won't you?"

Chung nodded, and reached across the table for her hand. "I appreciate all you are doing for me. Please, just promise me that you won't be too disappointed if the doctor here says the same thing as the one in Korea."

Kang's head bobbed up and down, and she wiped a tear from one eye.

Chapter Fifty Seven

En Route from Beijing to Washington Dulles

Bert Fowler frowned as he looked over the weather report that had just been transmitted to him, and turned to his copilot, Tim Shields.

"So, what do you think, Tim? We can make it through the storm ahead at our current course and speed, if we're willing to put the passengers through some turbulence. At our altitude, there's no real danger to the plane. Avoiding the storm will add time to the flight, and cost us some extra fuel. If you were in this seat, what would you do?"

Shields knew that this was another of Fowler's tests, a kind of on the job training that never stopped. Having flown with Fowler for over a year, the answer to this one was easy.

"The storm could strengthen while we're in it, and go from no real danger to a serious threat before we could fly through it. The cost of the extra fuel is worth it to avoid the risk of either damaging this plane or the death or injury of its passengers and crew. It's even worthwhile if all we do is avoid turbulence, which reduces the lifespan of this aircraft and makes our passengers miserable. As for the lost time, even the few passengers who might miss a connection wouldn't mind if they knew it was to avoid bouncing around the not so friendly skies."

Fowler grinned. "It's good to know that great minds think alike. As your reward, you can contact Narita Air Traffic Control to let them know we'll be changing course and speed to avoid the storm. Let me know as soon as they confirm we won't run into any other flight doing the same thing."

Shields nodded and flipped the transmit switch to call Narita ATC.

En Route to North Korean Coast

Getting out of Pyongyang had not turned out to be much of a challenge for Shin Yon Young. His papers had stood up to scrutiny at each checkpoint, helped by the guards' distraction by military traffic that was heavier than Shin had ever seen. Of course, he knew that exercises were scheduled, but was surprised even so. It was almost as though this time it was for real.

Shin shook his head. South Koreans had been sure that this time the war would finally restart for over seventy years. It hadn't happened yet, and wouldn't this time either. Even the lunatics running North Korea were smart enough to know that they could never win a war against the South. It was all part of the posturing that helped the government justify their ferocious repression, and blame North Korea's poverty and famine on the rest of the world.

He had made good time, but now he had a hard choice to make. Shin was exhausted, since he hadn't slept or rested since the night before killing the guard. He had memorized the guard's real name as soon as he saw it on the papers he took off his body, but still thought of the guard as "Sunshine." So, he could either try to press on, or find someplace to rest. Another issue Shin had to deal with was that though he had lashed an extra tank of gas to the scooter, he would need more before reaching the coast.

Dusk was quickly deepening into night, which meant he had been up for about thirty-six hours. In spite of his youth and excellent physical condition, Shin reluctantly concluded that he would not make it to the coast without at least a few hours of rest. In the rapidly dimming light, Shin spotted a possible solution to both of his problems.

Hotels in North Korea were few and far between, and papers presented by every guest checked with great care. Shin had already concluded he would not risk staying at one, even if it was on his route. To the right of the road, though, he saw what looked like an equipment shed on a farm, with the wheel of a tractor peeping through a partly open door.

The shed had many potential advantages. It was unlikely to be used at night, and would provide shelter from wind and rain. Best of all, there was likely to be a gas can for equipment like the tractor. If not, he could probably rig a siphon to get at least some gas from the tanks of the tractor and whatever else might be in the shed.

His decision made, Shin pulled off the road, and pushed the scooter a short distance into the field. Laying the scooter on its side, Shin laid down beside it. He would wait until it was fully dark to push it the rest of the way to the shed, to get the gas and rest he so badly needed.

This should be my last stop, thought Shin. If I have just a little luck here, I should be able to get back home.

Tunnel No. 1, North Korea

Lee Ho Suk was sweating as he ran up to the foreman, who was over-seeing excavation of the final stretch of the tunnel. Gasping for breath, he was barely able to force out the words, "Have to stop...train."

Staring at Lee, the foreman slowly shook his head. "We've talked about this. The train is the whole reason the tunnel was built. We're only a couple of days from being ready to break through to link up to the southern devil's tunnel. The officer in charge of this mission wants his troops and the train ready to go as soon as he gets the order to proceed with his mission. Frankly, I don't blame him."

Still bent over with his hands on his knees, Lee struggled both to regain his breath and to control his temper. "I have just finished checking all the brace points between here and the entrance. I found at least four that will never take the weight, and there are three others I'd like to shore up as well. I've got men working on the first four already, but I need more time!"

The foreman shook his head decisively. "No, Lee, you don't under-stand. This isn't up to me. The officer in command is Captain Yoon, and he's not going to listen to anyone who tells him anything that will slow him down even a little."

Lee nodded, and then looked the foreman straight in the eye. "Let me try," he said.

CHAPTER FIFTY EIGHT

On Patrol Off the Chinese Coast

Any NATO airman in the 1990s who had been shown the outline of the KJ-2000, NATO code name Mainring, would have immediately and incorrectly identified it as an IL-76, NATO code name Candid. That airman would have been blameless, though, since the airframe of the KJ-2000 was in fact IL-76s purchased from Russia. They were so good for the purpose that Russia realized they could raise the price considerably after the first few Chinese purchases, in spite of a signed contract.

Russia drew the line at providing the electronic monitoring equipment that made the plane capable of carrying out its mission, but the Chinese had decided to use their own technology anyway. China's previous experience with attempting to buy Israeli radar equipment, an effort foiled by American objections, had already convinced them of the value of self reliance.

The active phased array radar mounted on the KJ-2000 was designed by the Research Institute of Electronic Technology, popularly known as the 14th Institute, at Nanjing. It drew on lessons learned from the 14th Institute's previous development of the Type H/LJG-346 SAPARS (Shipborne Active Phased Array Radar System). Designing around the limitations on size and power aboard a ship proved to be good preparation for mounting a radar on board an aircraft. The capabilities of the final product could not match the American AWACS, but the KJ-2000 was well able to meet its basic mission of detecting and tracking airborne threats to China.

The airman at the tracking console of this particular KJ-2000 had good reason to be nervous. It was only his third mission, but the regular operator of his console was sick with the flu, and there had been no time to find a more experienced replacement. He had no idea why the officers were so nervous, but it was obvious this was no ordinary mission. Nobody had explained why it was so crucial to monitor the movements of a particular American commercial flight, but his orders were clear enough – report on any change in speed or direction.

To say that this mission was boring was a considerable understatement. Normally he was required to multitask at a pace that few could have managed without his training, as he tracked and assessed multiple aircraft to determine which were commercial flights on known headings and destinations and which were potential threats. Now, though, he had been directed to ignore every flight but this one, which like every commercial airliner crossing the Pacific was flying straight as an arrow at the same altitude, and had been for hours.

He had been diligent. He really had. But hours of staring at a dot on the screen that crawled endlessly and monotonously forward had finally caused his concentration to waver, and for a period of time he would never be able to specify, he started to think about his girlfriend back home.

"Airman! Report!," his lieutenant said, breaking into a pleasant memory of the airman's last date.

"No change in course or speed," the airman said automatically. The lieutenant nodded briskly, and went forward to report to the KJ-2000's commander.

The airman looked again at the dot on the screen and felt his blood freeze. The flight had changed both its heading and its altitude, though its speed remained constant.

He couldn't report this shift immediately without making it obvious that only his lieutenant's request for a report had caused him to pay attention to his console.

Just a few minutes, he decided. What difference could it really make?

Moscow, Russia

"So, where are we headed?" Grishkov asked, as they drove away from the Strategic Rocket Forces headquarters building.

"Back to our hotel so I can freshen up a bit, and then on to see my old boss at the FSB office here in Moscow," replied Vasilyev.

Grishkov grimaced. "Lubyanka Square? Seriously? Is there a place in all Russia I or anyone with sense would want less to visit?"

Vasilyev sighed. "Yes, you made it clear in Vladivostok that like most Russians you are not especially comfortable inside FSB offices. But at least it's not still Dzerzhinsky Square, and the 'Iron Felix' statue of the founder of Soviet security services was removed after the failure of the coup against Gorbachev in 1991. Plus remember, we're not the KGB. We're the FSB, and we've reformed!"

Grishkov couldn't help himself. Maybe it was that he was so tired after failing to sleep on the long flight from Vladivostok. But there was just one way he could respond to Vasilyev's statement. He threw back his head and laughed louder and longer than he had in a long time. After a few moments, Vasilyev joined him. After a full minute, both wound down, with Grishkov wiping his eyes.

"OK, seriously, what are you expecting from this visit?" Grishkov asked.

Vasilyev shrugged. "Perhaps nothing more than fulfilling my obligation to check in with my superiors. But, if I find who I hope to, we may get support for taking action on the information we have just obtained."

"Well, I know you read the documents on that shipment, but how much could you have committed to memory? And besides, do your bosses really trust you enough to act on whatever you can remember?"

Vasilyev shrugged again, and smiled. "We shall just have to see. Now, we are coming up to the hotel. I will take no more than ten minutes."

Grishkov grunted. "Good. From you I believe it. From Arisha, I would not!"

Vasilyev nodded. "I heard how she handled herself when dealing with the man behind our current difficulties. I must say I am impressed. You are a very fortunate man to have such a wife."

"I could not agree with you more. I am looking forward to ending this business, so she and my children can go back home."

"Yes. Well, we are here," Vasilyev said, as they pulled into the hotel parking lot. "I will be back shortly."

Vasilyev checked the tell-tales he had planted both inside and outside the hotel room door, but saw nothing indicating that they had been disturbed. It was still morning, so he was not surprised to find that the maid had not yet cleaned the room. He had already swept the room for bugs, and took a chance now that the two he had found in the lamp and the phone were the only ones in the room. He had found none in the bathroom, and after picking up a clean shirt and a small notebook case that is where he headed now.

Closing the bathroom door, Vasilyev removed his cuff links and changed shirts. Then he removed the notebook from its case, booted it, and entered his password. Next he twisted the cufflinks and removed a microSD card from each one, and placed each in an adaptor card from his notebook case. He slid each one into a port on the notebook in turn, and copied the contents. Finally, he replaced the microSD cards in his cuff links. This time, he placed the notebook case that he had previously left in his suitcase in the room's safe. The entire operation took less than five minutes.

Vasilyev slid into the seat beside Grishkov a few minutes later. Smiling, he said, "Next stop, Lubyanka Square!"

CHAPTER FIFTY NINE

On Patrol Off the Chinese Coast

The airman at the KJ-2000's tracking console finally judged that the time was right to make a report.

"Sir! The target has changed both heading and altitude!," the airman said.

The nearest lieutenant quickly moved beside him. "Show me its current position."

As soon as the airman had done so, the lieutenant moved to a console used exclusively for tracking PLAAF aircraft. The airman had often thought that this separation of functions made no sense, but his instructors had insisted it was vital to ensure security. Using the position fix from the airman's console, the lieutenant was able to place the target's position relative to the Mig-29Ks moving to intercept. It was obvious that the Mig-29Ks had to change course, and quickly.

"Airman! Are you sure that the target has just changed course and altitude?"

The airman knew he had only one chance of escaping punishment. "Yes, sir! Absolutely sure!"

The lieutenant nodded shortly and turned his gaze back to his console. It was possible that the MiGs had veered off course, since only a small mistake in course heading at these speeds equaled hundreds of miles. He would worry about assigning blame if the MiGs failed. For now, though, there was still a chance of salvaging the mission.

The lieutenant strode forward to the radio communications station, and handed them the MiGs' encrypted frequency and the target's new course and altitude. The chances of the transmission being intercepted mid-Pacific were small, and in any case the MiGs had to have the information to have any chance of success.

Besides, who in all this empty ocean could overhear in time to stop them?

Tunnel No. 1, North Korea

The train driver nodded as the foreman entered the engine car, but frowned when he saw Lee Ho Suk follow him in. "Prisoners aren't allowed in the engine room. In fact, Captain Yoon has given orders that they are not allowed anywhere on the train."

The foreman sighed. "Yes, I know. He is here under Colonel Park's authority. Another officer is bringing Captain Yoon. In the meantime, we have a few questions about this train."

The train driver adjusted his cap, and then shrugged. "Ask your questions."

Lee cleared his throat nervously as he looked over the glowing numbers that covered the display in front of the driver. "What kind of power does this train use?"

The driver nodded. "That's a good question. Normally a train like this would draw electric power from a third electrified rail, which of course there was no time to install. This one, though, was designed to carry maintenance crews. Since sometimes they would be going to fix a section of rail where power had failed, this model has its own battery power. With our current full charge, we can keep moving for at least one hundred fifty kilometers."

Lee was impressed, and said so. Then he asked the most important question, "How fast does this train go?"

The driver smiled. "Its cruising speed is 100 kilometers per hour." Seeing the look of horror on Lee's face the driver laughed and quickly added, "Don't worry, I've heard about your safety concerns and agree with them. Captain Yoon doesn't like it, but he's agreed to go much more slowly to the end of the tunnel."

Lee sighed with relief, and the driver continued, "I pointed out to him that even at 20 kph, as long as we don't have to stop we'll be at the end of the tunnel in about an hour. We're scheduled to begin in half an hour, so this should be over quickly."

The driver frowned as Lee paled and swayed, grabbing the edge of the control console to steady himself, and turned to the foreman. "What's wrong with him? I can't risk anyone being sick near these controls." Lee waved a hand shakily in an attempt to reassure the driver, while the foreman carefully responded, "I think you have different definitions of the word 'slowly.' How slow can this train go?"

The driver shrugged. "The controls are digital. I could set it to one kilometer per hour if I wanted to, though of course that would be ridiculous."

Seeing Lee grin and visibly collect himself, the driver shook his head vigorously. "Captain Yoon would never agree to go at such an absurd speed." Looking out the train window he smiled and added, "Here he is to tell you in person."

Los Angeles

Chung Hee Moon turned his head from the TV when he saw Kang Ji Yeong entering the apartment. Chung had been watching American TV as part of his training, which called on him to learn everything possible about his environment. There were dozens of channels to choose from, and so far each had done more to raise questions than to provide him with mission-essential information.

Many channels were devoted to what was called "reality TV". Much of this confirmed the worst of what Chung had been told about Americans and their obsession with material possessions. One program that had small children competing in beauty pageants he found particularly disturbing, both for the evident suffering of many of the children and for the conduct of their parents.

On the other hand, the sheer quantity of information available was astonishing. There were entire channels devoted to scientific and historical topics, broadcasting programs nonstop on a variety of topics at many different levels of difficulty.

Even more surprising was the variety of news sources. These included news channels from Europe, the Middle East and Asia. Chung would have expected these to have a wide range of viewpoints, but not to find them all on an American TV set. He was amazed, though, at the range of opinions expressed on American news channels. These ranged from fairly objective, to general approval of the American government, to actively hostile to the government in a tone so sharp and unrelenting that Chung had to check to be sure it was in fact based in the US.

Chung had been careful to minimize his questions to Kang, because of the danger that one might be a question no South Korean would ever ask. One he had asked, though, was whether there were channels controlled by the American government. Kang had laughed and said that there was one that received public funding, but was not controlled by the government, called the Public Broadcasting Service. Chung had smiled and been careful not to say what he thought, that Kang was hopelessly naïve.

What Chung saw on PBS only confused him further. The channel had appeals to its audience for money, and was apparently the only one that relied on cash from its viewers for much of its budget. Why people would give money to a channel that received money from the government was never explained, but it appeared that some viewers did in fact send contributions.

Even stranger were the PBS news programs. None were uncritical of the government, and one was even produced by the British government, not the American! And the BBC program was probably the relatively most critical one, even though it was produced by a government that Chung knew was a close US ally.

It was all very puzzling.

At least Kang was smiling, though Chung had no idea why, or what was in the small bags she was carrying.

"Well, I have good news," Kang said. "I got the doctor to agree to waive his initial examination based on your diagnosis in Korea, and so he will go straight to the colonoscopy. He had a cancellation, so he can fit you in day after tomorrow."

Chung nodded, though he was actually not quite sure what a colonoscopy was. Obviously, a medical procedure of some sort.

"Now, I have all the medications you need to prepare for the procedure. I'm sure they're the same as the ones you had in Korea, or similar. The instructions for times and dosages are all there. Just let me know if you have any questions."

Chung nodded again, smiled and said, "Thank you." Then he thought to ask, "How long do you think it will take?"

Kang shrugged and answered, "Probably about an hour for the anesthetic and the procedure itself, plus another hour or so of observation afterwards, mostly to make sure you don't have a reaction to the anesthetic. The doctor will give me the results while we're there, if you don't mind signing this waiver." Kang pulled out one piece of paper from a pile she had in her arms, along with the small bags, which she also handed to Chung.

"Now, the rest of these forms are straightforward, about medical history and insurance. Don't worry about the insurance forms. I know this doctor, and he will bill me directly at a price we agreed for cash. Since he doesn't have to declare cash as part of his income, he doesn't have to pay federal or state taxes on it. That plus avoiding insurance paperwork makes this a good deal for him too."

Chung nodded, and began to study the forms. He realized he also needed to do an Internet search whenever Kang was out of the room on the term "colonoscopy" so he would know what to expect. In North Korea, all they had done prior to his diagnosis had been a blood test, and that had been quick and painless. He wasn't sure just what a colonoscopy was, but if it only took a couple of hours, how bad could it be?

CHAPTER SIXTY

En Route to North Korean Coast

At first Shin Yon Young was completely disoriented. As his eyes flew open, Shin realized that waking up thanks to a boot in the ribs from sleeping on a dirt floor might have that effect. The first thing his eyes did after opening was to focus on the sharp metal prongs of a pitchfork held a hands breadth from his face.

Shin did the smartest thing he could have done under the circumstances. He lay completely still, and said nothing.

After a few moments, the pitchfork jerked upwards, and was accompanied by a man's voice.

"Who are you, and what are you doing here?"

Shin was careful not to move. "I am a guard at an important government building in Pyongyang, and am on my way to visit my family at a village near Haeju. I have papers, if you will let me reach for them."

The man holding the pitchfork nodded, and added, "Slowly."

Shin pulled out his papers and handed them to the man, who read them and then gave Shin a look that was still anything but friendly.

"I see nothing in these papers that allows you to steal from me."

Shin stiffened. "I did no such thing!"

The man shook his head. "Do you think I am a fool? I checked the gas can, and it is bone dry. It was full when I put it here yesterday."

Shin nodded and said, "Yes, I used the gas for my scooter over there, which is how I am getting to my family. Did you lift up the gas can?"

The man cocked his head sideways. "No, I just shook it to see if it was empty." Still holding the pitchfork on Shin, the man reached sideways with his other hand and lifted up the gas can. Shin heard his intake of breath when he saw the money Shin had left lying there. Shin had estimated it would be about double the value of the gas he used, and he could see the man make the same calculation.

The man lifted the pitchfork away from Shin's face, and held out his hand to help Shin up. "My mistake," he said roughly. "Come, you can have some breakfast before you go."

Shin's heartbeat slowly settled, as he pushed the scooter behind the farmer. One of the many lessons he had drummed into him by his instructors was always to pay for anything he took, if at all possible.

Shin was glad he had paid attention.

CHAPTER SIXTY ONE

Tunnel No. 1, North Korea

Captain Yoon scowled as he pulled off his gloves, and glaring at the three men in front of him, pointed first at the driver. "Are we still ready to leave on schedule?" His head bobbing up and down, the driver said, "Yes, sir!".

Nodding, Yoon turned to the foreman. "Let me save you some time. I spoke to Colonel Park before I entered this tunnel, and I know all about the authority he has given this prisoner in safety matters. However, my control over this operation comes directly from Marshal Ko. He told me - in person - not to allow anything or anyone to interfere with my mission. Colonel Park has told me he understands this. Do you?"

Swallowing hard, the foreman nodded vigorously, and said nothing. Yoon turned to go, but stopped when he heard a voice behind him.

"Do you know what they call me, sir?"

Yoon smiled and nodded. "Yes, Colonel Park told me the story. 'Lost Bet.' Very amusing."

"And did he say how long I've been in these tunnels?," Lee asked.

Yoon nodded sharply.

"However, he may not have told you how many tunnel collapses I have survived. That number is seven. By my count, I have been able to help prevent eleven others." Lee paused, and visibly collected his thoughts. "I understand that you and your men have courage, and that you are not afraid to risk your lives to carry out your mission. You need to understand, though, that the tunnel doesn't care about your courage. When you try to move through it too fast, it will bury you and your mission under tons of rock and earth, and it will be many days before anyone can try again. Unless the tunnel collapse destroys this train, and even trying again becomes impossible."

Yoon turned to the foreman. "Is this tunnel really as unstable as this man says?"

The foreman nodded. "We have done everything we can to brace the key weak points. But a collapse is still a real risk."

Yoon turned back to Lee. "What do you propose?"

"We will not set the charges to join with the other tunnel for at least two days. Start when you planned, but go at the slowest speed possible. You will still get to the other end ahead of the breakthrough. I will walk alongside the train as it moves to spot any sign that the tunnel is having trouble taking the train's weight, and have men and material on the train to add bracing as necessary. Another team will be ahead of us, continuing work to brace weak points we have already identified. This plan will give you the best chance to succeed in your mission."

Yoon nodded thoughtfully. "Very well." Turning to the driver, he said, "Do as he has described. However, if I receive orders to carry out this mission immediately, be ready to speed up at my command." The driver nodded, but was clearly seething at having been successfully contradicted by a lowly prisoner.

Turning back to Lee, Yoon frowned and asked, "If this tunnel is so unstable, how do you expect it to survive the explosion that will join it to the one being built by the Southern devils?"

Lee smiled, and shook his head. "I don't. When the blast opens a hole big enough to get us through, we need to be going as fast as this train will move to have any chance of getting to the other tunnel before this one collapses. There's only one thing I know for sure. However this turns out, it will be a one-way trip."

Shaking his head, Yoon stalked off to brief his troops. Once he was gone, Lee was startled by the foreman's outstretched hand. As Lee took it for the offered handshake, the foreman said gravely, "My name is Mun. You may call me by it from now on."

Lee stared at Mun, both from surprise and incomprehension. Prisoners never called anyone by name who was not also a prisoner. It was one of the most basic rules there was, and one that now felt as natural as breathing.

Mun smiled bleakly. "I still don't think it's likely we'll pull this off. But you have given me at least a chance to see my wife and children again. I really don't want to die in this hole."

Lee nodded and said simply, "Me neither."

CHAPTER SIXTY TWO

On Patrol Off the Japanese Coast

The Boeing E-3 Sentry AWACS had been built around the old Boeing 707 airframe, but by the time it had been sold to the Japanese Air Self Defense Forces, 707s were no longer available. So, it was the only air force in the world to use the newer Boeing 767 airframe, though otherwise its E-3 mission package was nearly identical. This gave it additional mission time aloft, as well as extra room for the AWACS crew and equipment. That fact became particularly important once a new AWACS crew addition found productive use for the extra space.

Haruto Takahashi would have never been on board one of his country's AWACS a generation earlier. If he had grown up in his parents' Japan of world beating companies and lifetime employment, his test scores and strong work ethic would have guaranteed him rapid placement in some corporate executive suite.

Another key change had been the Japanese public's view of their country's military. Japan's Self Defense Force had been seen as a necessary evil at best after the disastrous outcome of World War II. Along with defeat and occupation had come the revelation of atrocities committed by the military against Allied prisoners and Korean "comfort women".

Attitudes began to change as China became increasingly assertive over claims to Japanese islands connected to substantial offshore oil deposits, North Korea began test firing ballistic missiles over Japan, and as it became clear the US would not automatically intervene to protect Japan's interests. Although everyone wearing a uniform in the JSDF was still considered a "special civil servant" and the titles of "officer," "NCO" and "enlisted" still did not exist, the JSDF had once again become an honorable career choice for a graduate of one of Japan's top universities.

The JSDF had one unique attraction for Haruto. It gave him the opportunity to test a concept that Haruto had started to work on at university he called "integrated situational awareness." This meant tying together all the data available from multiple sources to form a complete picture, and using each source to reinforce the other in real time. The JSDF had the assets Haruto needed to turn theory to reality, and its unique Boeing 767 AWACS airframe gave him the room to install the extra equipment needed.

In particular it had equipment to maintain control over heavily modified RQ-4 Global Hawk surveillance drones, with their already formidable capabilities enhanced by upgraded Japanese optics and radar. The RQ-4s had first been deployed to Misawa Air Base in 2014 under American control, but a few years later the US had agreed to sell Japan its own RQ-4 squadron. Loitering above the waters surrounding Japan at 60,000 feet, well above the maximum commercial airline altitude of 40,000 feet, the RQ-4s gave Japan capabilities no one else in the region could match.

Just as important were some of the JSDF's oldest assets, its fleet of YS-11EB electronic intelligence aircraft. Turboprop aircraft that had seen decades of service, they were nevertheless an effective and reliable platform for collecting foreign military signals.

Normally, the Japanese AWACS that Haruto was aboard would rely exclusively on its massive rotating radar to detect possible threats. Haruto's "integrated situational awareness" concept incorporated the radar and optical data from the RQ-4s as well as electronic intercepts from the YS-11EBs to give him a complete picture at a single console.

At least, that was the theory.

Haruto had anticipated the first problem, getting the JSDF bureaucracy to take his proposal seriously. After all, he had nothing more than his university research to back up his concept. Two points, though, helped him succeed.

First, his proposal was cheap. It only required giving Haruto access to data from the YS-11EBs and RQ-4s, one extra display console and two additional servers. Haruto would write the software needed to integrate the data on a single console display himself. Second, the overall concept appealed to the senior leadership of the JSDF. It was 100 percent defensive, and so ran no risk of disturbing pacifist politicians or the public. And with threats multiplying from China and North Korea, anything that cheaply provided more advance warning was welcome.

Haruto's real problem was that he had underestimated the difficulty of integrating data from three very different platforms. Though as one month followed another without success Haruto was tempted to abandon the project, his innate stubbornness kept him hard at work. After nearly a year of writing and rewriting code the turning point was the assignment of a university classmate and friend to his squadron. Another set of trained eyes to spot software bugs proved invaluable, and Haruto thought they were finally ready to give his concept a real test.

He was looking forward to the challenge.

En Route to Rendezvous With USS Theodore Roosevelt

Captain Jim Cartwright opened his eyes, as he often did, to Lieutenant Fischer's knock on his cabin door. "Enter," he said, rising in his bunk.

"New orders, sir," Fischer said, handling Cartwright a single piece of paper.

Cartwright didn't need long to read them. "Rendezvous with the *USS Theodore Roosevelt* carrier group, and provide perimeter security. Coordinates as follows. Well, that's clear enough. How long before we get there at best speed?"

Fischer grinned. "Some genius at headquarters can actually read a map. We can get to the rendezvous point in just a few hours, and then wait another few hours for the lead escorts to reach our position. Then, we plow straight ahead."

Cartwright grunted. "You're right. Somebody at PACOM realized we were closer to the carrier group than Honolulu, so why not get some use out of us. Very well, Lieutenant, inform the crew of our new orders, and advise Mr. Spencer that he and his team will be our guests a bit longer. I'm on my way to the bridge."

Cartwright shook his head as he strode towards the bridge. Escort duty for a Block IV *Virginia* class sub? Somebody back at PACOM expected trouble, and was throwing everything they had at it. But who would be crazy enough to tangle with a U.S. carrier group?

Maybe that was the wrong question, Cartwright mused. Maybe the right question was how they would do it.

CHAPTER SIXTY THREE

Moscow, Russia

Grishkov frowned as they walked past an unadorned stone placed on Lubyanka Square in front of the FSB headquarters building. Before he could ask, Vasilyev answered his question. "That was placed there in 1990 as a memorial to the victims of the Gulag. The stone comes from the Solovki Prison Camp at the Solovetsky Islands in the White Sea."

Grishkov shivered. "The White Sea? You mean the sea that is *north* of Siberia. Very appropriate."

Vasilyev nodded grimly. "I will not deny that terrible cruelties have been inflicted in the name of state security, sometimes without need or justification. However, none of that lay behind the construction of the building that now serves as our headquarters, and the KGB's before it. In fact, it was finished in 1898, and was originally used by the Rossiya Insurance Company. My first boss used to say that now the KGB insured the future of the Soviet Union."

After seeing Grishkov's expression in response, Vasilyev grinned. "Well, my first boss was something of an ass."

With that, they entered the building, and Vasilyev handed over his ID to the guard at the entrance. After carefully examining it and comparing the man before him with the photo, the guard wordlessly jerked his head towards the reception desk.

Once again Vasilyev handed over his ID, and this time indicated to Grishkov he should hand over his as well. Then, he told the receptionist who he was there to see. The man nodded, and called his office. After saying yes twice, the man straightened, and raised his eyebrows as he rummaged for the correct passes. "I can't remember the last time I handed one of these out. You will both need to leave your IDs until you return these passes."

With that, the receptionist handed over two passes. One had no writing, just an elaborate hologram of the FSB's seal and a number. The other had "Escort Required" in large red letters. Speaking to Vasilyev he said, "Make sure you stay together, or that he has another authorized person with him at all times. I take it you know the way?"

Vasilyev simply nodded.

"Good. Welcome back, Colonel. Whoever you are here to see obviously likes you." He then pressed a buzzer, and they walked inside the FSB's headquarters.

"What was that all about?" Grishkov asked. "Is it such a big deal for you to be allowed in to your own headquarters?"

Vasilyev smiled. "Well, yes and no. In reality, it doesn't make much of a difference that I'm coming to see Smyslov without an escort. It is, though, an act of faith on his part that I won't go elsewhere in the building without his knowledge, or even worse let you see something you shouldn't."

"So, you have obviously worked here before."

"Well, yes," Vasilyev acknowledged. "Time at headquarters is a career must for anyone with ambition in most organizations, and the FSB is no exception."

"And you are still on good terms with your old boss. Do you think he will tell us anything we don't already know?"

Vasilyev shrugged. "If Smyslov was that easy to predict, he would never have risen so high in the FSB. He will decide whether to share what, if anything, he knows based on what he sees as the FSB's best interests. My main hope from this meeting is that he will authorize the additional man I want for the encounter I have planned with our Korean friend later today."

Grishkov was obviously not pleased to hear this. "Why do we need help? The two of us should have no trouble, particularly since there is no way he can bring a weapon through airport security, and we will have the advantage of surprise."

Vasilyev's short, sharp bark of laughter only deepened Grishkov's frown. "My friend, I know that in dealing with criminals you have been very effective. Few men could have survived the attacks that have been launched against you over the past week, and so please believe that I have the deepest respect for your abilities. But your experience and training has not been in dealing with men like this Korean. For a start, there are weapons made of materials that will not be detected by an airport scanner. And as for surprise, it is precisely at a moment like exiting a scheduled flight that this man will be most alert. Another point is that my primary concern is not that he will either escape or injure us when he attempts to do so."

"So, what then?"

"He is very likely to attempt to kill himself, so that we cannot extract information from him."

"Are you saying all intelligence agents are that dedicated?"

"Not at all. But there are two factors at play here. First, North Korean agents allowed to operate outside their own country are subject to a level of indoctrination that surpasses even what we do in the FSB. And we are not gentle. But perhaps more important, he has to know that there is no chance he will survive our captivity, and that the time he would spend with us before his passing would not be…pleasant."

Grishkov did not like the look of Vasilyev's smile as he said that.

"So, we are here. Please speak to Smyslov only if he asks you a direct question, and let me handle the rest."

As they walked into Smyslov's outer office, they saw his secretary immediately pick up the phone and speak a few words into it in a voice too low for them to hear. No sooner had she put the phone back down than the door to the inner office flew open and a burly figure with a thick shock of black hair, bushy eyebrows and open arms came hurtling towards them. "Vasilyev, it has been too long!" Smyslov said, wrapping his arms around him and pulling him towards the ceiling. "We need to get some meat on these bones!" Smyslov then dropped Vasilyev, and turned to Grishkov. "I understand that I have you to thank for keeping my favorite agent alive in Vladivostok. A Mosin-Nagant is no laughing matter."

With that Smyslov wrapped one arm around each of them, and nearly dragged them into his office. Grishkov couldn't help thinking that he finally understood the foreign stereotype of the Russian bear.

Smyslov dropped them into a huge red leather couch, and perched on the edge of a matching chair right next to it. On a large wooden coffee table was spread a feast of warm black bread, caviar, a dozen assorted snacks and a large bottle of vodka. They all fell to the food with a will, and after less than ten minutes were toasting each other over the crumbs of the meal. Smyslov's secretary had just served them coffee, and everyone was leaning back with a cup in hand.

Smyslov grinned and said to Vasilyev, "I told you I would get some meat on your bones! You look even skinnier than I remember!" Vasilyev smiled back and said, "Nobody in Vladivostok treats me as well as you always did."

Smyslov shook his head. "I always warned you that life was hard in the provinces. Still, from what I have heard you have done well there. And how did you fare with our comrades at the Strategic Rocket Forces? Are they still stuck in the 1960s, or have they perhaps advanced to the Reagan years?"

Vasilyev shrugged and said, "Well, I got the information we were looking for, and that was more than I expected. I would not have been surprised if the records had been lost after all this time, or if they had refused to share them with me."

Smyslov's bushy eyebrows reached for the ceiling. "Really? They shared the records with you? That sounds most unlike our military friends. Please tell me everything that happened."

After Vasilyev had finished his account of their visit, Smyslov concluded with the same observation Grishkov had earlier. "So, you saw the records, but they would not let you make copies. That means we only have your memory to go on, which I trust, but cannot take much farther than my office."

Vasilyev smiled, and twisted the tops off his cufflinks to reveal the two microSD cards inside. Smyslov threw back his head and roared with laughter. "Of course! I should have known that you would have a trick like that to fall back on!" Smyslov then went to his desk, pulled out a laptop, and inserted one of the microSD cards. An image of one of the documents on the stolen nuclear device immediately filled the screen.

Smyslov nodded as he read, and then shook his head. "It is as bad as we feared. There is no way to track the device, and no way to disarm it remotely. If it is found intact, there will be no doubt we manufactured the weapon. If it is detonated, analysis of the fallout will easily demonstrate that the materials used to build it came from Russia. Our only way out of this mess is to find the device before it is detonated. You said you have a plan to do so?"

"Yes, but we must move quickly."

"You have made a copy of these documents, of course," Smyslov stated rather than asked.

Vasilyev just shrugged.

Smyslov roared with laughter, and slapped his hand on the table hard enough to shake the plates and glasses. "That was the right answer. You were always too smart to lie to me. To others, naturally, but never to me. So, what do you need?"

"Not what, but who. I need an experienced operator I can trust absolutely, to help us quickly and quietly do an airport interception. The target is the man who has tried to kill me once in Vladivostok, and who we believe was responsible for multiple attempts against Grishkov and his family. We think these attacks were to prevent our investigation of the device's theft, because he is the one who bought it from Vladimir Timoshenko, and then killed him."

"How will you know him?"

"Well, we don't have a picture. But we do know which flight he is likely to take from Vladivostok to Moscow, and we believe he is Korean. I doubt there will be more than one or two people fitting that description on that particular flight."

Smyslov rubbed his hair and frowned. "That sounds pretty thin, but if that's what you have we must go with it. As for the operator- Evgeny?"

Vasilyev started with evident surprise. "He is available? He's nearly always overseas."

Smyslov nodded. "True. You happen to have caught him between assignments. Normally I would not use someone with his unique talents on a domestic assignment, but this case is obviously special. Now, what about equipment?"

"Well, we need to be sure that the target is able to talk after he is apprehended, and we need to prevent him from killing himself to avoid interrogation."

Smyslov grinned. "I have just the thing. The latest toy from our friends in the US. While we were partners in the war against terror, I had American companies giving me free samples of their products, and no more pesky export license issues to sidestep. Not, as you know, that avoiding such restrictions was ever much of a challenge."

With that, Smyslov went to his desk, and returned with a neatly sealed cardboard box, which he handed to Vasilyev. "The latest stun gun model, guaranteed to instantly incapacitate anyone. A range of four meters, 50,000 volts and a power output of 26 watts. Includes a laser sight, but at a range of four meters, I doubt that you'll need it."

"The power source?"

Smyslov's grin grew even wider. "Eight AA batteries."

Vasilyev frowned. "I have seen these work, but are you sure it is reliable?"

"Well, there is one way to make sure. Care to test it? Perhaps on your friend Grishkov?"

Grishkov looked up and blinked. "No thank you, please. I was a test subject when I was an ordinary patrolman, and it was an experience I have no interest in repeating. Our host is quite right to call these weapons reliable. There are only two reasons we do not use them more frequently. First, not every criminal is willing to remain four meters away during pursuit. An even bigger problem is cost. The weapons themselves are not so expensive, but the cartridges are quite pricey. It's bad enough when they are used for real, but getting enough cartridges for anyone to practice with it was a budget killer. When I complained, the company told me the compressed nitrogen in the cartridge used to fire the darts attached to the wires containing the electric charge is what drives up the price. So, we mostly stick with bullets."

Vasilyev threw up his hands in surrender. "Very well, I am convinced. Is Evgeny familiar with this weapon?"

"Of course," Smyslov said, nodding. "He has used an earlier version of this weapon in the field, and told me that he is looking forward to using this one. In fact, I was saving it for him to use on his next overseas assignment. He will just be using it a bit earlier than he had planned."

Vasilyev looked down at his watch. "Can he meet us at Sheremetyevo Terminal C in an hour? That will give us a half hour to brief him on the target and get in position."

Smyslov opened his arms so they were even wider than his smile. "Anything for my best agent!" Lumbering to his feet, he added "Good hunting!" as he walked them out of his office. The outer office door closed behind them as they heard Smyslov barking orders to his secretary.

Vasilyev smiled at Grishkov and shook his head as they strode rapidly out of the building, barely pausing to return their IDs. "Just like old times," he muttered to himself.

CHAPTER SIXTY FOUR

Tunnel No. 1, North Korea

Lee Ho Suk frowned as he examined the delicate lattice of cracks that had spread in the tunnel walls ahead of the advancing train. He lifted up his right arm towards the train's driver, who was only a dozen meters behind him, in a gesture the driver had grown to dread. It meant "Stop the train, and have the work crew leave the train and join me." This would be their fourth stop.

So far, to Lee's surprise, there had been no complaints from Captain Yoon. Maybe he had finally understood the point that a tunnel collapse at this stage would spell disaster for his mission, not just for expendable prisoners.

As the work crew moved bracing materials into position with a speed helped by repeated practice, Lee couldn't help thinking about what would happen after they had the train in position to make the final race to the South after the explosion cleared the way. Would they still see any need for him or the other prisoners? Or would it be, he thought with a wry smile, truly the end of the line?

En Route to Attack Trans Pacific Flight 898

Major Ma looked up in surprise as the message came in with the target's new altitude and heading, and then swore softly under his breath as he calculated the new intercept point. Ma and his wingman had only had minutes to make contact with the sub that was supposed to be in this area after firing their missiles at the target. Now the target's unexpected course change meant they would have to rely on their missiles' engines to cover the final distance to the target, since they would barely be able to get in range to lock on to the aircraft. They might not now have time to make a broadcast to the sub after firing, let alone wait for a response.

After some additional calculations, Major Ma breathed a sigh of relief. They would make it. He and his wingman each carried two Vympel NPO R-77 missiles, called by NATO the AA-12 Adder. The variant they were carrying had an upgraded solid-fuel ramjet engine and was designated as the RVV-AE-PD, with "PD" as short for the Russian "Povyshenoy Dalnosti", or "improved range." The increase in range from 80 to 110 kilometers was going to make the difference between success and failure for this mission.

A brief flicker on Ma's threat warning indicator came less than a minute after receipt of the message. Did the radar paint on his MiG-29K mean that the message had been intercepted? Ma looked at the indicator closely, but to his relief it stayed dark.

At least they should be able to complete this mission successfully without interference, Ma thought, even if it was looking less and less likely that he and his wingman would survive it.

Los Angeles

Chung Hee Moon came close to taking his chances on the street once he found out through his Internet research exactly what a colonoscopy involved. Not because of any pain or discomfort caused by either the preparation or the procedure itself, though both sounded quite unpleasant. Rather, Chung was well trained in the operational risks he would be running under either sedation or general anesthetic, and everything he had read made it clear those would be his only two alternatives. Either one could result in a drug-induced slip that would either betray his North Korean origins, or even his mission. That is why his orders, as always, specified he was not to allow the use of anything more powerful than a local anesthetic on him while on assignment.

Now, though, Chung had to weigh the risks to the mission of leaving Kang Ji Yeong's apartment against the possibility that drugs could cause his cover to slip. That would mean finding some other place to stay.

However, Chung didn't have the money to rent another apartment, and his cover might not stand up to a credit check anyway. Though there were abandoned spaces in various buildings throughout Los Angeles, he had been briefed that these were often already occupied by drug addicts and other criminals, and most were well outside the target area selected for his mission. Cheap motels were a possibility, but some managers cooperated with the police, and he couldn't take the chance on being reported. Another unpleasant thought that occurred to Chung was that once on the street looking for a place to live, anyone looking for easy cash could call a newspaper or TV station to say they'd spotted the man in the grocery store video.

After all the trouble and expense she had gone to, there was no chance that he could talk Kang out of his going through with the procedure. The only result would be to further arouse her suspicions.

No, there was really no alternative, Chung decided. He would have to go through with the colonoscopy, and hope for the best.

CHAPTER SIXTY FIVE

Escort Duty, USS Theodore Roosevelt Carrier Group

Captain Jim Cartwright looked up as the pilot announced that they had arrived at the rendezvous point.

"Lieutenant, let's give some thought to likely threats to the carrier. I think we can rule out surface ships."

"Agreed, sir," Fischer grinned.

"Ok, we're obviously here primarily on anti-sub duty. And we will certainly do that. Other threats?"

Fischer shrugged. "Well, air attack. There's not much we can do there, though."

Cartwright smiled. "Ordinarily, I'd agree with you. But we do have a couple of AIM-9X anti-aircraft missiles, right?"

Fischer frowned. "Well, yes sir. We're due to participate in a test launch exercise a few months from now. But those are short range missiles, and the exercise is to use them for self defense against anti-sub helicopters. To have any chance of hitting a fighter jet they'd have to fly almost on top of us. Well, within about 20 miles, anyway."

Cartwright nodded. "Good points. But we're directly in the path of any land based fighter and the carrier, correct? Plus, we're tied into the carrier's defense data network, right?"

Fischer slowly nodded. "Yes, sir. It's good practice for us. We can see everything that the carrier and its escorts can. If we loaded a couple of the AIM-9Xs in the stern tubes, we could be ready to use them as soon as an enemy plane is spotted."

Cartwright smiled. "Good. Let's do that."

Fischer grinned back at him. "Do you really think we could become a first sub to bag a fighter?"

Cartwright laughed. "I think the odds are pretty long against it. But it's like buying a lottery ticket - you can't win if you don't play."

Moscow, Russia

"So, what makes you think our Korean friend is headed to Sheremetyevo Terminal C at precisely this time?," asked Grishkov, looking at the scenery whipping past as Vasilyev's foot ground down on the sedan's gas pedal.

"Simple," Vasilyev replied. "We know when your captain communicated with his counterpart in Moscow. We know that the first flight available from Vladivostok to Moscow after that news could have been relayed to the target was operated by Aeroflot, and departed Vladivostok about seven hours ago. It is due to arrive in about an hour and a half at Sheremetyevo Terminal C."

"And if he is not on it?"

Vasilyev shrugged. "I have faith in his efficiency, which has been very nearly successful several times in bringing his mission to conclusion. In any case, there is another flight from Vladivostok two hours later, arriving at the same terminal."

Minutes later, Vasilyev pulled into a small parking lot directly adjacent to Sheremetyevo Terminal C, right next to a sign that said in bold red letters "Authorized vehicles only. Clearly marked authorization required!"

Vasilyev exited the unmarked vehicle, and as Grishkov eyed the sign strode towards the terminal entrance.

"Say, are you sure our car will be here when we get back?"

Vasilyev smiled, and nodded. "Things are a bit different in Moscow. No placards or marking. The guard just calls in any unfamiliar vehicle's plate. For ours, he will be told to forget he ever saw it."

Vasilyev waved his arm at the ceiling as he walked "This terminal has 430,000 square feet of floor space and the capacity to handle five million passengers a year, and so is considerably larger than either of Vladivostok's two terminals. However, it is less than a quarter of the size of Aeroflot's Terminal D, built to take in up to twelve million passengers a year. So, our target has some room to maneuver, but it could have been worse."

Grishkov nodded. "Know your environment, right?"

Instead of responding, Vasilyev veered to the left, and Grishkov followed. They passed a small, nondescript brown-haired man waiting at a baggage carousel, and then walked into the nearest restroom. Vasilyev checked to make sure it was unoccupied, and then placed a nearby "closed for maintenance" sign on the door.

A minute later, the door opened.

"Evgeny!" Vasilyev exclaimed quietly, grasping his right hand and pumping it quickly. "I can't tell you how glad I am that you are here to help us with this."

It was the small, nondescript brown-haired man they had passed at the baggage carousel. Grishkov couldn't help staring and thinking to himself, this is the highly capable agent normally reserved for the most important overseas assignments? Seeing his expression, Vasilyev laughed.

"Yes, he doesn't look like much, does he? That may be his greatest strength. Bond, James Bond, stands out in a crowd. Evgeny doesn't."

A thin smile crossed Evgeny's face quickly, and just as quickly left it. "I understand you have a weapon for me?" Nodding, Vasilyev handed him the stun gun, which quickly disappeared in Evgeny's jacket.

"Description of the target?"

"Definitely Asian, probably Korean. An experienced intelligence agent, highly dangerous, almost certainly armed. He must be captured alive, and we must not allow him to kill himself."

Evgeny nodded. "Yes, I have heard this, and that you believe you know which flight he will arrive on. However, it is likely several Asians will be on this flight. How will you identify him?"

"We believe he will identify himself by his reaction to seeing us in the corridor he must walk through to reach the terminal exit. We will pick a moment to show ourselves when there are as few people as possible in the corridor, to give you the cleanest shot. You will be on the opposite side of the corridor."

Evgeny cocked his head sideways. "Understood. You will both be ready in case I miss?"

Vasilyev laughed. "My friend, we both know that will never happen."

Evgeny smiled and shrugged, and all three left to greet the man who had made life so difficult for Vasilyev and Grishkov.

CHAPTER SIXTY SIX

On Patrol Off the Japanese Coast

Haruto Takahashi looked up at his console display, as a harsh buzz sounded in the AWACS workspace he shared with three other operators. He had programmed the sound to be discordant and attention-getting, and it had worked. Everyone nearby was staring at the display with the same amazement as Haruto.

Here is what had happened in the eighty-five seconds before the image appeared on Haruto's display.

First, a YS-11EB electronic intelligence aircraft had intercepted the message sent to the MiG-29Ks, and generated a bearing leading to possible enemy forces operating in the area. That bearing had been forwarded to Haruto's AWACS, which had directed a focused low-energy radar sweep in that direction. The sweep was successful in detecting the MiG-29Ks' location, which was then forwarded to the nearest RQ-4 Global Hawk surveillance drone.

The next step took fifty of the eighty-five seconds. The RQ-4 took multiple images of the MiG-29Ks, before selecting the best one to send to Haruto's dedicated console display, along with location and bearing data for the moment that image had been taken.

In truth, luck was with Haruto that day. Conditions for optical capture were near perfect, with low humidity, bright midday sunshine and an excellent viewing angle all cooperating with the latest Japanese optics to produce a crisp, clear image.

Haruto and the three other operators stared for several seconds in silence at the image of the two MiG-29Ks flying close enough to the surface of the Pacific to generate "rooster-tails" from their jet wash behind them.

Kaito Watanabe had been Haruto's supervisor since Haruto had first joined the AWACS crew nearly a year before. With over a decade of service behind him Kaito had not bothered to hide his skepticism of Haruto's project, though after the approval of the Ministry of Defense he had done nothing to obstruct it.

Everyone looked up as Kaito stepped into the AWACS workspace from the cockpit where he had been discussing course adjustments with the air crew.

"Haruto, I heard the alert…" Kaito's voice died away as he took in the image on the screen, complete with the software's identification of the image as Russian Navy MiG-29Ks and their position relative to the AWACS.

"What are they doing out here? How did they get out this far?," Kaito asked, as much to himself as to anyone listening.

Haruto nodded. "I was wondering the same thing. First, let me overlay other air traffic in the region on the display," he said, as he typed quickly on his keyboard. A new display replaced the image of the MiGs, which were now shown as a blinking, moving dot relative to all of the other aircraft in the region. It was immediately obvious that they were heading towards an aircraft heading nearly due east across the Pacific at high altitude.

Pointing at the aircraft that was obviously the MiGs' target, Kaito ordered "Confirm details on this flight."

All commercial aircraft carry a transponder that, when interrogated by a properly coded radio signal, will give details on the flight. The AWACS had all transponder codes for aircraft flying in the region, so that its crew could quickly focus only on potential threats. Less than thirty seconds later Haruto confirmed that the aircraft was a Trans Pacific 787 on a regularly scheduled flight from Beijing to Washington DC.

"How long before they intercept?," Kaito asked.

"They should be within missile range in about thirty-five minutes, sir," Haruto replied.

Kaito shook his head. "None of this makes any sense. Why should the Russians want to attack an American flight heading to their own country, that is flying nowhere near Russia? How did their aircraft get here so far from Russia? There is no Russian aircraft carrier operating in this area, and no refueling tanker could have flown low enough to escape our radar."

"Sir, everything you have said is true. However, I must respectfully point out that time is short if we wish to prevent this attack," Haruto said, pointing to the rapidly advancing dot representing the MiGs for emphasis.

"Yes, yes, you are of course correct," Kaito said. "What is the nearest aircraft capable of intercepting the MiGs?"

With a small smile, Haruto tapped on a dot less than a hundred miles from the MiGs. "A patrol of two American F-22s out of Kadena, sir."

Kaito grunted. "Americans to save Americans. Fitting. Radio their squadron command at Kadena, and provide them with full details."

"Yes, sir," Haruto said, quickly moving to obey Kaito's orders, which were exactly what he had expected.

"One more thing, Haruto," Kaito said.

"Yes, sir?," Haruto asked, as he continued to type.

Kaito bowed. "Congratulations. Let's hope we save some lives today."

Chapter Sixty Seven

Moscow, Russia

Kim Gun Jun wasn't simply tired. He was exhausted. Though he was in excellent physical shape, maintained by a rigorous exercise regime and a spartan diet, he had been managing this crisis on his own for days with little sleep. Though he had tried hard to at least doze on the flight from Vladivostok to Moscow, he had failed completely.

All Kim could think about were the consequences of failure. His promotion to deputy director of the RDEI had come as a direct result of his success in obtaining the nuclear device now in place in Los Angeles. The plan to do so had been his from start to finish, in every detail. He was the only one besides the RDEI director and Marshal Ko who knew both where the device had come from and where it was now. And they did not have the precise address in LA where the agent with the device was located, simply because they had no interest in knowing. Of course, he knew exactly where the agent and the device were supposed to be.

However, Kim also knew that the agent as well as the device were no longer at the assigned location, and the agent had not checked in. He planned to find out where the device was now and why the agent had moved it as soon as he finished with these two troublemakers.

Kim was well aware that security requirements for this operation dictated that he avoid lone wolf missions like the one he was undertaking now. Ordinarily, he would have already called upon the resources of North Korea's sizeable Embassy in Moscow, or as he had done in Vladivostok and Khabarovsk hire local criminals to either assist him or to carry out the mission in his place. There had simply been no time. Once he had obtained the tip from his source, he had been fortunate to secure a seat on the flight and board before its departure.

Ironically, getting one of the last available seats meant that he had been forced to fly first class. Ordinarily Kim avoided this simply because anyone in first class attracted more attention from the airplane's staff. Even if that attention was intended to be helpful, it also meant he was more likely to be remembered. In this case, though, it couldn't be helped.

The food was no doubt better than whatever was being served in coach, though Kim found little to his taste. Beet soup? Mayonnaise-based salads? Kim ate the black bread served with the meal and the pastry served for desert, and left most of the rest on his tray.

So, it was with bleary eyes and a rumbling stomach that Kim left the plane and headed towards the terminal exit. This operation could still be saved, he thought to himself. He had hours to arrange a warm reception for the two troublemakers who were threatening his career, and was lifting his cell phone to his lips to call the Embassy when he saw... Grishkov and Vasilyev. This was a trap!

But wait. They could have no idea what he looked like. If he did not react, and proceeded to the exit normally, they should not be able to distinguish him from the dozen or so other Asians walking down the corridor with him. And that assumed they even knew he was Asian.

Kim's bad luck was that both Grishkov's experience as a detective and Vasilyev's as an intelligence officer had picked up on Kim's reaction to their presence, well concealed though it was. They nodded to someone behind Kim, and the next thing he felt was an electric shock that froze all his muscles, followed by an immediate slide into darkness.

Chapter Sixty Eight

En Route to Protect Trans Pacific Flight 898

Major Mark Haskell was looking forward to the end of another uneventful patrol out of Kadena, where F-22s had been based starting in 2007. Though that same year F-22s from the 90th Fighter Squadron intercepted two Russian TU-95MS Bear-H bombers over Alaska, Haskell knew his chances of seeing enemy aircraft were slim, and that they were almost certain to be Chinese instead of Russian. After all, the Russians' closest base on Sakhalin Island was over 1,500 miles away.

At least, that's what he had always thought.

"Bravo flight, acknowledge."

Haskell frowned. He had been doing patrols out of Kadena for over a year, and had yet to be contacted by squadron command during a mission.

"Bravo flight, acknowledged. On patrol, nothing to report," Haskell said.

"Bravo flight, new orders are being transmitted to you now. Acknowledge and confirm."

Haskell read quickly through several paragraphs of text that appeared on one LCD display, while another showed the position of Haskell and his wingman relative to their new targets.

"Acknowledge receipt of new orders. Confirm that the use of deadly force is authorized if targets refuse to break off their pursuit of the Trans Pacific aircraft."

"Confirmed. You are to first intercept the targets and attempt to warn them away from the Trans Pacific aircraft. If they refuse or fail to acknowledge your communication and continue pursuit you are authorized to use deadly force to protect the Trans Pacific aircraft."

"Acknowledged. Will report after encounter with targets."

Haskell then contacted his wingman, Captain Peter Markus, who had just joined the squadron the previous month.

"Did you copy all that?," Haskell asked, as he changed course to intercept, noting with satisfaction that his wingman smoothly matched his maneuver.

"Yes, sir. How did two Russian Navy MiG-29Ks get all the way down here without anyone spotting them? For that matter, how did they get down here at all? And why are they trying to shoot down a Trans Pacific flight heading for the US?," Markus asked.

"All good questions, Peter. The answer to all of them is 'I have no idea.' The only thing I know for sure is that we have to stop them, and we're the only chance the passengers and crew on that Trans Pacific flight have got," Haskell replied.

"Yes, sir. We can only guess at the range of whatever those MiGs are carrying, but by my calculation supercruise should get us to intercept before they'll be able to fire on the flight. Since AWACS sees no active radar switched on the MiGs and they're only using passive detectors, our stealth capabilities should put us on top of them before they know what happened," Markus said.

"I hope you're right. It's finally time to see if the American taxpayer got his billion worth," Haskell replied.

"Roger that, sir," Markus said, with a short chuckle.

Haskell's comment was a reference to a General Accounting Office estimate that each of the US Air Force's F-22s cost $412 million, a calculation made in 2012 after the delivery of the 195th and final F-22, of which eight were test and 187 were operational aircraft. Including a $100 million per aircraft "structures retrofit program," the total F-22 price tag was about half a billion dollars. So, each two-plane F-22 patrol represented an investment of about a billion dollars, a fact well known to all F-22 pilots.

Markus' reference to "supercruise" was the F-22's unique ability to fly well above the speed of sound, in fact at Mach 1.82, or 1,220 mph, without afterburner. By contrast on afterburner at normal cruising altitude the MiG-29Ks could fly at about Mach 2, or 1,370 mph, and had in fact done so while still in Chinese airspace as they burned through their first two drop tanks. Now, though, they were quite a bit slower, since their maximum speed at low altitude was only Mach 1.2, or 870 mph. If the

Trans Pacific flight had not encountered significant headwinds at altitude from the storm system it was now skirting, the MiGs might not have been able to catch it at all.

The other feature Markus referred to, stealth capability, accounted for a good chunk of the F-22's half-billion cost. Radar signature reduction steps included airframe shaping such as planform alignment of edges, fixed geometry serpentine inlets to prevent line-of-sight of the engine faces from exterior view, using radar absorbent material, and minimizing the exposure of elements such as hinges and pilot helmets that could provide a radar return.

The payoff for all these steps was highly classified, but one project engineer was on record estimating that the radar return on the F-22 was the same as a "steel marble." Haskell wasn't sure whether that was accurate, but had racked up a lopsided score in exercises against F-16 and F-18 pilots, who in after action reports had ruefully admitted they never saw the plane that "killed" them.

Still, Haskell thought to himself, exercises were one thing but reality often another. They had never run exercises against MiG-29Ks, and had no real idea of their capabilities. They could also be sure that the Russians would send only their best pilots on a mission like this.

Yes, Haskell nodded, he'd bet his skills and his F-22 against anyone. He just had to remember the words of his first flight instructor- "Never underestimate your enemy, or think you know what he'll do. Keep your eyes open and your brain engaged, and you may live to come back here and teach someday."

Haskell nodded again. That actually sounded pretty good.

CHAPTER SIXTY NINE

Tunnel No. 1, North Korea

Lee Ho Suk paled as he saw the deep cracks in the tunnel walls, and earth drifting down from the walls to the tunnel floor in thin, dusty clouds. No, this can't be, he thought. Lee had scouted ahead just a few hours before, and this made no sense...

No sooner had he started the thought than he shut it down. Understanding wasn't what was needed here. Action was.

Lee ran to the train driver's cabin, and threw open the outer door. At the same time he leaped inside, Lee yelled, "30 kph!" To his credit, the driver did not hesitate, and with a smoothness that surprised Lee the train surged forward. Seconds later the door connecting the driver's cabin to the rest of the train flew open, admitting a scowling Captain Yoon.

"Why have we increased speed?," Yoon asked, looking at Lee with obvious concern.

Lee was staring out the window at the tunnel walls, trying and failing to see whether the deep cracks he had spotted were continuing. At the speed they were going, his eyes simply couldn't focus fast enough. Without turning, Lee replied to Yoon. "I'm trying to outrun the tunnel collapse that's coming. It may not work, but I know we'd have been buried for sure if we'd stayed."

"What made you think..." was all Yoon had time to say before they could all feel as much as hear a deep rumbling. Lee said calmly, "50 kph."

It felt as if the train was flying, though in a car above ground the speed would have seemed slow.

After about fifteen seconds, the rumbling slowed, and then stopped. Lee gently lowered his right hand, and the driver eased the train to a stop. Lee nodded approvingly, and left the train, with Yoon following right behind. They walked together to the end of the train, and looked behind them. All they could see was a distant cloud of dust. To Lee's relief, it did not appear to be moving towards them.

Lee turned to Yoon and said quietly, "I suggest, Captain, that you try to use your radio to see if anyone can tell us how bad the collapse is, and how long it will take to dig through it."

Yoon had been transfixed, staring down the tunnel at the distant dust cloud. "Good idea," he growled, straightening himself as he raised the radio up to his mouth. After several tries, he clipped it back onto his belt in disgust. "Nothing but static," Yoon said, shaking his head.

Lee had been examining the tunnel walls, and nodded with satisfaction. "Well, we're in luck. The collapse doesn't seem to have affected this section of the tunnel. We can still move forward."

Yoon nodded absently, obviously thinking about something else. "How long before we reach the end of this tunnel?," he asked.

Frowning, Lee peered ahead, and then said, "I can tell you in a moment, Captain." With that, he walked slowly forward about ten meters, and then returned.

"The good news is that our sprint forward has taken us to less than a kilometer from the end of the tunnel," Lee said.

Nodding impatiently, Yoon asked, "And the bad news?"

Lee shrugged. "Well, first off, we will have to make do with the bracing materials we have on the train. We may be able to stretch those out to cover two more weak stretches, but no more. The other obvious problem is that we can't rely on resupply, since the scale of that collapse means it will be days or even weeks before they can break through to us."

Yoon gestured dismissively. "All of my men are carrying food and water, and the last car is a supply car with additional stores. We can stretch those out for weeks if necessary."

Shaking his head, Lee said, "I'm sorry, Captain, but I wasn't finished. None of those issues are our biggest problem. I can only guess, but I doubt that we have more than two days of air left on this side of the tunnel. Since no rescue crew can possibly get to us in that time, we have to break through to the other tunnel by then."

Yoon frowned. "My orders specified that we were to proceed to the end of the tunnel, and wait for further instructions."

Lee just stared at him. "The air in this tunnel doesn't care about your orders. If we wait until it runs out we'll all die, and then your mission is sure to fail."

Yoon shook his head. "No, I do have additional sealed, written orders to be opened only in case of emergency."

Lee said nothing, but just smiled.

Yoon nodded. "Yes. This obviously qualifies."

CHAPTER SEVENTY

Pyongyang, North Korea

Shin Yon Young's luck was both good and bad. The good was that if it had been summer, decomposition from the guard's body would have prompted calls from his neighbors to the police within one to two days. Shin's training had helped him there, by prompting him to wrap the body in a sheet to contain the smell to the extent possible. The guard's body, though, did not have time to betray him. That was good luck indeed, and accounted for Shin's success in getting as far south as he did before a warrant was issued for his arrest.

The bad was that the guard's supervisor was both alert and intelligent. Guard service in North Korea was neither high status nor high paid, with the result that even supervisors in the guard force were often not particularly capable. Sunshine's supervisor, however, was an exception. What was not a surprise was that someone like Guard Captain Yeong Su Lee had been assigned to duty at the Personal Secretariat building.

"Captain Yeong! The missing guard has still not been located!"

Yeong scowled at the trembling Guard Lieutenant standing at attention before him.

"You have searched his apartment, questioned his friends and neighbors, and checked hospital, police, and mortuary records." Yeong did not ask this as a question, but rather as a statement he expected to be quickly confirmed. He was not disappointed.

The guard's head quickly bobbed up and down. "Yes, Captain, we have taken all of those steps. There is no trace of the missing guard, and nobody has any idea of where he is."

Yeong nodded, and then leaned back in his chair. He had not previously given this matter much thought, having expected the usual methods to reveal the missing guard's whereabouts, as they almost always did.

"Is any other employee missing from the Personal Secretariat building?" Yeong asked.

"Sir?," the guard asked, clearly confused.

"Lieutenant, our normal steps to locate the guard have failed. We must now check other possibilities. Go to the Personnel Office and ask them whether any other employees in this building have failed to report to work. If so, check them out as thoroughly as you did the missing guard. Their disappearance at the same time may be a coincidence. More likely, it will not be."

Now that he understood what he was doing and why he was doing it, the guard immediately saluted. "Yes, sir! At once, sir!" He left the office so quickly Yeong had to grab a letter to keep it from flying off his desk in the draft caused by the opening and closing door.

Yeong sighed and shook his head. It was hard to remember being that young and enthusiastic. Still, he was sure the lieutenant would carry out his orders within a matter of hours. With luck, then he would know just where this troublesome guard was, and what should be done about him.

En Route to North Korean Coast

Shin Yon Young had made good time towards Haeju since leaving the farmer's shed, and thought there was at least a chance his remaining gas would be enough to get him to the pickup point. After the crush of military traffic in and around Pyongyang, the road he was on now was eerily empty. It had been over two hours since he had even seen a checkpoint.

After giving it some thought, Shin decided to risk powering up the satellite phone to see if he had any hope of connecting to the nearest South Korean cell phone network. The risk wasn't so much detection out here in the countryside as it was running down the battery. But once he had turned it on and looked at the display, he could see that the battery, at least, was in good shape. It didn't surprise him that no bars had yet appeared on the display for a network connection. He was close to home, but not quite close enough.

Shin knew how dangerous optimism was for an agent, particularly one fleeing a manhunt. But he couldn't help grinning to himself as he thought, I'm actually going to make it home!

CHAPTER SEVENTY ONE

Los Angeles

Chung Hee Moon's eyes slowly opened to reveal the clinic's recovery room, well lit by buzzing florescent lights. After a few moments, the room stopped spinning and he could see that Kang Ji Yeong was sitting in a chair next to the bed where he was laying on his side.

Kang smiled and asked, "How are you feeling?"

Chung did his best to smile back. "A little dizzy, but fine otherwise."

Kang nodded. "That's normal, of course. It's why someone has to come with you for the procedure. You aren't allowed to drive until tomorrow." She bowed her head. "I would have come with you anyway."

Chung nodded gravely. "Thank you. I appreciate everything you are doing for me."

Kang just waved her hands absently.

Chung frowned. "How long do you think it will be before the test results come back?" *And I can establish my alibi for my departure in the near future,* he added to himself.

Kang shrugged. "Not long. We should see the doctor very soon."

On cue, the white-coated doctor walked in who had administered Chung's colonoscopy. To Chung's confusion, he was smiling broadly.

"I have excellent news. I have examined you very thoroughly following the lab tests we ran last week, and I can say without a doubt that your cancer is in complete remission. In fact, I can find no trace that you ever had cancer at all."

Chung sat bolt upright, as the greatest shock he had ever experienced passed through his body like an electric current. "Are you absolutely sure, doctor? The doctors in Korea told me that not only did I have colon cancer, it was also incurable."

The doctor nodded. "I understand your surprise. There are two possibilities. One is that their diagnosis was simply wrong, which could have been due to a wide range of possibilities, such as mixed-up lab samples. The other is that you went into total remission, which is uncommon but not unknown. There are documented cases where the body has been able to fight off cancer on its own, without any external help from drugs or chemotherapy. The fact that your physical fitness is excellent would help to support that conclusion. Either way, I make my diagnosis with no hesitation or doubt- you do not have colon or any other type of cancer. I would, though, like to see you back here in three months for follow up, just in case."

Chung nodded, still dazed. "Thank you, doctor. I will certainly do so."

"Well, it's not every day I get to deliver such positive news. I hope this will be a good omen for the rest of this day." Still smiling, the doctor went on to his next patient.

Kang reached over to Chung's hand, and gave it a quick squeeze. "I am very happy for you."

"Thank you. I still have trouble believing it."

Kang looked at Chung levelly. "I am glad I was here to see your reaction. If I hadn't seen how surprised you were when you got the news from the doctor, I might have thought you had invented the whole business."

Chung flushed with embarrassment and anger. "And why would I do such a terrible thing?"

Kang regarded Chung for a few seconds, and then shook her head and smiled. "You'd be surprised at the lengths some men would go to just to exit a relationship gracefully. Don't be angry though – I believe you really did think you were sick."

Chung nodded and said stiffly, "Thank you for that."

Kang shook her head again. "I thought medicine had advanced farther back home. I'm really surprised they could have been so completely wrong in their diagnosis."

"Well, you heard what the doctor said. He seemed to think it was more likely that my body was able to beat back the cancer on its own."

Kang looked thoughtful for a moment and then shrugged. "Maybe. It does happen, though a lot less often than we'd like. We're probably better off being thankful and moving on than wasting time trying to understand what happened."

Chung forced a smile. "Now, we are in complete agreement."

However, this had nothing to do with what Chung was actually thinking. Instead, Chung was evaluating two sets of facts. The first was that Kang and her doctor friend took it for granted that before making a colon cancer diagnosis the patient would have a colonoscopy, not just a blood test as he had. He might have dismissed that as due to the relatively primitive state of medical care in North Korea, except that he thought it was very unlikely that a soldier would be sent on a mission of such importance without his superiors being sure he was physically capable of seeing it through.

Chung had thought the blood test he took at the military hospital back home had given them all the information they would need to make that decision. Now it appeared that was not the case.

So, if he had never had cancer, why lie to him about it? The answer there was simple – to make sure he detonated the device, even though he would not have sufficient time to escape the blast. Chung had no trouble picturing his superiors doubting his resolve, and making up a reason for him to embrace a quick death. And he had to admit to himself that instant death in a nuclear fireball did strike him as very preferable to months of suffering.

That left one final question – why him? The answer there was obvious. The fact that both of his parents had died of cancer accomplished two goals at once. First, it made him more willing to accept without question that he had cancer, since everyone knew that the genes for the illness were often passed down to the next generation. Second, they knew that he had helped to care for both of his parents during the final stages of the disease, since those were the only times he had requested leave of more than a few days during his entire career. Once they reviewed his record, his superiors must have concluded he was perfect for the task at hand.

Oddly, that was what bothered him the most, he decided. A soldier's willingness to die could always be doubted. Chung believed he had proved himself at least as much as any other soldier, but he could accept his superiors wanting to be completely sure he would go through with the mission. But picking him because they thought he would want to avoid his parents' suffering made him feel unclean. Chung wasn't sure of the right word to use. Exploited? Violated?

Chung was sure of only one thing. He would have to think more about his superiors, the lie they had told him, and what if anything he was going to do about it.

CHAPTER SEVENTY TWO

Tunnel No. 1, North Korea

The train had continued moving slowly forward for the past hour, and Lee Ho Suk could do nothing but wonder what was in Captain Yoon's orders. He doubted that even the military would command its troops to passively suffocate, but nobody grew up in North Korea without developing an almost unlimited capacity to believe in human stupidity.

Finally, Lee saw Yoon moving towards him, and they stood examining the tunnel walls together.

Yoon gestured towards the wall in front of them. "Do you see any signs that the collapse has affected this section?"

Lee shook his head. "No. We have been lucky so far. If our good fortune holds, we should make it to the end of the tunnel in time. I have also confirmed that by then the work crew there will have the tunnel complete and the charges set, and be ready for the breakthrough. If, that is, your orders allow it." That last part Lee said as neutrally as he could, and with his gaze firmly fixed on the tunnel wall.

Yoon nodded. "It's about time I had some good news. In return I will give you some. My written orders specify that I am to carry out the breakthrough and complete our mission if for any reason I am cut off from communication for twenty-four hours. At our current rate, we will be ready well before then, correct?"

Lee hesitated, but then slowly nodded. "Yes. But that actually makes another issue I was going to raise even more awkward."

Yoon gestured impatiently. "Yes, yes. What is this new problem?"

Lee lowered his voice. "There are over two dozen men ahead at the end of the tunnel. Some are prisoners, some are guards, some are miners, and a few are explosives technicians. The plan had been that once the tunnel was finished and the charges were set, they would leave the area. But..."

"Now they can't," Yoon finished for him.

Lee nodded. "So the question is..."

Yoon frowned and finished for him again. "What do I do with them?"

En Route to Protect Trans Pacific Flight 898

So far, it could hardly have gone better, Major Mark Haskell thought. He and his wingman were now within missile range of both MiG-29Ks, and there was no hint that the MiGs had spotted their pursuers. Now a single coded command to his wingman would set a series of actions in motion they had practiced dozens of times in exercises and simulations.

The pilots of both F-22s readied their AIM-9X Block II Sidewinder missiles for firing. With development starting in 2008, this Sidewinder variant provided yet another upgrade to a missile first fielded in the 1950s. Ironically, one of its new features was that it could be fired from an internal bay without first locking onto its target.

Ironic, because today Haskell and Markus would announce their presence by locking their missiles, as well as opening their weapons bays and dramatically increasing their radar cross section. At the same moment, Haskell keyed the radio transmit switch to the international emergency frequency monitored by all aircraft.

"Unidentified Russian Navy aircraft at my 12 o'clock. You have been tracked in hostile pursuit of a United States commercial aircraft. Lower your gear immediately and slowly turn right 90 degrees to break off your pursuit. If you disobey this order, you will be destroyed by the United States Air Force fighters at your 6 o'clock. This warning will not be repeated."

Major Ma was jolted by the simultaneous activation of every warning system on his MiG, just as they finally came within launch range to attack their target. A bit late, he thought acidly, while the voice of the American pilot behind him ordered him to abandon his mission. English language instruction was a routine part of pilot training, since English was the language of international air traffic control. Nice to see that at least some of his training was being put to use, Ma thought bitterly.

Though the sudden appearance of American fighters was a surprise, Ma knew exactly how it had happened. All Chinese pilots had been briefed on American stealth technology. Well, the Americans weren't the only ones who could pull surprises.

For this high-priority mission, their planes had been equipped with their only R-76s featuring the latest avionic upgrade devised by the Russians - a fire and forget capability that did not require advance lock on. Unlike similar American missiles that depended on subsequent target guidance from the firing aircraft, these missiles would simply attack whatever aircraft was in front of their radar seeker head. It was a design that the Americans, with their worries about friendly fire and civilian casualties, would have never used.

Today, though, it was a design that would allow him to complete his mission.

Ma did not think for even a second of complying with the American's demands. In part this was because he was determined to carry out his orders. In part it was that he knew the consequences for his family of failure and capture by the Americans, when he knew how important it was to have this attack blamed on the Russians.

Besides all that, Ma also knew that if a Chinese sub were in these waters it would certainly not surface with American fighters in the area, even if by some miracle they could escape pursuit.

No, if it was Ma's time to die, it would be with one final success to add to his many others.

Ma might have felt better had he known that there had never been a Chinese sub anywhere near. Then again, perhaps not.

Major Haskell stared in disbelief as both of the lead Russian pilot's missiles fired. At the same moment, his display advised that the other plane was attempting to fire on the Trans Pacific flight.

"Fox One," he called, hearing Marcus repeat the call as they each fired AA-9X missiles at their targets. The MiGs had no time to even attempt escape. In seconds both MiGs were expanding clouds of smoke and debris, that Haskell and Markus had to maneuver quickly to evade.

That left the two R-76s still heading towards the Trans Pacific flight, now flying at the same altitude about thirty feet apart and accelerating rapidly.

"You take right, I'll take left," Haskell said.

"Copy," Markus said tersely.

In fact, Markus' destruction of his targeted missile was nearly textbook perfect. The R-76 was still well within range of his AIM-120 AMRAAM missile, and he locked onto it without difficulty. Less than a minute later, the R-76 missile was no longer a threat to the Trans Pacific flight.

However, though much smaller than the MiG-29K debris field Markus had just successfully avoided, the R-76's remains were consciously designed to cause maximum damage to any nearby aircraft. And, Markus' sharp turn away from the destroyed missile almost avoided damage to his aircraft.

Almost.

The missile fragment that was sucked into the F-22's jet turbine would ordinarily have been too small to cause extensive damage. The Pratt and Whitney F-119 turbofan engine was designed to withstand contact with a small amount of debris, such as fragments from the MiGs' explosions. No engine, though, could have survived the shaped and hardened R-76 fragment. It did exactly what it was designed to do.

Markus' training saved his life. By quickly shutting down the wounded engine, he prevented an explosion that could have led to the catastrophic destruction of his aircraft. Even a successful ejection would have been problematic, given the length of time he would have had to survive mid-Pacific before a rescue helicopter could arrive.

As it was, Markus could try to limp back to Kadena on his remaining undamaged engine.

"Return to base. I'll get the other one," Haskell said.

"Copy," Markus replied, as he focused all his attention on keeping his damaged plane in the air.

Haskell had also had to maneuver to escape the destroyed missile's debris, but a quick look at his instruments reassured him that he had avoided damage. Haskell was now too far away for a lock on his target missile, but hit his afterburners to close the range. Within a few minutes he had the missile back in sight and locked. Haskell hit the trigger - and to his horror a warning tone and a flashing red box advised him that the door to his missile launch bay had malfunctioned. He correctly guessed that the failure was due to the debris from the R-76 explosion.

Grimly, Haskell realized he only had one chance to stop the remaining R-76, his M61A2 Vulcan 20mm cannon. Since he had only 480 rounds for a cannon firing 6,000 rounds per minute, Haskell would have a total of just twelve and a half seconds to hit his target. Even worse, to have any chance of hitting the missile he would have to close to a range where damage from its debris - if he managed to destroy it - was practically guaranteed.

Haskell moved his throttle forward as far as it would go.

CHAPTER SEVENTY THREE

Moscow, Russia

"So we have him. Now how do we get the truth out of him?"

Both Grishkov and Vasilyev were looking through a one-way mirror at Kim Gun Jun strapped to a table in an interrogation room in one of the Lubyanka's prison floors, though they didn't yet know that was his name. In fact, Kim was still unconscious, though he was breathing normally and the doctors who had examined him had said he could be revived soon.

A fake tooth containing a poison no doubt designed to provide Kim a quick death had been extracted minutes after his arrival at Lubyanka.

Vasilyev looked at Grishkov and shrugged. "I have given that much thought. I think we will try drugs first."

Grishkov nodded. "I had the same thought. We have used them on occasion in very high priority cases where obtaining information quickly was vital, such as kidnappings. However, for us they are not always successful."

Vasilyev smiled thinly. "Nor for us. What do you use?"

Grishkov pursed his lips. "I am no expert, but I think we normally use scopolamine."

Vasilyev laughed. "Ah, the original 'truth serum.' Do you know where its use started?"

Grishkov shook his head.

"It was first used in interrogation in 1922 by a Dallas, Texas, obstetrician. He had used the drug to help sedate women in childbirth, and noticed that they often made surprisingly candid statements while under scopolamine's influence. He somehow arranged to administer the drug to two prisoners being held in a local jail who were thought to be definitely guilty. Both protested their innocence at length while under the drug's influence, and upon trial both were acquitted. The good doctor subsequently enjoyed national success, published numerous articles, and became known as the 'father of truth serum'."

Grishkov nodded. "But…"

"Yes. But. It turned out that scopolamine's side effects, including hallucinations, headache, rapid heartbeat, and blurred vision made for difficult interviews, particularly since those effects far outlast the psychological relaxation that sometimes provides candid statements. Even more annoying is the painfully dry mouth brought on by the drug, which is not exactly helpful when we want a talkative prisoner."

Grishkov shrugged. "Yes, as I said I'd heard it didn't always work. What are the alternatives?"

"Most of our chemical interrogations use barbiturates, either singly or in combination. The three principle varieties are sodium amytal, pentothal sodium, and seconal. All have a calming and sedating effect, and we have found that resistance to interrogation is reduced in nearly all subjects. However, it is a matter of trial and error to find the correct dosage, and particularly with a trained intelligence officer we may still expect difficulty in obtaining the information we seek."

Grishkov frowned. "And if drugs don't work?"

Vasilyev sighed. "There are two principle alternatives. The first is sensory deprivation. It is quite effective, but takes more time than we may have, and even though subjects are closely monitored there have been cases of cardiac arrest. The second is direct physical pressure, which has obvious limitations and risks."

Grishkov shook his head. "Normally I am strongly opposed to everything we are about to do to this man, and even his attempt to both kill me and kidnap my family would not change my mind. But he is our only chance to stop the detonation of a nuclear device that will kill an unimaginable number of people. And it is our weapon – whoever is the target will be certain to retaliate against Russia. If that target is the United States, it could even mean the world war we thought we had finally avoided."

Vasilyev spread his hands. "You do not need to remind me what is at stake. We will do what is necessary. And besides, it is not as though there is any question of what will happen to this agent after we complete his interrogation. Not only is he a spy who has stolen one of our nuclear devices,

Russian citizens have died at this man's hand. He deserves death many times over."

Grishkov nodded agreement. "On that point there can be no doubt. When will we begin the interrogation?"

Vasilyev's eyebrows raised high with astonishment. "For a matter of this importance, neither of us will be allowed involvement with that process. In fact, we may never be told what they discover, if anything."

Grishkov felt a combination of anger and frustration so strong it threatened to shake him apart. "But this man tried to kill me and kidnap my family! This case has been ours from the beginning!"

Vasilyev shrugged. "So, the outcome may be neither fair nor right. Even in law enforcement I am sure you have seen this. In matters of national security, it is even more common."

Both men stared through the mirror as technicians began to hook up Kim to an IV drip. With luck, the answers to their questions would soon be known, though perhaps they would never hear them.

Chapter Seventy Four

Los Angeles

Chung Hee Moon sighed as he looked down at the remains of his breakfast, while Kang busied herself in the kitchen. Spending time with Kang Ji Yeong had been pleasant in many ways, but being with her was like creeping through a minefield. Any wrong move might end his mission. He resolved again to leave as soon as he was sure the attention from that thrice - cursed online video had died down. Chung wasn't sure why, but his instincts told him someone was still looking for him.

More because he wanted a conversation on a safe topic than from genuine curiosity he asked Kang, "What's in the bag?". The plastic shopping bag contained a small cardboard box with a round plastic ball in its center, with its front covered in a clear sheet of plastic holding the ball in place.

Kang made a face. "My headache for today. I'm going to try again to return this security camera. I'm surprised you didn't recognize it - they're all over the place back home."

OK, Chung thought to himself with annoyance, not such a safe topic. He was careful, though, not to let the annoyance reach his face. "Of course I know what it is. I meant I didn't understand why it's still in the bag."

Kang shrugged. "Well, I did get as far as taking the box out of the bag, and into the hallway. I was holding the box up in different places to try to decide where to put it when Park saw me."

Chung nodded. "And he had some objection?"

Kang sighed. "Did he ever. First he said I had no right to use the building's electricity. When I told him it runs on a battery, he said he didn't want to trip on its wires. When I told him it was wireless, then he got really mad. Said he didn't want it spying on him any time he walked out his door, and that if I installed it he'd report me to building management. I honestly don't think they'd care, but I just don't need the grief."

Chung cocked an eyebrow and asked, "Why did you say you were going to return it again? Was there a problem when you tried to return it before?"

Kang nodded glumly. "I dealt with a clerk at the store who insisted I'd opened the box and resealed it, violating their return policy for electronics, even though I really never did. I was on my way to work, so I didn't have time to deal with his manager. Today, though, I do."

Chung stood up and brought his breakfast dishes to the sink, where without conscious thought he washed, dried and put them away. Lost in thought, it was only after a moment that he became aware of Kang looking at him thoughtfully.

Puzzled, in spite of himself Chung asked, "What is it?"

Kang laughed and said, "You're the only man I've ever seen clean up after himself. Not that I've had so many men in my kitchen," she said, blushing furiously, "but Korean men are famous for never going anywhere near a sink."

Chung had an answer ready for this, at least. "You said you never knew anyone in the Army, only the Navy. Well, I don't know how they do things on ships, but in the Army you get meals two ways. In an Army mess - and I don't know why in English they say that instead of cafeteria - you give your dirty dishes to the men who have the duty to clean them. That's not you."

Intent on his explanation, Chung didn't notice Kang's soft intake of breath at his last statement.

"In the field, you clean after yourself, and you do it quickly and quietly without leaving a trace that might be noticed by the enemy." Shrugging, Chung added, "It's the only way I know how."

Kang stepped closer to Chung, her eyes shining. "So, it's not my duty to clean your dishes?"

Chung shook his head, confused by her reaction. "No, I just said it's not."

Kang nodded, smiled, and held both of Chung's hands. She then said in a low voice, "I don't have to go to the store right away."

CHAPTER SEVENTY FIVE

Tunnel No. 1, North Korea

Lee Ho Suk sighed with relief as the train pulled around the last turn in the tunnel before its end. Blazing lights, dust, and workers rushing in several directions at once revealed exactly the chaos that Lee had expected to see.

Turning to Captain Yoon, Lee said "I will check on their progress," and then jumped from the train.

After a few minutes, Lee was able to find the foreman Mun, who was talking to a prisoner holding a length of bracing material. As Lee walked up to him, Mun gestured dismissively to the prisoner, who hurried off.

"So, Mun, I thought by now all the work would be done," Lee said, looking around at the continued frantic activity. Mun shrugged, and then nodded. "The tunnel is finished, and the charges are set. However, there is the small detail that anyone not on that train has nowhere to go, and the remaining air won't last much longer. The only constructive thing I could think of to do was using our remaining bracing materials to try to keep the whole tunnel from immediately collapsing when you set off the charge to break through to the other tunnel."

"Good thinking!," Lee said, nodding approvingly. "That should give everyone a fighting chance."

"Well, maybe," Mun said, dubiously. "We'll run out of air in a matter of hours. How long before those charges are set off? Captain Yoon isn't just going to park here and have us all suffocate, is he?"

Lee shook his head. "No. He's setting off the charges within the next few hours. Once the tunnels are joined, at least whoever survives the explosion should have air to breathe."

Mun smiled bleakly. "That is, if the tunnel on this side doesn't collapse completely."

Lee simply nodded in agreement.

Mun frowned. "So, what is Captain Yoon's plan? Has he told you?"

Lee shook his head. "No. I don't think he knows himself, or at least he didn't before we got here. Once I tell him the status here, though, I think you'll find out where you stand pretty quickly. Yoon may have his faults, but I don't think indecision is one of them."

Mun grunted. "Good. Whatever our fate is to be, I would like to know it sooner rather than later. We have all worked very hard for a very long time. One way or another, I have a feeling that now we will be able to rest."

Pyongyang, North Korea

The encrypted cell phone sitting in a charger on top of Guard Captain Yeong Su Lee's desk almost never rang. In fact, in the three months since he had received it the phone had only rung twice. There was a good reason for this. Only one other person had such a phone, and he had given that person instructions to use it only for urgent official business. If either phone broke, Yeong had a pessimistic view of how quickly, if at all, it would be replaced.

On the plus side, when the phone did ring as it just had, he knew exactly who would be calling.

"Yes, Lieutenant? Have you located the missing guard?"

"Yes, Captain! He is dead!"

Yeong grimaced. This was news both unexpected and unwelcome, for many reasons.

"Where are you now, Lieutenant?"

"At the apartment of a Personal Secretariat janitor named Shin Yon Young. You were right, Captain. He was the only other employee in the building who had failed to report to work. I came straight to his apartment, to find the missing guard dead in the living room, and no trace of Shin Yon Young."

"What steps have you taken so far, Lieutenant?"

"I have issued a nationwide, high-priority arrest warrant for Shin Yon Young on suspicion of murder. I have questioned his neighbors and the apartment building manager. All say they heard nothing suspicious, and had no reason to believe Shin Yon Young was a criminal. I have also called for a forensics team and medical examiner."

"Lieutenant, you have done well."

Yeong paused to allow the lieutenant to take in the compliment, which from the stunned silence on the other end of the line appeared to have been a good idea. In Yeong's view praise, to be truly effective as a motivator, had to be doled out sparingly. He did not recall having praised this lieutenant before, but in this case it was warranted. His initial steps were exactly what he would have done.

"Describe the scene, Lieutenant."

"The guard appears to have died as the result of multiple blows, in particular one to the head which matches blood and hair on the concrete kitchen counter. There are many indications of a violent struggle. It appears to have been hand to hand, since there were no weapons recovered at the scene, and the only bleeding appears to have been from blows, not the larger quantities to be expected from gunshot wounds or from edged weapons."

"Have you recovered any evidence or discovered any material that might give us a starting place to look for the suspect?"

"Captain, only one thing about the scene makes me think that this is more than a personal dispute of some kind. The guard's body was wrapped in a sheet."

Yeong felt as though an electric current had passed through him.

"Explain the significance of that, Lieutenant."

"The only reason to wrap the body in a sheet was to prevent the smell of decomposition reaching the neighbors, who would then have called the police. If this had been a personal dispute of some kind with an ordinary janitor, it seems to me unlikely the killer would have had the presence of mind to take the time to wrap the body in a sheet. Instead, a typical janitor would have fled in panic, at most closing the door behind him."

"You are correct, Lieutenant. Did you find any ID papers on the guard?"

"No. I have already added the guard's identity to the nationwide arrest warrant for Shin Yon Young, in case he is attempting to use the guard's ID papers to make his escape."

"Good, Lieutenant. Did the guard own a vehicle?"

"Yes, a scooter, but we have been unable to locate it. I have already sent out a notice separately on the scooter, and also linked it to the arrest warrant for Shin Yon Young."

"Well done, Lieutenant. Also, send men immediately to Shin's home village, with instructions to question his parents and any other relatives, as well as officials at all schools he attended."

"Yes, Captain. What do you expect them to find?"

"Give your men no preconceived ideas, Lieutenant. Otherwise, they will tend to confirm whatever you tell them. However, I will tell you that I suspect nobody will be found who is able to confirm Shin's existence."

A long silence followed Yeong's statement.

"But Captain, surely Shin's background was checked before he came to work at the Personal Secretariat."

"Yes, Lieutenant, it would have been. But that would have been just a records check. Pull Shin's file, and arrest whichever clerk signed off on his clearance. Also, arrest the clerk's spouse, parents and children. I will question this clerk personally, as soon as your men report back on what they find at Shin's home village."

"At once, sir. You will have my report shortly."

Yeong trained his men to hang up once they were done speaking, and to waste no time on either pleasantries or normal communications protocols. He was pleased to see that in this as in other matters, the lieutenant recalled his training.

An icy chill ran down Yeong's back as he thought about what the sheet-wrapped body of the guard meant. Dead was bad enough. Killed by a cleared Personal Secretariat employee was worse. Murdered by someone either smart enough – or well trained enough – to wrap the body in a sheet and use his papers and transport to escape strongly suggested a spy.

Unless he caught Shin Yon Young very soon, Captain Yeong realized that his career was likely to come to a quick and inglorious end.

CHAPTER SEVENTY SIX

En Route to Protect Trans Pacific Flight 898

As Major Mark Haskell continued to squeeze every bit of speed he could from his F-22, he went over in his head everything he could remember about his cannon, a weapon that in modern air combat saw hardly any use. He knew that it used the standard round for US Navy and Air Force aircraft, the PGU-28/B. The round was designed to reduce in-flight drag, with a speed of over a thousand meters per second. The PGU-28/B is an armor piercing high explosive (HE) round containing an incendiary charge in the nose that sets off the HE behind it with a slight delay to increase damage. As a final touch, a zirconium pellet at the bottom of the HE charge increases fire damage from each round.

Haskell also knew that he had computer assistance available to help him put those rounds on target. However, experience in exercises had taught him that the graphic on his Heads Up Display (HUD) was only useful as a guide. There were just too many variables for the computer to track, and in the end it was instinct that separated high and low cannon scores on the test range. Haskell's self confidence was not helped by the knowledge that his cannon scores had been average at best and, except for one hit on a practice drone, against ground targets. He had genuinely believed he would never fire his cannon in combat.

Haskell's HUD was now telling him that he was almost in range of the missile. He knew he would only have one or two chances at destroying it, both because he only had seconds to fire his cannon before running out of ammo and because the missile would soon outrun his F-22. Like any air to air missile, it not only built speed and momentum over time, it also went faster as the weight of its fuel went down.

And that was not his only problem, Haskell realized. There was a straightforward tradeoff to make between the likelihood of successfully destroying the missile and surviving its explosion. His wingman had already taken damage while stopping the other missile, but Haskell would have to get closer.

A lot closer.

There was really no choice, Haskell decided. Over two hundred passengers and crew would be on a typical 787 flight. If he had to sacrifice himself and his plane, so be it.

Haskell closed until he was sure he could hit the missile, and saw from his HUD that he was just in time. Within a few seconds, the missile would have begun to outrun him.

Haskell smiled to himself as the missile was perfectly centered in his gunsight. His finger began to squeeze - but before he could complete the motion, the R-76 disappeared! Haskell's head swiveled as he tried to find it, and precious seconds went by before he was able to locate it again. Fortunately, its maneuvering had cost it speed, so Haskell was able to line up for another shot while he thought about what had just happened.

Haskell realized, correctly, that he had just seen a demonstration of a concept never previously incorporated in a missile. A proximity sensor, linked to software that had the missile carry out evasive maneuvers once an aircraft was detected behind it. It would have saved the missile from most attacking fighters, but maybe not one with the F-22's speed and agility.

There were now three variables Haskell had to calculate. His rate of closure with the missile. The range he could reach with the best chance of hitting the missile without setting off its proximity sensor. The number of seconds left before he ran out of ammo.

His first attempt was a failure that cost him half of his ammunition, as he misjudged the sensitivity of the R-76s' proximity sensor. Cursing as it veered away, Haskell reacquired the missile and forced himself to calm and focus by reminding himself of what was at stake. This time his plan was to stay at the edge of the cannon's range, center the missile in his gunsight, and squeeze the trigger until he was out of ammo.

It worked on what must have been one of the last rounds, because the missile exploded just as his trigger clicked on empty. Haskell then maneuvered the F-22 as quickly as he could from the debris field.

Unfortunately, he had even less luck than his wingman.

Haskell immediately lost one of his two engines, his primary navigation system, and his cockpit radio transmitter. Normally, this would have left him unable to call for assistance. A recent avionics upgrade, though, had given him a chance at survival. Sardonically called "Fighter Onstar" after the General Motors feature, it automatically sent out a distress signal on a discrete encrypted frequency.

One reason most pilots thought little of the feature was that chances were usually low in combat that help would be close enough to hear the distress call, or able to do anything concrete to assist even if they were nearby. In Haskell's case, though, both happened to be true.

Haskell's first surprise was discovering that though he could not transmit, he could still receive over the emergency data link.

"Bravo patrol flight from Kadena, this is a JSDF AWACS flight fifty miles to your north, authentication code foxtrot delta tango four. We have received your automated distress call, which contained details of the damage you have sustained. Turn to bearing one six niner now."

As Haskell fought the F-22's damaged controls to reach the new heading, the message continued.

"The aircraft carrier *USS Theodore Roosevelt* has been advised of your status, and is en route in your direction. At your current speed you should rendezvous in about twenty minutes. Two rescue helicopters will be launched as you approach. Since you lack arrestor gear you will have to eject."

No kidding, Haskell thought. Though there had been a planned naval variant of the F-22 to replace the F-14, it had been canceled to reduce the program's cost.

"Eject within sight of the carrier, but ensure that your aircraft does not endanger its operations."

Translation, please don't bend our carrier, Haskell thought. Fair enough, since at about six billion dollars, it was one of the few items in the US military inventory more expensive than his F-22.

Now all Haskell had to do was keep his fighter flying and on course for another twenty minutes, and survive an at-sea ejection from a damaged aircraft.

Haskell grit his teeth as he gripped the F-22's throttle and continued to scan his instruments. The AWACS and the carrier turning up in time to help gave him a fighting chance. He was going to make the most of it.

Kaito Watanabe turned from the screen that everyone had been breathlessly watching and asked Haruto Takahashi, "Has all of this been recorded?"

Haruto smiled. "Absolutely, sir."

Kaito nodded. "Excellent. I am going to ask for a refueling tanker. I don't know what's going on out here, but I have a feeling it's not over."

CHAPTER SEVENTY SEVEN

Los Angeles

Chung Hee Moon propped himself up in bed on one elbow, and turned toward Kang Ji Yeong. Her eyes were closed, but Chung knew she wasn't sleeping.

"I think I have a way you can avoid going to the store today," Chung said.

Kang's eyes opened slowly, and she asked skeptically, "And how will you manage that?"

"Simple," Chung said. "Keep the security camera, and I'll install it in the hallway."

Kang shook her head. "I told you I don't want to deal with either that busybody Park or building management when he complains."

Chung smiled, and said "Why would they complain about something they can't see?"

Kang frowned and punched Chung in the arm. "What, now you are a magician? Are you making fun of me?"

Chung laughed and shook his head, rubbing the spot where Kang had hit him. Still laughing, he said, "You are stronger than you look."

Kang tried unsuccessfully to fight back a smile. "You had better explain yourself, or you will get more of the same."

Chung held up both hands in mock surrender. "Here is how I will do it," he said, and went on to explain. When he had finished Kang frowned and nodded. "Are you sure that will work?," she asked.

Chung shrugged. "I don't see why not. If you agree, I will do it later tonight, after you and everyone else on this floor has gone to bed."

Kang smiled and nodded. "I agree."

"Good," Chung said, with an answering smile. "That just leaves us with the question of what to do with the time you were going to spend at the store."

Kang answered by giggling and burrowing under the covers. Chung followed her.

Tunnel No. 1, North Korea

Captain Yoon looked out at the crowd surrounding the train. He had called them together to tell them what would happen before and after the charges were set off to join the two tunnels. There wasn't a single sound as everyone waited for what he had to say. Not even his own men, who stood guard over him and the device, knew what was coming next.

"All of you have heard that explosives have been placed that, when detonated, will join this tunnel to another one. That creates an obvious risk to the stability of this tunnel. The plan had been to evacuate all of you from this end of the tunnel before setting off the charges. However, the collapse of the tunnel midway to the exit now makes that impossible."

Yoon paused. There was still not a sound from his audience.

"I considered waiting for rescue crews to reach us before setting off the charges. However, your foreman has told me there is no hope that rescuers will break through before we all run out of air."

If anything, the silence was now more absolute.

"If there was room on the train, I would take you with me. There is not. However, I have decided to take the three explosives specialists with me, along with their remaining materials. There may be obstacles that need to be cleared in the other tunnel."

Now there was a low murmuring in the crowd, as many started to realize options they thought open were in fact closed.

Yoon paused again, looking out over the assembled prisoners, guards, and miners with a grave expression.

"I have decided that the best chance is to set off the charges before we all run out of air. Once the two tunnels are connected, there will be enough air for everyone. Now, that leaves the question of the stability of this tunnel after we set off the charges. Many of you have worked to brace this end of the tunnel to help it withstand the impact of the explosion. No matter how hard you have tried, though, you all know that after such a blow this tunnel won't stay intact for long."

Now the murmuring had stopped again.

"So, I am authorizing all of you to move forward into the other tunnel once the charges have been detonated and this train has cleared the new entrance. There is, however, one condition."

Yoon looked sternly out over the silent crowd.

"You must stay away from this train once it is in the other tunnel. I and my men will not be able to take the time to distinguish you from the Southern enemy. The simplest way to do this will be to wait for four hours. You may then move forward, since by then we will have cleared the tracks and be on our way. You should then be able to reach an exit from the Southern tunnel."

There was an excited buzz from the crowd, as they realized that they had a chance to survive after all.

"You will all hear an announcement ten minutes before detonation." Pointing at several men near the front of the crowd, Yoon added, "Explosives specialists gather your materials. My troops will show you where to put them."

With that, Yoon turned abruptly and went back into the driver's cabin, where Lee Ho Suk stood waiting.

Lee bowed to Yoon, and said, "With respect, Captain, your speech came as a pleasant surprise."

Yoon gave Lee a thin smile, and asked, "Really? How so?"

Lee hesitated, and then said, "You have obviously thought carefully about the best way to save as many lives as possible. It is not the priority I would expect from a military officer."

Yoon laughed, the first genuine sign of amusement Lee could remember seeing from the man. "Lee, you know a lot about tunnels, but very little about command. If I thought killing every man out there was the best way to accomplish my mission, that's what I'd do. However, there are quite a few guards among them, and they all have guns. Besides, dozens of men bringing up our rear may prove to be a useful distraction if any Southerners try to sneak up behind us once we're in their tunnel."

Lee slowly nodded. "And most of what you said was just a description of our situation, and everyone already knew the facts about the tunnel collapse and our running out of air."

Yoon shrugged. "Never lie if you don't need to, and especially don't lie if everyone already knows the truth."

CHAPTER SEVENTY EIGHT

En Route to USS Theodore Roosevelt

Major Mark Haskell finally had the carrier in sight, and breathed a sigh of relief. Rescue would have still been possible if the rescue helicopter had to search for him, but his chances for survival were much better with the rescuers' eyes on him from the moment he ejected. Now, he had to hope his ACES II ejection seat system had not been damaged by the shrapnel that had hit his plane.

He ran through what he could remember about the version of the ACES II aboard the F-22, which had been modified in anticipation of likely high altitude ejection. It had a faster deploying drogue parachute, housed in the enclosure behind the headrest. A pair of nets rolled into nylon enclosures on either side of the seat backrest area served as arm restraints. These nets would be mechanically deployed as the seat moved up the rails by a set of nylon lines running through fittings attached to the cockpit floor. They would detach through shear-pin action once the arm restraints were fully deployed. There was also a larger oxygen bottle for longer lasting emergency oxygen supply, which fortunately he wouldn't need. He was wearing the anti-G vest, anti-G pressure pants, and Combat Edge helmet pressure system designed to see him through both combat maneuvers as well as ejection.

Haskell frowned. He was forgetting something. Right...due to the larger oxygen bottle, both disconnects for the canopy jettison system had been relocated to the right side of the seat.

Everything he could see appeared to be in order, and none of the many caution lights glowing in front of Haskell related to the ejection system. He was as ready as he was going to get.

As if reading his mind, his headphones crackled to life. "This is *USS Theodore Roosevelt* flight operations control, calling Bravo flight from Kadena. We understand you have sustained damage, and can receive but not transmit. We have your aircraft in sight, and rescue helicopters are taking off now. You may eject at your discretion." There was a short pause. "Good luck, Major Haskell."

Haskell grunted with surprise. In his experience, it wasn't often that the right information made it that quickly to the people who needed it. He resolved that if he made it through this, he would look up whoever was responsible and buy them a drink.

Maybe several.

Reaching down for the ejection lever, Haskell steeled himself for what would come next. Having done ejections before in simulators, he knew it would be rough.

At least, Haskell thought he knew what to expect.

His ejection seat rocketed upward at a velocity that made his most violent combat maneuvers seem tame, and Haskell's vision blurred. Before he even had a chance to worry about it, though, his parachute deployed.

Though Haskell still had trouble focusing, he had no trouble hearing the rapidly approaching helicopters. He had barely touched the water when he could see one of them directly overhead.

Less than five minutes later, a Navy rescue diver had him connected to a harness and on his way up to the helicopter.

"Welcome, Major!," the medic examining Haskell said. "How are you feeling?"

Haskell shook himself and tried to take stock. "OK, I guess. I was having trouble focusing and had the breath knocked out of me, but I'm fine now."

Ripping off the blood pressure cuff, the medic shined a pen light into Haskell's eyes. After a few moments he nodded. "You'll get a complete physical once we're on board, but from what I can see you've come through ejecting without lasting trauma. Still, take it easy until the flight surgeon gives you clearance to return to duty."

Haskell nodded, and looked out the window at the rapidly growing bulk of the carrier. On the one hand, it always amazed him that something the size of an aircraft carrier could float, let alone make speeds in excess of 35 miles per hour. On the other, as an aviator he didn't envy the challenge Navy pilots faced landing on the carrier's flight deck. Not only was it small, but Haskell could see the deck moving up and down with the waves.

Thank goodness I don't have to deal with that, Haskell thought, as the helicopter touched down on the carrier.

CHAPTER SEVENTY NINE

Moscow, Russia

Smyslov was not nearly as jolly as he had been on their last visit. It didn't take them long to discover the reason.

"I heard you were both unhappy with my decision not to pass what the interrogators learned to you after chemical interrogation failed, and they had to move on to other methods. In fact, you both made something of a nuisance of yourselves."

Vasilyev and Grishkov looked at each other, but said nothing. "Nuisance" was a considerable understatement.

"Well, under the circumstances I might have done the same in your place. Fortunately, as it turns out, I can share that information with you. In fact, I must."

Vasilyev and Grishkov both leaned forward and it was hard to tell who was more eager to hear more, though Vasilyev perhaps hid it better.

Smyslov laughed. "My argument was simple, and in the end it persuaded the Director. The fewer people who know of this matter, the better. So, though we have agents in place who could deal with this matter directly, it has been decided that it is better to avoid briefing others on this matter, no matter how trustworthy they may be. It helps that you both already have high security clearances. However for you, Grishkov, it needs to be both elevated and updated." With that, he slid a stack of papers and a pen towards Grishkov.

Grishkov did not bother reading the forms, and instead signed each page and handed them back to Smyslov, who smiled and asked, "Aren't you in the habit of reading what you sign?"

Grishkov did not smile back. "They say if I breathe a word of this matter to anyone, I may be executed without trial. Correct?"

Now Smyslov laughed aloud. "Vasilyev, I now see why you two get along so well. Yes, my friend, that is quite correct."

His smile quickly faded as he added. "And now I have papers for both of you." With that he handed each of them a folder.

As Vasilyev and Grishkov examined the contents, they saw that each contained diplomatic passports, paperwork identifying them as newly assigned temporary staff at the Russian consulate general in San Francisco, and their itinerary. It showed that they would be flying to Paris via a four hour Aeroflot flight at noon, and then have 90 minutes to get to the terminal where their eleven hour Air France flight would fly them nonstop to San Francisco.

Vasilyev looked at his watch and frowned. "We must head for the airport shortly. So the device is in San Francisco?" Shaking his head, Smyslov said, "No, we have a location in Los Angeles. However, it appears it is no longer at that address."

Vasilyev opened his mouth to ask another question, but Smyslov held up his hand first, and pointed to the LCD screen on his wall. "It will help to explain if I show you this first." Punching a few buttons on his remote, Smyslov brought up a poor quality black and white video showing a foiled holdup where the gunmen managed to shoot each other.

"I must caution you that what you have just seen may have nothing to do with your mission. However, the store where this attempted robbery took place was within a block of the address provided by the North Korean agent. He also told us that after this video was shot the agent reported that he was changing locations, but provided no explanation and did not report his new address. The North Koreans have had no contact from him since, but that is normal procedure since there has been a heavy police presence in the area attempting to locate the survivor in this video."

The confusion on Vasilyev and Grishkov's faces would have been comical under other circumstances, Smyslov thought to himself. Vasilyev spoke first.

"So, we think that the man in the video who helped those two idiots to shoot each other was an agent responsible for detonating our stolen nuclear device on command? How could a man chosen for such a mission be so irresponsible?"

"Yes, that is one reason why I cautioned you it may not be the man you seek. However, I should note that according to news reports the thieves had knocked a pregnant woman unconscious just before this man confronted them. Faced with such barbarity, he may not have been able to restrain himself."

Vasilyev thought about it, and then nodded. "Particularly if the man was a soldier, rather than an intelligence agent."

"Very good," Smyslov said. "Our Korean friend says he is special forces."

Grishkov then asked, "Will our Korean friend be able to offer us any additional assistance?"

Smyslov shook his head. "Sadly, no. The interrogators did their best to keep him alive, but with the time constraints placed on them were fortunate to obtain as much information as they did." He then handed each of them a blow up of the face in the video.

"The quality is poor, but it may help as a starting point. Likewise the address. Even though the agent is no longer there, since he appears to have had no help from other agents he may not have moved far."

Smyslov stood up to signal the end of their meeting, and said "My technical staff tells me that they might be able to improve the image further if they could get access to the source recording, rather than what is available from the upload to the Internet. That may be one place for you to start." Cocking one eyebrow, he added "Of course, this or any other step is strictly to aid you in recovering the device. We have no interest in this man or any other part of what the North Koreans may be planning. Recovering our device is your first and last priority. Understood?"

Nodding, both Vasilyev and Grishkov headed for their flight to the US.

CHAPTER EIGHTY

Washington, D.C.

Tom Browning had worked in the CIA's Operations Center for three years, and had seen many situations requiring quick action and coordination with multiple agencies. As he put together the two reports, though, he realized this challenge would eclipse them all. First he had to convince his boss, Center Director Mike Pupols, that this really was a crisis requiring immediate action.

It helped a lot that both Browning and Pupols had served in the military, Browning in the Army and Pupols in the Marines. Both had served in overseas combat tours, Browning in Iraq and Pupols in Afghanistan. They both joked that their hardest tour had been as Pentagon staffers, where unlike combat overseas you were never sure just who the enemy was, sometimes until it was too late. They shared the same frustration with bureaucracy, and had come to the CIA because it had a reputation for being less obsessed with rules than the other national security agencies.

Pupols, though, had more time in at the CIA, having worked as a highly regarded analyst before making the move to the Op Center. Browning had always found him ready to listen, and to act quickly when needed. He prayed that the same would be true today.

"Mike, did you see the report on the MiGs attacking that Trans Pacific flight?," Browning asked.

"Yeah, it didn't make much sense. Why would the Russians want to destroy that particular aircraft?," Pupols replied, shaking his head.

"Well, that's just it. I don't think the Russians had anything to do with it. I think it was the Chinese," Browning said.

Pupols looked at Browning dubiously. "And you think this because..." Pupols prompted.

"The two defectors from Beijing are on that flight," Browning replied.

"What! That wasn't in the report on the attack!," Pupols exclaimed.

"Right, because nobody at Defense knew that. Nobody but the Chinese would have known that these two were on that flight, or would have had any reason to care. Certainly not the Russians," Browning said, tapping the CIA's file on the defectors for emphasis.

Pupols grunted acknowledgement. "So, MiGs were used to make us blame the Russians, who make believable fall guys because they've shot down passenger jets before."

"Right," Browning nodded. "Now, if the Chinese were willing to shoot down a commercial flight to stop these defectors from getting here, what would they be willing to do to stop them at Dulles Airport?"

Pupols frowned. "We've coordinated with the Bureau?"

Browning shrugged acknowledgement. Whenever agents with guns and badges were required within the United States the law required that the FBI take action, not the CIA.

"And the number of agents assigned to meet the defectors?," Pupols asked.

Browning grimaced. "Two."

Every organization has its shorthand expressions, that mean nothing to outsiders, but save time inside it. The expression Pupols was about to use went back decades to a scene in a movie when its star, a great white shark, first raised its head into view of the people hunting it.

"I think we're going to need a bigger boat."

CHAPTER EIGHTY ONE

San Francisco

"I don't understand why we are arriving in San Francisco, when our information says the device is six hundred kilometers away in Los Angeles," Grishkov said.

"Operational security," Vasilyev responded, in a tone that sounded as though the answer should have been obvious.

The glare he received in response from Grishkov could have stripped paint.

Vasilyev sighed. "I could tell you in detail, but I assure you that once we arrive at the consulate, the reasons will become obvious."

"Tell me again why you are the one driving," Grishkov grumbled, while their rented car sped from San Francisco Airport to the Russian Consulate.

Vasilyev laughed, and shook his head. "First, though your English is not bad, mine is better. Second, I have driven in the U.S. before, in fact to this very consulate, while this is your first trip outside Russia. No matter how much the Chechens might wish it were not so, Chechnya is still part of Russia. Finally, I won the coin toss."

"OK," Grishkov said grudgingly, "but next time we use my coin!"

"Ah, now you take paranoia about FSB treachery a bit too far! I assure you, trick coins are not part of my equipment. In any case, we have a straight shot up from the airport on US 101 North, and should reach our consulate in San Francisco within half an hour. Be grateful the Americans finally allowed us to reopen it."

"Straight shot?" Grishkov repeated, obviously as amused as he was puzzled.

"American slang. It means we do not have to make multiple exits or detours prior to reaching our destination."

With a grunt Grishkov settled back in his seat. Just as Vasilyev had said, it was not long before they were pulling up in front of a building flying the familiar Russian flag. It struck him for the first time that the white, blue and red colors in the Russian flag were the same as the colors used in the American flag.

There were two long lines in front of the consulate, one for Russians seeking passports and another for foreigners seeking visas. Vasilyev strode forward confidently past both of them, and Grishkov followed. Vasilyev showed the guard at the gate his diplomatic passport, and after a bit of fumbling Grishkov did the same. Both were passed through at once, and the guard gestured them towards a door on the far left side of the lobby. As they reached it, the door swung open.

Vasilyev fell into the open arms of a man who looked enough like him to be his brother, and it was obvious that they already knew each other. Grishkov had a sudden image of rows of cloning vats for producing FSB agents, and then shook his head. Paranoia really could go too far!

"Oleg, let me introduce senior detective Anatoly Grishkov, who will accompany me on this trip," Vasilyev said, sweeping his hands in a grand gesture towards Grishkov. They shook hands while Oleg favored Grishkov with a half smile. "I would dearly love to know how you ended up traveling to America with this scoundrel on a mission classified at a level above the Consul General himself. Ah well, I understand speed is of the essence," he said, glancing towards Vasilyev.

"Quite right," Vasilyev nodded.

"Then, onward and upward," Oleg said, pushing the nearby elevator button.

The elevator doors opened to the consulate's top floor, where a man was waiting for them who looked disturbingly familiar to Grishkov. After a few moments, Grishkov realized that the man looked as much like him as Oleg did to Vasilyev, though like him his hair was quite a bit longer. The man, who pointed to himself and said simply "Yakov", gestured to a room behind him and said "You will find your clothes in there."

Before Grishkov could respond, he heard Vasilyev laughing behind him. "Yakov, you must pardon my friend's inexperience. He is not an intelligence agent, and has never been through this routine before."

Turning to Grishkov, Vasilyev gestured towards the open door. "You will find a set of clothes inside that should fit you. Please put them on, and lay the clothes you take off as neatly as you can in their place. Please hurry."

Grishkov shrugged and did as he was told. Once he finished changing and left the room, Yakov came in right behind him and shut the door. Grishkov saw that Vasilyev had already finished changing, and Oleg was nowhere in sight. Grishkov frowned when he heard a faint buzzing noise, which sounded familiar but which he couldn't quite place.

Once Yakov and Oleg came back in the room, the point of the past half-hour's effort became obvious. "So, you are to take our place," mused Grishkov. "You have done an excellent job of reproducing our haircuts. The clothes are ours, and you started out with the same build and similar facial features. The only thing I don't understand is who we are trying to fool!"

Smiling, Vasilyev gestured towards the nearest window. Tapping on it, he said "The ballistic film used to coat all of the consulate's windows is also tinted in such a way that you can easily see out, but no one can see in."

Grishkov peered through the window, and with his long police experience said immediately, "The white van."

Laughing, Vasilyev accepted a five dollar bill from a scowling Yakov. "I bet you would spot it within three seconds. I doubt that you needed one."

Grishkov shrugged. "The local authorities? Why would they be interested in us?"

Vasilyev nodded. "More specifically, they are the FBI. They are in fact not that interested in us, at least not as much as they used to be. Their top priority these days are Islamic militants, and anyone associated with them. But, since we are new they will always start out by following us around. We usually let them, since most of the time we truly have nothing to hide. On this mission, though, we obviously don't want company."

"I presume we are also switching vehicles?"

Vasilyev tossed a set of keys to Oleg, who tossed another set of keys back. "Let's see if our friends have left us anything in the trunk."

A quick elevator ride to the consulate's basement later, they were opening the back of a Cadillac Escalade with diplomatic plates. Vasilyev smiled. "Note that our American friends scrupulously observe the Vienna Convention, so anything we carry in this vehicle is immune from search." Having said that, he removed a large metal case, and quickly worked the combination. Glancing at Oleg, he said "I'm glad to see they haven't changed it."

Grishkov frowned as he examined the weapons contained in the case. "Aren't these M-16s? Certainly they are not legal for us to possess in this country!"

Vasilyev laughed, and said "I am not surprised at your reaction, but neither statement is correct. These are semi-automatic AR-15s expressly manufactured for sale to civilians. They are internally different from the full automatic M-16, although almost identical externally. The hammer and trigger mechanisms are not the same and the bolt carrier and internal lower receiver are milled differently, so that the firing mechanisms are not interchangeable. This was done to prevent the easy conversion of these civilian weapons to full-automatic."

"And, this is obviously not a 9mm weapon," Grishkov said, lifting one of the handguns from the case.

"Indeed not," Vasilyev acknowledged. "These are Colt 911A1 .45 ACP guns, which I have chosen both because they are quite common in the US, and because they use a single-stack magazine. As you can see, that makes for a thinner pistol which is easier to conceal. Also, a hit anywhere with .45 caliber ammo will usually incapacitate the target. If the target happens to be our Korean friend, please try to hit him in an area which will leave him both alive and able to talk."

Grishkov grunted. "The only way to make sure of that is not to shoot him at all."

Vasilyev clapped him on the back and said, "That's the spirit! I'm sure your unarmed combat skills will prove more than equal to the task."

Vasilyev then turned to Oleg and Yakov. "We will wait until you have drawn off our would-be escort in the white van, and then be on our way."

Oleg nodded, and then both agents climbed into the sedan that Vasilyev had rented at the airport. Fifteen minutes later, Vasilyev received an "all-clear" text from Oleg.

Firing up the Escalade's engine, Vasilyev grinned at Grishkov. "Next stop, Los Angeles!"

CHAPTER EIGHTY TWO

Los Angeles

Chung Hee Moon looked carefully both ways down the hallway, but saw or heard no one. At three AM, even in LA most people are in bed, he thought to himself with satisfaction. He didn't know why, but it comforted him to know that at least one expectation he'd had was accurate.

Removed from its packaging the security camera was remarkably small, which was critical for where Chung planned to place it. Now to see if his guess that it would fit in its new home was accurate.

Stepping carefully on the small step ladder Kang Ji Yeong had provided, Chung inserted his screwdriver into the first of the exit sign's six fasteners. In less than a minute, Chung was holding the plastic sign, and carefully using one of his many knives to carve a hole in the letter I just large enough for the lens to function. The choice of that letter was not optional, since the space was otherwise occupied by light bulbs.

The feed from the camera went directly to Chung's phone, which to his chagrin had been made in South Korea. It took another minute of adjustment to get the coverage of the hallway and the apartment door the way he wanted it, but after replacing and securing the sign, Chung could step back and check his handiwork. Fortunately there was a hallway light blazing directly over the exit sign that discouraged direct examination, but even squinting and looking for the camera Chung could not spot it.

Of course, he had set up Kang's phone with a feed to the camera as well, but as the camera's administrator could cut that off whenever it became inconvenient. It would be easy to blame any coverage gaps on "technical problems" that he could quickly "fix."

Satisfied, Chung quietly went back into the apartment. Raised as an atheist from childhood, Chung would never have thanked a deity for unexpectedly providing this free boost to his security. Like every soldier he knew, though, Chung was a firm believer in luck. After the disaster at the grocery store and being forced to move, though, he had started to doubt luck was on his side. With the unexpected news that he was cancer free plus the gift of enhanced security, Chung was starting to think that maybe his luck had changed.

As he slipped under the sheets next to a gently snoring Kang, Chung winced inside as he had every time after his new diagnosis at the thought of his mission. Lee had said he might not be ordered to detonate it, and in that case would return to retrieve it.

Looking at Kang and thinking about her son in the next room, Chung asked himself the question again. If the order came instead to set off the device, could he still do it?

Tunnel No. 1, North Korea

Lee Ho Suk looked nervously over the explosive charges set into the wall at the end of the tunnel. Turning to Captain Yoon, he asked, "Are you sure these charges won't go off until they're supposed to?".

Yoon laughed and patted Lee on the shoulder, with a familiarity that made Lee wince. He didn't care for his new status as Yoon's good luck charm, but had enough sense not to object to anything that might help him stay alive.

"You may have noticed I'm standing right next to you. My men know their business, or I wouldn't be anywhere near these charges. We will be waiting out the remaining hours in perfect safety," Yoon said, with a carefree assurance Lee wished he could share.

"And how many hours will that be?," Lee asked.

Yoon frowned and said sternly, "That is a military secret." He then grinned and shook his head. "But who are you going to tell?"

Yoon then checked his watch. "A little over four hours, unless I receive orders to stand down before then."

Lee nodded and asked, "Do you think that could still happen?"

Yoon shrugged. "Years of military service have taught me never to rule out any possibility. However, the men I have right next to our side of the tunnel collapse have reported to me within the past hour. They say there has been no indication that the rescuers on the other side are anywhere close. You told me we should hear some noise, feel some vibrations, several hours before they reach us, correct?"

Lee nodded.

"Well, that's your answer. It's still possible we won't go, but with every passing minute, it becomes more likely we will."

CHAPTER EIGHTY THREE

Beijing, China

Song Hailong's stomach lurched when he saw Liu Jie's expression as he stepped into his office. "I regret that there has been no word from our fighters, and we have monitored the Trans Pacific flight's routine check in with Anchorage Air Traffic Control. Our fighters must have run out of fuel by now. Their mission has failed."

Song nodded. "Are our men in place at the American airport where the plane will arrive?"

"Yes, sir," Liu answered. "I have told them to use whatever force and resources are necessary, and not to be concerned about the reaction of the Americans."

Song nodded again. "Good. If the traitors are allowed to talk, the Americans will be even angrier, and will know exactly who to blame. Now, how are we going to prevent the American aircraft carrier that appears to be on its way to waters near Taiwan from interfering with our plans?"

Liu hesitated. "Sir, I have spoken with our supporters in the military. In the time we have available, they are unanimous that an air attack is the only option."

Song grimaced. "That didn't work so well the last time, and then the target was a commercial airliner. Isn't an aircraft carrier accompanied by ships and planes that will defend it from any hasty attack we could organize?"

Liu nodded. "That is exactly what I said. However, it appears that a new missile we recently acquired from the Russians may be able to make it through the American defenses. Called the Brahmos, the Russians actually developed it jointly with the Indian military, which also uses the missile. It has a range of nearly three hundred kilometers and skims just above the ocean's surface, going as low as ten meters above wavetops. At a speed of Mach 2.8 it is the world's fastest low altitude missile, and that speed at impact combined with a payload of 300 kilograms of high explosives means even a single hit could disable the carrier."

Song grunted. "And do we try to point the finger at the Russians for this attack too?"

Liu shrugged. "We have no reason to think the Americans even know we tried to attack their aircraft, let alone the planes we used. Their missiles may have fallen short, and the fighters almost certainly fell into the ocean without witnesses when they ran out of fuel. We do know that the Trans Pacific flight never reported being under attack."

Song tapped his pencil on his desk, which Liu knew from experience meant he was uncertain. "So, we send up some of the planes we just got from the Russians with these Brahmos missiles, and hope one of them gets through?"

Now Liu looked uncomfortable. "We just received both the planes and the missiles. If we are to strike immediately, I am advised we only have a single plane and a single missile available. It is part of a squadron that had been in the process of testing the missile."

Song looked at Liu incredulously. "One? You seriously propose to place the success of all our plans in the hands of a single pilot?"

Liu shrugged. "The Americans should have no idea we have this missile. It can be launched beyond what our military advisors call their normal defense perimeter. Since it is a "sea skimmer" missile they believe the Americans will have less than a minute from the time the missile is detected to impact, and that it is very unlikely they will be able to stop it. In an absolute worst case the plane is shot down, and any wreckage discovered is of a Russian fighter. What are we really risking?"

Song frowned, but then slowly nodded. "I see little alternative. Very well, give the order for the attack to begin immediately. As you say, at least we shouldn't be risking much."

Liu stood. "At once, sir."

Once he had left the office, Song resumed tapping the pencil against his desk. A single plane! Had it really come to this?

Chapter Eighty Four

On Patrol off the Japanese Coast

Haruto Takahashi had been nursing his jury rigged monitoring setup for several hours after the strange encounter between the F-22s and the MiG-29s. It had been fully functional about half that time, and Haruto knew there was a lot of work to do before it could be considered reliable.

Work there was zero chance he could complete by himself on this flight.

Haruto shook himself. That wasn't the way to think. He needed to concentrate on getting the most out of the assets he had strung together. Kaito Watanabe was the aircraft commander for a reason, Haruto thought. He also had the feeling that something else was coming, though he had no idea what.

There! What was that? It was coming from the same direction as the MiG-29s had, but considerably further south. At least it was well away from any commercial aircraft routes. And it looked like a single aircraft, making it unlikely to be a serious threat. Fighters nearly always traveled in pairs. Maybe this was nothing.

Haruto shook his head, and routed one of the RQ-4 drones at his command to take a look. Whatever this plane was, it had no business being in this part of the Pacific. Fortunately, the drone he had selected was in range for an easy intercept.

Haruto's lips thinned as he had no sooner had the thought than the feed from the RQ-4 went dark. Ok, he had the half hour before the RQ-4 reached monitoring range to fix the problem.

It took 40 minutes. It did mean, though, that when the plane appeared on the screen, it had not just come into range. In fact, the drone was within a few miles and had an excellent view of the aircraft, though due to the target's speed that wouldn't last long.

Once again, a MiG-29 painted in Russian Air Force colors filled the screen. Kaito Watanabe had been walking past the screen, and now froze. "This is a recording, right?"

Haruto shook his head.

He had never heard his commander curse, or for that matter imagined that he ever would. He had to admit, though, that he had never dreamed of a situation like this.

"So, what could this fighter possibly be doing in the middle of the Pacific? What planes or ships are in the area?"

Haruto answered immediately. "No commercial aircraft in the area. The only ships are the *USS Theodore Roosevelt* and its escorts, but it can't possibly reach attack range before it runs out of fuel. There are no refueling aircraft in the area except our own. I can't imagine what it could be doing out here."

Kaito grunted, obviously unconvinced. Haruto didn't blame him. He also thought he was missing something, but had no idea what it could be.

Suddenly Kaito's head snapped up. "We're getting a view from overhead. Can we change the angle so we can see under the wings?"

Haruto nodded, his hand delicately grasping the joystick controlling the RQ-4 as he moved it to a new vantage point. Two minutes later, the view stabilized, and they could see a single missile under the right wing, tucked close to the fuselage.

"That's an anti-ship missile," Kaito said quietly, as he took in the missile's size.

"Yes, sir," Haruto said, frowning as he used another screen to pull up a chart of anti-ship missile types.

After a few moments, his frown deepened. "This doesn't make any sense. It's a Brahmos anti-ship missile, currently in service with the Russian and Indian navies."

Kaito shrugged. "A Russian missile on a Russian plane. What's the surprise?".

Haruto waved in exasperation at the MiG-29 image on the screen. "The problem, sir, is the same as with the other MiGs. The Russians only have one aircraft carrier operational, and right now it's off the coast of Syria. Getting a MiG out here from the closest Russian air base would have taken multiple mid-air refuelings, and there's no way we would have missed that. On the other hand, a plane taking off from China could have been refueled once out of range of our surveillance, since we have to stay well clear of their airspace. I think that plane's Chinese."

Kaito nodded. "Very well. That's what you think. How are you going to prove it?"

Haruto shrugged. "I don't know, sir. But I am sure that its target is the American aircraft carrier. That missile has recently been upgraded to a range of 600 kilometers, and at its current speed the MiG will be in range to launch in about half an hour."

Kaito nodded. "Inform the Americans. Continue to monitor the MiG, and give the Americans continuing updates. Can we connect with their defense system?"

Haruto shook his head. "Not from this range, sir. However, if we were to fly towards the carrier group, we should be able to link up in about fifteen minutes."

Kaito nodded. "We will do so." He paused. "If the MiG does fire that missile, what does your chart say about the Americans being able to stop it?"

Haruto looked uncertain. "The Brahmos reaches a speed of nearly Mach 3. Advance warning will help, but I wouldn't want to be on that carrier," he said, as he quickly typed the warning notice to the Americans.

"Warning sent, sir."

Kaito nodded. "I hope it will be enough," he said, as he hurried back to the cockpit.

CHAPTER EIGHTY FIVE

Washington Dulles Airport

After over twenty years in the FBI, Bob Hansen sometimes thought he had seen it all. Then a day like today would come around to prove him wrong.

First, the CIA had actually been forthcoming, which was already unusual enough. Then, the details they'd provided had made it clear just how far the Chinese would be ready to go to stop the defectors from making it out of Dulles Airport alive. Hansen had realized just how much firepower he would need to respond, and even more important, how much smart and effective planning.

Hansen knew that the CIA's priority was the safety of their defectors, and he respected that. They had a job to do. But that wasn't his priority.

First and foremost, Hansen was determined to avoid any innocent loss of life at the airport. Second, he wanted everyone who posed a threat to those innocents in custody, or dead.

If the defectors survived, that would be good, too.

As he thought it over, Hansen realized there was a way to make the CIA happy, and achieving his other objectives a lot easier.

Smiling to himself, Hansen picked up the phone.

Pyongyang, North Korea

Guard Captain Yeong Su Lee's nose wrinkled as he entered the high security detention center, as it did every time he entered. No matter how many times his duty took him there he could never get used to the stench, a combined odor emanating from unwashed prisoners forced to live in their own waste, the metallic tang of blood, and the almost visible smell of mortal fear. He always thought that the prisoners were comparatively lucky, since few survived long enough there to have a chance to pay much attention to the odor. This center was reserved for threats to national security, and North Korea took such threats very seriously indeed.

The clerk cowering in front of him had already been beaten, a process that had begun even before his men confirmed that the clerk had signed off on a records check having no basis in reality. Even if the records check had been verified and Shin Yon Young had turned out to be exactly who he said he was, the lives of the clerk and his family would have still been forfeit.

False arrest was an unknown concept in North Korea. Its government never made mistakes. None that it admitted to anyway.

The interview room was like those found in prisons around the world. A buzzing florescent light, a metal table, and two metal chairs. The clerk sat in one of them, his wrists handcuffed behind his back to the chair.

Yeong glanced through the file again in his right hand. Nothing was in any way remarkable about the clerk. As with any prisoner, he neither gave his name nor used his.

Yeong thrust the form on which the clerk had signed off on Shin Yon Young's records check towards him.

"You signed this form stating that you had checked government records and confirmed Shin Yon Young had lived in a village and attended a school that in fact he had not. We are not here to discuss whether or not you did this. We know you did. What I need to know from you is who paid you, how much he paid you, and how he made contact with you."

"Please, Captain. There has been some misunderstanding. Perhaps the records have been misplaced," the clerk said, trembling.

Yeong sighed with frustration. He simply did not have time to waste.

Yeong's fist connected with the clerk's jaw at an angle designed to hurt, but not render unconscious. The clerk's head snapped back along with a small spray of blood. Yeong's blow appeared to have loosened at least one of the clerk's teeth.

"Now, I hope I have your attention. Let me make your situation clear to you. You will be tried and convicted of treason. There is only one punishment for that crime. The only question that remains is what will happen to your family."

"No, sir, please!" The clerk's eyes were round with panic. "They had nothing to do with this!"

Yeong nodded. "Very well. Make me believe you. Start by telling me everything I want to know."

Of course, no matter what the clerk said his family would be executed as well. Part of what kept the regime in power, in spite of miserable living conditions for most people, was fear of the consequences of opposing it. Punishment for families was routine, and for cases of treason death for all its members was automatic. After all, it was unlikely you could live with a traitor without being one yourself.

The clerk straightened in his chair, and Yeong was gratified to see in his eyes that he had resigned himself to his fate. It often took longer than this, and time was not on his side. Yeong felt in his bones that every second counted.

"The man who paid me said to call him Kim. I only saw him twice. Once was the day when he asked me to verify a record, and the next was the day he paid me."

"How much did he pay you?"

Yeong nodded when the clerk named a sum. High enough to be certain to tempt someone with the clerk's low salary, but not so high as to make him think the bribe was more than routine.

"Why did he say he was paying the bribe?"

"Because Shin had a cousin who had been arrested, and he was afraid that if his real record was used that relative's record would prevent him from working in the capital."

Yeong nodded again. That tracked too. North Korea had thousands of people who had no record against them, but the bad luck to be related to someone who did. Most of the jobs that paid enough to eat were in Pyongyang, especially for someone looking for unskilled janitorial work.

"How did this man Kim contact you?"

"I was eating my lunch on a bench outside my office, trying to get a little fresh air. He came up to me and started talking, and before I knew it he was asking for my help. A little favor, he called it."

"How did he know you were a clerk able to help him?"

"He asked what I did after we had been talking for a few minutes. He said it was really lucky for him that he came across me."

"So, his meeting you was just random chance." The clerk visibly wilted under Yeong's skeptical glare.

"I had no reason to suspect him. He was just trying to get a janitorial job for his relative."

"How did he say they were related?"

"He said he was Shin's uncle, and that it was his son who had been arrested and caused problems for Shin. He said that his son had been released and was a good boy, but that the arrest record would always be a problem for his nephew."

Yeong shook his head with admiration for the man who had paid the clerk. The story was plausible in every respect, and the image of an uncle trying to smooth over problems for his nephew caused by his son was one guaranteed to draw sympathy in Korean society.

"Describe the man who paid you."

The clerk went into a long description which amounted to what Yeong had expected. The man had been a middle-aged Korean with nothing significant to distinguish him from any other. Average height, average build, ordinary clothes, no scars, no tattoos, no missing fingers or teeth. Based on the clerk's description, Yeong mused, he could have been the man who paid him the bribe.

"I have told you everything. Will you keep your promise? Will my family be safe?"

Yeong turned his attention back to the clerk. For now, it was important that he not lose all hope, since others would soon want to question him as well.

"As long as you continue to cooperate, your family will be well. Keep that in mind, when you are questioned again," Yeong said sternly.

Tears welled in the clerk's eyes as he babbled his thanks. Yeong marched out of the room, eager to leave the pathetic scene behind him now that he was convinced he had all the information the clerk had to offer.

Yeong would have loved to be able to tell himself for even a second that the story the clerk had been told might be true. That somewhere there really was an uncle who just wanted to help his nephew.

But the sheet wrapped around the dead guard's body stopped him. His lieutenant's judgment on that point was absolutely correct. An ordinary janitor would have fled in panic after killing someone in a hand to hand struggle, or sat down with the door open to wait for the police. He would not have carefully wrapped a sheet around the body to prevent the neighbors noticing the smell for as long as possible, and then closed the door behind him after taking the dead man's ID and scooter.

No. Shin was not an ordinary janitor. So it followed that the person who had bribed the clerk to enable him to get his job was not an uncle.

And Shin worked at the Personal Secretariat.

That left only one possible conclusion.

Yeong swallowed hard as he realized where he had to go next.

CHAPTER EIGHTY SIX

On Patrol Off the Japanese Coast

Haruto Takahashi had been thinking logically about how he could prove the Russian plane was being flown by a Chinese pilot. Getting his picture seemed pretty unlikely. That left intercepting a radio transmission in Chinese, which seemed almost as farfetched - after all, out here in the middle of the Pacific who could he possibly be talking to? More to say he'd tried everything than because he expected a result, he directed the RQ-4's directional radio antenna to monitor the MiG on their screen.

And to his astonishment, got a result. Not that he could hear the pilot saying anything. That would have been a bit too much to hope for. No, it was that among the literally hundreds of controls available to a MiG-29 pilot, this one had left on the switch for short-range transmission. The sort that a pilot would use to speak to a wingman. Since this pilot didn't have one, right now Haruto could hear nothing except something that sounded like the pilot's breathing.

Haruto shrugged. The chances were that the pilot wouldn't say any-thing, since there was literally no one around to talk with. Still, now Haruto could say with a clear conscience that he'd tried everything he could to prove what he knew in his bones - the pilot of that MiG was no more a Russian than Haruto.

En Route to Los Angeles

The Escalade had smoothly eaten up the miles on I-5, and they had just reached the stretch of US 101 that would take them to their destination.

"I understand the North Korean agent in Los Angeles may no longer be at the address we have for him, correct?" Grishkov asked.

Vasilyev simply nodded.

"If that turns out to be the case, where do we go next?"

"First, we will question his neighbors, posing as friends. If that turns up no leads, then I have a contact in Los Angeles who may prove helpful."

In response to Grishkov's questioning look, Vasilyev smiled. "He is our contact within the yakuza."

"But I thought that the yakuza were Japanese?"

"Correct," Vasilyev said. "However, it is not well known that about ten percent of the yakuza in Japan are of Korean ethnic origin. Even though born in Japan, they are still considered aliens due to their different ethnicity, which helps explain why some turn to crime. That has helped them to coordinate well with Korean gangs in California."

Grishkov frowned. "Why not go to one of these Korean gangs directly?"

Vasilyev laughed. "Well, I considered that. However, we have no established contact with them, so we would be going in cold. Even if we did, there is a major advantage in going through the yakuza. They are respected by all of the Korean gangs, so all will help us in the search for this agent. Also, we have to consider it likely that at least one of the Korean gangs is working with the North Koreans. If so, we could end up asking for help from the very people most interested in concealing his location."

"I see your point. Well, let's hope we can avoid that route. As you may imagine, I have no particular fondness for the yakuza."

"From a policeman I would expect no other reaction. Even for intelligence agents, dealing with criminals is not our preference, but it is sometimes a regrettable necessity."

"Understood. There have been times when we have played off one mafiya faction against another, and you can't do that without talking to them. Still, the one constant I have found is that you can't trust any of these criminals."

Vasilyev nodded. "And if we keep that in mind, we are much more likely to profit from any contact with the yakuza."

Washington Dulles Airport

The name "Hostage Rescue Team" was not intended to be misleading. It did in fact carry out successful hostage rescues, and much of the team's training was focused on rescue scenarios. As Bob Hansen knew, though, it was not the primary reason someone like him called HRT.

Instead, it was because as an FBI field commander he needed men that were both heavily armed and who could be counted on to use that firepower with discretion. At a major international airport like Dulles, avoiding an incident was just as important as succeeding in his mission.

It also helped that HRT was based in Quantico, just minutes away from Dulles Airport. Since the team's deployment standard was four hours to be en route to any location nationwide, getting them quickly to Dulles was no challenge. Though they could have easily driven, Hansen specified that the team should come by helicopter, and that he would explain why once they arrived. Hansen could almost hear the team leader shrug as he agreed.

Once the HRT chopper arrived, Hansen explained the deployment plan, and the need to accomplish all its objectives quickly and quietly. As he put it to the HRT team leader, "Good would be to save the defectors and arrest the kidnappers without any innocents being hurt. Better would be to do it without firing a shot. Best would be if nobody but the kidnappers knew we'd been there."

The HRT team leader grinned, and said "Can do, sir!," as he hurried off to place his men around the airport. Shaking his head, Hansen looked at him rushing off and wondered to himself whether he'd ever been that young and enthusiastic.

Hansen glanced at his phone and sighed with relief. Twenty minutes to spare until the plane touched down. He thought about the number of spots they had to cover and nodded to himself. With luck, they just might make it.

CHAPTER EIGHTY SEVEN

Pyongyang, North Korea

An encounter with North Korea's State Security Department (SSD) was neither sought nor welcomed by any of its citizens, but Guard Captain Yeong Su Lee had finally concluded avoiding it any longer would be even worse. He could no longer plausibly claim to have been unaware that Shin's case fell under SSD jurisdiction.

This was true in particular because once Yeong had been promoted to Guard Captain, he had received additional training that included details on the North Korean security and intelligence agencies he was expected to coordinate with in cases like Shin's. As he approached the SSD headquarters compound, just a short walk from his own office at the Personal Secretariat, Yeong mentally reviewed what he remembered about the SSD.

Yeong knew that the SSD serves as a secret police force responsible for detecting political and some economic crimes through both surveillance and investigations. To carry out that mission it monitors, reports, and acts on political or public activities critical of the regime. The SSD also has border policing functions, pays close attention to the activities of North Korean citizens traveling to and from China, and taps both landline and cellular communications at the country's borders.

Outside North Korea the SSD collects intelligence and provides security for North Korean diplomats and their embassies. It also owns two corporations for carrying out trading activities outside North Korea.

The SSD is divided up into multiple "Bureaus," many with administrative tasks such as managing the SSD's hospital. The three most important are the 7th Bureau, responsible for operating the political prison system, the 16th Bureau, manager of electronic eavesdropping - particularly on the country's leadership - and the 2nd Bureau, responsible for monitoring the activities of all foreigners.

The fact that Shin's North Korean identity had turned out to be bogus, as well as the sophisticated way the clearance had been obtained, made Yeong certain that Shin was a foreign agent. He was just as sure that the man who had bribed the clerk was a foreign agent as well. That made them a 2nd Bureau problem.

Yeong had made an appointment to see the 2nd Bureau deputy commander, Colonel Jong. He carried a hefty folder under his arm that contained copies of all the reports and arrest warrants generated by Shin's case so far. As he presented his ID papers to the lieutenant at the 2nd Bureau headquarters entrance, Yeong thought to himself that he had done everything he could to prepare for this encounter.

Yeong just hoped it would be enough to let him exit the 2nd Bureau as easily as he had entered.

A corporal escorted Yeong to Colonel Jong's office, which Yeong was surprised to see was not very different than his own. Jong glanced up from the file in his hand, which Yeong could see from the photo on the cover was of Yeong himself. Well, that wasn't much of a surprise. The 2nd Bureau might be exclusively concerned with foreigners but it obviously coordinated with other security offices, including the one that maintained a file on him. The fact that Jong was studying the file could be seen as simple preparation for their meeting, or as a message that Yeong himself was under investigation. Most likely, Yeong thought, a bit of both.

Yeong saluted and stood at attention.

Jong frowned and waved dismissal at the corporal, and then gestured at Yeong to sit in the sole chair in front of his desk.

"So, Captain, I understand you have some information for me on the case involving one of your men killed by a janitor working at the Personal Secretariat."

Yeong nodded, and passed over the bulky file folder.

"I will of course read these documents with interest. However, please summarize their contents for me."

Yeong proceeded to summarize all of the actions he and his men had taken to date, including issuing the arrest warrant for Shin and Yeong's interrogation of the clerk who had provided Shin's clearance.

Jong nodded. "And when did you conclude that this was a case that should be brought to the attention of the 2nd Bureau?"

Yeong spoke without hesitation, sensing that the confidence he displayed in answering the question would be more important than his words.

"When the clerk who signed off on Shin's clearance described how the man who had bribed him justified his actions. Pretending to be related to Shin gave him credibility, and helped ensure his success. I also believe his total lack of distinguishing features makes it more likely that he was a foreign agent."

"Is that right? What makes you so sure?" Jong's face was impassive, and his tone gave Yeong no way to know whether Jong was truly skeptical, or if he wanted to be sure Yeong was not just guessing.

"Any reasonably intelligent person can find something memorable about nearly anyone they encounter, especially someone that is paying them to break the law. The clerk could recall their meeting nearly word for word, but his description of the man who bribed him is completely useless. It is not that he was trying to protect the man. In fact, because he believed a useful description of the man might help his family avoid punishment I am sure the clerk did the best he could. That says to me that the man was a spy."

Jong nodded. "One detail about the guard Shin killed was interesting. Shin wrapped the guard's body in a sheet before leaving. Why do you think he did that?"

Yeong did his best to remain impassive, but he knew this was the key question. If Jong believed that Yeong suspected Shin was a spy as soon as details of the guard's murder had been reported to him, then he could have Yeong arrested right now for failure to report that immediately to the SSD.

"The most obvious reason would be to conceal the smell of decomposition from Shin's neighbors."

"Agreed. Did you draw any conclusions from Shin's action?"

Yeong shrugged. "It was clear that Shin's reactions were more carefully thought out than we would have expected from an ordinary janitor. However, wrapping the body and stealing the guard's ID papers and scooter could have indicated nothing more than above average intelligence. It was only after Shin's background failed to check out and I questioned the clerk responsible that I suspected he might be a foreign agent."

Jong appeared to pay no attention to Yeong's reply, and continued to study Shin's file. After several more minutes, Jong looked up, and closed the folder.

"There appears to be little more you could have done. In fact, I would say that so far you have done quite well." Jong said.

"Thank you, sir," Yeong said as calmly as he could, while his mind raced for an explanation. It was not long in coming.

Jong pressed a buzzer on his desk, and a young lieutenant appeared about fifteen seconds later.

"Sir?" the lieutenant said, saluting.

"Lieutenant, you are aware that our military forces are conducting exercises to the south of us, near the American puppet regime?"

"Yes, sir."

Jong handed Shin's file to the lieutenant. "Have this man's description and that of the scooter he is using distributed to all military units involved in these exercises. Ensure that this is understood to mean not only military police, who should have already been informed, but instead each and every soldier."

"Yes, sir! At once!"

"And make sure that all reports relevant to the search are sent to the officer in charge, Guard Captain Yeong," Jong said, gesturing towards Yeong.

Saluting, the lieutenant left to carry out his orders.

Jong nodded with satisfaction. "Now Shin, or whatever his name truly is, will find making his way home quite a bit more difficult."

Yeong's head bobbed up and down, as he struggled to grasp what was happening.

"You will of course need to delegate your regular duties to your second in command, while you continue to carry out the search for the spy. Do not hesitate to call on me for any resources required to find him. I'm sure I don't need to stress the importance of your succeeding in this mission," Jong said, his eyes glittering.

"No, sir," Yeong said, swallowing hard.

"Excellent," Jong said, saluting dismissively.

Yeong wasted no time leaving Jong's office, his mind already racing to think of additional steps he could take to find the spy, before he escaped and condemned Yeong to a slow and unpleasant end.

CHAPTER EIGHTY EIGHT

Escort Duty, USS Theodore Roosevelt Carrier Group

Captain Jim Cartwright's head turned involuntarily towards the warning tone that had just sounded throughout the sub. Lieutenant Fischer was already hurrying towards him with a message form in his hand. "Sir, the *Roosevelt* is under attack by a MiG-29 armed with a long range anti-ship missile. They've launched fighters to intercept, but it's doubtful they'll be able to stop the MiG from launching."

Cartwright nodded. "And what about us, Lieutenant? We're tied into the carrier's defense network, and are ready to use the AIM-9Xs we have in the tubes. But will the MiG fly into range?"

"Yes, sir. But it will be reaching what the *Roosevelt* says is launch range at about the same time."

Cartwright grunted, and then smiled as he thought back to the exercise when the commander had tried to set him an impossible target.

"We're going to be firing these missiles straight up, and then they're going to search for a target, right? And the MiG is flying straight at us, right?"

Fischer looked confused, but nodded agreement.

"Good. So, instead of waiting until the carrier says the MiG is in the missile's 20 mile range, launch when it's about 30 miles out. By the time the missiles reach altitude, the MiG should be in range."

"Yes, sir. But what if the MiG changes course after we fire?"

Cartwright nodded. "Then we'll miss. That's just a chance we'll have to take."

"Understood, sir. I was going to tell you the MiG will be in range in about five minutes. This will make it about a minute less."

"Very well, Lieutenant. Launch when ready."

North Korean Coast, 40 Kilometers North of DMZ

Shin Yon Young first smiled, and then scowled as he looked from the edge of the road at the sea nearby. Of course, reaching the coast accounted for the smile. The transparent glint he had seen on the surface of the water, though, had caused the scowl.

Jellyfish. Shin had particular reason to hate them, having been badly stung as a teenager. They had just been an annoyance back then, but now jellyfish numbers had exploded, both on the Korean coast and around the world. Shin had read explanations ranging from global warming, to overfishing having removed species that eat jellyfish and reducing competition for food, to fertilizer runoff helping jellyfish out compete other fish in newly nutrient-rich, oxygen-poor waters.

There were so many jellyfish now that they had gone from a nuisance to a worldwide menace. Several children had been stung to death on Korean beaches. A Swedish nuclear power station had to shut down because jellyfish had clogged pipes it used to draw in cooling water from the Baltic Sea.

After reintroducing natural predators proved ineffective, Shin was particularly interested to read about a Korean solution developed at the Korea Advanced Institute of Science and Technology. This was the JEROS (Jellyfish Elimination RObotic Swarm), autonomous robots working together to track down jellyfish and grind them into pulp. Each JEROS is held afloat by two pontoons fitted with motorized propellers, with a square net suspended underwater that pulls nearby jellyfish into it using its own propulsion. Any jellyfish that get scooped up are guided straight into a separate propeller, which instantly chops them into small pieces.

Through both GPS and inertial guidance the JEROS determines its location and orientation in the ocean within one and a half meters. Controllers can wirelessly upload data on current jellyfish locations to the JEROS so it can navigate to these areas on its own. An on board camera scans the surface of the water, and the JEROS uses image recognition software to identify any jellyfish within range. Using all these features, a controller can either have the JEROS steer itself autonomously towards higher concentrations of jellyfish or manually issue commands from a distance.

The first successful test had a swarm of three JEROS bots moving at a speed of four miles per hour, and was able to eliminate about 2,000 pounds of jellyfish per hour. Subsequent improvements both increased efficiency and collected the jellyfish remains for processing as fertilizer. The Swedes were among the first export successes, with even Swedish environmentalists agreeing that a nuclear disaster would be worse for the environment than grinding up jellyfish.

Unfortunately, success in South Korea had not translated to the peninsula's northern coast, Shin thought glumly. If anything, efficient eradication in the south appeared to have translated to even more of the pests here. And at some point, I'm going to have to go right through the middle of them to get on a small boat out of here.

Great.

CHAPTER EIGHTY NINE

Washington Dulles Airport

More than two decades of experience had taught Bob Hansen that an operation went smoothly or became a disaster almost entirely based on the quality of the preparation done beforehand. Of course, there was always plain bad luck, but Hansen had always found that fortune favored the better prepared.

From what he had already discovered, Hansen was feeling lucky.

First, he had checked to see which flights would be using the arrival gate for the Trans Pacific flight, as well as the gates around it. Though the Chinese seeking to intercept the defectors could have purchased tickets for any flight to get through security, and even though there was almost no chance that they would be asked to show their boarding pass again after being screened, Hansen knew how professionals would think. Better to have boarding passes that gave them a reason to be where they were, just in case.

That made finding them fairly easy. First, he limited the search to people who had bought tickets in the past eight hours for flights leaving from the target gates with Asian last names. Though Hansen knew the Chinese team leader could have easily hired help from any ethnic group, he knew from experience he probably would stick with his fellow Chinese. Among other advantages, this would allow the Chinese team to communicate in a language spoken by relatively few Americans.

Then, Hansen matched those names against those of known Chinese agents, on the chance they had not had time to produce bogus ID good enough to get through airport screening. Once he had a hit, Hansen looked to see who else among his candidates had purchased tickets within fifteen minutes of the known agent. There were three others, all four tickets for the same flight, all purchased within five minutes using the same credit card.

They were all for a departure leaving by the same gate that would be used by passengers exiting the Trans Pacific flight arriving from Beijing.

To find the rest of the Chinese team, Hansen thought the way their leader would, given the same goal. So, what if one or both defectors made it past the team at the gate? The obvious answer was to have men at the next choke point, baggage pick up. Hansen correctly guessed that the defectors would have checked luggage, since anyone on a long flight without it would have been automatically suspect.

A quick look around the baggage carousel designated for the Trans Pacific flight was all it took to spot three muscular Asians waiting patiently for bags that never seemed to come.

Next, the Chinese team clearly needed transport. But, idling at an airport curbside post 9/11 was not going to work. The solution wasn't hard to guess. Ten minutes was all it took to identify the two full-size SUVs that pulled up, dropped off a passenger, and then were back minutes later to pick up the same person. They did it in tandem, so that one SUV was replaced curbside by the other seconds after the first had pulled away, though never at exactly the same spot. In the constant traffic outside the terminal, nobody would have noticed unless they were looking for that exact pattern.

As Hansen was.

Finally, Hansen knew that the Chinese team leader would have realized the defectors might be brought out through one of the airport's service exits, ordinarily used only by airport employees and their vehicles. This would have presented a special challenge, since a vehicle could not wait inconspicuously outside a service gate. Hansen realized that the roads leading to the gates were the place to look.

Sure enough, he thought to himself with satisfaction. Drones were normally not allowed anywhere near a commercial airport, but HRT had one of the very few blanket exceptions. There were several reasons for this, starting with their lead role in responding to hijackings. It also helped that HRT's drones were small, low altitude, and operated by some of the most experienced technicians available.

Hansen was looking at two screens, one for each HRT drone. The first showed a car with a flat tire being changed. The second was a rotating infrared view between two men in the drainage ditches on either side of a road. The men were well concealed, and the drone operator had told Hansen admiringly that he would have never spotted them without the FBI agent's insistence that they had to be there.

A baker's dozen, Hansen thought to himself, shaking his head in wonder. The Chinese were obviously serious about making sure that these defectors never made it out of Dulles Airport.

Well, they were in for quite a surprise.

CHAPTER NINETY

En Route to Attack USS Theodore Roosevelt

Lieutenant Wang Yong was not the first choice for the mission to attack the American carrier, and he knew it. He would have happily skipped the honor, too, since his commander had made it clear he was unlikely to make it back to the refueling tanker that had topped him off just before leaving what China expansively called "its" airspace.

Since he was the only one in the squadron who had ever test fired the Brahmos missile, though, he was the only one who could really be sent. Even though he didn't have that much flying time yet, ironically most of it had been in the MiG-29Ks the squadron had obtained only a few months ago.

And that mattered, since flying the MiG with the missile weighing down his right wing left the fighter unbalanced and difficult to control. There wasn't a second Brahmos fully assembled and ready to load on the other wing, and anyway the added weight would have made reaching the target impossible.

No, instead he had to be focused 100 percent of the time on keeping the controls balanced for the extra weight on his right wing. Otherwise, he might have noticed that he'd accidentally hit the short-range radio transmitter switch.

Well, at least he was almost in range of the target. As soon as he had a lock on tone he was going to launch this missile, do a 180 degree turn and hope against hope that he could get back. His head knew he didn't have the fuel, but as long as he was alive he was going to try.

At least his commander had promised that his parents would be cared for, and that made this mission easier. A big part of why he had signed up had been to send back money to his parents, who weren't so young anymore.

Wang was so startled when his threat warning radar reported two anti aircraft missiles straight ahead and moving towards him that he said, "Where the hell did those come from?"

Naturally, he said that in Chinese.

He then quickly got on with trying to stay alive. The MiG-29K's engines had been shielded to reduce their thermal signature, and it carried flares, which Wang used successfully to decoy one of the AIM-9X missiles.

He was not able to avoid the other.

The anti-aircraft missile flew straight into one of the MiG's two engines, exactly as it had been designed to do. It happened to fly into the engine on the right side, and its explosion detonated the Brahmos missile's warhead.

The one consolation for the men who had sent Wang on his mission was that the resulting fireball left very little for later investigators to discover.

Los Angeles

Vasilyev reached out to knock on yet another door, as Grishkov became more and more impatient. So far they had received reactions ranging from blank staring incomprehension from Asians who obviously did not speak English, hostility from people who simply didn't want to be bothered, and quite a few doors that didn't open no matter how hard they were pounded on, though noise and movement inside made it clear that someone was at home.

"Are we going to knock on every door in this whole building?" Grishkov muttered, not really expecting an answer.

Vasilyev gave him one anyway. "I understand your impatience, my friend, and I'd be lying if I didn't say I was beginning to share it. Two things, however, keep me going. First is that I would prefer to avoid dealing with the local yakuza, if we can. Second is that I have an instinct, or I think the word in English is hunch, that there is something here worth finding."

Grishkov nodded. "Those are both good answers. Knock away."

The scowling face of the Asian man who appeared at the door did not inspire much hope that this conversation would be any different.

"I'm sorry to bother you, sir. We are looking for a friend of ours who we understand was living in this building, but the manager has no record of him. I have a picture of him here, but I'm afraid it's not a very good one. Maybe you saw how he helped that pregnant woman on the news, recently?"

The man laughed. "Him? No wonder the manager had no record. I sublet that apartment, since I have the lease. It's right next door."

Vasilyev nodded. "Excellent. He told us he might have to leave, and that his apartment might become available. Is there any chance we could see it?"

Grishkov had to fight back a grin at the immediate transformation in the man's expression and attitude, which went from hostile to nearly fawning as soon as he realized Vasilyev might be a source of income rather than annoyance.

"Absolutely! Let's go have a look! Just give me a second to get the key. Wait here, please."

Less than a minute later the man, who had introduced himself as Mr. Park, was opening the door of the apartment that had been occupied by Chung Hee Moon.

"Your friend left in a hurry, so some of his things are still here. Maybe you know where I can send them?"

Vasilyev shook his head. "No, we were hoping that you might know. Have you heard from him at all since he left?"

Park scowled. "Not a word, and no trace of him either. I've got utility bills coming for this apartment, and nobody to pay them." Then he smiled. "So, let's have a look around!"

Vasilyev and Grishkov looked carefully around the small apartment, but saw quickly that nothing the size of the device they sought could possibly be there. Vasilyev engaged Park in conversation while Grishkov looked through the few papers he found lying on a kitchen counter. Grishkov, though, saw quickly that the papers were only unopened junk mail that hadn't yet been thrown out.

Vasilyev gave Park a card with his cover name and the number of a burner phone he had purchased at the airport. "We are very interested in the apartment, but have promised to look at two others in the neighborhood. Also, we still want very much to get in touch with our friend. If anything happens with the apartment, or if you hear from our friend, please give me a call."

Park smiled. "I will certainly do so. I am sure once you compare this apartment to any other in its price range, you will find this one is a bargain."

Vasilyev smiled back, shook Park's hand, and headed for the elevator. After pushing the down button, they heard the door to Park's apartment close. Vasilyev moved back to the door of the apartment between the one they had just seen and the elevator. Though he had no way to know it, it was Chung Hee Moon's new residence.

Vasilyev knocked on the door. Not only was there no response, this time there was absolutely no sound or movement suggesting anyone was home.

For the first time since Grishkov had known him, Vasilyev appeared indecisive, chewing on his lower lip as he fingered something in his pocket.

"So, what have you got there?" Grishkov asked, jerking his head toward Vasilyev's pocket.

Vasilyev withdrew a lockpick.

"I was trying to make up my mind whether to use this," he replied.

Grishkov raised his eyebrows. "So, what's stopping you?"

Vasilyev shrugged. "Many points. It's very unlikely that the man we're looking for would have moved just one door away. The fact that we don't hear anything doesn't mean that nobody's home, and in this country that person could very well be armed. Being caught for breaking and entering by the police would not help us accomplish our mission. Also, I keep expecting Mr. Park's head to pop out of his door any minute."

Grishkov nodded. "Well, you've convinced me. Why are we still standing here?"

Slowly, Vasilyev nodded too. "Yes. We have at least confirmed our target's prior location, and that the device is no longer here. I see no choice but to carry through with our plan to contact the local yakuza."

Grishkov grimaced and punched the elevator's down button again. "Agreed." They both got on, but as the doors closed Vasilyev had a feeling that he was missing something. After a few moments he shrugged, and decided it was because they were still far from accomplishing their mission. Only later would he find out how close he had come to completing it.

Escort Duty, USS Theodore Roosevelt Carrier Group

Lieutenant Fischer gripped the sides of the console displaying information from the carrier's combat data network as though he could shake more information from it. Captain Cartwright smiled in spite of himself, and asked the obvious question. "Any word on the missiles we just fired, Lieutenant?"

Fischer grinned and nodded. "Yes, sir. The Japanese AWACS is reporting that the MiG has disappeared from radar. They had a drone monitoring it for a while, but lost coverage by the time we launched the missiles. Their pilot is reporting a flash of light along the same bearing as the MiG, but due to the distance can't confirm it was a hit. Bottom line - I think we got it. F-18s from the *Roosevelt* will be at the MiG's last known position shortly, and tell us for sure."

Cartwright nodded. "Good. Once we get confirmation, please pass the word to the rest of the crew."

Fischer's grin grew even wider. "Yes, sir! This will be quite a story back home, I bet!"

Cartwright smiled and shook his head. "Actually, I'm expecting us to be ordered to consider the entire encounter highly classified, and never to speak of it again once we dock."

Fischer looked genuinely confused. "Sir, I know things happen all the time on patrol the crew of a submarine is told not to talk about. But how could they hope to keep all the thousands of crew on the carrier and its escorts quiet?"

Cartwright cocked his head and tapped the console. "The data feed to us from the carrier group is one-way, right?"

Fischer nodded. "Yes, sir. We can receive data without surfacing, but the system doesn't have the capability to transmit our data...."

Cartwright smiled. "Did it ever occur to you, Lieutenant, that could be by design?"

From the expression on Fischer's face, it clearly had not.

Cartwright shrugged. "Maybe I'm wrong. But I'm betting that PACOM won't want to advertise that US Navy subs can take shots at attacking aircraft. Especially since I think if we did get this one, it took quite a bit of luck. Not to mention a heads-up from that Japanese AWACS we're not likely to get very often. How did the MiG disappear? Its missile launch system malfunctioned, or maybe it crashed after running out of fuel. Who knows?"

Fischer slowly nodded. "Makes sense, sir. So, we just congratulate each other on a job well done, and that's the last anyone will hear of it?"

Cartwright laughed, and said "Now you're starting to understand the real reason we're called 'The Silent Service'."

CHAPTER NINETY ONE

Washington Dulles Airport

The People's Liberation Army General Staff Headquarters had a wide range of responsibilities, including military intelligence. The General Staff's Second Department included such programs as military espionage, with agents at all Chinese embassies. However, their activities were normally geared towards obtaining intelligence directly relevant to military operations.

The Ministry of State Security, China's equivalent of the Russian KGB, would have ordinarily carried out an operation like the one now underway at Dulles Airport. MSS had not even been informed of the operation, though, because its leadership was not yet fully committed to the plan to use a second Korean War as cover for Taiwan's reunification by force with China.

The agent in charge of Chinese military intelligence activities in the U.S. was, naturally, one of the best the organization had to offer. Xu Guotin had just completed a successful tour in the United Kingdom, where he had organized the theft of highly classified data from a British company's work on the new F-35 Lightning II. Blackmail, kidnapping and murder had all figured in that accomplishment, so Xu could be considered highly qualified for this assignment.

Xu was a perfectionist, and it annoyed him that an operation of this importance had to be carried out with only a few hours available to plan. He had agents at every Chinese consulate, and with more time could have drawn on experienced and reliable men from New York City, Chicago, Houston, Los Angeles, and San Francisco. As it was, along with the few agents Xu had immediately available from the Chinese Embassy, he had been forced to call on a number of freelancers.

Xu had only taken that risk after checking with an old friend in Beijing over the embassy secure phone. The one word he had spoken about the mission's importance had immediately convinced Xu. That word was re-unification.

The good news was that many of these freelancers would be unknown to American intelligence and law enforcement officials. Though the FBI only followed Chinese agents in the U.S. for a long term assignment on an intermittent basis, they had an annoying habit of turning up at exactly the wrong time.

Tonight, though, luck seemed to be with Xu. He had seen no evidence that he had been followed to Dulles Airport, and as they reported in, the rest of the team gave the same report.

Helping to balance the rushed nature of this operation was one stroke of genuine good fortune. Their most capable undercover agent, purely by chance, was on shift at her job in a duty free shop. Ping Jing-Wei was an attractive woman in her late twenties whose dress, artfully applied makeup and flawless English made her one of the best performing workers in the shop. Ping picked up a number of interesting tidbits at the shop, particularly from the many Chinese businessmen making last minute purchases before going back home. However, that was not her main purpose at the airport.

The duty free shop was within the secure zone of the airport, so Ping could go anywhere that a ticketed passenger could whenever she wished. Once she had established herself as an airport employee and become a familiar sight at security, it had been easy to bring in weapons in a box disguised as containing duty free goods, and hide them in the duty free storage area. Ping had already discreetly distributed these guns to Xu and his team even before they reached the Trans Pacific arrival gate.

Even better was that customs requirements did not allow a purchase to be handed directly to a customer. Instead, they had to be brought by a shop employee like Ping to the jetway connecting the waiting area at the gate to the plane. After presenting his receipt and ID, the customer would receive his purchase just before boarding the plane. This ensured that duty free purchases actually left the country, instead of being resold in the U.S. for profit.

As a result, nobody thought twice about Ping being in the jetway where the plane from Beijing was due to arrive. They just assumed, correctly, that another flight would shortly depart from the same gate. They were wrong, though, to think that this time Ping's presence in the jetway had anything to do with handing out liquor and perfume.

Ping was also an accomplished assassin. Her last assignment in Tokyo had given her practice on several targets, two corrupt businessmen as well as a particularly annoying dissident. She had used her cover there as a geisha to great advantage. Up to now, she had thought this tour was quite boring by comparison, but it appeared that was likely to change. Her instructions were clear - if Xu decided it was practical to abduct the defectors, she would assist in that effort by pressing gifts into their hands with a drugged coating that would render them disoriented and easy to control.

If Xu decided abducting the defectors was too risky, Ping was to press different gifts in their hands. The coating on these contained a poison that would kill them in minutes. If they refused the gifts, Ping was to shoot them in the jetway using her silenced 9 mm pistol, and make her escape in the panic that would follow. With her airport employee ID, Ping thought her chances of getting away clean were good, although the poisoned gifts were obviously preferable.

Ping spotted Xu and his team at the gate as she readied herself in the jetway, being careful to put on her thin, elegant leather gloves. Naturally, she did nothing to acknowledge him. No matter how routine Ping's presence in the jetway might be, there was still no need to do anything that might attract attention.

Now all that was left was to wait for the flight's arrival, just minutes away. Ping nodded to herself with satisfaction. Finally, this boring assignment was about to get interesting.

CHAPTER NINETY TWO

Los Angeles

Grishkov looked dubiously at the decrepit warehouse in front of their car. Most of the streetlights in this industrial district were out, and the building itself had only a single working light attached. It wasn't exactly an inviting location for a meeting, which now that Grishkov thought about it, may have been precisely the point.

"Are we sure this is the right address?"

Vasilyev smiled. "Yes, I am quite sure. Believe it or not, I have been here before, for a similar purpose."

Grishkov shrugged. "And you obviously survived the experience. Well, let's get this over with."

Vasilyev laughed. "Please, my friend, contain your enthusiasm! You may embarrass me! Seriously, though, you know from your own experience with organized crime that its members are interested in two things above all. Reputation, and money. If we convince them that helping us will do their reputation no harm, and that the money we offer is worthwhile, they will increase our odds of success by a substantial margin. And we have to project the right attitude to make that happen, for in the end we need them – and they don't need us."

Grishkov nodded. "Understood. As I mentioned before, it is not the first time I have had to deal with such criminals. I will back you, no matter what is said or done in there," he said, nodding towards the warehouse.

"Excellent. I expected nothing less."

Grishkov followed Vasilyev to the warehouse door, which opened at their approach.

They walked through the door, only to find that whoever had opened it was no longer there. Peering through the gloom inside the warehouse, they saw what looked like an office at the far end of the building. Nothing but unpainted drywall with glass set inside on all sides and a single door, it had been constructed as cheaply as possible for the purpose. Vinyl blinds were drawn on all sides so that they could not see inside, but it was clear that a light was on in the office.

Grishkov jerked his head towards the office. "And this is where you met these people last time?"

Vasilyev nodded. "Cheery, isn't it?"

Grishkov grunted, and they both moved forward. Vasilyev tapped on the office door, and then gently eased the door open.

Inside there were three Asian men, one seated at a desk with his back against the wall, and two others standing at each side. None were smiling.

Each of the men had ornate tattoos visible on their arms, and the two standing men were each missing a pinkie finger. Tell-tale bulges said all three men were armed, and weren't taking much trouble to conceal that fact.

The seated man waved to Grishkov and Vasilyev that they should enter, and once they had, pointed to the two battered chairs in front of the desk.

"I am Hiroshi Sato," the seated man said, gravely, using the name that was probably the most common in Japan.

"And my name is John Smith," Vasilyev said, just as solemnly.

Sato nodded, and then smiled. "OK, you're not complete idiots. So, John, what can we do for you?"

"Very similar to the last time I called on your colleagues for help, but even easier. This time no violence is called for, or even desired. Just as before, locate an individual. This time, though, simply call me once you have him and I will take it from there."

Sato raised his eyebrows, and shook his head. "Well, you say this will be easier, but I say harder. I can shoot a man and disappear, and that's five minutes' work and if I plan it right, little risk. Kidnapping is much harder. I have to be ready to restrain the target, but not kill him, or from what you say even hurt him. I have no one I could trust to be so...restrained. That means I will have to lead this job myself, and that will definitely cost you extra. In fact, it will cost double."

Vasilyev frowned, and then shrugged and nodded. "Done."

Sato regarded Vasilyev with a level stare. "So, you really want this guy. Want to tell me why?"

Vasilyev smiled, and said nothing.

Sato grunted. "Well, that's your business. What can you tell me that will help us find him?"

Vasilyev slid the picture from the video screen capture and a piece of paper with a name and address across the desk. "Though that is the man's last known address and the name he used to rent it, we have been to the apartment and spoken to the person who rented it to him, and I am satisfied he has no idea where the man is at this point. Of course, he could be using any name by now."

Sato looked intently at the picture. "The quality of this image is terrible, but somehow it looks familiar."

Vasilyev nodded. "It's from the grocery store holdup."

Sato laughed. "This is that guy? We heard the cops were looking high and low for a while, but since the clip isn't being played on the news anymore they seem to have lost interest in him. But not you, eh?"

Vasilyev just smiled.

"Well, you were smart to settle a price before showing me this picture. I saw the video, and this guy moves fast. But, we have agreed on a price, and I think double is fair. Your contact number?"

Vasilyev handed over a card with only a phone number, and added "I am working on getting you a better picture, but don't count on it."

Sato nodded. "Any particular deadline on this, or just the sooner the better?"

"The sooner the better is about right. To make the point clear, if you find him in the next two days, I'll pay triple. But if he can't talk, I'll pay nothing."

Sato stared at Vasilyev. "Right. You really want to talk to him. Got it."

As Vasilyev and Grishkov walked back to their car, Grishkov couldn't resist asking, "What if we can't get the original grocery store video, or the techs back in Moscow can't improve the image?"

Vasilyev shrugged. "That's why we came here first."

CHAPTER NINETY THREE

North Korean Coast, 25 Kilometers North of DMZ

Shin Yon Young had been walking for hours along the coastal highway, keeping one eye on the satellite phone's display and the other on the road, his head swiveling in both directions to try to get enough notice of an oncoming vehicle to take cover. The gas in his scooter had finally run out, and dragging it well away from the road and concealing it had taken precious time he was now trying to make up. However, it did not take long to discover that in spite of his youth and his extensive physical training, his legs would only take him so far so fast.

Shin's heart leapt as a single bar flickered to life on the phone's display. His fingers trembling, he texted the four digit code that requested a coastal extraction and hit send. He then began setting up to transmit the contents of the SD card. A few minutes later, he received a single digit text that translated to "request approved." The wide grin that had been on Shin's face soon faded, though, as the SD card data transmission stubbornly refused to transmit. This was not really a surprise, since the signal was both weak and intermittent. Good enough to send a few characters, but not megabytes of data.

So be it. Shin would just have to make sure that the card itself made it to the hands of his superiors in Korean intelligence. He was optimistic, because having failed to check in should have alerted them to have a sub ready to pick him up on the coast at the prearranged site. All he had to do was get to the site by nightfall, since pickup was set for twilight the same day the code was received. That gave him about twelve hours, which he should be able to make easily at his current pace.

If he could keep it up. And, he thought glumly, if this mission had no more unpleasant surprises.

Washington Dulles Airport

Bert Fowler had been pushing his Boeing 787 at close to its maximum rated airspeed for most of the flight, and had only eased off after they were over the US mainland. He had explained this to his copilot Tim Shields by saying they needed to make up time for detouring around the storm, and that was true as far as it went. The real reason, though, was that he'd had a nagging feeling of danger he couldn't explain to Tim or the rest of the crew, or even to himself.

Fowler was glad that in a few minutes, this flight would finally be over.

"Dulles control, this is Trans Pacific flight 898, requesting clearance to land and runway assignment," Fowler said, beginning to relax as the reality of making it back safely started to sink in.

The feeling didn't last long.

"Trans Pacific flight 898, you are cleared to land on runway 4. Taxi to the end of the runway and await further instructions."

"Ah, Dulles control, please repeat that last transmission," Fowler said, frowning in confusion.

"Trans Pacific flight 898, you are cleared to land on runway 4, repeat 4. Taxi to runway end and await further instructions."

"Roger, Dulles control. Will land on runway 4, taxi to runway end and await further instructions," Fowler said, shaking his head.

His copilot turned to Fowler and asked the obvious question. "So, why do you think they're having us land on the cargo side of the airport?"

"Tim, I have absolutely no idea," Fowler replied with a deepening scowl.

"Do you think it could have anything to do with the passenger, or passengers, that we were guessing the Chinese wanted back?," Shields asked.

Fowler shrugged, and looked thoughtful. Finally, he nodded. "You may have something there. When one flight has two odd things happen, chances are they're connected. Even though I don't see how. Anyway, I guess we'll see soon enough."

Fowler didn't have to wait long. As soon as they had completed landing and taxied to the end of the runway, Dulles control was on the radio again.

"Trans Pacific flight 898, mobile stairs are en route to your aircraft. Two FBI agents will board and assist two of your passengers to exit the aircraft. After they escort these two passengers off the aircraft, you are to proceed to your regular assigned gate."

"Dulles control, are these passengers being put into custody? Do they present any security threat we should be aware of, and should we make any announcement to the other passengers?," Fowler asked.

"Negative to all three questions. Respond to any inquiries from the rest of your passengers with the statement that you do not know why these two passengers left the aircraft early. You should now have the stairs and the vehicles with the agents in sight. Please prepare the exit door adjacent to the cockpit."

"Roger, Dulles control," Fowler said, shaking his head.

"Well, at least we'll be telling the passengers the truth when we say we don't know anything," Shields said acidly.

Fowler grunted, still shaking his head. "I wonder if we'll ever know what this was about." With a shrug, he turned to call the lead flight attendant to prepare the exit door.

CHAPTER NINETY FOUR

Los Angeles

The grocery store was about to close, as demonstrated by the woman who walked up to the door with keys in her hands right after Vasilyev and Grishkov stepped in. Both noticed the poisonous glare she directed at them. It made them feel as though they had committed some crime by sliding in just ahead of closing time. As though to emphasize the point, they could hear the doors being vigorously slammed shut, and the keys in the lock jingling furiously with the impact.

Vasilyev raised one eyebrow. Grishkov shrugged and said, "Must have been a long day."

The counter at the front of the store had cigarettes and a large sign proclaiming that the Powerball lottery's jackpot had now reached a value of $320 million, a sum that made both Vasilyev and Grishkov shake their heads. It was more than the gross national product of many countries, but here it was a lottery prize that could go to a single person who had bought a $2 ticket.

What the counter did not have was anyone manning it. As far as Vasilyev and Grishkov could see, as both of their heads swiveled back and forth, there were a grand total of two other people in the store. One was the cashier, and the other was a customer, a young Korean man wearing a ball cap, sunglasses, and a dark T-shirt with something written on its front.

As the cashier stalked back to her register, she glared at Vasilyev and Grishkov and snapped, "Lottery machine closed. Store will be closed in five minutes, so please bring your items to the register as quickly as possible."

Vasilyev and Grishkov looked at each other. Vasilyev nodded towards Grishkov, saying without words, "She's all yours."

"Actually, miss, we aren't here to buy anything. We have a few questions about the robbery attempt here the other day. It shouldn't take long."

The cashier shook her head emphatically. "I already told the police everything. If you read the paper, you know everything there is to know. If you are not here to make a purchase, please leave so I can close up and go home."

Grishkov spread his hands and nodded. "I hear what you're saying, so I will make this simple. We are friends of the man who stopped the robbery, and we're trying to find him. All we want is the original recording of the incident. We are ready to pay you for your time and trouble."

With that, Grishkov noticed the attention of the man who had been browsing through a rack of magazines nearby was now clearly focused on their conversation. A glance at Vasilyev confirmed that he had noticed this too.

"Look, you can see the recording online for free. There's no need to pay me, or waste my time."

Grishkov shook his head. "We need to make sure this is our friend. The original recording will let us see his face in more detail, so we can confirm we're not looking for the wrong man."

The cashier scowled. "Why should I believe you're his friend? Maybe you're one of the ones who are after him!"

Grishkov cocked his head sideways, as though puzzled. At last they were getting somewhere. "After him? What gave you that idea? Who would be after him?"

The cashier clearly regretted having said as much as she had. "Never mind. I have no idea, and I don't care. Please, just leave."

Before Grishkov could say more, the young Korean man in the dark T-shirt slid forward. "Listen, I may be able to help you guys out. How much for our time and trouble?"

The cashier rounded on him angrily and began speaking very rapidly in Korean. The man said nothing to her in response, but instead just blinked and shrugged. Turning again to Grishkov, he asked "So? How about it?"

Grishkov looked thoughtfully at the young man. "May I ask what this lady just said to you?"

The man shrugged again. "She says you could be the men this guy was afraid would find him, and that all he wanted was to be left alone. She also says I should be ashamed that I'm selling out the man who saved her and the pregnant woman from those thieves."

Grishkov nodded. "But you don't think we're the men he was afraid of, right?"

The man looked at him frankly. "You look like a cop, but I guess you're not because you're not waving an ID, and I see no badge. Plus, you got some kind of accent, like maybe Russia or Eastern Europe. You got no tats, and you're polite. Bottom line is, I got no idea. So want to answer my question?"

"How do you have access to the original recording?"

"Because I'm the son of the store's owner, and I set up the camera that made the recording. And I'm the one who posted it online. That good enough?"

Grishkov glanced at the cashier, who continued to glare at the man, but had contradicted nothing he said. It was the best confirmation he was likely to get.

"Two hundred dollars, cash right now."

The man shook his head. "Worth more than that. Five hundred."

Grishkov frowned and chewed his lip, but it was just for show. He'd been ready to go as high as a thousand dollars on the spot. Smyslov had been generous with their expense money, telling them that their goal made it worthwhile.

"Done. When can we get the recording?

"As soon as you give me the cash."

Grishkov pulled out his wallet and carefully counted out five one hundred dollar bills.

The man nodded. "OK, give me your cell phone number."

Vasilyev silently handed the man his card with the number.

The man pulled out his cell phone, pressed a number of buttons, and a few seconds later Vasilyev's phone began to vibrate. The phone was new, with a large clear display. Grishkov could tell that the image's resolution was better than what he had seen before online, but the difference was not that dramatic.

"This recording's not compressed the way the one online was as soon as I uploaded it, so maybe that will help. Either way, this is all I've got."

Grishkov nodded. "Understood. If by any chance you see our friend, please call the number on the card. It will be worth a thousand dollars to you if you help us find him."

"OK. By the way, what's his name?"

Having looked before for unidentified criminals, it was a question Grishkov was ready to answer. Smiling, he said "We always called him Lightning, because he moved so fast. But I'm not sure what name he'd be using now. It's been a while since we've seen him."

As they left the store and the doors closed behind them, they could still hear the cashier shouting at the man who had given them the recording.

Vasilyev lifted one eyebrow. "I don't think you convinced her that we mean her savior no harm."

Grishkov shrugged. "I don't think I convinced that guy either. Fortunately, money speaks louder than words."

Vasilyev smiled and clapped Grishkov on the shoulder. "Don't sell yourself short, my friend. If you had come across as an obvious threat, no amount of money would have done the trick. Now we will put the technicians at Moscow Center to work, and with a better quality image to work with should have a fighting chance to find this man in time to locate the device."

Grishkov nodded. "You mean, before it goes off, probably taking us with it."

Vasilyev smiled even more broadly. "That's exactly what I mean."

CHAPTER NINETY FIVE

Los Angeles

Kang Ji Yeong grimaced with annoyance at the knock on the door. It came while she was in the middle of fixing dinner, which she was determined would be a genuine made-from-scratch meal rather than the pizza and take out usually forced on her by her busy schedule. Chung had just started a shower, and she didn't want to have to tell him to stay put. Maybe if she ignored whoever it was, they would go away.

No such luck. The pounding continued, probably because she was making enough noise in the kitchen that it was obvious she was at home. Looking through the peephole, she was surprised to see a man she recognized as a neighbor, but one she had never spoken with. He didn't look threatening. In fact, he looked nervous and frightened. She decided to get rid of him quickly, while Chung was still in the shower.

Kang opened the door. The man spoke immediately.

"You don't know me, but there are a few things I think you should know, if you have a minute."

Kang said nothing, but gestured for the man to enter.

"Maybe you know I'm your neighbor on this floor. My name is Mr. Park."

Kang nodded, and pointed to the sofa, while she sat on a chair. The man sat down, his hands twisting in his lap as though he wasn't quite sure what to do with them.

"This is about the man who was living in the apartment I was subletting. The man the police are looking for, after the shooting I'm sure you saw on TV."

Kang looked up. "I saw that on TV. That man didn't shoot anybody."

Park's head bobbed up and down nervously. "I didn't say that he did. Just that the police are looking for him."

Kang chewed her lower lip. "You're right. I'm sorry."

"I understand. Look, the man's name was Chung Hee Moon, but I guess you know that since he's staying with you now."

Kang paled, but said nothing.

"You don't have to worry. The man who rented the apartment for him paid me extra to keep quiet about it, but I wouldn't have told anyone about him anyway. The thugs who shot each other got exactly what they deserved, and there was no reason to punish Chung for helping them do it. If I saw him today, I'd shake his hand and congratulate him."

Kang looked up. "So, then, why did you decide to come to see me today?"

"To tell you that the police aren't the only ones looking for him. Two men came to see me asking about Chung. They weren't cops, though they seemed like government types. I don't think either were American, though if I'd heard one of them on the phone I might have thought so. I'm not sure where they were from. Maybe eastern Europe or Russia. They didn't say why they were looking for Chung, and I didn't ask."

Kang didn't bother trying to hide her confusion. "So, what did you tell them?"

"The truth at the time. That I didn't know where Chung was. It was only later that I saw him get into the elevator with you, just as the doors were closing. Like I said, I wouldn't have told them anything anyway, but it worked out for the best. They looked like men who would have been able to tell if I'd been lying."

Kang frowned. "And what about the man who rented the apartment for Chung? Who was he?"

"I have no idea. He paid me cash up front for the first and last month's rent plus a security deposit, signed the lease, and told me when to expect Chung. I never saw him again."

Kang was silent for a moment, continuing to twist her hands in her lap while she thought over what Park had said. Finally, she nodded.

"Thank you for telling me this. If these men come back, I'd appreciate it if you could let me know."

Park stood and made a small bow. "I am glad to help a neighbor. I wish you both the best of luck."

Kang held the door open as Park left. She had a jumble of thoughts running through her head, as well as a growing list of questions for the man in her shower.

Chung, who had been listening against the bathroom door as the shower continued to run since he first heard the apartment door open, couldn't see Kang's face. But he had no trouble guessing she would have questions. He had no idea where he would find answers.

Washington Dulles Airport

Li Weimin and Park Won Hee were separated by several rows in the Trans Pacific flight that had just landed, but were having much the same thoughts. Both were thinking about the relatives they had left behind, and were wondering whether they would ever see them again. Both were wondering what would happen next. They each had guesses, but neither were anywhere close.

The two FBI agents boarded the plane in first class, and quickly moved back to the economy seats where both Li and Park were sitting. One agent each went straight up to them, clearly knowing exactly who they were looking for.

"Sir, I'm with the FBI. Please come with me." Each time it was said politely, and with a display of credentials.

In less than a minute, Li and Park were both on the stairs leading to the tarmac, where they saw a car was idling in wait.

As they were getting in the vehicle, Li couldn't resist asking, "Please, where are we going?"

One of the agents smiled reassuringly and said, "To a safe place not far from here. In fact, we'll be there in about fifteen minutes."

The car sped across an airport service road, and stopped in about three minutes in front of a helicopter with its rotors already spinning. The plain black helicopter had numbers and letters on the tail, but no other markings. Moments later, Li and Park as well as the two FBI agents were soaring over the Virginia countryside.

CHAPTER NINETY SIX

En Route to North Korean Coast

Shin Yon Young was right to think that his failure to report would prompt action by the South Korean Navy. A Type 214 sub was on its way to the rendezvous point less than a day later, and held just outside North Korean waters to await further orders. Those came shortly after Shin's text had been received at National Intelligence Service (NIS) headquarters.

The Type 214, a diesel-electric sub designed by Germany's Howaldtswerke-Deutsche Werft GmbH, used an air-independent propulsion system and Siemens polymer electrolyte membrane hydrogen fuel cells. The Type 214 submarine was a variant of the Type 212, but as an export lacked the classified non-magnetic steel hull that made the Type 212 impossible to detect using a Magnetic Anomaly Detector.

The Korean versions were designated as the Son Won-Il class, and built in Korea by Hyundai Heavy Industries and Daewoo Shipbuilding and Marine Engineering. The first three Son Won-Il class subs entered service in 2007, and six more in 2012. Capable of diving 1,200 feet, the Son Won-Il class could operate without resupply for about eighty-four days, depending on how frugal her captain was with her fuel.

The most impressive feature of the Son Won-Il class was its SPHINX-D Radar System, supplied by Germany's Thales Defense Deutschland GmbH. The SPHINX-D used both conventional radar and an additional pulse transmitter in the top of the mast. The combination of high power pulse radar and a Low Probability of Intercept (LPI) transmitter using less power than a cell phone meant that during surface operations in home waters the sub sails with an easily detected open pulse fingerprint, but on a mission like this could switch to LPI mode and be nearly certain of remaining undiscovered.

The Son Won-Il class carried a variable mix of sixteen surface to surface missiles (SSMs) and torpedoes. These could be launched from eight 21 inch tubes, of which half were capable of launching SSMs.

Other Type 214 subs were operated by the navies of Greece, Turkey and Portugal, but none of these others were to be found in Asian waters. Of course, the captain of the ROKS *Baekdusan* thought with satisfaction, nothing the North Koreans had could compare in terms of the Son Won-Il class's capabilities, or stood any chance of detecting it while it remained submerged. Captain Yun Sang Chul was particularly proud of the fact that his sub carried the same name as the South Korean Navy's first warship, carrying on his navy's tradition into a new century.

Naturally, this mission would require surfacing in order to launch the Zodiac that would pick up the NIS agent. Then, Captain Yun thought glumly, all that would be needed to spot his sub was a pair of Mark I eyeballs. The North Korean Navy had plenty of those, and its coastal waters were perhaps the most heavily patrolled in the world, particularly the stretch closest to its border with South Korea.

The Zodiac Futura Commando that would be used for this mission weighed one hundred twenty kilograms fully inflated, and measured about 14 x 6 feet. It could handle a payload of about two thousand pounds, meaning six passengers well outfitted with weapons. Today five were on board the Zodiac that had just been set into the water, to provide room for the NIS agent they were set to retrieve.

"Captain, Huangfeng class missile boat off the port bow!"

Not unexpected, and not the worst news possible, since the North Korean Navy had ships with more advanced capabilities. The 205 ton Huangfeng class missile boat was an old direct Chinese copy of the Soviet Osa-class missile boat, and at 127 feet in length was a fairly tight fit for her crew of 28. Around 130 of this class were built, in several versions with different armament, all with a top speed of about 35 knots thanks to a Chinese engine that was a significant upgrade from the Soviet original. Like most this one was armed with twin 25 mm guns, while unlike most this one did carry fire control radar. That meant that it had either four Silkworm missiles, or four C-101 missiles. Both were supersonic anti-ship missiles that could not be outrun or decoyed. There was in fact only one defense. Making sure they weren't launched.

Captain Yun smiled grimly as he thought about what the age of the ship near him meant. Not that there was no need to fear its weapons. Instead, that it would not be led or crewed by the best the North Koreans had to offer. Otherwise, they would be on a newer ship. That meant he had a decent chance of firing first.

All these thoughts went through his head during the same second that he roared, "Fire tubes one through four at Huangfeng class boat, designate target Sierra One!"

The weapons officer's response was immediate. "Attack Sierra One, aye!" Two seconds later, the sub lurched as pressurized gas sped four torpedoes towards the missile boat. A few seconds after that, they could see their launch had been detected as the North Korean vessel sped up dramatically and began to zigzag in a desperate attempt to avoid destruction.

Captain Yun relaxed fractionally as he saw the boat begin evasive maneuvers, because it meant on a ship that old getting a firing solution for its missiles was nearly impossible. Since he had not seen the tell-tale smoke of missile liftoff from the deck of the North Korean boat, it appeared that his sub might live to fight another day. If at least one of his torpedoes made it to its target.

This was the first time Captain Yun had ordered weapons fired at a real enemy. As far as he knew, it was the first time any officer in the South Korean Navy had done so since the Korean War ended over half a century ago. He didn't realize he had been holding his breath until his chest started to hurt, and remembered to breathe just as a flash of light lit up the North Korean missile boat.

The first flash was quickly followed by two others, just as the sound wave from the first explosion made it to the ROKS *Baekdusan*. Captain Yun waited for a fourth explosion, but it never came. A miss, he thought at first, but then realized there was probably nothing with enough mass left in the water to activate the fourth torpedo's warhead. Nothing was visible now where the North Korean boat had been but drifting smoke.

However, Captain Yun knew he could not yet relax. In fact, much greater danger lay ahead. He was certain the North Korean missile boat would have radioed its headquarters that it had spotted an enemy vessel. That meant any minute he could expect a North Korean attack jet to appear, and against even a simple strafing run he had absolutely no defense except to submerge and abandon both the team on the Zodiac and the agent they were trying to retrieve.

As he ordered additional crew to the deck to maintain a visual lookout for aerial attack, Captain Yun silently urged on the team speeding towards shore on the Zodiac. He felt in his bones that seconds would separate complete success from abject failure for this mission. For the sake of his crew and his country, he prayed those seconds would be on his side.

CHAPTER NINETY SEVEN

Los Angeles

Kang Ji Yeong stood in front of Chung Hee Moon with her elbows out and her hands on her hips. It was a pose that told Chung nothing good was going to come from this conversation.

"So, did you hear what your landlord had to say?," Kang asked, with a glare that told Chung the answer she expected.

Chung simply nodded.

"Why are Russians or whoever they are looking for you? Do I need to be worried about them?," Kang asked, her voice trembling.

"I have no idea why anyone but the police would be looking for me, and you know the reason for that. These other men are as much a mystery to me as they are to you," Chung said, looking Kang straight in the eye.

It helped that Chung was in fact telling the truth, and after a few moments Kang nodded, evidently satisfied with his answer.

"What about the man who rented the apartment for you? Don't tell me you don't know who he is," Kang said with a scowl.

"Of course not. He is a friend from my days in the Army who offered to help me get settled in LA. I wired him the money and he took care of the rest. You never met him because his company transferred him to Portland the same week I got here. That's before we even met."

Some of that was...kind of true. The Army part was, since a military intelligence officer had rented his apartment. Not the South Korean Army, but he couldn't be blamed for other people's assumptions, could he? And the officer had left as soon as Chung arrived, just as he said. He had no idea where he had gone, but he could have gone to Portland.

Kang gave him a glare that let him know she had guessed his second answer had not been as true as the first. Chung decided that saying anything else would just make matters worse, demonstrating the judgment that had served him well over his career in the North Korean military.

"Was the story about you having cancer a lie to get my sympathy? Did you go through the colonoscopy hoping the doctor would give the results only to you?," Kang asked with a fierce scowl.

"I was as surprised as you were to hear I didn't have cancer," Chung said, with a sincerity he did not have to fake. Again, Kang appeared to have no trouble telling that this time he was telling the truth. Chung was smart enough not to speculate on how he came to believe he had the disease. He now knew the truth, and could hardly tell Kang that his superiors in the North Korean military had misled him to strengthen his resolve to carry out a suicide mission.

Kang waited for Chung to say more, and when he didn't shook her head and sighed. "I know you're a good man, both from living with you these past days and for what you did to help that pregnant woman. But I also know there are things you're not telling me, and that really worries me."

Chung stood up and gave Kang a small bow. "I understand. I would like to thank you for everything you have done for me. You have shown me greater kindness than I have experienced before in my entire life. I will have my things out later today."

Kang shook her head, and said sharply, "Idiot! Did I tell you to leave? In fact I'm the one who's going. I've been meaning to see my sister in San Diego for some time now, so I'm taking my son and driving down for the rest of the week. If I don't take the leave now I'll lose it anyway."

Kang paused. "Use the time to figure out who the men are who are looking for you, and what they want. I care about you, but I can't take risks with my son. And think hard about telling me whatever it is you're hiding. If you're not here when I come back, I'll know it's because keeping your secrets was more important than whatever feelings you have for me."

Before Chung could respond, Kang had run into her bedroom and closed the door. Chung could hear her opening and closing drawers, and was sure he was hearing her pack.

The truth was, matters had worked out perfectly. Chung had been trying and failing to reconcile completing his mission when ordered to do so with the feelings he had for Kang and her son. Given the blast radius of the device, just moving elsewhere in Los Angeles was not a solution. San Diego, however, was far enough away that even fallout was unlikely to affect them.

Of course, once they came back, so would his dilemma. That didn't worry him, though. Chung had no idea why, but somehow he was sure that one way or the other his mission would end soon.

So, Chung thought to himself, I should be pleased. I wonder why I'm not?

CHAPTER NINETY EIGHT

North Korean Coast, 15 Kilometers North of DMZ

Lieutenant Pang clutched a Daewoo K11 DAW (Dual-barrel Air-burst Weapon) assault rifle as the Zodiac bounced through the waves towards where they hoped the NIS agent would be waiting for pickup. The K11 was chambered to fire 5.56x45mm NATO rounds, as well as 20x30mm air-burst smart grenades from its over barrel launcher that would either detonate immediately on impact or after impact on a timed fuse. Another option was to fire a shell directed by the K11's integrated electronics to explode a few meters from the target, with an air burst capable of killing targets within a six meter area and seriously wounding others for an additional two meters. This meant Pang could enter a detonation range on the rifle, so he could destroy targets in ditches, in buildings, or behind walls without a direct hit. Pang had been delighted to get his hands on the Korean made K11 when it was first distributed to South Korean forces in 2010, when they became the world's first army to use an airburst rifle as standard issue.

Pang grimaced as he thought about the reason for both the K11 design and the decision to issue two of these expensive weapons to every South Korean squad. This was the expectation that the South's forces would be heavily outnumbered if the North Koreans ever decided to replay their 1950 invasion. It would be an interesting contest between quantity and quality, Pang thought with a thin smile.

The rest of Pang's unit was carrying Daewoo K2 assault rifles. Though externally similar to the AR-18, it was actually an odd hybrid of the American M-16 rifle and the Russian AK-47. The K2's bolt carrier group was not only derived from the American rifle, some of the parts were actually interchangeable with the M-16, and it used the same magazine. The fire control system was derived from the M-16 as well. However, the gas operating system was derived entirely from the AK-47.

On firing ranges and in exercises both the K2 and K11 had performed well. Neither had ever been used in combat. Pang clutched his weapon nervously at the thought, and hoped that their first real test would be a success.

Shin Yon Young's first notice that something was badly wrong was when he noticed little spouts of mud and dirt rising from the ground around him. Confused, his first thought was that hailstones were hitting nearby, since the clouds and the cold certainly made hail possible. He grimaced at the thought of being caught in the open during a hailstorm. A second later, the sharp crack of gunfire from a distance made it clear that his situation was much more serious.

As Shin began to run, a quick look around confirmed his initial impression that there was nowhere to run to that offered any real cover. At the same moment that he wondered what had prompted the patrol to begin shooting at him without even checking his papers first, a massive explosion in the waters nearby answered his question. The sub that had been sent to collect him had obviously been spotted, and all nearby patrols alerted. The only question left was whether the sub or one of the ships attacking it had been destroyed in the explosion.

Well, there was one other question, Shin thought glumly as he weaved his way towards the surf. If the sub had survived, would it continue trying to pick him up, or head for safety?

Lieutenant Pang's Zodiac was at full throttle as it raced towards the shore to pick up the NIS agent. As the boat crested a wave, Pang could see that one of his worries had been groundless. There would be no trouble with signaling and counter signaling with flashlights, as planned. The man he saw headed for the beach while a three-man patrol fired at him from a distance was, Pang thought grimly, very likely the agent he was supposed to retrieve.

Just as Pang had that thought, the man made it to the water, throwing himself in while the soldiers continued to run towards him. The professional soldier in Pang cringed at the amateur performance displayed by the patrol. They had long since been in range for a careful shot to have made short work of the NIS agent. Instead, they tried to fire on the run, expecting that out of dozens of bullets fired in the agent's general direction one would have to find its mark. From the steady way the man was now swimming out to sea, it appeared unlikely that he had been hit, at least so far.

And now the patrol was just in range for an unpleasant surprise. Pang steadied his K11 DAW, setting its 20x30mm smart grenade on air-burst. Though Pang knew he was at the limit of the weapon's range and unlikely to score a direct hit firing from a rapidly advancing and bucking boat, he thought that at least he would shift the patrol's focus away from the agent.

Pang would later acknowledge that the results of the grenade's detonation were both unforeseen, and the result of a generous helping of luck. To his considerable surprise, after the smoke of the grenade's explosion cleared Pang saw that all three soldiers in the North Korean patrol were down. At first he assumed that one or two were just seeking cover, but after a few seconds realized that none were moving or firing. Pang would never know whether they were dead or injured, but all he really cared about was that they would no longer interfere with his mission.

No sooner had he congratulated himself on the success of his shot than one of Pang's men waved his K2 assault rifle at something on the top of a nearby wave top. Actually, at many glistening somethings. At first Pang wasn't sure what he was looking at, but his brain supplied the answer at the same time as the soldier waving the K2 said the word aloud – jellyfish. Pang's heart sank as he realized that they would be even thicker closer to shore. Where the NIS agent was swimming through them.

Snarling a curse, Pang twisted the Zodiac's throttle even harder, and did his best to will the boat to close the distance while the agent was still conscious and afloat.

CHAPTER NINETY NINE

North Korean Coast, 15 Kilometers North of DMZ

Captain Yun spotted the rapidly advancing shape at the same moment that one of the lookouts roared "Enemy aircraft!" He was about to order the sub to submerge when he recognized the model as a North Korean MiG-29. Nearly all were configured as air superiority fighters, not ground attack aircraft. In fact, the only weapon such a MiG-29 carried that could hurt his sub was its single GSh-30-1 30mm cannon, carried in the port wing root with a 150-round magazine. Yun knew that nearly all North Korean MiG-29s were original production MiG-29B aircraft, which could not fire the cannon when carrying a centerline fuel tank, because it blocked the shell ejection port. Though this flaw was corrected in the MiG-29S and later variants, as far as he knew North Korea had never purchased those versions. Yun was nearly certain this MiG would be using an additional fuel tank, because as the best fighter North Korea had, it was always on patrol duty near the capital Pyongyang. To stay on patrol for any length of time, the tank was a must. Already being in the air on patrol also accounted for the MiG-29's rapid arrival at the coast, since there had been no time to scramble a flight from the ground to attack his sub.

If Yun was right, the MiG would have just enough gas to make one pass over his sub before it had to return to its base near Pyongyang to refuel, and would have nothing to fire except AA-10 "Alamo" medium-range air-to-air missiles and AA-11 "Archer" dogfight missiles that would be unable to lock onto his sub. If he was wrong about the plane being a MiG-29B with a centerline fuel tank, or if it was a MiG-29S with a working cannon, his sub would shortly become floating debris.

Ordinarily a submarine sailor like Captain Yun would have had little knowledge of or interest in aircraft. The MiG-29 was an exception, though, because of its special place in Korean history. North Korea bought its first dozen MiG-29s from Belarus in 1995, as the worst part of the Great Famine began, at a cost of nearly half a billion dollars. That would have been enough to feed every hungry North Korean man, woman, and child for two years. Estimates of Great Famine deaths ranged between two to three and a half million. As a result, these dozen MiG-29s had probably killed more people than any others in history, without firing a shot.

All this passed through Yun's thoughts in about two seconds. In that time, he decided to give Lieutenant Pang's men more time to carry out their mission.

"Sir?," the lookout asked, leaving silent the obvious question. Yun mutely shook his head, and then the heads of all of the sailors on deck swiveled to follow the MiG as it turned and lined up on the sub. It was now too late to submerge in time, even if he gave the order.

The MiG quickly grew from a small speck to a large V kicking up a large plume of seawater behind it as it passed low over the water towards his sub. With a deafening roar it passed directly overhead, and then it was gone, with the sub rocking in its wake and salt spray drenching everyone on deck. A rapidly retreating dot, it was obvious it was not coming back.

Yun was certain, though, that their position and identity had been confirmed and radioed to every North Korean base with ground attack aircraft in range. Their life expectancy could be measured in minutes. Yun hoped there would be enough of them to let Lieutenant Pang and his men succeed in their mission.

Shin Yon Young heard the explosion behind him, but did not stop to look, instead grimly swimming towards the Zodiac he could see bobbing through the waves straight at him. Shin had already been stung by jellyfish several times, and the pain and swelling were making progress increasingly difficult.

Shin had no way to know whether the information he was carrying was important or not. The leadership gathered at the conference table he had bugged might have discussed the next massive public spectacle celebrating the regime's greatness, or ranted about the enemies encircling the People's Paradise on all sides. Legend had it that North Korea's founder, Kim Il

Sung, carried on diatribes to the rest of the Party leadership about the perfidy of the USA and South Korea lasting an entire afternoon.

So, the recordings he was bringing home might be vital, but might not. The truth was, they weren't what kept his arms and legs churning through the waves, in spite of the pain.

No, for that he had to thank Sunshine, the North Korean who for Shin had come to symbolize everything he hated about the regime. His red, enraged face as he burst through Shin's apartment door was the image that kept him going. There was no way Shin was going to let men like that have the run of his country. Not as long as he still had breath in his body.

Lieutenant Pang reached into the water to pull out the dripping NIS agent, noting with dismay the welts caused by jellyfish stings covering every inch of exposed skin. As soon as the agent was safely in the Zodiac, Pang twisted the throttle as far as it would go. He had been surprised that Captain Yun had left his sub on the surface when the MiG appeared, and knew that with every additional second he was pushing his luck.

The noise made by the engine and the boat slapping up and down on the waves prevented him from hearing it, but one of his men further away from the engine and closer to the agent's head finally gave Pang some good news.

"Sir, I think he's trying to say something," the soldier said, leaning his head down towards the agent's barely moving lips.

Pang internally breathed a sigh of relief, since until that moment he hadn't been sure the man was still alive.

"So, can you make out what he's saying, Sergeant?" Pang asked.

"Something about his phone, sir," the soldier answered.

Pang nodded. It made sense that either the agent's phone contained important information, or that he wanted to call his superiors to pass on such information. Or both.

Without taking his eyes off the rapidly growing image of the sub or loosening his death grip on the throttle, Pang gave the agent what he considered the only possible response.

"The surest way for us to lose your phone would be for us to try to find it in your clothing while we're bouncing up and down on these waves. In a few minutes we'll be on our way home, and you'll be able to call anyone you like." Pang didn't add that there was no way the man would be contacting anyone until his identity had been confirmed, but the circumstances of his pickup made him confident that would be a formality.

"Sir, I think he's passed out," the soldier said.

Pang nodded. Who could blame him? He wouldn't have relished the swim the agent had just made, and he imagined getting to the coast hadn't been easy either. No, all things considered, he'd have to call the rest well earned.

Shin Yon Young opened his eyes a crack, and almost immediately closed them again against the fluorescent glare assaulting them. He then heard a chuckle, followed by an order to lower the lights.

"My apologies, Shin," Captain Yun said. "Corpsmen need to see what they are doing in the infirmary, and until just now, you were in no condition to object. I understand you were asking about this?"

Smiling, Captain Yun held up Shin's phone.

Shin reflexively reached towards it, but shaking his head, Captain Yun kept it out of reach. "Let me save you some time, and tell you what we've done so far. We extracted the memory card from the phone, and confirmed that it contained data. We communicated with our headquarters, which then contacted your superiors. Our HQ then ordered us to transmit the contents of the memory card to your headquarters on an encrypted frequency we had never used. In fact, I had to help our radio technician retrieve instructions held under seal in my personal safe to make the transmission. I think it's the most interesting experience he's had in his Naval service. Naturally, none of us know what was transmitted."

Shin shifted uncomfortably, and started to speak, but Captain Yun just shook his head. "I know, you can't say what was on the card. Don't worry, I'd really rather not know."

Shin shook his head as well. His voice was shaky as it passed through lips still swollen from jellyfish stings. "Actually, sir, I don't know myself."

Captain Yun stared at Shin in disbelief, and started to speak, but couldn't manage to get a word out. He had risked his ship and crew, and this man didn't know...

Yun couldn't help it. He started laughing uncontrollably, and a few seconds later, Shin was too. As both of them slowly recovered and wiped their eyes, they had the same thought. I hope to God this was worth it.

CHAPTER ONE HUNDRED

Washington Dulles Airport

It wasn't often that Bob Hansen received exactly the news he'd been hoping for, but this time he was pleasantly surprised. He heard over his earpiece that the pickup of the two defectors had gone off exactly as he'd planned it when he insisted the HRT use a helicopter to get to Dulles Airport. Now that the CIA's primary mission had already been accomplished, he could move on to the FBI priority - arresting anyone who threatened American lives.

Hansen's only regret about removing the two defectors from harm's way was that it would now be almost impossible to make attempted kidnapping charges stick. On the other hand, he was certain the Chinese team was armed, and that would be enough with the laws passed post 9/11 regarding weapons possession at airports.

With a few terse words, Hansen ordered all teams to move in on their targets. As he did so, he said a silent prayer that he and his men had spotted everyone on the Chinese side. In fact, they had done an excellent job, and missed only one Chinese agent.

Ping Jing-Wei.

Los Angeles

Park grimaced as he heard an all too familiar knock at his apartment door. It was the annoying thud thud thud of his nephew, a punk teenager named Bae who imagined himself to be a gangster.

Park's sister had been smart to divorce her no-account husband, but that had been her last smart choice in men. Park blamed Bae's stupidity on his lack of a proper male role model, though he had done his best to fill that gap.

There was a reason Korea had no real equal to the Japanese yakuza or the Chinese triads. Most Korean children believed that education was the way forward in life, not violence and drug dealing. Crime existed in Korea, including organized crime. It was simply not on the same scale as in much of the rest of Asia.

Sighing, Park stood up and walked to the door, running his hand through his thinning hair in a gesture his late wife had often told him meant he was not happy.

"Greetings, uncle," Bae said, a smirk decorating a round, overfed and acned face, crowned with a bowl-shaped head of greasy dark hair.

"And what can I do for you, nephew?" Park said tartly, adjusting his gold wire framed glasses to send his glare more accurately in Bae's direction.

"Hey, slow down, Pops! Can't a man just come by to say hey, check how you're doing?" Bae's air of injured innocence was so contrived, it almost made Park laugh. Almost.

"First, you're not a man, you're a punk kid. Second, anytime you come to see me you want money or a favor of some kind. So, spit it out. What do you want this time?"

"You got me all wrong! All I want is a little information, and it won't cost you a thing. In fact, for a change maybe I'll give you a few bucks for your trouble. How's that sound?"

Park frowned. It sounded extremely suspicious. Still, better to find out what the little thug was up to, if only for his sister's sake.

"OK, what do you want to know?"

Bae's smile became, if possible, even wider and less sincere. "Just this. Remember the guy who helped those two losers shoot themselves in the store not far from here?"

Park nodded, and with his right hand made a spinning motion that any Korean would understand meant to speed up the story.

"Yeah, well, that's it. I'm looking for the guy. I heard he was living in this building, right? You know anything about him? Like I said, there's good money in it if you can help me find him."

Park scowled at Bae, and all he could think of was the poor woman trying to raise a small child down the hall, and the man who had risked being shot by two armed men to save a pregnant lady. Grabbing Bae by the collar, he roared, "Who is paying for this information? Why do they want this man?"

Bae winced and tried to pull away, but years of watching TV and playing video games had done little to prepare him for physical confrontations. Shrugging, he said, "I don't know any names. Everybody knows, you got the info, go to anyone with the right tats for the payoff. These are real serious dudes, the kind you don't mess with if you know what's good for you. Don't know why they want him, and don't care."

Park knew the truth when he heard it. Releasing Bae, he glared at him and shook his head. "And why do you think it's smart to become involved with these 'serious dudes,' eh? Are you really that desperate for money?"

Bae shrugged again. "Look, I was just looking to make a quick buck. If you don't know where he is, just say so."

Park scowled at Bae, and gave him a shove towards the door to the hallway. "I do say so. And even if I knew where he was, I wouldn't tell you and your oh so serious friends. Now, get out!"

As the door slammed shut behind him, Bae rubbed his neck where his uncle had grabbed it. He still wanted the money. But now, he wanted even more to get even. And he had a good idea who could help him do it.

CHAPTER ONE HUNDRED ONE

Washington Dulles Airport

Ping Jing-Wei peered out from the edge of the jetway at the people clustered around the gate. From her perspective she could see what her team leader Xu Guotin could not. American agents were about to arrest him and the other members of the Chinese team waiting for the defectors.

Now Ping had a decision to make. She could remain in place, hoping to still have a chance to complete their mission. Or, she could try to help her teammates escape.

Ping chewed her lower lip as she worked through her dilemma. After only a few seconds, she realized that if Americans were here to capture the rest of her team, it was unlikely the defectors would be coming through the gate as expected.

Her decision made, Ping drew her silenced pistol.

Though Ping had correctly judged it impossible to succeed in their mission, she had missed one possibility that should have been obvious. That the Americans had placed an agent among the staff manning the counter at the gate. As her attention was focused on the man who appeared to be the American team leader, she missed the blur of motion to her right while her arm went up to fire.

Ping had nearly managed to focus her aim when she was tackled by the agent she had missed. The impact sent her gun flying, and her body flying backwards into the jetway, knocking over her cart and its packages. Including the ones Ping had prepared for the defectors.

As Ping lay dazed, the first thing her eyes focused on was one of those packages. Against her cheek.

Ping jerked upright, but she knew better than anyone there was no chance. The poison was designed to leave its victims alive for several minutes to separate them from the site of exposure. However, that presumed the toxin had to travel through the hands via the bloodstream to the heart and brain. Head exposure had not been tested, but Ping doubted she had minutes.

She was right. She was dead before the agent who had tackled Ping could remove his cuffs to secure her. Fortunately for him, he had enough sense to avoid touching her or the objects around her, instead reporting in that a Chinese agent appeared to be deceased.

The agent turned around as several gunshots suggested Ping might not be the day's only casualty.

Seoul, South Korea

The analyst at South Korean National Intelligence Service (NIS) headquarters in charge of transcribing the information Shin Yon Young had collected had a much easier task than would have been the case even five years earlier. Every word captured by the bug was transcribed with an accuracy of over 99 percent about three hours after the transmission from the sub had been received.

Key word analysis was then used to quickly focus on the parts of the National Defense Committee meetings of greatest interest. "Nuclear" was one obvious key word, and it helped the analyst quickly zero in on the meetings where sending one nuclear device to the United States and another to Seoul's subway system were discussed. He was about to write up an interim report when he saw another key term - Mount Paektu. One meaning was an actual Korean mountain that had supposedly been climbed by Kim Jong Un, who was subsequently photographed at the top of the mountain wearing remarkably shiny loafers.

Another was one of the many hidden headquarters prepared for the North Korean leadership in the event of war. The context of the conversation made it clear that was the meaning in this case.

Quickly adding this detail to his report, the analyst forwarded the report to his superiors, with security and urgency markings he'd never used before. Truly an amazing accomplishment, he thought, shaking his head at what it must have taken to obtain the recordings. I just hope I can get them to our leadership soon enough to make a difference.

CHAPTER ONE HUNDRED TWO

Long Beach, CA

Grishkov shook his head as he and Vasilyev pulled up to a warehouse in a dark and deserted corner of Long Beach. "Don't criminals here ever use residences or office buildings? Why are we always meeting them at warehouses?"

Vasilyev smiled. "Simple, my friend. In a warehouse, you are far from prying eyes and ears. Old ones like this can be rented very cheaply, and can be used to store goods or as admittedly not very comfortable accommodations. And then, there is the reason we are here today."

Grishkov nodded. "Do you really think the man they have knows where the device is?"

Vasilyev shrugged. "These men know better than to waste my time. Their captive may in fact know nothing useful, but the yakuza believe he does, or they would not have tried my patience with tonight's outing. In any case, the answer lies beyond that door."

Once inside, the warehouse appeared just as dingy and deserted as the one where they had met the yakuza the day before. It was, however, considerably larger. It took them about ten minutes to walk to the other end of the structure, where what had first appeared to be a pinpoint of light was revealed to be a single bare bulb suspended from the ceiling. Its light revealed a man slumped forward in a metal folding chair, with several men standing silently around him. One of the men was Sato.

"Ah, Mr. Smith. A pleasure to see you, and to be able to collect our agreed upon fee."

Vasilyev cocked one eyebrow upward, and shook his head decisively. "You appear to have forgotten two important points. I told you that I had already spoken to the landlord. Also, this man appears unable to carry on much of a conversation."

Sato smiled and shrugged. "You said that you were sure he knew nothing. I am just as sure that he does know something. I'll admit that he may need to rest a bit before he's ready to speak with you, but I'm sure you'll find the conversation worthwhile."

Vasilyev was about to object again, when Grishkov leaned forward and whispered, "He may have learned something after we spoke with him."

Vasilyev frowned, but then nodded. "Very well. I will still provide the agreed upon payment plus bonus, provided that you and your men depart immediately and provide us with privacy for our...conversation."

Sato laughed and spread his arms wide. "Of course! As they say here in beautiful southern California, mi casa es su casa."

Vasilyev withdrew a thick brown envelope from his jacket, and a few moments later he and Grishkov were alone with the landlord. Vasilyev reached forward to check the man's pulse, frowned and shook his head.

Grishkov sighed. "I suppose that frown means we're going to be here a while."

Vasilyev nodded. "That's exactly what it means. I have drugs that would wake him up immediately, but at his age I can't risk using them. We'll have to wait for him to regain consciousness naturally."

"And then? What makes you think he'll be more willing to talk to you than he was to Sato?"

Reaching into his jacket, Vasilyev pulled out a slim leather case, opening it to reveal several hypodermic needles filled with different colored solutions. "Why, I'm surprised at your lack of faith, my friend. You should know how persuasive I can be when I really try."

Washington Dulles Airport

Xu Guotin knew a trap when he saw one, and the professional in him almost admired how thoroughly all possible escape routes from the gate had been covered by the Americans. He was about to order his men to surrender when several things happened at once.

Ping foolishly attempted to come to their aid, and was quickly tackled for her trouble.

Two of the freelancers with Xu pulled out their guns.

The Americans, who already had their guns leveled at the Chinese hit squad, shot both men multiple times while everyone else at the gate ran away as fast as they could with much shouting and screaming.

Xu slowly and carefully held his arms straight up, as did his surviving team members.

A tall American strode up to the team and looked over all of the survivors, finally settling on Xu. Whirling him around, he placed Xu in handcuffs while other Americans did the same to the rest of his team.

Leaning into his ear, the American hissed, "You are in charge of these men?".

Xu simply nodded.

Pushing him forward, the American growled, "Let's talk."

CHAPTER ONE HUNDRED THREE

Pyongyang, North Korea

Guard Captain Yeong Su Lee stood at attention before 2nd Bureau deputy commander Colonel Jong. This time, he had not been offered a seat.

"Let me see if I understand your report, Captain. The spy has escaped by submarine. Four soldiers are dead, and a patrol boat has been sunk with the loss of all hands. We don't know for sure what information the spy had, but we do know he had access to the conference room used by the highest leadership for their most sensitive discussions. Would that be an accurate summary?" Jong asked.

"Yes, sir," Yeong said, standing and staring straight ahead.

"What would you suggest as a course of action, Captain?" Jong asked, his voice painfully neutral.

Yeong swallowed, and then said carefully, "I believe the leadership must be informed, sir."

Jong nodded. "Yes, I agree completely. And who should deliver that report, Captain?"

Even a blind man could see where this was headed, but though Yeong could see the noose, he was not quite willing to reach up and put it around his neck.

"Sir, it should be whoever you think could best explain both what happened, and all its implications. In short, someone who has not only knowledge, but also experience and wisdom."

With a thin smile, Jong nodded and said "Quite so. I could not have given a better description of you myself. I will let you know when to present your report. In the meantime, one of my officers will escort you to a desk where you can ready your presentation. I suggest you make it a bit more concise than your report to me, and do your best to anticipate likely questions."

Like, would you prefer a blindfold or a cigarette, Yeong thought to himself. Aloud, he said, "Thank you, sir," and saluted.

At least he wouldn't have long to wait.

Los Angeles

Detective Paul Valone frowned at the report on his computer screen. In itself, that was nothing unusual, and not necessarily because of anything in the report itself. It was instead because Valone was heartily sick of burying his nose in a glowing monitor, when he really wanted to be out on the street the way he had been as a patrolman.

It wasn't like his captain or anyone else was chasing him with a stick. Plenty of detectives spent most of their time anywhere but their desk, and they still did okay.

Valone's problem, though, was that for him okay wasn't good enough. It wasn't that he was gung-ho, or that he thought he was better than any other detective. In fact, if he'd been asked he'd say that he was average, no better or worse than any other.

Nobody else at the precinct would have agreed, though they would have never told Valone.

The truth was, two things made the difference between a good detective and a great one. The first was information, the kind Valone was getting by reading the day's reports. The second was the ability to see patterns in the information that helped to solve cases.

Like the missing person's report Valone was reading now. It seemed an elderly Korean man had been reported missing by his niece. Patrolmen had checked his apartment, and found signs of a struggle. There was no ransom demand. The niece had been asked to look at the apartment, but said she didn't think anything was missing, and that her uncle wasn't rich. The only source of income she knew of was another apartment on the same floor that he rented out.

It was a short distance from the grocery store where the mystery man had stopped the robbery just days ago.

The good news was that Captain Gonzalez had stopped asking about the missing "witness" whose interference had caused two gunmen to cease causing problems for either their fellow citizens or the overburdened justice system. Another more important case had come along, and then another one after that.

The bad news was that Valone still wanted to locate him. Now that he finally had a lead, he was going to follow it, even though the case was no longer active. Why, he wasn't exactly sure.

But Valone had learned to trust his gut. And right now it was telling him that a man who could do what he had seen in that video was one he needed to find.

Valone jotted down the name and phone number of the niece, as well as the missing man's address. This wouldn't be his top priority today, but he was determined to work on it before he went off shift, even if that meant working unpaid overtime again.

That willingness to work extra hours was one of a long list of complaints his ex-wife had against his job, which she'd said he loved more than her. She was wrong about that, because "love" was the wrong word. It was part of who he was, and he could no more change that than he could cut off his arm. No, scratch that, he'd seen the movie about the guy who did that, and in the same spot could imagine doing it too.

No, changing who he was would be harder than cutting off an arm.

She had also hated his habit of tinkering with broken toys, which he fixed and donated to orphanages all over LA. Since he had been an orphan himself, he said, it was his way of giving back.

Fortunately, now that his ex was history, there was nobody to give him grief over when he got home or what he did when he got there. The truth was, he didn't really think of the one-bedroom apartment he lived in as home, just as where he went when he was too tired to work any more.

Yeah, he'd find this guy. Valone had a good feeling about that, and his hunches were almost never wrong.

CHAPTER ONE HUNDRED FOUR

Long Beach, CA

Vasilyev snapped the plastic gloves off that he had worn while administering the injection and nodded with satisfaction. "He's no longer unconscious, just asleep. We won't have to wait much longer."

Grishkov looked at Vasilyev dourly. "How can you be so sure? His eyes are closed either way."

Vasilyev shrugged. "I can't be totally sure, but breathing, pulse rate and pupil reaction all suggest simple sleep. What I just gave him will bring him up to a kind of twilight about halfway between sleep and waking. His resistance to questioning should be much reduced, but I will have to tread gently to avoid waking him completely."

Grishkov grunted. "Whatever it takes to end this. I have a bad feeling that we're running out of time."

Almost as though he had heard Grishkov, the man in the chair stirred and his eyes fluttered open. Clearly disoriented, he whispered, "Where am I?"

Vasilyev sat down in a chair he had placed earlier right next to the man.

"You are Mr. Park, yes?" Vasilyev asked.

Park nodded. "Yes, that's right," he said.

"We're your friends. You remember seeing us before, don't you?" Vasilyev asked, in a soothing, pleasant tone.

Park frowned. "Yes, yes I do. It wasn't long ago."

"That's right!" Vasilyev said, beaming. "We came to see you because we were looking for another friend of ours. You were renting a room to him. But you didn't know where he went."

Park nodded. "That's right, I didn't know."

Vasilyev gravely nodded along with him. "But you just told us that now you do know. In fact, you said he was nearby."

Park chuckled groggily. "Yes, yes, he could hardly be any closer."

Vasilyev smiled encouragingly. "In fact, on the same floor, right?"

Park nodded vigorously but erratically, his head moving side to side as well as up and down. "Right, the nurse's apartment. Nice lady, has a young son. Raising him all by herself, the poor thing." Now Park's head was sadly shaking from side to side, and his eyes were closing.

Vasilyev lightly grasped Park's right shoulder and gave him a sympathetic squeeze. "Maybe I can do something to help. What was her name again?"

"Kang Ji Yeong," Park mumbled, in a voice that was barely audible.

"Yes, that's right. And you were going to tell me her apartment number," Vasilyev said with a confidence that had the hoped-for effect.

"Yes, yes I was. 4A." With that, his eyes fluttered closed.

Grishkov grinned. "I never doubted you for a second."

Vasilyev frowned. "A second was about all the margin I had. Still, I'm glad I got what we need without doing him any permanent damage."

Grishkov cocked his head to one side as he looked at Park, who was beginning to snore. "And what shall we do with our sleeping friend? I don't think leaving him here is a good idea."

Vasilyev snorted. "Hardly. I think Sato's curiosity would guarantee a rude awakening once he returns. Two men from the consulate followed us to LA, and aren't far away. I've just texted them to hold Mr. Park at their location until this is over. I think that will be soon, now."

Grishkov nodded. "So, still keeping secrets, are we? And here I thought we were such good friends."

Vasilyev laughed and clapped Grishkov on the back. "Old habits die hard. Tell your enemies nothing, and your friends even less. Lesson one from my training days. I have outlived many of my colleagues who forgot that lesson."

Grishkov grunted assent. "It's an important lesson for police officers and detectives too, especially since organized crime started spending so much time and money to infiltrate every Russian law enforcement agency. Once we get back home, I plan to follow up on some ideas I have on who was feeding information to the Koreans."

Vasilyev had been checking to make sure they had left nothing behind, and gestured for Grishkov to move with him to their car. "It's good to always be planning ahead. But first..."

Grishkov's grin reminded Vasilyev of a hungry wolf, as he interrupted to finish his sentence.

"Apartment 4A."

CHAPTER ONE HUNDRED FIVE

Washington Dulles Airport

Bob Hansen glared at Xu Guotin, who sat handcuffed across the table from him at one of Dulles Airport's several detention areas. "So, how do you explain leading a group of armed men in the airport serving this nation's capital?," Hansen asked.

Xu shrugged. "You have my identification. You know that due to my diplomatic status you must release me to the custody of our Ambassador. If your State Department is displeased with my actions, they may request that I return to China, which I am ready to do. I know that not all the men you arrested have diplomatic immunity. What you do with them is entirely up to you." Silently Xu added to himself, you are welcome to bury the two idiots you killed who started shooting without orders.

Hansen smiled unpleasantly. "So, you're ready to go, then?"

Xu stirred uncomfortably. "I just said that I would, if ordered to do so by your State Department."

Hansen nodded. "Good. I am happy to pass along those orders. We have a charter aircraft preparing for takeoff which will take you and all of your men directly to Beijing. It seems that there are quite a few people there interested in discussing this incident with you. Have a nice flight."

As Hansen stood up, Xu came to the quick realization that immediate return amounted to a death sentence, since the operation to reunify with Taiwan had not yet begun. The only question was whether they would be killed quickly by the men plotting reunification to keep them quiet, or slowly by those not aware of the plot, seeking to learn its details.

"I would like to request political asylum," Xu said, speaking slowly and carefully. He knew the wording mattered.

Hansen stopped before he reached the door, but put his hand on the handle. Grinning, he shook his head. "Oh, I bet you would. But that option is not on the table."

Genuinely confused, Xu tried to move his handcuffed hand to gesture. "I don't understand. You are police. You have to follow the law. I must have a hearing on my claim."

Hansen's grin just grew wider. Shaking his head again, he said, "Normally, you'd be right. But you know that diplomatic status you mentioned? Turns out that trumps everything else, unless the President or his duly appointed representative decides otherwise. And guess what? He didn't."

Hansen paused. "Of course, if you decide to tell us what you and your men were doing here tonight, he might change his mind. Personally, I'm hoping you don't."

Xu could see from Hansen's expression he was completely sincere about that hope. He wasn't exactly surprised. If the situation were reversed, Xu imagined he'd feel the same way.

"All right," Xu said. "I will tell you the truth," he said, hanging his head down low.

Hansen slowly sat back down. "I'm listening," he said.

"We were tracking Uyghur terrorists. We had information that there were two on that Trans Pacific flight, and that they were planning an attack inside the United States."

Hansen smiled and nodded.

"As you may know, the Uyghurs are Islamic fundamentalists who have carried out many terrorist attacks. They should be considered extremely dangerous. We did not notify you because, frankly, we wanted to question them ourselves without the constraints imposed by your legal system. I regret that decision, and will do everything possible to fully inform you now."

Still smiling, Hansen began to slowly clap his hands, and then stopped. "That was some world-class BS, masterfully delivered. Enjoy your trip home."

Hansen got up again and started to walk towards the door. Xu looked at him frantically, and said loudly, "All right! We were there for the two defectors."

Hansen turned the handle and began to walk through the door. "Wait!," Xu called, "I am telling the truth!"

Without stopping, Hansen called back, "I know, but I don't care." With that, the door closed and locked behind him.

Xu looked after Hansen in horror. There had to be something he could do, but his brain refused to cooperate. For the next few minutes, all Xu could think about was what would happen after the plane touched down in Beijing. He had been on the giving end of many Chinese interrogations. Until now, he had never imagined being on the receiving end of one.

The door quietly swung open. Before Xu could say anything, a different man walked in the room. Looking at Xu, he said in even tone, "Fortunately for you, I do care what you have to say. However, I also know that time is of the essence. So, the ground rules for our conversation are simple. You will tell me the truth. If you do not, I will put you on the charter flight to Beijing."

The man sat down across from Xu. "You may call me Tom." Tom Browning smiled. "You may be asking yourself how I will know if you are lying. The answer is simply that I already know quite a bit about what your government has been planning. We have already been talking with the two defectors, and obviously that conversation will continue. We also have other sources."

The door opened and another man stuck his head inside. He said nothing, and simply nodded. Then he withdrew and closed the door.

Browning smiled at Xu, a smile that had no warmth at all. "We're ready to go. But don't worry, we won't be going far, and that charter flight will stay right here and ready to go."

Cocking his head sideways, Browning looked Xu over carefully. "The man who arrested you really didn't want to give you this chance. He said you wouldn't know more than the defectors about what's going to happen next." Now Browning's smile looked even less pleasant. "Part of me is hoping he's right."

CHAPTER ONE HUNDRED SIX

Long Beach, CA

Sato looked out of the window at Vasilyev and Grishkov as they climbed into their car and drove off, waiting until they were out of sight to move. The abandoned factory Sato had chosen as a lookout post was far enough away that he was sure they couldn't have spotted him, even without the help of the grime coating the window.

Punching a single number on his cell phone, Sato sent his men a pre-programmed text message telling them to move in. As he left the abandoned factory, Sato looked up and down the street, and saw with satisfaction that it was completely deserted.

Entering their warehouse, Sato nodded towards the men on guard concealed inside near the entrance. He never relied on locks for security, knowing from experience how easily even the best devices could be defeated. Instead, Sato believed in what he called the home court advantage. This warehouse was his turf, and anyone coming here without knowing every nook and cranny the way he and his men did would not live to regret it. The proof was that if he hadn't known where his men were hiding, he would have never spotted them.

Sato turned a corner, and frowned as he saw that the hapless landlord's head was lolling forward with his eyes closed as the rest of his men stood around him, obviously unsure of what to do. Walking up to the man, Sato gently patted the right side of his face, saying in a clear and firm voice, "Mr. Park, it is time to wake up."

To his relief, Park's eyes fluttered open, though no expression registered on his face. Sato guessed correctly that the drugs that "Mr. Smith" had used were still in effect.

"Mr. Park, you were just telling me where the man had gone who you rented the apartment to, but I forgot the address," Sato said.

Park shook his head. "You know my address," he mumbled.

Sato was about to correct him, but then had the sort of inspiration that had helped him to become a gang leader rather than a follower. "I meant his apartment number."

Park sighed. "I told you," he said, his voice barely audible, "4A." With that, his eyes closed again.

One of his men looked at Sato in confusion as he saw him smiling, which made Sato actually laugh.

"Don't you get it? All this time he's been just down the hall!" But before Sato could say anything else, the bark of pistols answered by semiautomatic weapons made all of their heads snap towards the entrance.

As quickly as the exchange of gunfire started, it abruptly cut off. Sato and the two gang members with him had their pistols drawn and had started to move towards the entrance when two shots fired in quick succession threw both of his men to the floor, both bleeding from mortal wounds. Though he couldn't see a clear target, Sato emptied his pistol's entire 9mm clip towards where he thought the intruder had to be. He fully expected it to be the last thing he ever did.

Sato's belief in the importance of a home court advantage turned out to be well founded. As the silence that followed Sato's emptying his clip testified, he had guessed the intruder's location correctly. That didn't stop him from quickly reloading, in case the unknown gunman had only been wounded.

Sato moved forward carefully, keeping to cover as he moved to where he guessed the intruder was located. He started moving faster when he saw a shoe lying flat on the ground, but even then he didn't take for granted that its owner was dead. Experience had taught Sato that nothing was more dangerous than a wounded man.

This time, though, Sato had nothing to worry about. The gunman's open, staring eyes and the nearby pool of blood made it clear he posed no threat. Sato frowned with recognition as he removed the pistol from the limp hand of the dead intruder. It was a Makarov, a pistol used for decades by police in the old Soviet Union, but since replaced by the Yarygin PYa. Ejecting the clip, his frown deepened. The clip held twelve rounds, but every Makarov he'd ever seen only held eight.

Sato could hardly be blamed for his confusion, since in the US the eight-round Makarov PM was far more common. He was holding the Makarov PMM, a redesign of the original dating from 1990, which as well as increasing the clip to twelve rounds boosted muzzle velocity by about twenty-five percent.

In truth, though, the pistol just helped confirm what he'd already guessed. These were Smith's men.

Turning around, Sato saw that Park was still asleep. Shrugging, Sato decided to let him live. The drugs Smith had used would make it impossible for him to remember who had questioned him, and Park had done nothing to deserve death.

Walking more quickly towards the entrance, Sato soon came across the bodies of his two men, as well as the second intruder. Shaking his head, Sato thought through the results of this encounter, which had resulted in the loss of four of his best men. And two had been waiting in ambush with automatic weapons, against men with pistols. Sato had the uneasy feeling that only luck had kept him alive, even so.

Trembling with anger, Sato sent a terse text message telling the surviving members of his gang to meet him at Park's apartment building. The old man had done nothing to deserve death. The opposite was true for Smith and his friend. They might have a head start, but it wouldn't be long enough to keep Sato from getting the vengeance that four dead gang members demanded.

CHAPTER ONE HUNDRED SEVEN

Pyongyang, North Korea

Marshal Ko looked up from the orders he had been writing as the head of his chief of staff, Gye Tae Hyun, appeared in the partly opened door.

"So, Gye, I see from your expression that it's not good news. But then these days it seldom is," Ko said impassively.

"Yes, Marshal," Gye said nervously. "It is a report on the spy suspected to have been in the Secretariat," he added.

"Let's hope it's a report on his capture," Ko said. "Who is presenting it?," he asked.

If possible, Gye looked even more nervous. "Marshal, it is the captain in charge of the Secretariat's guard force."

A deathly quiet descended on the office. "So, the spy hasn't been captured, then. To add insult to injury, someone has sent me a guard captain as a sacrificial lamb," Ko snarled. That changed to a slight smile at the surprised expression Gye was too slow to conceal. "Yes, though I'm a soldier I have read some books. Even the Bible, at least some parts of it." With another small smile, Ko added, "Know thy enemy. Sun Tzu said much the same thing."

Ko paused, shaking his head. "Show the captain in." Nodding, Gye hurried out. In less than a minute, Guard Captain Yeong was standing and saluting in front of his desk.

"At ease, Captain," Ko said. "Please make your report."

Once Yeong had finished, Ko nodded and gestured towards one of the two chairs in front of his desk. "Have a seat, Colonel." Smiling at Yeong's obvious confusion, Ko said, "Yes, I imagine you came here expecting to be executed, not promoted. And heads will roll over this, you can be sure. But not yours. The poor aim of the soldiers on the beach, the incompetence of the patrol boat's crew, and sending out a fighter plane with no bombs was hardly your fault. No, it's clear we would never have come as close as we did to catching the spy without your quick action. I do, though, have some questions," Ko said, pointing again at the chair.

Still clearly trying to grasp his change in fortune, Yeong slowly sank into one of the chairs.

"Good," Ko said. "Now, you said that the only place the spy might have had access to sensitive information was the NDC conference room." Seeing Yeong's look of discomfort, Ko nodded. "Well, yes, that is where some of our most secret security issues are discussed. It's an obvious target. But you found no evidence of a listening device?"

Yeong nodded. "Correct, sir. But the device could have been removed. As a precaution, I have had the conference table and chairs removed, even though our technicians could find nothing wrong."

With a frown, Ko said, "We can't even be sure we'd be able to detect one of their devices. I've read they can be incredibly small."

"Yes, sir. Even though I have had every item in the conference room replaced, as an extra precaution I have prepared another room on the same floor in the Secretariat as an alternative meeting location. It is slightly smaller, but should still accommodate all NDC members."

"Good thinking, Colonel. I knew I was right to promote you," Ko said with a smile. "Please wait in the outer office while my chief of staff has your new orders prepared." Yeong swiftly rose, saluted, and exited Ko's office. Ko smiled with approval. He appreciated men, especially his officers, who wasted no time on pleasantries.

Gye entered without being asked, but as he knew Ko expected. He stood silently before Ko, knowing that orders would follow.

"Have orders drafted promoting Yeong to Colonel," Ko said.

Gye nodded. "And his new assignment?"

"Who ordered Yeong to present this report?," Ko asked.

Gye consulted one of the files he was holding and had the answer in three seconds. "2nd Bureau deputy commander Colonel Jong."

Ko nodded. "Yes, that doesn't surprise me. I never cared for the man. Have him executed. Put Yeong in his place."

Gye was busily making notes as Ko spoke.

"Have the commander of the MiG-29s guarding Pyongyang report to me later today. He'd better have a good explanation for why his planes patrol without bombs, or he'll be keeping Jong company."

Gye continued making notes, but then looked up as Ko fell silent. "Will that be all, Marshal?," he asked.

Ko looked thoughtful, and finally shrugged. "I suppose so. I was going to hold someone accountable for the poor performance of the soldiers assigned to coastal patrol, but ultimately it's really the commander of the army who sets standards and provides the resources necessary to maintain them."

Gye wisely remained silent.

Ko sighed. "Since I am Army commander, the responsibility is mine. Well, we'll soon see if any of our other troops can shoot straight. Yes, Gye, that will be all."

CHAPTER ONE HUNDRED EIGHT

Los Angeles

Sato's last encounter with Smith and his friend had made him even more cautious than usual, or his anger would have made him rush into the old man's apartment building as soon as the first two members of his gang joined him at the vacant shop across the street. They had grumbled when he told them they had to wait for the others, and even more when he told them to stay away from the windows. Even an idiot could see that this empty shop was a perfect spot to stage an assault on the nearby apartment building, and Smith was not an idiot.

Scowling, Sato carefully peeked through a gap in the newspapers taped across the store's front windows, but saw neither Smith and his companion or any of his missing men. One of the men already with him had been close enough to the building when Sato sent his original text that he was sure Smith could not have beaten them there.

Once again Sato considered simply going to Apartment 4A, kicking the door in, and finding out why the man Smith wanted was worth thousands of dollars to him. Several things stopped him. No matter how impressive Smith's target might have been in the video three to one odds would have been good enough, but Sato couldn't be sure the man would be alone. Also, Sato couldn't be sure that Smith would appear with only a single companion, since the encounter at the warehouse had demonstrated his organization had other capable men at his disposal. Finally, Koreatown was not a part of LA that had been written off by the police. LAPD response would not be that quick for a noise complaint, but there would be a patrol car on its way too soon for Sato's comfort.

No, Sato again decided. The smart play was to make sure Smith came with just one extra man, and then hit him from behind once the rest of Sato's men were here. A quick look at his buzzing phone told him that three more of his men would be there in ten minutes. Sato smiled grimly in acknowledgement of the news. Just a little longer, and he could finish this.

Pyongyang, North Korea

Marshal Ko looked up from yet another report in surprise, as his chief of staff Gye Tae Hyun entered the office. He had left orders not to be disturbed, and he could not recall Gye having ever violating such instructions. Gye's expression warned him that the interruption would not be good news.

"Minister of Foreign Affairs Sook to see you, Marshal. He says it is an urgent matter.," Gye said formally.

Ko swiftly realized that no minister had ever come to see him without a prior appointment.

"And he told you why it was so urgent," Ko said, rather than asked.

Gye nodded, but said nothing.

Ko pursed his lips, and made a "bring him in" gesture with his hands. Whatever Sook had to say could hardly be as depressing as the fuel availability report he had just been reading.

"Minister Sook, welcome, please be seated. What news brings you to see me today?," Ko asked.

Sook always wore a dark suit, white shirt with a dark narrow tie, silver colored wire frame glasses, and a perpetually worried expression. Today was no different, except that Sook appeared to be even more morose than usual.

Clearing his throat, Sook responded, "Marshal, I regret that it appears the envoy we sent recently to China has defected."

Ko nodded. "Yes, I saw a report saying that he had gone missing in Beijing. Still, though, no great problem I imagine. Surely our Chinese friends can be counted on to return him to us."

Sook shifted uncomfortably in his chair. "We have been informed by the Chinese that he has reached the United States, accompanied by a defector from their Ministry of Foreign Affairs. Both had detailed knowledge of our invasion plans."

Ko stared at Sook in horror. "Can anything be done to stop them?," he asked.

Sook looked as though he had bitten a lemon. "The Chinese tried twice, once with fighter jets and once with an assassination squad. Both failed. The traitors are now in the hands of the American government, in a location unknown either to us or the Chinese. Details are in the report I left with Gye."

Ko could not believe what he was hearing. "What did they know, exactly?"

Sook spread his hands. "Between the two of them? Everything. Our contacts in the Chinese government have made it clear that their defector knew about our plans for reunification."

Ko shook his head. "And our defector knew what use we were planning to make of both nuclear devices. The only thing he did not know was which American city would be the target of the Russian device."

Sook looked blankly at Ko. "Marshal, what are we to do?"

Ko stood up and walked to the office's large picture windows, which offered a commanding view of Pyongyang's Kim Il Sung Square. Gazing out at the space where the world had so many times seen North Korea's military might on display helped to firm his resolve.

"I will have the NDC meet later today, where I will announce my decision on how we will overcome this setback. And, Minister, your decision to deliver this news in person was a wise one. It is why you will be alive to attend this afternoon's meeting."

Sook correctly understood this as his cue to depart.

Ko continued to stand, looking out at the vista of central Pyongyang. The truth was, only one alternative made any sense. What he had to do now was explain that course to the rest of the NDC, and keep them believing in the North's final victory. Because, he thought, grinning fiercely to himself, I certainly do.

CHAPTER ONE HUNDRED NINE

Los Angeles

Grishkov frowned as he helped Vasilyev fill a second large rucksack with the contents of their trunk. Even though the corner of the parking lot they were in was totally deserted and the trunk's lid shielded them completely from view, Grishkov still felt naked.

He supposed it had something to do with being in a foreign country with a trunk full of weapons and explosives.

"So, I think we have everything but the first aid kit," Grishkov said sardonically.

Vasilyev laughed and said, "You are right! It's in the back seat, because experience has taught me to always have one in reach. I think there's just room in your rucksack for it."

Grishkov shook his head. "Ok, I saw the video, but do you think we'll need all this firepower to deal with one man?"

Now it was Vasilyev's turn to shake his head. "No. I've heard nothing from the men I sent to retrieve Park, so I have to assume Park told Sato what he told us. That means he and his men will attack us either on the way there, or more likely after we've arrived."

As they both entered the car with Vasilyev again taking the wheel, Grishkov couldn't help exclaiming, "Isn't it unlikely that we'll succeed in our mission if we have to take on the whole local yakuza by ourselves? Can't we ask for help?"

Vasilyev put the car into gear and nodded. "Yes to both questions. On the first, Sato is not the whole yakuza. I don't claim to have all the details of the operation of the yakuza in California, but I doubt he can call up more than a dozen men."

Grishkov just stared. "Oh, is that all. OK, then."

Vasilyev laughed, and shook his head. "I doubt very much that there will be an even dozen. I sent two of our best men to get Park, and even if they didn't succeed, I'm certain they took at least a couple of Sato's men with them."

"On your second question, I have asked for reinforcements from the consulate in San Francisco, but I doubt they will arrive in time to be much use. We couldn't empty the consulate without attracting FBI attention we really didn't want, and I admit I thought the four of us could handle this. With what we have in the rucksacks, I still think we can."

Grishkov grunted. "Well, whatever we've got won't be enough against that many men if we go waltzing up to the front door. Did you notice the vacant shop across the street from the apartment building on our last visit?"

Vasilyev grinned and nodded. "I knew I picked the right man for this mission! There are plenty of excellent FSB agents I've known who would have missed that little detail. So, why does this shop matter?"

Grishkov snorted. "It's obvious. That's where Sato and his men will gather."

Vasilyev nodded. "Just so. Now, what can we do with that knowledge?"

Grishkov frowned and was still for a moment. "Well, we could call the local authorities and report a break in at the store. I don't know how long they would take to come, but it might give us the distraction we need."

Vasilyev cocked his head sideways and said, "A good start. We need more, though. Both of us will call, a couple of minutes apart. One crucial detail we will both add - we think we heard gunshots. Keep the call brief, both to avoid any attempt to trace the call and to add to the call's authenticity."

Grishkov nodded. "Do you think that will be enough for the police to take action?"

Vasilyev punched the button on the car's dashboard that connected its hands-free calling system to his phone. "There's only one way to find out."

CHAPTER ONE HUNDRED TEN

Pyongyang, North Korea

Ko looked up from his desk in annoyance. "Gye, I must finish preparing for the NDC meeting, and have no time for interruptions." His heart sank as he saw Gye's expression. "But it's someone I have to see right away."

Gye simply nodded.

"Very well, show him in. Who is he?," Ko asked.

"Colonel Park, sir. Commanding construction of Tunnel No. 1," Gye answered.

Well, he had heard before that bad news came in threes. Maybe he should have expected this.

Park strode confidently to Ko's desk and rendered a crisp salute. He gave Ko the impression of being an officer who knew what he was doing. Maybe the news wouldn't be so bad after all.

"Marshal, I regret to report that at least the middle portion of Tunnel No. 1 has collapsed," Park said.

And maybe it would be worse, Ko thought bitterly. Keeping that sentiment from his expression, Ko gestured for Park to continue.

"We have all the men and equipment that will fit in the undamaged portion of the tunnel working to reach possible survivors at the far end of the tunnel. We have found only a few bodies so far, so there is still hope that most of the men and much of the tunnel may still be intact. Also, the special train and its cargo had progressed well over half way through the tunnel at the time of the collapse," Park said.

Ko nodded. "There has been no contact with anyone who may have survived on the far end of the tunnel?"

Park shook his head. "Though we have not heard from survivors, that doesn't mean there are none. In every tunnel collapse so far some made it out. I think there is a good chance that the train had gone far enough to avoid damage."

Ko thought for a moment, and then asked, "How long before we know for sure?"

Park was visibly uncomfortable. "I will not lie to you, Marshal. I do not know. The work is proceeding as quickly as possible. However, we must be careful to avoid additional damage on the near side of the tunnel that could set us back even further."

Ko nodded. "Never apologize for telling me the truth, Colonel. Give me your best guess."

"At least two days, though more likely three to four. It may take longer."

Ko's expression was completely impassive, but Park had been an officer long enough to know that his answer was not the one Ko wanted to hear.

"Would more men or different equipment help?," Ko asked.

Park shook his head. "We have all the men and equipment we need. Now it is just a question of time."

Ko nodded, while thinking to himself that Park was far more right than he knew.

Los Angeles

Detective Paul Valone frowned as he saw the reports, and the note that a patrol car had been dispatched to investigate. Valone was no fan of computers, but he knew a useful tool when he saw one. For years the LAPD had used software designed to help investigators see patterns, and it was simple for someone like Valone to set up alerts for areas where they planned to visit later the same day.

Like that apartment building next to that Korean grocery store.

But the report made no sense. The shop where the break in had been reported had been closed for months, and certainly had nothing worth stealing. And shots fired? This was one of the quietest areas in LA. No, something didn't add up.

Valone looked over the rest of his case files, and made his decision. He'd planned to wait until the end of the day to check out the report of a disappearance, but again decided to trust his gut. He'd go now.

CHAPTER ONE HUNDRED ELEVEN

Pyongyang, North Korea

Marshal Ko entered the NDC conference room with a confident stride that had become second nature. Normally, being the leader of North Korea meant total confidence was more than justified. Today, though, he had to make sure that the news he brought did not start a rebellion among the elite caused by the one thing they feared more than death.

Losing power.

Ko swiftly looked around the room as he sat down, as always, the last to enter. The room's location had been changed, as well as all the furniture in it, but the faces around the table were the same.

Well, almost. Someone with less experience in reading the tight-lipped expressions around the table might have been fooled. But with a skill that came from a lifetime of observation, Ko could see the two emotions that prevailed. Uncertainty. And fear.

Ko looked sternly around the table, and tapped on a folder in front of him. "I assume everyone has read the files that were sent to you on the discovery of a spy in this building, the defection of a member of this committee, and the collapse of Tunnel No. 1. Before we proceed further, I will begin by telling you how we will proceed from this point, and then give you additional information that will help to explain my decision."

Ko paused, and could practically feel the expectation that he would call off the invasion.

"We will proceed exactly as planned."

Into the stunned silence that followed, Ko's voice continued with quiet authority.

"First, it is not certain that the spy who fled from this building learned anything important. No documents are missing, and no listening device has been found. Both our defector as well as the Chinese one left with nothing but the knowledge in their heads. That will make them good storytellers, but who will believe them? Plus, it will take time to question them, and then to report the findings of the interrogation to decision makers. And time, comrades, is on our side."

Ko could see that his words were working, but he hadn't won them over yet. Well, he'd never thought this would be easy.

"Second, do not underestimate the Americans' ability to ignore valuable intelligence, even when it is staring them in the face. Remember the FBI memo over a month before the September 11 attacks titled 'Bin Laden Determined to Strike in U.S.' with its specific reference to hijackings. The Americans did precisely nothing."

Good, that got some heads nodding around the table.

"As for the tunnel collapse I have been advised that the train, as well as its men and cargo probably survived. However, it must be admitted that we will probably not be able to communicate with them by the time of the planned invasion of the South. And that brings me to the first reason we must proceed on schedule."

Well, Ko thought, that certainly got their attention.

"The commander of the detachment with the device is under orders to proceed with his mission if he is cut off from communication with headquarters for twenty-four hours. He is under further orders to detonate the device immediately if his force is under attack and he may lose control over the weapon."

"Another factor is that our Chinese comrades have failed to provide us with the promised additional fuel stores needed for a successful invasion. As a result, I have been forced to commit our agricultural fuel stocks to our military forces now at the Southern border. Without gas for farming equipment, the only planting and harvesting will be that done by hand. The same will be true for applying fertilizers and pesticide."

Into the horrified silence that followed, Ko said, "There is only one place where we can get the food and fuel that our people and our military must have. We must go south."

Hwan Ji Hoon, the Interior Minister, was as Ko had expected the first to speak. "But Marshal, all along we have counted on the element of surprise to make up for the enemy's vast military capabilities. We all saw what happened to the Iraqi Army in 2003. No one doubts the courage of our brave soldiers. But how can they succeed, if the Americans and their southern puppet allies know they are coming?"

Ko shook his head. "Hwan, you give the enemy far too much credit. Certainly a few intelligence agents may soon have some idea of what we plan. But by the time their leaders are informed, bicker among themselves and finally send orders to their troops, we will already be in Seoul."

Hwan was clearly not convinced. "There is no doubt that our enemies often chatter among themselves like old women at the marketplace." Ko nodded impassively, while Hwan's allies politely chuckled. Ko was disturbed to see several more around the table laughing than he expected.

Hwan continued, "But once they do make a decision, we have seen they can act on that decision very quickly. Perhaps we can make an agreement with the southern devils where in exchange for calling off the attack through the tunnel, they will give us the food and fuel we need. After all, they did it before when all we gave them were empty promises to halt our nuclear weapons program."

Ko tapped the table in front of him impatiently, and said in a calm voice, "I see I was not clear when I said that the commander of the detachment with the device would proceed with the mission. You appear not to recall the mission orders specify that once underway, unless the detachment is recalled within twenty-four hours the device is to be detonated wherever in the Seoul subway system they are, even if they have not reached the target location."

As Ko looked at all of the NDC members, all he saw was blank incomprehension. Sighing, Ko asked, "Did none of you read the orders drafted for this operation? Copies were sent to each of you."

Hwan said slowly, "So, you are saying that unless we can make contact with the men in that tunnel with the device, they will set it off in...less than twenty-four hours."

Ko nodded. "Correct. Also, do not forget that we still have the device available in Los Angeles. The Americans will pay a heavy price if they stand in the way of our people's reunification. I don't think they have the courage to pay it."

Hwan and Ko both looked around the table at their supporters and those who were uncommitted, and saw that everyone was sitting perfectly still, and looking straight ahead.

Ko said sharply, "I propose that we carry on the plan for reunification under the orders already issued. Are there any objections?"

This time, even Hwan was silent.

Ko rose, signaling that the meeting was over. "Thanks to all of you for your service. I will make sure that all NDC members are kept informed of our progress."

CHAPTER ONE HUNDRED TWELVE

Los Angeles

Sato looked down at his buzzing phone and swore. One of the men he had left as lookout was reporting a patrol car nearby, and heading straight towards the shop. He'd known that even a quiet break in at the back door carried the risk that someone they hadn't spotted might call the police, but a response this quick was truly bad luck.

Sato ordered his men out the same way they'd come in, and shrugged. Well, sometimes you had to switch plans. Fortunately he'd known this was a possibility, and had another plan ready.

It was straightforward enough. One of his men had spotted a "For Rent" sign in a nearby building for a second floor apartment, and it had proved to have no security system. The vantage point for watching the target apartment building wasn't as good, but it would do.

In less than five minutes, they'd once again be ready to go.

Tunnel No. 1, North Korea

Lee Ho Suk looked at the men working on the explosive charges as Captain Yoon stood next to them with arms folded, supervising their progress with an impassive expression.

Yoon glanced in his direction. "So, you are back from the site of the tunnel collapse. Any communication?"

Lee shook his head glumly. "I wish I could tell you there is any sign that rescuers are nearby, but there aren't." Gesturing towards the men working intently on the charges draped across the end of the tunnel, Lee asked quietly, "Do your orders truly give you no choice?"

Yoon shrugged. "They don't. The point is that the Southerners and their cursed American allies could be behind the collapse. Nothing can prevent us from carrying out our glorious mission."

Lee said nothing in response, instead just quietly shaking his head.

Yoon grinned and patted Lee affectionately on the shoulder. Lowering his voice, he said "Look, I know it's hard for someone who has lived on luck for so long to think that it's finally run out. But you have to look on the bright side."

Seeing Lee's look of blank incomprehension, Yoon's smile grew both deeper and sadder. "You see, no soldier worth the name puts on his uniform expecting a comfortable retirement. The most he can hope is that his death will count for something."

Pointing at the subway car with its mysterious cargo, Yoon said in a low voice, "Believe me, our sacrifice will mean more than you can possibly imagine."

CHAPTER ONE HUNDRED THIRTEEN

Loudoun County, Virginia

Bob Hansen stood next to a seated technician, who was busy making adjustments to dials on the equipment console in front of him. The rest of the room was full of similar equipment, all with glowing displays that meant absolutely nothing to Hansen.

"Are you sure they can't hear us?," Hansen asked the technician in a low voice, gesturing towards the empty table on the other side of the glass. Of course, as an FBI agent he had been on the other side of such one way mirrors many times. Somehow, though, being in a house that looked a lot like his home in Alexandria compelled him to ask the question.

The technician grinned and shook his head. "Yeah, I asked the same question my first time here. Talk as loud as you like, no one on the other side will hear a thing. By the way, the name's Frank," he said, extending his hand.

"Bob," he said automatically as he shook it. "So, Tom told me you could fill me in on what you do here while we're waiting for him to get here with the defectors."

Frank nodded, and then waved his hands towards the roomful of equipment. "With this, we can see into a person's soul," he said solemnly.

Seeing Hansen's expression, he quickly changed tack.

"Ok, sorry, I really thought Tom would have covered the basics. I mean, maybe we can't see into someone's soul exactly, but we can sure see everything else. This setup is absolute bleeding edge. Let's take it one step at a time. First, microexpressions."

Frank hit a few keys, and a person's face filled the screen.

Hansen nodded, and said, "We do this at the Bureau too. In fact, we even train other agencies in using unconscious facial tell tales to determine whether a subject is being truthful."

"Yes," Frank said, "That's why I started with microexpressions. Years ago, some of your people trained some of ours at the Agency. You warned us, though, that some of these facial cues were culturally specific. That limited the value of the technique when dealing with foreign nationals."

Hansen shrugged, and said "That's true, but only a handful of our interrogations involve suspects who aren't American. Not enough, anyway, for us to justify the expense involved in creating a database of microexpressions tailored to different nationalities."

Now Frank's grin was even wider. "We, on the other hand..."

Hansen wasted no time finishing his sentence. "Only interrogate foreigners. So, how long have you had this database, and have you ever considered sharing it with other agencies?"

Frank stopped smiling. "Ok, first, what we've got is a work in progress. For some nationalities with cultural and value systems that aren't too different than ours, like Europeans and Latin Americans, we think it's pretty good. I'd even include Africans. For people out of Asia and the Middle East, though, we've still got work to do. As far as sharing the database with other agencies goes, you need to talk to Tom about that. I'm just a contractor."

Hansen held up his hands. "Fair enough. Since the people we have coming are Asians, why are they harder to read?"

Frank shook his head. "I wouldn't say that, exactly. It's that the cultural reference points are different. So, in Western cultures, there is an absolute positive value to telling the truth, no matter what. The Confucian moral code, on the other hand, makes the good of the family what determines right and wrong. So, if telling a lie will help your child or your spouse, it's not just OK to tell that lie. It would actually be wrong to tell the truth."

Hansen frowned. "But not all Asian societies are based on Confucius' teachings."

Frank nodded. "Absolutely. We really shouldn't even be using terms like Asian at all. The Philippines, for example, spent centuries as first a Spanish and later an American territory. Thailand never lost its independence. We do our best to account for all these differences, but thankfully we have other measures to fall back on."

Hansen looked at a monitor that was filled with a close up image of a single eye. "Such as pupil dilation?," he asked.

"Exactly," Frank said, nodding. "We also measure heartbeat, respiration, and galvanic skin response."

Hansen pursed his lips in disapproval. "I don't think either of these defectors are going to appreciate being strapped into a lie detector straight off the plane."

Frank laughed, obviously now back on familiar ground. "No, no, nothing so primitive. Sensor quality has come a long way over the past few years. The entire room, including the table and the interview chair, are rigged with sensors that relay to the monitoring equipment in this room. None of it is visible to the subject. Honestly, the main reason we do it that way is not because we're worried about whether someone will like it. It's because we get more accurate readings that way."

Hansen slowly nodded. "I'd always thought that most people wired up in a lie detector would have to be nervous and upset, just from being strapped in like that."

"Well, of course it's possible to compensate," Frank said. "But I think 'strapped in' readings are always more suspect, simply because you have to allow a wider range of variation. This way is just more accurate. Of course, the failure to detect Aldrich Ames was a wake up call that got a lot of people thinking about building a better mousetrap. Without it, I doubt we'd have been given the resources to do all this," he said, looking around him at the roomful of equipment.

Hansen frowned as he followed Frank's gaze. "How long is it going to take you to analyze all of this data? Time is really critical here."

Frank laughed. "Wow, Tom didn't tell you anything, did he? I'm sorry, you're the first person I've briefed from another agency on this setup. I really need to start with the basics. I analyze nothing. Everything picked up by these cameras and sensors is transmitted over a dedicated line to where the analysts do their work. My job is to make sure the data flow to the analysts is high quality and uninterrupted. That means calibrating, adjusting and swapping to backup equipment as needed."

"So, how long before Tom gets the analysts' readout?," Hansen asked.

"He's getting continuous analyst input through a receiver implanted in his right ear. There's a difference between 'continuous' and 'constant'. One of the first lessons we learned is that nonstop analyst chatter is very distracting to interrogators. Now they are only told high priority detail, most often that the subject is lying or nervous." Frank shrugged. "Like I said, it's a work in progress, but I think it's the best of its kind anywhere."

Hansen did his best to keep his skepticism off his face. "Has there been any post-interview analysis to try to establish accuracy?"

Frank nodded vigorously. "Not only is there such analysis, there's a separate contractor doing the work to avoid the obvious conflict of interest. Believe me, they'd love to show up the current analysts, because they beat their company out for the contract, which is worth about three times what they're getting paid. So far, they haven't found a single missed call."

Hansen let his silence do the talking for him, a technique that had often worked well in questioning suspects. It did just as well here.

"OK," Frank said with a grin. "I know just as well as you do it's impossible to be sure the analysts caught every lie. All we know for certain is we haven't found any evidence that a lie hasn't been caught. And there's always the possibility the subjects believe things are true but have been deceived themselves."

Now Frank held up an index finger. "But Ames wasn't the first or the last failure we knew about with the old 'strap em in' lie detector, just the most spectacular. For you, the most important thing to keep in mind is this - if the analysts say these defectors are telling the truth, a lot of people who matter are going to believe them."

Chapter One Hundred Fourteen

Los Angeles

Chung Hee Moon looked down in dismay at the text message from Kang Ji Yeong. It was short and to the point - she and her son were back in LA, and would be at the apartment in a matter of minutes. The truth was, he'd had plenty of time to think about what to do next. He had in fact thought of little else for days. Chung had started to picture his brain as like a hamster on a wheel, full of energy and spinning and spinning and getting exactly nowhere.

Even though his superiors had lied to him about having cancer, a lifetime of military discipline made failing to follow orders the same as failing to breathe. He knew he could do it in theory, but he couldn't imagine actually following through.

Chung also didn't know how he could allow Kang and her son to die when they had done nothing to deserve it. The only logical way he could see around that was to force them to leave LA, but could see no way to do so and carry out his mission. In fact, aside from hoping that the order would never come, Chung had no plan.

Part of him had ached to see Kang again, while at the same time he had hoped he never would. For the first time in his life, Chung had no idea what to do.

Loudoun County, Virginia

Li Weimin and Park Won Hee had both been offered tea as soon as they arrived at the CIA safehouse, a large and well kept home deep in the Virginia countryside, about thirty miles from Washington DC. Both had accepted, and found that their low expectations had been completely justified. The most positive thought was Park's, who thought the tea was at least better than what they had been served on the Trans Pacific flight.

Park was then shown to his quarters, while Li was escorted to a room dominated by a large dining room table, which had only two chairs, one on either side. The table stood on a deeply piled oriental carpet. Two unremarkable pictures were on the wall near the door, while a massive mirror with a gilt edge occupied the wall in front of Li. A man stood up from the chair on the other side of the table as he entered, and reached across the table to shake his hand.

"My name is Tom Browning, Minister Li. Please call me Tom," the man said with a smile.

As he nodded and shook Browning's hand, Li thought to himself that this introduction was quite interesting. Li had no doubt the man knew he would have preferred an exchange of bows to a handshake, but the choice did underline one point. He was no longer in China.

"Please, have a seat. You have come a great distance, and I know you must be tired. However, I understand you have information you believe it is important to share with my government," Browning said, as he sat down himself.

Gesturing towards the large mirror behind Browning, Li asked dryly, "And how many others will I be sharing with today?"

Browning laughed, and glanced behind him at the mirror. "There is a technician who will be recording our conversation. Do you have any objection?"

Li shook his head. "I would have been surprised if you had not made such arrangements. I suppose I just wanted to make it clear I am not a fool who is unaware of his surroundings."

Browning nodded, and said, "I understand, sir. Now, I understand that there are actions planned by some members of your government that you do not agree with. Please give me as many details as you can, and then I will have some follow up questions."

Li took a deep breath, and visibly gathered himself together. "Well, I have to go back about a month…"

Los Angeles

Vasilyev nodded as the patrol car pulled up to the vacant shop, guns drawn. "That should keep our friends busy for a while," he said with satisfaction, peeking around the building's back right corner.

Grishkov grunted assent. "Yes, with luck long enough to get into the building unseen, even with these ridiculous burdens," he said, hefting his rucksack.

Vasilyev laughed, and then winced as he lifted his own bag. "Yes, well, perhaps I'm being too pessimistic. I haven't reached this age, though, without learning to trust my instincts. And mine tell me we're not seeing this through without all the help we can get."

Grishkov nodded. "Yes, I've felt it too. I wonder if Sato and all his friends would be so eager if they knew what we're really trying to recover."

Vasilyev shrugged. "Maybe not. After the men he's lost, though, I'm certain Sato won't stop until either he's dead, or we are."

Grishkov grinned as they both quickened their pace towards the building's entrance. "Well, now that you put it that way, my bag feels as light as a feather!"

Vasilyev shook his head, and moved even faster.

Chapter One Hundred Fifteen

Camp Mobile, South Korea

Technical Sgt. Josh Pettigrew looked over the latest drone shipment, another two hundred Miniature Air Launched Decoys (MALDs), which brought their stock at Camp Mobile up to over five hundred. The MALD, a nine-foot, 300 pound drone designed to mimic the flight profiles of US military aircraft to confuse enemy anti-aircraft systems, was Pettigrew's personal favorite. He had seen the press release from the company that built the MALD, Raytheon, back in 2014 announcing delivery of over 1,000 of them to the US Air Force. Now that Iraq and Afghanistan were again finally winding down, it was nice to be getting more of them in Korea.

Launched from an aircraft in-flight to save fuel, the MALD flew a pre-programmed course of up to 100 checkpoints over a 500 mile range, so Pettigrew didn't have to worry about assigning a drone operator. While in flight its Signature Augmentation Subsystem (SAS), made of active radar enhancers covering a range of frequencies, sent out signals identical to the radar signature and flight profiles of US military aircraft. These could be anything from an F-16 Falcon to a B-52 Stratofortress. Multiple MALDs gave enemy anti-aircraft batteries the unpleasant choice of either remaining inactive, and perhaps allowing real US military aircraft to proceed on their mission unmolested, or opening fire and revealing their positions.

Sgt. Pettigrew smiled as he saw that these were "MALD-J," for "jammer." The original MALD design had been augmented in the past few years to also include jamming capabilities. This additional signal output further confused SAM sites by accurately replicating the jamming signals from stealth aircraft.

Yes, Pettigrew thought to himself, with these US forces could completely confuse North Korean air defenses. He had seen plenty of technology come and go during his time in the Air Force. If these worked in the field as well as in the demonstrations he'd seen, they could make the contest for air supremacy over the Korean Peninsula...brutally short.

Osan Air Base, South Korea

First Lieutenant Dave Fitzpatrick looked down the runway at the F-16 as it taxied towards the hanger. No doubt about it, his wingman needed more airtime, but at least he'd brought the plane back in one piece. Better than his last wingman, who had been forced to eject when a botched maneuver caused an engine flame out. In a single engine jet like the F-16 there wasn't much room for error, and that pilot had been lucky to survive the ejection with only minor injuries.

Osan Air Base was a front line unit. That meant it wasn't just the question of competence, though the F-16 was a demanding aircraft that took real skill to fly to the edge of its capabilities. It was also that no one, including the squadron commander, wanted an unlucky pilot. Stateside bases had the luxury of retraining and reassigning pilots who made mistakes. At Osan, where they had it drummed into them constantly that "Any day could be The Day," everyone understood that wasn't going to happen.

As the wind whipped across the runway, bringing with it the familiar smell of jet engine exhaust, Fitzpatrick smiled to himself as he thought about how many pilots had stood here waiting for The Day. Well over half a century since the end of the Korean War. In fact, he couldn't think of anyone on base who had even been born when the war ended, not even the squadron commander.

Then Fitzpatrick frowned as he thought back over the war's history. Fighting had finally stopped when the newly elected President Eisenhower made a threat, secret at the time, to use nuclear weapons. Though the North Koreans believed he was bluffing and wanted to continue the war, their Chinese allies weren't willing to run that risk, and forced them to accept what amounted to a ceasefire in place. Even now, North and South Korea were technically still at war.

And now both China and North Korea had nuclear weapons too.

Fitzpatrick shook himself the way a dog shakes off water after a bath. Not even the North Koreans were crazy enough to start a nuclear war. Probably.

Lieutenant Herb Dremer finally taxied up to the hanger where Fitzpatrick was standing. As Dremer exited the F-16, Fitzpatrick slowly clapped, with just a hint of a smile to underline his sincerity. As Dremer removed his helmet, he shook his head and asked in a resigned tone, "OK, what was wrong with that one? "

Fitzpatrick looked down at his clipboard, and then at Dremer's F-16, which already had two mechanics starting post flight service. "Well, let's start with what went right. Wings still attached, check. Pilot carried out the letter of his mission, check."

Dremer scowled. "So, what's the problem?"

"The problem, *Second* Lieutenant Dremer, is that you carried out your patrol exactly as ordered, way point by way point. That's fine in a stateside exercise. It's not fine here."

Fitzpatrick could see Dremer was genuinely confused, and didn't really blame him. South Korea had over fifty million people, with domestic and international air traffic criss-crossing an area that was only the size of Indiana. Every newly arrived pilot got the "busy skies" lecture from the squadron commander, and it was obvious Dremer had paid attention.

Fitzpatrick tapped on his clipboard, which contained among other papers a copy of Dremer's patrol orders. "Did you notice the part of your orders allowing you to call into ATC during flight to request authorization to change one or more way points?"

Dremer shrugged and nodded. "I did, but why would I? It's not like I didn't have enough to do."

Fitzpatrick had to suppress a grin because it was true. Especially for a new pilot the challenges of navigation, mission completion and situational awareness in a single seat fighter were nothing to laugh at.

"Did it occur to you that the North Koreans might be looking for patterns, and if you just fly the way points maybe someday they'll have someone waiting for you?," Fitzpatrick asked.

"Isn't it the job of the mission planners to avoid patterns the NKs might spot? Why bother having way points if we're not going to fly them?," Dremer retorted, folding his arms.

"Think there's any chance the enemy has spies on this base, maybe with access to your orders?," Fitzpatrick asked.

Dremer just stared at him. "Are you serious? What makes you say that?"

Fitzpatrick shook his head. "Every war has spies, and the Korean War was no exception. Why should it be any different this time?"

Dremer was still staring. "You're talking like the war is going to start tomorrow."

Fitzpatrick nodded. "Now you're starting to get it. For all you know, it is. If you want to have a chance of living long enough to make First Lieutenant, that's where your head needs to be."

Fitzpatrick paused. "The North Koreans do exercises every year, just like we do. They're doing one right now. I've been reading the intel reports and talking with some of the analysts. No one can point to anything specific. But nobody's happy."

Dremer nodded, and Fitzpatrick was relieved to see he was getting through.

"Now, let's get something to eat. You can tell me about your mission, and I can tell you stories about my childhood in Korea," Fitzpatrick said.

Dremer went back to staring.

CHAPTER ONE HUNDRED SIXTEEN

Los Angeles

Vasilyev knocked on the apartment door, receiving as expected no response. He had already decided on their approach to the man holding the nuclear device. Now to see whether this was a rational military man, or a suicidal fanatic.

"I don't blame you for refusing to open your door to two strangers. I will also admit that we are here to recover property stolen from our government. However, you should also know that criminals will be here very shortly who are also determined to take what you have. We can face them together, and then decide how to proceed. Or, you can fight them alone. It is your choice, but you must make it quickly."

After about ten seconds the door slowly opened, and a man on the other side gestured to them to enter with one hand. A pistol was in the other.

Grishkov and Vasilyev entered the apartment one at a time, both being careful to keep both hands in plain sight.

The man nodded approvingly, and cocked an eyebrow towards their rucksacks. "Weapons?," he asked.

Grishkov and Vasilyev both mutely nodded.

"My name is Chung. Yours?," Chung asked.

"Vasilyev," he said, pointing at himself. Grishkov did the same.

"Russian?," Chung asked.

Vasilyev and Grishkov both nodded.

Chung looked at them thoughtfully. He was still holding the pistol loosely at his side.

"Yes, I saw the Russian characters on the device. So, stolen, not purchased?," Chung asked.

Vasilyev shrugged. "Purchased, but not from an authorized seller."

Chung nodded. "Do the criminals following behind you know?"

Vasilyev shook his head. "No, but they know you have something worth taking. Our fault, I'm afraid."

Chung glanced at the smartphone he had laying on the counter. "Well, they're not here yet."

Grishkov looked at the phone's display, which was closer to him than to Vasilyev.

"A feed from a camera in the hallway? I didn't notice one," Grishkov said.

Chung just shrugged.

"Could we get the feed on our phones too? We're going to be outnumbered, and will need every advantage we can get."

Chung nodded, and a few minutes later they all had the same view of the hallway on their phones.

"And just in time," Vasilyev said, as a head peered around the corner of the hallway and was quickly withdrawn.

Chung gestured toward their rucksacks and asked, "Are you willing to share?"

Vasilyev looked at Chung levelly. "I was just about to ask you about the device. If we do give you something more useful than that pistol you're holding, do I have your word that you won't turn it on us later? Obviously, I am assuming we all survive the upcoming encounter."

Chung didn't hesitate. "Yes. I'd rather have it in the hands of its rightful owners than a bunch of thugs."

Vasilyev smiled. "Yes, we've seen video of how you deal with them."

Chung frowned as he looked at the smartphone's screen and lowered his voice.

"Those men were fools. These are not."

They could all see five men slowly advancing down the hallway towards the apartment, using hand signals to communicate as they moved. Movement was visible at the end of the hallway behind them.

"Five men in front, with reinforcements behind," Chung said calmly.

"Let's see what you have in those bags."

Chapter One Hundred Seventeen

Pyeongtaek, South Korea

Fitzpatrick looked on with amusement as Dremer tried to figure out the Dunkin Donuts menu. Though it included English as well as the Hangul characters used to write the Korean language, many of the items were unique to Korea.

"Having trouble deciding between the Potato Meat Sandwich and the Jalapeño Sausage English Muffin?," Fitzpatrick asked innocently.

Dremer glared at him. "When you said let's go somewhere American for lunch, I thought you meant a burger place. I don't know what half this stuff is supposed to be."

Fitzpatrick laughed. "Well, it's not a menu that's really aimed at Americans. I like the food though, and the prices aren't bad. Plus, I like to buy American, even here."

Dremer grunted. "OK, we agree on that at least. Guess I'll try the Jalapeño whatever."

Fitzpatrick nodded. "Good choice." Signaling to the cashier, he ordered two and two coffees. Turning back to Dremer, he added, "You'll learn that anything spicy here is usually pretty good."

After picking up their order and sitting down to eat, Dremer asked, "Say, you said you were here as a kid, so maybe you know the answer to something that's been bugging me. Our base is here in Pyeongtaek, and there is another town called Osan about ten miles from here on the way to Seoul. So, why has it been called Osan Air Base since it opened during the Korean War?"

Fitzpatrick nodded gravely, and said, "Yes, a long and complex story."

As Dremer looked at him expectantly, Fitzpatrick said, "Osan was easier to say."

Dremer responded by punching him in the shoulder.

"Hey, no striking a superior officer!" Fitzpatrick said with a laugh. "You've got to remember, it was the 50s."

"Yeah, OK," Dremer said with a grin. "So, how was childhood in Korea?," as he took the wrapping off his Jalapeño English Muffin.

Fitzpatrick smiled, and sipped his coffee. "My dad was a major in the Army stationed at Yongsan when I was in elementary school. Because he was on the staff of the general commanding US forces in Korea, he was one of the lucky few allowed to bring his dependents."

Dremer nodded. "Haven't been there. In Seoul, right?"

Fitzpatrick nodded back. "Right. When the base was built it was way outside the city, but Seoul grew up around it in the decades that followed. We got to Yongsan the year before the handover of the golf course."

Dremer grinned. "We had a golf course inside the capital city? Really?"

Fitzpatrick shrugged. "Like I said, Yongsan used to be way outside of town. Now over 40 percent of all Koreans live in the Seoul metro area."

Dremer chewed thoughtfully. "So, what did they do with the golf course?"

Fitzpatrick smiled. "They turned it into a city park. As a bonus, we kids on base could stop worrying about getting hit by a golf ball."

Dremer laughed. "That really happened?"

Fitzpatrick smiled. "Yeah, it did. I didn't say everyone on base was a *good* golfer. Of course, now almost everyone who used to be at Yongsan has moved to Camp Humphreys."

Dremer nodded. "Any other fond childhood memories?"

Fitzpatrick immediately said, "Tear gas."

"Really?," Dremer asked, laughing. "You say it like it happened a lot."

"It did," Fitzpatrick said with a shrug. "You have to remember that I was a small kid here when the generals had just exchanged their uniforms for suits and declared that democracy had arrived. Nobody outside the Korean military was happy with that, and anti-government demonstrations happened a lot."

Dremer nodded. "Yeah, I remember now. And to stop the demos, the police would always use tear gas. But you weren't in those demonstrations, right?"

"Right. Sometimes, though, they used so much that the gas would end up drifting into the base. If you were inside you were OK, but outside it would be on you before you knew it," Fitzpatrick said.

"Didn't you get any warning?," Dremer asked.

"Sometimes, but demos could pop up almost anywhere, anytime. People did adapt, though," Fitzpatrick said with a smile.

"How do you mean?," Dremer asked.

"Well, if you were in a department store in town and gas started to drift in, the shop attendants would pass out little plastic packs of Kleenex to wipe your eyes so - they hoped - you'd tough it out and keep shopping. If you were on the street when the demo started and far enough away not to be participating but close enough to get gassed, there were guys with the demo holding wicker baskets piled high with the same little Kleenex packs handing them out to anyone walking past. My dad told me they did it to help keep the people on their side."

Dremer laughed. "It sounds like your dad was on their side, too."

Frowning, Fitzpatrick shook his head. "No, he never said that, exactly. But I know the tear gas annoyed him. Actually, it was a really fine powder, not a gas. One time, a demo happened downtown late at night, and my father took a subway train early the next morning. Because it was a powder, it had drifted through cracks onto the subway platform, and when he walked on it he kicked it up into his face. I'll never forget how mad he was when he got home."

Dremer nodded. "Well, in the end the protesters got what they wanted, right? A real democracy, rather than generals wearing suits."

Fitzpatrick shrugged. "You're right. South Korea has democracy and an economy that works. It's a success story, plain and simple."

Dremer smiled, and rocked his hand back and forth. "Except for our being here, and the reason why we have to be here."

Fitzpatrick scowled. "North Korea. Yeah, if we could finally just be finished with it."

Chapter One Hundred Eighteen

Two Kilometers North of the DMZ, North Korea

Captain Hong Sang Ook sat in the cupola of his M-2002 main battle tank and stirred the food in his ration cup with the dubious air of a soldier who hadn't decided whether he was hungry enough to risk eating its contents. Sergeant Cha squeezed next to him, a feat that would have been impossible if both had not been rail thin, and small even for tankers.

"The food here on the front lines not to your liking, sir?" Sergeant Cha asked with a smirk that back in Pyongyang would have ensured a quick trip to a labor camp. Things were different now, though, with battle finally about to begin against the southern devils. Sergeant Cha knew more about operating the M-2002 Pokpung-ho "Storm Tiger" tank than anyone else in Captain Hong's regiment. Developed in North Korea from reverse engineering the Russian T-72, T-80 and T-90 tanks, they were an attempt to improve on the Iraqi Army's disastrous performance in the Gulf War using T-72s. Hong's regiment was equipped with the most advanced version, the Pokpung-ho III. Armed with a 125mm 2A26/46 smoothbore main gun and fitted with reactive armor on the front glacis, the turret front and the forward part of the turret roof, it was a serious threat to the American M1A2 Abrams tank.

An upgrade program had just fitted AT-5 Spandrel wire-guided anti-tank missiles to every tank in the North Korean Army, including the M-2002. Though none of the troops knew it, this was thanks to an arms dealer eager to trade new, still crated Libyan munitions for high quality counterfeit US currency produced in a Pyongyang print shop. As a happy bonus, the North Koreans were already familiar with the AT-5.

Hong scowled at Sergeant Cha, as much out of annoyance at the food as Cha's insolent attitude. "I always thought the best food went to the troops at the front."

Now Cha laughed out loud. 'When we were back at base camp your wife cooked for you, right, sir?"

Hong nodded. When he hadn't been able to get home in time for a meal, she'd usually been able to pack something he could take with him.

"And I'm sure your wife did her best to make whatever she found at the market as tasty as she could. These guys?" Cha gestured towards the men still lading out food to a long line of soldiers. "They're doing their duty with what they've got. No more, no less."

Hong shrugged. "I see your point, Sergeant. It doesn't make me any happier to be eating this slop. I'm actually worried that some of the men may get sick. You know as well as I do there's no room for a sick crewman in a tank."

Now it was Cha's turn to shrug. "Believe me, the men have had worse. Besides, at least there is some kind of food to eat." Cha looked around and lowered his voice. "I've heard that's why we're finally headed south. I've also heard that if anyone here would know the truth it would be you, sir."

Hong scowled even more deeply than he had at the disgusting food. It was true that his family was well connected in the Party, and that it was no accident he was both an officer and in command of a regiment of North Korea's most advanced tanks. Fortunately for Sergeant Cha, Hong was aware that he could no more maintain or repair a Storm Tiger tank than Cha could command the platoon. With combat only hours away, re-placing Cha was out of the question.

And at this point, maybe the truth would help motivate the men.

"I've heard the same thing. Everyone knows the drought this year has been bad. Not many know just how bad." Hong paused and looked straight at Cha, and was grimly pleased that the sergeant did not flinch. "You can let the men know that they are not just fighting for their lives, and their nation. They are also fighting for the survival of their families."

With a sharp nod, Cha disappeared back inside the tank. Hong was sure word would spread through the regiment before they moved out. Normally he would have been worried about arrest for his "defeatist attitude." Not now. Only one thing mattered - making it to Seoul. If any of his tanks made it to the enemy's capital, he was sure the southern cowards would surrender.

It would be even better, Hong thought with a wry smile, if one of the surviving tanks was his.

Chapter One Hundred Nineteen

Los Angeles

Chung and Grishkov were both quick to load the AR-15s Vasilyev handed them, as they kept an eye on their smartphone screens at the gang members who had taken up position on both sides of the apartment door. They appeared to be waiting for a signal.

Vasilyev did not plan to wait.

With a brisk nod he brought his Mossberg 500 pump action shotgun to his shoulder. In the plan they had hastily prepared Grishkov and Chung each had two designated targets, while Vasilyev had only one. They knew the drywall separating the apartment interior from the hallway would prove to be no obstacle for rounds from the AR-15s, and even less so for the Mossberg 500. Vasilyev had only one designated target both because his weapon's rate of fire was much slower than the AR-15s, and because he had an additional task. Once he had fired the Mossberg, Vasilyev had a surprise for the thugs assembled in the hallway.

Grishkov and Chung readied their AR-15s, knowing that to have any chance of evening the odds against them they all had to fire simultaneously. One last check of their smartphone screens told them that their targets were obligingly still.

All three fired at nearly the same instant, and Chung was able to dispatch his second target as well. Grishkov's second target's reflexes were better, but it didn't help him. With the elevator door at one end of the hallway, there was only one direction for quick retreat. Using the hole newly created by the Mossberg's blast, Vasilyev tossed an M-67 grenade as far down the hallway as he could.

Vasilyev was correctly concerned that with an effective fatality radius of 16 feet, the grenade could be just as dangerous to them as to their enemies.

Vasilyev would have been the first person to admit that his throw's accuracy owed far more to luck than skill. It hit the wall at the end of the corridor where it formed an L with the adjoining hallway, and then bounced into that hallway.

Sato's good fortune was that he and a half dozen of his men were covering the building's street level exits to prevent their prey's escape. His bad luck was that he had four men in the hallway upstairs as backup, who saw two things arrive at exactly the same moment. The first was the man with excellent reflexes who Grishkov had missed. The second was a round metal sphere that none of them had time to register as a grenade before it exploded.

There were no survivors.

Grenade fragments also sliced through the drywall of three adjoining apartments, as well as the floors of two apartments on the floor above. Fortunately, since it was midday on a Wednesday all five were unoccupied, with their residents either at school or work. In fact, that was true for every apartment on the floor where the grenade exploded.

It was not true on the floors above and below the explosion. One apartment contained a teenager who had faked illness to stay home from school and play video games. His headset's simulated gunshots and explosions were ironically perfect cover for the real thing one floor below.

A housewife one floor below the explosion was in an apartment next to the elevator, and so far enough away that instead of hearing distinct sounds only felt a vibration which she dismissed as one of LA's frequent minor earthquakes.

So, incredibly, no one called the police.

On the ground floor where Sato and his remaining men were covering the exits, the only hint of what had happened was that several small pieces of glass had fallen where they had been dislodged by grenade fragments. While in most cities the windows would have shattered, the apartment building had recently been brought up to code, which in LA included impact resistant glass. Californians had learned the hard way that one of the principle killers in earthquakes was flying glass.

Frowning as he saw the glass fragments fall, Sato thought that they showed his men firing before he gave the order. Having just secured the exits he had been about to call his men with the order to enter the apartment. Now, seething, he called with a single clipped word, "Report."

The call went immediately to voice mail without even ringing, as did each subsequent call to other gang members. Finally, one of Sato's calls reached a cell phone that had not been destroyed, so that he was at least rewarded with a ringing phone. Its very dead owner, however, was unable to answer.

Sato stood rooted to the exit he was covering, trying to understand what was happening. There was no way all nine men he had sent upstairs were dead. A cell phone jammer? No, a call to one of his men at another exit went through immediately. So, what was happening?

Sato knew without even having to think about it that going up with his remaining men was his only option. If he and his men ran at this point, it would be only a matter of time before one of them turned on him. In fact, it would probably be all of them. And he wouldn't blame them.

But just he was about to hit the call button on his phone, he saw that a woman and a small boy were about to enter the building. Sato pretended to study the building's directory as they moved towards the elevator.

"Excuse me, ma'am," Sato said with his best attempt at a sincere smile, as he blocked the way to the elevator. "I'm looking for my friend Mr. Oh, but I don't see him here in the directory. Do you know him, by any chance?"

Kang Ji Yeong looked at him suspiciously, liking neither the man she saw before her nor the obstacle he represented. Chung had sent her a text just minutes before telling her to stay away from her own apartment, but had not given a reason or answered her calls since. She was going to get to the bottom of this, and had no time to waste on pointless questions.

"I don't," she said curtly. "Sorry, I need to go."

Sato nodded, and said "Certainly. Just one question - what is your apartment number?"

In a flash Kang knew why Chung had told her to stay away, but it was too late. Sato could see the realization in her expression, and his gun was pressed against her ribs before she could think of moving.

"Now, hand me your phone please. For your son's sake, you will want to cooperate," Sato said with a neutral tone that Kang found far more threatening than shouting.

Her son started to cry.

Sato gestured at the boy as Kang handed over her phone. "He needs to stay quiet."

Sato's smile contained no warmth as he looked through her texts and said, "When he told you to stay away, you really should have listened."

CHAPTER ONE HUNDRED TWENTY

Loudoun County, Virginia

Tom Browning's head was throbbing as he opened the door to the room with the monitoring equipment for the interview he had just finished with Li Weimin. Bob Hansen and the CIA technician looked up as he entered with expressions that told Browning they had been paying attention.

Hansen shook his head and said, "I'd ask whether we should believe him, except that I was there at Dulles when his own government tried to take him out. So, interview Park next and then report?"

Now it was Browning's turn to shake his head. "From what Li is saying minutes may count here."

Turning to the CIA technician, Browning said "Ok, Frank, Protocol AA for the entire interview, distribution list 23. Subject line reads High Value Chinese Defector Provides Intel on Imminent Threat to National Security." The technician nodded and began typing rapidly. Less than a minute later he looked up and said simply, "Done."

Hansen looked at Browning quizzically, but didn't ask. He knew if their roles were reversed he might have easily decided not to tell Browning anything.

Browning, though, didn't hesitate. Turning to Hansen, he said "Frank just sent a recording of that interview complete with detailed analyst confirmation that Li believed every word he said was true to all our top decision makers, including the Director. Most of the people on that distribution list already knew it was coming."

Hansen nodded, but still asked nothing. Instead, he let the silence ask for him.

"You're wondering why I'm telling you any of this," Browning said flatly. "Well, in a way you've already said it. You believe this incredible story because of how many men were thrown at trying to stop them telling it. All of the top people here know about the verification process for high value interrogation, including the Director. Once we start repeating this story outside the CIA, though, the word of a senior FBI agent is going to count for more with quite a few people."

Hansen shrugged. "It really wasn't like the Chinese to act so boldly in such a public space. Now, though, the risks they were willing to run at Dulles make a lot more sense. How long do you think it will be before someone with the authority to make decisions about this wants to hear from us?"

Before Browning could answer, the phone on his belt buzzed. After he looked at the screen he grimaced. "Well, there's your answer. We go with your Director and mine to the White House four hours from now. That will barely give me time to finish interviewing Park before we go."

Hansen stared at him. "And who, exactly, are we going to be briefing?" he asked.

Browning grinned and clapped him on the shoulder. "You know, the guy who lives there. Plus whoever else he decides needs to know. You wanted decision makers? You're going to get them."

CHAPTER ONE HUNDRED TWENTY ONE

Two Kilometers North of the DMZ, North Korea

It was finally happening. A part of Captain Hong Sang Ook had insisted that this was just another exercise, and that they would end up heading back to base in spite of their war orders. The armored bulldozers that had just taken up position in front of the tanks of his regiment, though, had convinced Hong that this time it was real.

Sergeant Cha poked his head up next to Hong's, and for a moment they stood together silently looking at the rank of armored bulldozers taking up position in front of them, and as far to the right and left as either one could see.

"So, Sergeant, I'm guessing you've never seen these bulldozers before in an exercise," Hong said.

"Sir, I didn't know we had this many. All they're good for is clearing mines. This is it, sir, we're really going."

Hong nodded gravely. "Yes, Sergeant, I had the same thought myself. The men and the tanks are ready?"

Cha's head bobbed up and down with a nervous energy Hong knew was unusual for such an experienced soldier. "Yes, sir. Gas and ammo is full up in all tanks, and we're ready to move out on your command."

"Good work, Sergeant. I'm sure I'll be hearing from command shortly. In the meantime, pass this word on to all the men." With a wolfish grin that had no humor in it, Hong said softly, "Next stop, Seoul."

Los Angeles

Detective Paul Valone had agreed to cover a shift for another detective who was having the marital problems that seemed to afflict any colleague Valone considered even halfway decent at his job. So, when following up on one of his cases drug on Valone thought about putting off the Korean witness business for another day. After all, it wasn't even an active case anymore.

Two things stopped him. First, there had still been no ransom demand for the Korean man missing from the apartment building near the shop where the attempted robbery had taken place. Second, he still thought that the man who could do what he saw in that video needed to be checked out - if he could just find him.

So, here he was headed to the apartment building where the missing man had lived. A lifetime of habit made Valone park a block away and take a hard look at his surroundings before making his approach.

Not for the first time, that habit probably saved his life.

CHAPTER ONE HUNDRED TWENTY TWO

Five Kilometers South of the DMZ, South Korea

A massive artillery barrage and the work of hundreds of armored bulldozers had cleared most of the anti-tank mines from the path of Captain Hong Sang Ook's M-2002 regiment. The ones they missed cost him only one tank, though Hong winced as explosions to the left and right of his regiment told him others in the advancing force had not been so lucky.

Though he knew the danger beneath him from mines was serious, Hong also knew he could do nothing about it. Instead, he focused on the other threats he could address - tanks ahead and planes above his regiment. The tanks he could fight, but the planes he could only try to evade. Hong respected but did not fear the M1A2 tank. A-10 and F-35 ground attack aircraft were another matter. He briefly wondered which they would face, before dismissing the thought with a shake of his head. Either way, only the division's truck mounted and infantry handheld antiaircraft missiles would protect his regiment. Though he would have never said so aloud, Hong had no faith in the North Korean Air Force's ability to keep the Americans from destroying the tanks moving forward to liberate the South.

Hong was right not to spend time wondering about whether his regiment would face A-10s or F-35s. Years before the Americans had debated which was superior for ground attack, and held a series of war games to settle the question. Their conclusion had been that the A-10 was superior in a low-threat environment where its long loiter time gave it the best chance to make effective use of its 30mm cannon and 2.75 inch rockets. Facing more capable air defense, though, the F-35 had better odds of survival with a lower radar cross section, faster speed and superior maneuverability.

So, the Americans had decided to base A-10s in South Korea, and the North Koreans knew all about these 50 year old planes. They did not know, however, that fully half of the F-35s stationed in Japan were dedicated to Korea's defense in the event of invasion from the North. With a range of 1,379 miles and a top speed of 1,199 miles per hour, F-35s from American bases in Japan could be over the DMZ in a little over 30 minutes. Midair refueling could keep them on station for hours.

The only catch was that launching F-35 strikes from Japan required clearance from the Japanese government, and coordination with US Forces Japan. Not much time was needed for either step, but it meant that the first planes to attack Hong's regiment were A-10s. Hong had read about the A-10's weapons, but thought that his tanks' primary and reactive armor would give them a good chance to survive an attack.

However, Hong had never been on the receiving end of an attack from the A-10s' GAU-8 seven-barrel autocannon. A 4,000 pound monster carrying 1,150 rounds of ammo mixed at a five to one ratio of PGU-14/B armor piercing incendiary and PGU-13/B high explosive incendiary, in the hands of a capable pilot it could place 80% of those rounds fired at a range of 4,000 feet within a 40 feet diameter circle.

In the A-10s' first pass Hong's regiment discovered two things. An M-2002 tank fit almost perfectly inside a 40 feet diameter circle. And the pilots flying the A-10s from Osan Air Base were capable of using its GAU-8 cannon exactly as designed.

As for the division's antiaircraft defenses, multiple hits from Hydra 70 2.75-inch fin-stabilized unguided rockets fired from the A-10s just before switching to cannon fire had reduced their effectiveness considerably.

Hong, though, did do one thing right. It was the reason most of his regiment survived the A-10s' first pass.

"Left!" Hong shouted, as he had to if he wanted to be sure of being heard over the noise being made by his tank and the rest of the regiment. Though there was an internal communications system in the tank to let him talk to the soldiers in his tank through a mouthpiece and headphones, it hadn't worked in any of the regiment's tanks in over a year. Fortunately, the separate radio system allowing him to give orders to the rest of the tanks in his regiment did still work.

To compensate, Hong had worked out a simple set of commands that could be shouted within each tank and sent over the regiment's radio net with little chance of misunderstanding. "Left" meant that every tank in the regiment veered five degrees to the left for two minutes, before once again driving straight ahead. By calling "left" and "right" to the other tanks in the regiment at irregular intervals, Hong's regiment zigzagged while still moving forward with the rest of the division.

Hong swore viciously as explosions bracketed his tank to the left and right.

"Smoke!" Hong shouted, both to the soldier with the trigger for the smoke dispenser in his own tank, and over the regiment's radio net. A few seconds later, Hong shouted, "Right!".

Those commands gave the tanks in Hong's regiment a higher survival rate than any other in the vanguard of the North Korean attack. By the time the A-10s headed back to base with their ammo exhausted they had lost only a single plane, to a hit from an SA-7 Grail man-portable missile.

They had left in their wake dozens of destroyed and disabled North Korean tanks. Though the North Korean advance continued, it had taken a serious hit.

Hong unconsciously mashed down his radio's transmit button almost hard enough to break it. "Report!" he shouted into the handset. One by one the tanks of his regiment responded, until Hong was finally satisfied that he knew what he had left. Two of his tanks didn't respond at all, and though it could be that their radios were out, Hong doubted that answer. One reported severe damage and the death of several crew members. A quick look out the hatch at the tanks nearby confirmed that he had in fact lost three tanks to the A-10s. Listening to the reports coming over the division's radio net made it clear that he had gotten off lightly.

Hong swore again at the thought. They had barely crossed the DMZ. What else did the enemy have waiting for them?

CHAPTER ONE HUNDRED TWENTY THREE

Washington, DC

President Hernandez wanted a war even less than he wanted another root canal. And that last one had really hurt, no matter how many times they shot Novocain into his poor abused mouth. But it looked like it didn't matter what he wanted. The North Koreans had just come rolling south, and he was about to hear from a roomful of experts what was happening, and the bad options he had to choose from to get the United States out of this disaster.

Hernandez hadn't even believed he'd make it through the primaries, let alone the general election. The truth was, Hernandez had spent most of his life as a businessman, and had turned to politics only because he saw no choice if he was going to fix the problems he saw all around him. He had little patience for any of the established political parties. Running as an independent to reach the Senate, he called himself the leader of a party now only because running for President had required it.

Everything Hernandez wanted to accomplish fell into what politicians called "domestic policy." In particular, he was obsessed with fixing the country's crumbling roads, bridges and other critical infrastructure. Hernandez was also determined to improve the quality and relevance of American education, once the highest ranked in the world. One idea he had was formal apprenticeships of the sort that had been successful in Germany and many other countries in helping new entrants to the workforce get high quality jobs. The list went on and on.

The problem was that addressing any of these issues meant legislation, and that meant dealing with Congress. If by some miracle a law was passed it was immediately challenged in court, usually all the way to the Supreme Court. Every year was a struggle in Congress to get new money for the few programs that had not been stopped by the courts.

Hernandez had seriously begun to question whether he wanted to run for another term, even though his wife and kids were pushing for him to do it, and he was still fairly popular.

Now this war threatened to make every one of his goals impossible to accomplish. It was already certain to cost billions, and who knew how many billions more before it was over. The only prayer he had to get his agenda back on track in even a second administration was to end the war quickly. He had been told he'd get a briefing on just how that could be accomplished.

First though, he'd been promised an explanation of just what had caused the North Korean invasion, and why they believed it would succeed. Apparently two defectors had the inside story. Hernandez hoped they could make sense of this mess, because so far nobody else had managed anything better than "we sure didn't see this coming."

CHAPTER ONE HUNDRED TWENTY FOUR

Los Angeles

Chung, Vasilyev and Grishkov all stared intently at their smartphone screens, and then more cautiously through the gaping holes in the apartment's wall. Their ears were still ringing from the gunshots and explosions, and by contrast it now seemed unnaturally quiet.

Into that quiet came a very faint ringing from the bedroom behind them. If they hadn't been completely quiet and straining to hear any sound it's doubtful any of them would have heard it.

Vasilyev was the first to speak, looking at Chung. "Is that your alarm?"

Chung shook his head. "I don't have one, and the apartment's owner has one that is much louder."

Grishkov interrupted immediately. "I think it's time we saw the device."

Vasilyev's eyes widened. "You don't think..."

Grishkov shrugged. "That was way too easy, and you knew we'd have to pay for it."

Chung nodded. "Russian fatalism. I've heard of it, and now I know it's true. Let's take a look."

Each of them continued to check their smartphone screens as they moved to the adjacent bedroom, but nothing moved in the hallway.

Chung opened the door to the closet, and they saw that the trunk at its floor barely fit inside. Grunting with effort Chung pulled it out, and then unlocked the trunk and lifted its lid.

All three of them were mesmerized by the faint mechanical click, click click of the numbers on the device as they moved backwards second by second. They now read 1:58:32, which clicked down to 1:58:31, 1:58:30 as they watched.

"So," Vasilyev whispered, "it appears we have a little less than two hours to disarm the weapon."

Grishkov frowned. "I have used a lot of our military equipment. I wouldn't trust this ancient display to be totally accurate. I think the only thing we know for sure is that it's been armed."

Chung's smartphone display switched from its view of the hallway to notice of an incoming call. "It's the apartment owner. I've told her to stay away by text, but not why. I have to make it clear to her that she and her son must avoid the area."

Grishkov and Vasilyev looked at each other, and nodded at the same time. A mother and her son were the last thing they needed right now.

Chung answered the call, and they saw from his expression that he was not happy with what he heard. Other than saying "Yes" a few times, along with one "No" Chung said nothing before returning the smartphone to its view of the hallway.

"They have her and the child," Chung said grimly. "They want me to come downstairs unarmed, give them the apartment keys, and then they'll let us go. I told them I'm the only person here. I doubt they believed me."

Grishkov nodded. "And you don't believe them, right?"

Chung cocked one eyebrow upward, and said nothing.

Vasilyev gestured towards the weapons piled near the shredded apartment wall. "You are welcome to whatever you like. We would go with you but..."

Chung nodded. "Can you disarm it?"

Grishkov shrugged. "I have the code. If that doesn't work, I have a few other ideas."

Chung nodded. "I wish you luck. I will buy you as much time as I can."

With that Chung scooped up two pistols, and quickly strode out of the apartment.

Vasilyev looked at Grishkov. "First I'll say the code, and then you say it, so we can be sure we memorized it correctly. As you recall from the instructions we read in Moscow, we'll only get one chance to key it in."

Grishkov nodded, and listened as Vasilyev recited the code, then followed it with the same one.

Vasilyev sighed in relief. "It's good to know that even in my old age I can still remember the important things. I think, though, that your younger fingers are better suited to keying in the code."

Grishkov bent down to the keypad, and immediately frowned. "Look at this! These screws have been replaced! Someone's been inside this weapon!"

Vasilyev bent down next to Grishkov and swore softly. The bright shiny screws certainly didn't match the rest of the case.

"Well, let's put the code in and hope for the best."

Grishkov nodded and began to carefully key in each letter and number in the sequence of ten. After each keystroke there was a distinct "click" which the weapon's manual had said meant it was correct. When Grishkov keyed in the seventh character, though, there was no click.

Both Grishkov and Vasilyev immediately froze.

After a few heart stopping moments, they each looked at each other. Vasilyev whispered, "The manual said any mistake in keying in the disarming code would detonate the device."

Grishkov nodded. "Whoever opened the case and replaced the screws may have dislodged a wire or contact for this particular character on the keypad. Or there may be corrosion from over half a century in storage. Either way, I need to open the case. Do you happen to have a screwdriver?"

Vasilyev mutely handed Grishkov his Swiss Army knife.

CHAPTER ONE HUNDRED TWENTY FIVE

Five Kilometers North of Camp Mobile, South Korea

When First Lieutenant Seth Younger had been growing up in the back-woods of Kentucky, hunting was a serious business. In good times whatever he shot for the pot would stretch the family dollar, so that now and then he might get candy, or be able to go to a movie. In bad times it just meant having something to eat, especially if his dad had been drinking again.

Younger had treated his battered Winchester Model 1890 .22 caliber rifle with love and care, because he'd known if anything happened to it he would never get a replacement. A slide action rifle that Winchester stopped making when the U.S. entered WWII, it still worked flawlessly. Younger, though, had always dreamed of having a bigger gun.

Standing up in the cupola of his M1A2 tank, Younger absently patted the side of its M256 120mm smoothbore cannon as he looked north for any sign of advancing North Korean forces. Well, Uncle Sam has sure given me a bigger gun, he thought to himself wryly. Now let's see if I know how to use it.

The US Army had been preparing for a North Korean invasion for well over half a century, and a lot of thought had gone into the position of Younger's platoon. Though the naval and air options available to both sides had changed a great deal since the last Korean War, for ground forces choices were much more limited. The terrain was basically the same, and tanks and Armored Personnel Carriers might be faster and better equipped, but their options for crossing that terrain had not changed much. There were only so many places a significant body of troops and equipment could cross.

That made the defenders' job much easier, but the flip side was that there weren't very many American and South Korean tanks to go around. Younger mulled over the numbers he had received from the rushed briefing he had received that morning, and grimaced as he thought about where they left his platoon. The best estimate was that the North Koreans had about 4,200 tanks, though it was anyone's guess as to how many were fueled and combat-ready.

Not counting M1A2 tanks sidelined for repair or maintenance, 121 were now deployed along the DMZ. Joining them at the DMZ were 2,500 South Korean tanks, about half the latest K-2 Black Panther and half the older K1A1. Both were based on the M1A2, which Younger thought was a great choice. Younger also understood the Koreans' desire to produce their own version, because he had seen plenty of evidence since arriving in Korea that they were capable in both engineering and manufacturing.

After a few days of hands-on experience with the K-2, Younger was both impressed with its performance, and just as happy to go back to his M1A2. Some things weren't better or worse, just different, like the engine and the viewing system. Younger had been careful not to say anything about the engine, knowing that it was a sore point with the Koreans. The locally produced version had failed in field testing, so they had been forced to turn to a German manufacturer.

One capability the Americans had insisted on with the M1A2 was that it be able to run on any fuel, because of past experience where continuing an advance had depended on the ability to use captured fuel supplies. As a result, the M1A2 could run on any grade of gasoline, diesel, kerosene, or jet fuel. The tradeoff was poor mileage, but what did you expect from a multi-ton tank?

Younger had heard rumors about the K-2's composite armor performance, and they weren't good. The fact that some K-2s also had explosive reactive armor, while others had the more advanced additional non-explosive reactive armor complicated the assessment even further. Younger knew how the M1A2 had performed against Russian designed tanks in Iraq, and was very happy to be in one to face similar tanks operated by the North Koreans.

About the only thing Younger did envy was the K-2's Korean Smart Top-Attack Munition (KSTAM). Designed specifically to attack a tank's thin and vulnerable top armor, it had an effective range of up to five miles. It was fired from the K-2 in a high arc like a mortar. When it reached the top of the arc a parachute opened, giving the munition's radar and infrared sensors time to find an enemy tank. When the tank was acquired, a penetrator round was fired straight down, with devastating results. Younger had been impressed by a demonstration he had seen of the KSTAM'S capabilities, and privately thought they went a long way towards making up for the K-2's engine issues. He had been smart enough, though, not to say so after the demonstration.

The tanks in Younger's platoon were carrying the M829A4 kinetic energy round as their tank killer. The number 4 at the end might make someone think it was the fourth in the M829A series of rounds that had first seen combat use in 1991 during Desert Storm. Younger smiled to himself as he remembered his instructor's lecture at the Armor School in Fort Benning. "You would be wrong to think it's the fourth, for the simple reason that the first M829A didn't have a number at the end. So, the M829A4 is actually the fifth in the series. Let that remind you - again - not to make assumptions, which are the gateway to jumping to conclusions." The instructor had gone on to explain that each round in the series had been in response to an improvement in Russian armor, the latest being an embedded radar unit that blew up the tank's reactive armor just before the round hit, in most cases deflecting it enough to avoid penetration.

The instructor then said that nobody in the classroom, including himself, had the clearance level needed to know just how the M829A4 managed to defeat radar-reactive armor. All he would add was that the M829A4 had a depleted uranium payload like the M829A3, and weighed about the same. Younger talked over the lesson with several of his classmates later and agreed with the consensus. As long as it works, that's all that matters.

As Younger continued to scan the distant treeline through his binoculars, he thought again that he was just as happy to be in his M1A2. It might not have fire-and-forget rounds that could destroy a tank he couldn't even see. But it could run on just about any liquid that burned, had armor that could shrug off most hits and fired rounds designed to defeat the latest armor.

Now, where were these guys?

CHAPTER ONE HUNDRED TWENTY SIX

Los Angeles

The first thing Detective Paul Valone noticed when he peered cautiously around the corner of the apartment building's front door was what at first appeared to be a Korean family, but another look made that unlikely. Plenty of families Valone had seen weren't happy, so the sniffling Korean boy was not a surprise. Neither was an unhappy Korean wife.

But the Korean woman wasn't just unhappy. She was clearly terrified. The man gripping her arm appeared more Japanese than Korean, and was at least a decade younger than the woman. It wasn't impossible that they could be a couple, but from what he knew of Korean society, it was very unlikely. Valone knew that some people might have regarded such an observation as stereotyping, or worse. In fact Valone, without thinking about it, divided everyone he encountered outside the office into one of four groups regardless of race, religion, gender, or sexual orientation - law enforcement, victims, perpetrators, and actual or potential witnesses.

If he had done anything but work, he might have thought about some other group. As it was, Valone's observations were keyed to solving cases, and nothing else.

This time, Valone was pretty sure he was seeing a woman and child being held against their will by someone who was neither father nor husband. They would have already spotted him, if not for their attention being completely focused on the stairwell leading down to the lobby.

Then Valone spotted the gun.

It was only a glimpse, because it was stored inside the man's jacket, but its presence told him a lot. It made a hostage situation much more likely. Koreans and Japanese, as opposed to many other ethnic groups in LA, were far less likely to have and use a concealed carry permit. In fact, with the partial exception of Korean shop owners, they were unlikely to have guns at all.

Valone was not a fan of technology, but he made a grudging exception for the new LAPD text system to call for backup. The system recognized his phone, and its GPS automatically gave his location. All Valone had to do was enter the appropriate code, in this case "Hostages held by armed suspect - not domestic dispute" and another code confirming it was Valone sending the backup request, not someone who had found or stolen his phone. There was even a separate code Valone could use if someone was holding him under duress and wanted to lure backup into an ambush.

It certainly beat moving out of the suspect's earshot to make a phone or radio call, or trying to whisper a backup request.

Valone had every intention of waiting for backup to arrive. The gun signaled to him that its Asian owner was probably a gang member or leader, and either way probably not alone. It would be foolish to walk alone into an armed confrontation with an unknown number of gunmen.

Just as Valone had that thought, he saw the man pull out his gun with his free hand, keeping the other firmly on the woman's arm. He saw the man looking towards someone in the stairwell Valone couldn't see from his angle, and snarl "Walk forward slowly with your hands raised."

The woman yelled something in a language Valone didn't know, but if he'd had to guess would have been something like "Run away, save yourself."

The gunman's attention was still on the stairwell, so it looked like whoever was there wasn't following her advice.

Ten Kilometers North of Camp Mobile, South Korea

Captain Hong Sang Ook had no idea how many of the tanks in his regiment had survived. Relentless air attacks had both reduced their number and scattered the survivors, so what had started as a well orga-nized and disciplined force was now groups of two or three tanks fighting to stay alive. Nonstop jamming on all frequencies made any attempt at co-ordination impossible.

In spite of this, Hong and two other tanks in his unit were still moving south. For the first time, Hong was actually able to make use of the intelligence included in the map he had been given of their primary objective, a place called Camp Mobile. According to the map, there were several likely ambush prepositions just north of the installation, which was an enemy drone base.

Hong grinned as he looked over the map. If the enemy was where it showed, he could finally start to pay them back for the misery they had endured since crossing the DMZ.

Chapter One Hundred
Twenty Seven

Camp Mobile, South Korea

Sgt. Josh Pettigrew prepared another Miniature Air Launched Decoy (MALD) for launch, the latest in a never ending stream that had reduced North Korean air defense effectiveness by over 90%, according to an intelligence assessment an Air Force colonel had shared with him while he was still on the flight line. The colonel, whose twang said "Texas" and whose closely cropped gray hair told Pettigrew he was at least twice his age, told him "You're confusing the hell out of the North Koreans with these things. You're doing God's work, boy! Keep it up!"

Pettigrew thought it was certainly the most colorful motivational speech he'd heard, suppressed an exhausted smile and said the only response possible, "Yes, sir!", coupled with an enthusiastic salute.

It seemed to make the colonel happy. At least, he let Pettigrew get back to work.

He had just been resupplied from Kadena Air Base, and had every intention of continuing to make the North Korean air defense networks' task as miserable as possible. Camp Mobile had been badly damaged by a flood in 2011, and before his UAV company had been stationed there it had nearly been closed altogether. Now that he had more MALDs, Pettigrew was sure he could do his part to make this war as short as possible, and make his division commander happy he had decided to keep Camp Mobile open.

Los Angeles

Valone spotted movement near the mailboxes mounted in the walls in the far left of the lobby. As he'd suspected, the gunman wasn't alone.

And with an imminent threat to civilians, there was no way he was waiting for backup.

In one fluid motion Valone drew his .40 caliber Glock Model 22, opened the door, crouched into a firing stance and yelled "LAPD! Lay down your weapon!"

Several things then happened very quickly.

Valone had his weapon pointed at the gunman he could see, but one eye to his left. As the gunman cursed, let go of the woman and turned towards him, he saw more motion to his left. Instinct dropped him to the floor just as he could feel multiple rounds pass overhead.

Valone looked up at the gunman whose weapon was now pointed straight at him, and his only thought was regret that he wouldn't be able to save the woman and her son.

The gunman then pitched over dead, just after several bullet holes appeared in his torso. Valone wasn't certain, but the figure pressed against the wall near the dead gunman looked like the man in the convenience store video.

Valone fired several shots to the left, as did the man from the video. He thought that he heard a body hit the floor, but wasn't sure through the noise of the gunfire.

The gunfire stopped. It sounded as though whoever was left from the men who had been firing were exiting through the back.

After the door slammed behind them, the silence was echoing. Valone looked across at the man who had saved him from the gunman, and saw that he had laid his gun down on the floor beside him. As Valone watched, he kicked the gun towards him.

As Valone picked up the gun, the man asked "Are you police?"

Valone nodded.

The man said, "I need to check on my girlfriend and her son. They are the ones who were being held hostage by these gangsters."

The book said he should be placing this man in custody, both as a material witness and participant in a gunfight with at least one fatality.

But the man had saved his life. No civilian had ever done that before. Well, Valone thought to himself grimly as he looked at the shot grouping on the corpse in front of him, probably not really a civilian.

Valone made his decision instantly. "Go ahead," he said. "Any second a lot of other police are going to be here. I suggest you find someplace else to be by then."

The man made a small bow, and then visibly hesitated. "There are two men upstairs in Apartment 4A. I think they are police, and could use your help."

With that, the man hurried off in the same direction the woman and child had fled earlier.

Valone quickly confirmed that the sound he had heard earlier had indeed been a dead body hitting the floor near a bank of mailboxes. Approaching sirens confirmed that there would be plenty of help to secure the scene shortly. The book said he should stay put to brief the new arrivals on what had happened.

Normally Valone did what the book said. He couldn't remember the last time he'd ignored it twice in one day. But his gut was telling him that checking out Apartment 4A couldn't wait.

Part of it was that Valone knew whoever was in the apartment, they weren't LAPD. The other part was that Valone had the strong feeling the man had told the truth as he knew it, both about believing the men were police and about their needing his help. Maybe feds?

Valone shrugged and strode towards the elevator. Only one way to find out.

CHAPTER ONE HUNDRED TWENTY EIGHT

Camp Casey, South Korea

South Korea was a far more open society than North Korea. For nearly every purpose that mattered including industry, trade and culture this gave the South a substantial edge over the North. There was only one major exception - spying. While it took heroic efforts to get a spy to anywhere where he could gather worthwhile intelligence in North Korea, in South Korea it was far easier.

That was not to say there were no risks for North Korean spies, or that none were ever caught. South Korea kept entry and exit records going back to the 1960s, so anyone claiming to have been born in South Korea who tried to enter without a record of having previously left had some explaining to do. The South Korean national ID card included a fingerprint, so even a perfect forgery wouldn't work once the fingerprint was checked.

There were ways around these problems, though. Hundreds of thousands of Koreans were born outside Korea every year, most in the United States and Japan, but in dozens of other countries as well. Even though parents were supposed to report the birth of a Korean child right away to the closest Korean Embassy, it didn't always happen, especially if the child had no immediate need for a passport. So, someone who applied for a Korean passport for the first time outside Korea to study at a Korean university was not at all unusual.

Forging the necessary documents for the Korean passport, such as foreign birth certificates and ID cards, was no challenge. The best part was that armed with a genuine Korean passport issued outside Korea, upon arrival in South Korea the North Korean spy could then apply for a genuine national ID card, complete with the spy's own fingerprint.

The main limitation of this infiltration method was that to avoid unwanted attention the spies needed to appear around 20 years old or less, the typical age for a university student. For older spies, there were two primary alternatives.

The first was to be smuggled in by minisub. This method had the advantage of allowing the spy to bring in equipment and weapons as well. It had the disadvantage of extreme risk, as South Korean coastal defenses improved every year. Plus, every discovery reminded the South Koreans of just how eager the North was to place spies in their country. As a result, it was rarely used.

The second alternative was to come into South Korea as the citizen of another country. Since thousands of ethnic Chinese were born in North Korea every year, Chinese citizenship was the most frequent choice. However, there was also a smaller number of ethnic Japanese born in North Korea, a population dating back to the Korean Peninsula's status as a Japanese colony prior to World War II. It was easy for North Korean spies pretending to be Chinese or Japanese to blend in, since there were hundreds of thousands of real Chinese and Japanese citizens living in South Korea.

There were three main disadvantages with this approach. First, the fact that so many real Chinese and Japanese lived in South Korea made them difficult to avoid, and even a casual conversation could arouse enough suspicion to prompt a call to the authorities. Second, the South Korean government monitored all foreigners resident in the country. Finally, some jobs in South Korea were closed to foreigners, and these included many with access to the information of the greatest interest to North Korea.

The top of that list was military information, for example where American and South Korean tanks were likely to be deployed to defend against an invasion. It was possible to get a general idea simply by living in the area where American and South Korean forces held joint exercises, since Korea was too tightly packed to keep everyone far enough away not to see anything, and the exercises were always held in the areas near the border where fighting was actually expected.

To get detailed information that would help a North Korean invasion force, though, there were few realistic approaches. The first was to infiltrate either the American or South Korean military by convincing a soldier to work as a spy for North Korea. Several attempts had been made using large cash payments as bait, but this approach was abandoned after the soldiers turned in the North Korean agents making the offers.

Several agents attempted to enlist in the South Korean military. Most were arrested after failing their background check, though two passed initial screening after claiming to be orphan brothers raised at an orphanage that had in fact burned down with all of its records. Unfortunately, neither one was able to convince skeptical investigators who questioned them separately and at length, until both finally confessed.

The most productive approach turned out to be applying for work in low-level labor and clerical positions on U.S. and South Korean military bases. Working at a commissary, PX, bar or restaurant on base required nothing more than a criminal records check which North Korean agents had no trouble passing, since they really didn't have a South Korean criminal record. Though this gave them no direct access to classified military intelligence, it provided close contact with Americans and South Koreans who did.

Bae Jung Wook had been lucky enough to get a job at a forward U.S. Army base, Camp Casey. The base had been open near the DMZ since the Korean War, and though there had been a plan to move most of the forces there to Camp Humphreys, increasing tensions with North Korea had forced reversal of the move. Forty miles north of Seoul, it was by far the closest major U.S. Army base to North Korea.

Bae had the good luck to have been looking for a job when the Officer and Enlisted/NCO Clubs were converted to the Gateway Club and Warriors Club, and made available to all military personnel. Some of the existing staff at both of the old clubs hadn't cared for the change and moved on to other jobs, and Bae was picked for one that called for a little bit of everything. Need to move bottles or kegs of beer from the truck to the bar? Get Bae! Need clean glasses, floors or toilets? Get Bae! Need to rearrange the tables and chairs for a party? Well, who else?

Bae started at the Gateway Club, but sometimes worked at the Warriors Club as well. He was popular with the managers of both clubs because he would work any shift offered, never complained, and took care of any job given quickly and competently. He might have been offered more responsible work, except for his withdrawn personality. Bae spoke only when spoken to, and only about work. He had no social life or family that anyone knew of, and seemed to spend all of his time outside his sixty hour a week work schedule in his tiny apartment.

This perception was inaccurate. Bae wasn't a conversationalist, but he was a very good listener. As at bars worldwide, US military personnel had one topic that dominated all others - they talked about work. Much of the time, they did so within Bae's earshot.

Bae's problem was not collecting facts about U.S. military operations near the North Korean border. It was sorting through the mountain of information he collected every day to find the data of greatest interest to his superiors in North Korean intelligence. In order to do that, he had to understand what he was hearing, and that meant putting the information in context.

For example, one of his highest priority collection tasks was information on US Army planning for a North Korean invasion. When Bae heard soldiers talking about the results of the latest exercises, though, much of what he listened to was useless without knowing where what they described was happening. They didn't talk about prepositioned defenses near a particular village, but instead about map references and grid coordinates that made sense to them but left Bae angry and frustrated.

Over time, though, Bae learned to pick up mentions of terrain features and other landmarks that gave him a place to start. He found reasons to go through exercise areas that would not attract suspicion, and was careful to go outside the camp only when no exercises were either underway or recently concluded. Bae wasn't doing anything as crude as counting tank tracks. He was after information that wouldn't shift from one commander to another.

All armies developed habitual ways of doing things in a particular place over time. Some were dictated by terrain, others by what had worked in the past. Bae was determined to learn whatever he could about the plans of the U.S. invaders who had been in his country since long before he was born, so the stalemate that had persisted since the 1950s could finally be ended.

Bae hardly ever heard from his superiors in North Korean intelligence. The reason for this was simple. Bae had been given detailed instructions on the information he was to collect, and any contact included some degree of risk. A week before, though, he had been given an urgent, single line instruction. Update and expand on the expected positions of enemy armor attempting to ambush an invading tank force.

Bae had already provided an extensive readout on this topic, but agreed it couldn't hurt to see if anything useful could be added. Unlike much of the other information he had been asked to collect this at least was knowledge that could help a North Korean liberation force, as Bae unironically thought of it, succeed in its mission.

If, Bae thought bitterly, anyone back home had the guts to use it.

CHAPTER ONE HUNDRED TWENTY NINE

Camp Mobile, South Korea

First Lieutenant Seth Younger had struck up a friendship with Sgt. Josh Pettigrew over beers at the Gateway Club that would have never happened in the old days when officers and NCOs each stuck to their own clubs. Once they each knew what the other did, Pettigrew wasted no time telling Younger that he was happy to have his tanks between Camp Mobile and the North Koreans. Younger was just as quick to tell Pettigrew how impressed he was with the drones he had at Camp Mobile.

There was no formal link between intelligence collected by drones and tanks at the platoon level. The staff needed to manage that information flow and to distribute it on a real time basis simply didn't exist.

However, when it came to securing Camp Mobile and the drones that Pettigrew rightly thought were helping them win the war, he decided to try an ad hoc solution. He detailed one of his best soldiers, Corporal Martz, to watch the feed from an AeroVironment RQ-20 Puma, an old model that was due for retirement and had no other mission tasking. It had no sophisticated jamming or offensive capabilities, just high quality optical and infrared cameras. This variant, the "Solar Puma" had solar cells that increased endurance to about nine hours.

Corporal Martz kept an eye on the drone's feed along with his other duties, with instructions to let Younger know first about any enemy activity, and then Pettigrew. At first, he had trouble believing what he was seeing. Then, he quickly carried out his instructions.

"Sir, it looks like three M-2002 Pokpung-ho tanks are advancing on Lieutenant Younger's position. It's almost as though they know where they are."

Pettigrew frowned. "No, it's exactly as though they know. You've already notified Younger?"

Corporal Martz nodded. "Yes, sir, and received acknowledgement of transmission receipt."

Pettigrew grunted. Younger's platoon ought to be able to handle the North Koreans. But it might not be a bad idea to plan for a worst case scenario.

CHAPTER ONE HUNDRED THIRTY

Washington, DC

Tom Browning and Bob Hansen ushered Li Weimin and Park Won Hee into the Situation Room, where they were met by the frank stares of the nearly full room. Looking over the seats available, Browning and Hansen saw the four at the table that had been set aside for them. The only other vacant seat was at the head of the table.

The moment they sat down the door opened and President Hernandez strode into the room. Everyone rose, and quickly sat down as Hernandez gestured impatiently to do so.

The colonel standing at the briefing display switched on the first slide, which showed the last reported positions of North Korean and Allied forces. Hernandez held up his hand.

"Colonel, I want to hear your briefing, but first I want to find out how we got here, and what possessed the North Koreans to start a war they should know they can't win."

Turning his gaze to Tom Browning, Hernandez said "I understand the gentlemen with you have some light to shed on this."

Browning nodded. "Yes, Mr. President. What we have been able to piece together from their accounts is as follows. .."

Twenty minutes later a stunned silence filled the Situation Room.

Hernandez said, "OK, so I'm going to sum up what I've just heard. The North Koreans are about to detonate a nuclear weapon in a subway tunnel in downtown Seoul. They have another smaller nuke stolen from the Russians prepositioned in an American city, but we don't know which one. And a rogue faction in China is planning to take advantage of our being occupied in Korea to invade Taiwan."

Browning and Hansen both nodded. Li and Park wore similar grim expressions.

Though most in the room still looked stunned one of the generals sitting at the table looked thoughtful, which Hernandez noticed immediately.

"Something to share, General Wilson?"

"Yes, sir," the Army Chief of Staff replied. "We'd been expecting the North Koreans to shell Seoul to create chaos and panic. With all the high rise buildings there mass casualties would be practically guaranteed. But so far they've only shelled military targets, and plenty of them. If they were planning to set off a nuke in Seoul though, that choice makes more sense."

Into the sudden silence Wilson said awkwardly, "As much as any of this does."

Hernandez smiled tiredly and shook his head. "I understand what you mean, General. And Admiral, I suppose you agree this helps explain the mysterious attack on our carrier?"

Admiral Carter looked up from the tablet he had been examining. "Yes, sir. We couldn't see how it fit into the conflict in Korea, but now it does. If we're going to head off an invasion of Taiwan, we need to get new sailing orders to that carrier group ASAP."

Hernandez nodded. "Consider the order given."

The President paused, and then looked at Park Won Hee. "Mr. Park, when do you think your government is likely to detonate the nuclear device in Seoul?"

Park looked at Hernandez bleakly. "Mr. President, it could be any time now. It was supposed to be announced as a threat to the South Korean government, but I understand that never happened. I suggest you check to see whether all is normal with the construction crew at Tunnel Number 7. If not, you must act immediately."

One of the men sitting against the wall rose and left without a word. Not for the first time, Hernandez gave thanks that popular perception notwithstanding, there were at least a few people in government who knew what they were doing.

"I know we've already increased our terrorist attack level to its highest readiness level. What else can we do to find this nuke that may be in an American city?" Hernandez asked.

Park spoke again. "I was not told where the device would be sent. But I think it would be by sea instead of air, since security is much less. Once at a port, I don't think they would risk moving it far overland. That probably means a large port city on your Pacific coast."

Hansen nodded. "I think that makes sense, sir. If you agree I suggest the Bureau coordinates a search in cities from San Diego to Seattle with local law enforcement. Once we locate it, we'll call in a Nuclear Incident Response Team."

Hernandez looked at the Attorney General. "Bob, I don't need to tell you to do this as quietly as possible, do I?"

Attorney General Robert McKimmon looked back at Hernandez unhappily. "No, sir. But it's only a matter of time before the press finds out, no matter how tightly held we keep this."

Hernandez nodded. "I know, Bob. We just have to find it fast enough to make it a good news story. Because if we don't, I think panic will be the least of our problems."

After a pause he looked again straight at the Attorney General, and asked, "Bob, with all we've heard, you agree that a mission specifically targeting the North Korean leadership is legally justified?".

"Absolutely, sir," McKimmon said without hesitation.

Hernandez nodded. "Good. Admiral Carter, you have men ready to carry out this mission to the location identified by South Korean intelligence?"

Carter nodded. "Yes, sir, as we discussed. Just waiting for your command."

Hernandez nodded again. "Let me know once the mission is complete."

Hernandez turned to Secretary of State Fred Popel. "Fred, make sure that the Japanese recordings of the MiGs' attack on both the Trans Pacific flight and the carrier are given by our Ambassador to the Chinese Foreign Minister personally. Now, our response to the Chinese demand that we negotiate with the North Koreans..."

CHAPTER ONE HUNDRED THIRTY ONE

Five Kilometers North of Camp Mobile, South Korea

Younger swore as soon as he finished acknowledging the message from Camp Mobile, and immediately ordered his platoon to move out from their positions. He had argued against fixed emplacements for the tanks in his platoon, insisting it reduced them to little more than mobile artillery.

Command invoked "doctrine," which said that an attacking enemy could be ambushed effectively from a camouflaged position along a route that terrain forced them to cross before reaching their objective.

That sounded great, as long as the enemy didn't know where they were. Younger had argued that the North Koreans could also read maps, and could easily guess likely ambush spots. He'd also pointed out that though the North Koreans had far fewer drones than the U.S. did, they did have some. That was an inarguable fact, since North Korean drones that had malfunctioned had been picked up inside South Korea as early as 2014. One discovered in 2017 had even been found to have specifically targeted the Terminal High Altitude Area Defense system, also known as THAAD, taking ten pictures of the system without being detected before it crashed on a mountainside near the North Korean border.

Younger had never even tried to suggest that North Korean spies might have discovered their ambush preparations, since he didn't believe that himself.

The problem with prepositioning tanks in a location that made them hard to see and gave them some protection from attack was that it took time to move out of the positions. Not much time, but when under attack every second counted. Also, if the enemy knew exactly where you were, you were easy to target.

No sooner had Younger had the thought than the first AT-5 Spandrel missile hit one of the M1A2 tanks in his platoon. With its nearly three kilogram load of high explosives, the AT-5 was rated as a significant battlefield threat, but the first hit was defeated by the M1A2's reactive armor. Though its crew was shaken, they were unhurt and the tank was still fully combat capable.

The second and third M1A2s to be hit were not so lucky. One suffered a penetrating hit that killed the gunner and driver, and seriously injured the commander and loader. The other was only slightly better off, with only the driver being killed, but all three others were too seriously wounded to continue the fight.

The surviving M1A2s, though, had now spotted the M-2002s. All fired on the move, which the Abrams did more effectively than any other tank. Smoke and flame erupted from two of the M-2002s, though Younger saw that one was still moving. Another had laid down smoke, but Younger decided to ignore it while he concentrated on finishing off the wounded M-2002.

Both Younger's M1A2 and the one that had been hit first by an AT-5 fired at the same moment at the same wounded tank. They were rewarded by a spectacular explosion, that threw the M-2002's turret into the air.

It had been a mistake, though, to ignore the smoking and unmoving M-2002 tank. Though only its commander remained alive, and even though he was wounded, he was the one who operated the tank's AT-5 launcher. The tank beside Younger no longer had reactive armor left to protect it, and the second AT-5 hit proved fatal.

Younger quickly remedied their earlier mistake with a round that left the M-2002 laying on its side and its commander just as dead as the rest of his crew, while wondering where the tank that had laid down smoke could be.

Hong Sang Ook's M-2002 announced its presence with a round from its 125 mm 2A26/46 smoothbore gun, which knocked off one of Younger's treads but did no other damage. Younger wheeled the Abrams' turret to counterfire, but to his frustration there were no targets visible, only smoke from both Hong's grenades and from the burning tanks.

Fortunately for Younger, Hong wasn't interested in continuing the engagement. He had an objective, and now his was the only tank left in his entire force with a chance of reaching it. Hong was going to use every round he had left on Camp Mobile, and do his best to make the sacrifice of all his dead comrades worthwhile.

CHAPTER ONE HUNDRED THIRTY TWO

Los Angeles

Grishkov frowned as he gently removed the plate surrounding the nuclear weapon's keypad. To his relief, the keypad's removal allowed him to see how it was attached to the rest of the device. The problem was obvious almost immediately.

Pointing mutely at a wire hanging loose from the keypad, Grishkov cocked an eyebrow at Vasilyev, who simply nodded.

Grishkov looked more intently at the wires that were still attached, and frowned even more deeply. "They're soldered," he hissed quietly.

Vasilyev grunted acknowledgement. "And that's important because. .."

"Well, I don't have a soldering gun or solder, and I doubt we'll find any in this apartment," Grishkov said impatiently. "And I can't just put the wire back, because the solder is probably designed to be part of the connection between the keypad and the device."

Vasilyev nodded. "Solder is metal, yes?"

Grishkov scowled. "Tin or lead, or a mixture of both. I only need a little."

They heard the elevator door open.

Both Grishkov and Vasilyev drew their weapons and crouched down facing what was left of the door.

"LAPD!" a voice announced. "Backup will be here any moment."

Valone knew this statement was a bit optimistic. While police would indeed be in the lobby very soon, it would take time to secure the scene and do a floor to floor sweep as far as the fourth floor. As he looked over the evidence of a gun battle that appeared to have included a grenade detonation, Valone found himself fervently hoping that the man who had saved his life in the lobby was telling the truth about these men being police.

After a pause, he heard one of the men say, "Please come forward holding up your ID in one hand, and your other hand clearly visible."

Valone briefly considered asking for their ID, but decided that it would make more sense to take the elevator back to the lobby instead. Unless he really wanted to give in to his curiosity.

A moment later, Valone shrugged and moved forward, holding up his badge in one hand and the other in plain sight. The two men inside rose and lowered their guns, though they didn't put them away.

The younger one said, "My name is Grishkov. My colleague here is named Vasilyev. We have Russian diplomatic identification we could show you, but there is no time to waste. It will be quicker to show you the problem."

Grishkov gestured towards the bedroom. Vasilyev entered first, followed by Valone and Grishkov.

Valone paled as he looked at the device, with its display counting down 1:47:22, 1:47:21. "Is it...?"

Grishkov nodded. "A bomb? Yes, a stolen Russian nuclear bomb, and it has been armed. We were sent here to retrieve it."

Several versions of "You're a bit late" raced through Valone's head but were discarded in favor of "How do we disarm it?"

Grishkov nodded approvingly. "We have the disarm code. A loose wire is preventing us from entering one digit. I need to reattach the wire with solder."

Valone thought, finally the tinkering that drove my ex crazy may come in handy.

"If I can find some toys, I may be able to fix this," Valone said, and rushed out to the other bedroom. He was back in a few moments with an armful of metal toys.

Valone pulled out a Swiss Army knife, and Grishkov followed with the one he'd been using. Valone handed over several of the toys, and said "Open up the battery compartments. Toss the batteries, and check for corrosion. If it's clean, pry out the metal lining. We'll go with the first one that looks decent."

In less than two minutes, Grishkov and Valone had both pulled out metal pieces from the toys. Valone looked over them, and picked one.

"I think this can work. Do either of you have a lighter?"

Vasilyev pulled out a battered metal lighter, and said, "I'm glad I still smoke an occasional cigar."

CHAPTER ONE HUNDRED THIRTY THREE

Camp Mobile, South Korea

Sgt. Josh Pettigrew had run a small risk of disciplinary action by concealing a reconnaissance drone for his unit's own use. Keeping a General Atomics MQ-1 Predator and its two Hellfire missiles hidden in a back repair bay was another matter altogether. It was not that anyone would miss the MQ-1, since it had been replaced in combat operations by the much more capable General Atomics MQ-9 Reaper, and this particular Predator had been designated for return to the U.S. and decommission. Instead, it was that an NCO was simply not authorized to operate his own private air defense force.

There was also the small matter of the two Hellfire missiles, which were still very much in the combat inventory.

Pettigrew's concerns about the wrath of his superiors, never that important in the past, now evaporated completely as he watched the recon drone's feed of the battle just north of Camp Mobile. When he saw that the net result had been that a North Korean tank had survived to attack the camp, he immediately turned to Corporal Martz.

"Help me arm and launch the Predator. You know where it is, right?"

Martz nodded. "I wondered why we hadn't crated it for return, but now I'm glad we didn't. Shouldn't we report that tank to somebody?"

Both of them were already running to the repair bay.

Pettigrew shook his head. "No time. This camp is either going to get hit with every round that tank has, and watch as it rolls over what's left, or we're going to take that tank out ourselves."

Martz nodded, as both of them reached the repair bay and he checked over the two Hellfire missiles stored in the rack next to the Predator. "How long do you think we have?".

Pettigrew bent down to check the fuel gauge, which read gratifyingly full.

"Maybe just long enough. We'll load the right Hellfire first, then get the left."

Martz and Pettigrew grunted with effort as they lifted the first 45 kilogram Hellfire onto the Predator's wing mount. In just a few minutes, they had both missiles mounted on the Predator.

Pettigrew's fingers flew over the keyboard as he input a generic attack profile into the Predator, while Martz hooked up the MQ-1 to a small cart used for towing drones to the taxiway. The recon drone's feed was still displayed on the overhead monitor, showing the North Korean tank's advance. Pettigrew didn't need to compare the image to any maps, since it was close enough to the camp that he knew exactly where the tank was. Way too close.

Chapter One Hundred Thirty Four

"Mt. Paektu" Secret Headquarters, North Korea

Gye Tae Hyun cautiously knocked on the heavy wooden door that opened onto Marshal Ko's office at the "Mt. Paektu" secret headquarters. Of course, it was in fact nowhere near the actual Mt. Paektu.

"Enter," a tired voice responded. Gye winced internally. Ko didn't sound ready for the news he was bringing. Just a few hours earlier, Gye had brought word that their forces had been fought to a standstill before reaching Seoul and were running out of fuel and ammunition.

Ko was as clear eyed and observant as ever. "So, Gye, more bad news. You know, I was just trying to remember the last time it was good, and I think it was when we were able to get that Russian man-portable nuclear device without even having to pay for it. But, we sent the radio signal that should have set it off remotely, and there's nothing on the radio about a fireball in Los Angeles."

Gye shook his head.

"Well, I suppose we'll never know whether the device malfunctioned, our radio signal failed to detonate it, or the Americans somehow found and disarmed it. In the end, it doesn't really matter."

Gye stood silently.

"There is still a chance that the device we built ourselves could detonate in the subway tunnel under Seoul. But we have not heard of either a detonation, or the device's capture."

Gye shook his head.

"All of our nuclear missiles have been destroyed by American air strikes."
Gye nodded.

Ko shrugged. "Firing them at the South was an option I seriously considered, but multiple hits would have resulted in a South not worth having. They might also have been intercepted by the American's THAAD anti-missile system, and made us look weak."

"One or maybe several of our ICBMs might have reached the US. If they had, we'll never know now if they would have worked. Whether or not they worked, I think the Americans would have reacted with a massive nuclear response no living creature in our country could survive."

Ko paused. "Our Chinese friends have passed on to the Americans that we wish a negotiated end to this conflict, based on a return of all forces to their previous borders, correct?"

Gye nodded. "Yes, sir. Do you think the Americans will agree?"

Ko shrugged. "After they kicked the Iraqis out of Kuwait and had thousands of troops inside Iraq with nothing between them and Baghdad, who would have believed they would let Saddam Hussein remain Iraq's ruler for another dozen years? Anyway, we have nothing to lose."

Gye looked thoughtful. "And if the Americans refuse to negotiate?"

Ko grimaced. "Unlikely. But if they do refuse, there is nothing for us to do but wait for them to find us. I don't think we'll have to wait long, either way."

CHAPTER ONE HUNDRED THIRTY FIVE

Outside "Mt. Paektu" Secret Headquarters, North Korea

Commander Dave Martins assessed this mission as one of the most difficult Seal Team Six had ever been assigned, primarily because aside from the location, they had very little intelligence on the target. One of the few concrete details on the headquarters where the North Korean leadership was hidden was that it could only be entered through a massive steel door, set into the side of a mountain within natural granite folds that made a direct bomb or missile hit impossible. Evidently, its design at least on the exterior was based on the Cheyenne Mountain Complex, but given the North Koreans' far more limited resources the mission planners were confident they would not meet the Cheyenne Complex's multiple 25 ton steel doors.

They did have one other crucial bit of intelligence - the door of this secret headquarters, like all the others, swung open on hinges. That was critical, because it meant that instead of blasting through several feet of metal, they just needed to blast the door off its hinges. Naturally, that meant applying shaped charges directly to the hinges.

One bit of good luck was that a new explosive had just been released to the Teams, a new combination of CL-20 and HMX that increased the proportion of the more powerful CL-20 in the mix, while retaining HMX'S stability. They had the new compound for both the shaped charges and incorporated into new grenades that testing had shown were several times as powerful as any others available worldwide.

And they would need every advantage they could get, Martins thought. They had no idea how many armed enemy forces they would be facing, just that they were certain to be outnumbered. Mines, booby traps, fixed gun emplacements - once they were inside, there was no way to know what defenses they could encounter.

The door could only be approached by helicopter. That had meant suppressing the enemy air defenses around the headquarters with a massive air assault before landing. Seals train exhaustively on gaining the element of surprise. Here that was missing from the outset.

Well, Martins thought, we're just going to have to succeed regardless.

"Lieutenant Lombardy, are the shaped charges in place?" Martins asked.

"Yes, sir," Lombardy nodded.

"Ok, let's get everyone back to the copters," Martins said.

"Aye, aye, sir," Lombardy said with a grin.

This was Martins least favorite part of the plan, but it was unavoidable. When the door blew there was no way to know where it would go, and no place in the small space in front of the door to shelter from the force of the explosion, shaped though it might be.

The results of the detonation were everything Martins had been promised. The door was thrown completely off its hinges, and laid flat on the ground a dozen yards away.

One of the AH-64E Apache Guardians flying escort immediately emptied its entire load of Hydra 70 2.75-inch rockets into the space revealed behind the blasted door.

"Nice work, Lieutenant," Martins said. "Now, let's head back and see how well the new grenades do."

"Yes, sir. I've thrown a few in practice, and agree with the instructor. The big thing to remember is - throw long!"

Martins smiled. "I'll keep that in mind, Lombardy."

The rockets has pulverized the interior they could see on entry, and for a good distance beyond. Whoever had organized the defense of the headquarters had made a bad mistake by placing a large force near the entry door, since anyone who had survived the breach of the door had no chance against the Apache's rockets. Not only were there no survivors visible upon entry, there were few recognizable bodies.

The Seals methodically cleared corridors leading into the mountain with their new grenades, finding few survivors of the explosions still capable of resistance. Finally, they came to a door about half the size of the one at entry.

"Still have breaching explosive left, Lombardy?" Martins asked.

"More than enough for this, sir," Lombardy said. "Once I'm done, though, we'll need to backtrack at least two corridors."

Martins nodded, and waited for Lombardy to complete his work.

The result this time was just as satisfying, with the door thrown well clear of the entrance to what Martins sincerely hoped was the end of the complex. He ordered more of the new grenades thrown through the open door, and could hear from the cries of pain and despair inside that their power came as an unpleasant surprise to those inside.

With the area near the door clear, several of Martins' men dove through it, grenades in hand and ready to throw. Though gunfire wounded one of them, they were all able to toss the grenades at their attackers. The survivors were able to hit Lieutenant Lombardy in the shoulder, but not before another round of grenades and machine gun fire silenced them.

In the echoing silence that followed, a heavy wooden door opened. A man in uniform came out with his hands raised, and strode towards Martins, who he had apparently been able to identify as the commander. The man said, "I am the President of Korea, and I demand to nego"

That was as much as he said before Commander Martins shot him in the head, as he had been ordered to do personally by President Hernandez, who had told him "We're not going to leave anyone alive who tries to set off a nuclear weapon against this country."

Martins agreed with that position completely.

CHAPTER ONE HUNDRED THIRTY SIX

Tunnel No. 1, North Korea

Lee Ho Suk looked over the mass of explosives, fuses and wires covering the end of the tunnel and shuddered. This was it, he realized. After so many close calls, his luck had finally run out. Numbly, he went where the shouting soldiers were pointing for him and the other workers to go, while most of the troops piled into the subway car. Lee shook his head at the lunacy of Captain Yoon's plan. Set off the explosives, and simultaneously run the subway car forward at top speed through the just created hole, before the tunnel had time to finish collapsing.

Well, he thought bitterly, they'll have a better chance than I will. Without even thinking about it, Lee's feet moved him to the edge of the area the soldiers were pointing to, towards the side closest to the end of the tunnel. This was made easier by the fact that everyone else was trying to stay as far away from the explosives as possible.

Finally, with a last shouted order and waving of rifles the few remaining soldiers piled onto the subway car. Lee could barely see through the dust raised by all the rapid movement, but could just make out through the car's rear window a soldier holding up two hands. When he dropped one of the hands, Lee felt like an electric shock had passed through him. Five seconds left!

Lee didn't think. He just ran. So did many of the other workers, though most were just curled up with their arms covering their heads.

Lee was the only one to run towards the subway car, parked directly behind the explosives. The last thing Lee saw before the explosives went off was the scowling face of a soldier lifting up his rifle as he ran to within a few yards of the back of the subway car.

The last thing Lee heard was a roaring that sounded like the end of the world, and then everything was blackness and silence.

Los Angeles

Grishkov held the keypad and its dangling wires clear of the weapon while Valone used the pointed end of the Swiss Army knife's wire stripper to place a drop of homemade solder on the faulty contact.

"We should give it a minute to harden," Valone said, looking at the advancing time display clicking 1:41:44 to 1:41:43 as he did. Grishkov and Vasilyev were looking too.

Grishkov finally shrugged. "Agreed. But no more than that. I really don't think we have that much time," he said, nodding toward the display.

Valone spent the next minute thinking about all the questions he really wanted to ask these two men, and what a bad idea it would be to allow a distraction of any kind before the bomb was disarmed.

Finally, Valone lowered the plate, at the same time that Grishkov lowered the keypad. Valone quickly replaced the screws, and Grishkov once again stood in front of the keypad. Visibly steeling himself, he pressed the next character in the code sequence.

Click.

From the look of relief on the two men's faces, Valone guessed correctly that they had successfully fixed the problem. It was almost anticlimactic when Grishkov pressed the final character on the keypad, and the clock obligingly stopped advancing.

The display read 1:40:09.

Grishkov and Vasilyev looked at each other.

Vasilyev spoke first, as he pulled out his phone. "Detective Valone, we need to remove this stolen Russian government property and return it to Russia as soon as possible. We have a plane waiting at LAX for this purpose. We are working on getting your government's assistance with appropriate transport and security arrangements. We are also recommending that the public not be troubled with this matter, since after all there is now no danger. I hope we can count on your assistance with any of your police colleagues who come upon this scene before those arrangements are complete."

Valone had already been thinking about what to do next, and certainly agreed that a citywide panic wasn't what LA needed.

"OK, I'll keep a lid on this with patrol once they make it up here, but my captain is going to have to get the word pretty quick if we're going to keep this quiet long enough to get this bomb on your plane."

Vasilyev nodded. "The man who asked you to come and help us. Did you arrest him?"

Valone shook his head. "If he has any sense, he's halfway to Mexico by now."

Vasilyev and Grishkov looked at each other, and shrugged simultaneously.

Valone thought, as he listened to Vasilyev speaking in Russian on his phone, that he had never heard anyone speaking faster in any language.

CHAPTER ONE HUNDRED THIRTY SEVEN

Camp Mobile, South Korea

Sgt. Josh Pettigrew's fingers twitched as they rested on the keyboard he was using to command the MQ-1 Predator that was now the camp's last line of defense. They had launched the attack drone in record time - nothing like your own skin on the line as motivation, Pettigrew thought wryly. The problem was that the North Korean tank commander had apparently spotted the reconnaissance drone, and ducked under tree cover. Corporal Martz had tried to use the drone's infrared sensors to pick up the M-2002 Pokpung-ho tank again, without any luck.

Now that the Predator was airborne it had joined in the search, but so far no success. Pettigrew was uncomfortably aware that every passing moment made it more likely they would fail to stop the tank before it attacked.

No sooner had the thought formed than both Pettigrew and Martz heard an explosion that was nearby, but not close enough to rock their small building.

Pettigrew pointed at Martz. "Time for looking is over. Take cover."

As he could see Martz getting ready to argue Pettigrew shook his head. "I don't need any help piloting the Predator, and it's obvious now where it has to be. Take cover - that's an order."

"Yes, sir. Good luck," Martz said, as he headed for the nearest shelter.

Pettigrew was already completely absorbed in redirecting the Predator. He knew he'd be lucky to launch even a single Hellfire if the North Korean tank continued its rapid advance.

Los Angeles

Chung Hee Moon only had to go a short distance to find Kang Ji Yeong and her son, who were both crouched beside a dumpster in the alley outside the apartment building. Chung silently approved; they had been out of sight when the survivors of the gang that had kidnapped them made their exit.

"I am going to take you there before I go," Chung said, pointing at the supermarket down the street. "You will be safe there until the police come to question you."

"And where will you go?," Kang asked quietly.

"To Mexico, at least for now. Maybe later I can come back," Chung said.

Kang then said something in a language Chung didn't understand, but sounded like Spanish.

"What did you say?" Chung asked, puzzled.

"I asked, how do you think you're going to survive in Mexico without being able to speak Spanish?" Kang asked, this time in English.

Chung's answer sounded weak, even to him. "I'll just have to make do. Also, I didn't know you speak Spanish," he said, trying to change the subject.

"Idiot!", Kang said, eyes blazing. "I'm a nurse at a hospital in L.A. How could I not know Spanish? We're coming with you."

Chung shook his head. "Too dangerous. Besides, I can't ask you to leave all your belongings behind."

Kang just looked more stubborn. "You're not asking. I'm telling. I don't want to be here when those goons come back. And you know someday they will come back."

Chung honestly hadn't thought of that. He could see that they very well might, to claim some sort of vengeance.

"Also, you've seen what I have in that apartment. There isn't much there worth keeping."

Chung remained silent, thinking to himself that after the pitched battle with Kang's apartment at its epicenter, she was more right than she knew. Not to mention he wasn't sure how much radioactive contamination there might be after they had opened the case of the nuclear device.

"Bottom line - I'd rather take our chances with the man who just saved our lives, and risked his own to do it."

Chung thought briefly about pointing out that it was because of him their lives were risked in the first place, but quickly decided against it.

He was sure it would come up later.

Aloud he said, "I agree with everything you've said. What will we do in Mexico?"

Kang laughed. "Mexican hospitals are happy to have experienced nurses with an American degree who speak Spanish. I've got a couple of friends we can stay with to start out who've already made the move, and I'm sure you'll figure out something while you're learning Spanish. I parked my car a block over."

Without looking behind her, Kang took her son's hand and started walking.

Chung wasted no time in walking beside her, and taking her other hand.

Kang nodded with satisfaction, and said, "Now you're starting to show some sense."

CHAPTER ONE HUNDRED
THIRTY EIGHT

Subway Line No. 7, South Korea

Lee Ho Suk started to slowly open his eyes and then immediately closed them again as thick clouds of dust made them burn like fire. After years in the tunnels Lee knew all about dust, and recognized this variety as more than ordinary powdered dirt. Though he had no way to know it the dust also included the chemicals used to make up the just-detonated explosives, and gunpowder residue from the rounds fired by Colonel Yoon's men to kill the South Korean subway construction workers who had the bad luck to be present when they made their dramatic entrance.

After a few minutes Lee tried again, and this time it wasn't so bad as long he just barely opened his eyes. He could feel fresh air reaching them from somewhere, and guessed correctly that this was thanks to equipment installed by the South Koreans. Though Lee could see many of the tunnel lights were shattered, there were enough still working to let him observe the scene around him.

Lee focused first on Colonel Yoon, who was shouting at an obviously unhappy soldier Lee had never spoken to with the uniform badges of a Lieutenant, but who Lee had heard whispered was the detachment's Political Officer.

"Lieutenant, I know all about the orders saying we were to kill anyone who was not a member of this unit once we reached this subway tunnel. I wrote those orders! But this man can help us see whether we need to move further into the tunnel immediately because this section is going to collapse. I want to check the subway car we are using first to be sure it is un-damaged before we get underway, but we may not have that time. Success of the mission is the first priority, and supersedes any other aspect of our orders. Do you understand that, Lieutenant?," Yoon asked, with a scowl that made it clear there was only one right answer.

The lieutenant looked even less happy, though Lee would have guessed that was impossible. He then stiffened to attention and barked, "Yes, sir!"

"Very good, Lieutenant. Now supervise the men checking over the subway car while I make sure the device is undamaged. We need to get moving before the enemy has time to react," Yoon said.

The Lieutenant saluted and hurried towards the soldiers who Lee could now see were looking at the underside of the subway car.

Lee slowly moved his head to the side, and could see that no one ap-peared to be watching in the direction of the tunnel that extended out of sight towards. ..freedom?

No sooner had the thought formed than Colonel Yoon was standing in front of him.

"So, Lee, I see you are still with us. Ready to shake off some of that dust?"

Lee grasped Yoon's outstretched hand, and only when he was standing noticed the soldier who had been standing in the shadows behind his head.

"Yes," Yoon smiled without warmth, as he followed Lee's gaze. "It's a good thing you didn't make a run for it. Not when there's still work to do."

"You need to check this section of the tunnel, both here and at what-ever distance you think might have been affected by the explosives. Before I move this subway car I have to be sure it won't collapse on top of us. Do this, and I promise you won't be shot when it's time for all of us to go."

Looking at Lee's expression, Yoon could not help laughing.

"Let me rephrase. You will not be shot, stabbed, strangled, or touched in any way by me or my men, on my honor as an officer."

Strangely, Lee believed him. He also knew that whatever Yoon said, there was no way he expected Lee to leave the tunnel alive.

He knew better than to say any of that, though.

"Yes, sir. Whatever I can do to help," Lee said.

"Good man," Yoon said with an approving nod. "These two men will assist you."

A second soldier emerged even more deeply hidden in the shadows than the first. Lee groaned inwardly as fantasies of wresting away the first soldier's gun and bolting down the tunnel died stillborn.

Yoon smiled as though he had read Lee's thoughts. Maybe he could, Lee thought bitterly.

"Once you have completed your inspection, report back to me. Take no more than one hour." Before Lee could say anything, Yoon grimaced and bent down over the body of one of the South Korean workers. In a moment, he tossed a watch to Lee. It was still wet with the man's blood.

Lee had seen blood before. He wiped it off on his pants, and put it on his arm.

Yoon grinned and nodded. "One hour. No more."

CHAPTER ONE HUNDRED THIRTY NINE

Camp Mobile, South Korea

Captain Hong Sang Ook had never been busier, or more satisfied, in his entire life. The enemy was defenseless before him, and all he had to do was make the most effective use of his remaining ammunition. Then, rejoin another advanced unit for resupply.

Hong then remembered one of their last briefings.

"Sergeant Cha! Keep an eye out for AT-4s!"

"Yes, sir!" followed in a tone that told Hong the sergeant had remembered the briefing well before he did. Called the M-136 by the Americans and the AT-4 by the Swedes who had developed it and the dozens of other countries that used it, it was a man-portable antitank weapon that posed only a limited threat to the M-2002 tank. That threat, though, did include knocking off one of their treads, which would not be ideal in the middle of an enemy installation.

Sure enough, no sooner had Hong warned Cha than he heard him announce "AT-4 Front," followed immediately by the rattle of his 7.62 mm PKT machine gun.

A few seconds later Cha said, "I don't know if I got him, but nothing's aimed at us anymore."

Hong grunted. Cha was right - they hadn't come this far to kill a few infantrymen.

Most of the rounds they carried for the 125 mm 2A26/46 smoothbore main gun were antitank, and designed to penetrate armor. Against buildings, they caused damage but usually left the structure standing.

Their smaller number of high explosive shells were far more effective.

Hong watched the second HE shell hit the closest building, and knew from the multiple secondary explosions that it had contained either fuel or military equipment, or both. In a matter of seconds the building was engulfed in flames.

As he ordered another HE shell loaded, Hong did a quick calculation of the number remaining against the structures he could see. They might have just enough...

An explosion rocked the front of the M-2002, knocking Hong out of his commander's chair and drawing a sharp curse from Cha.

The Pokpung-ho lurched forward as the driver, without waiting for orders, decided it was best not to stay where they were.

Hong agreed entirely.

CHAPTER ONE HUNDRED FORTY

Seoul, South Korea

News of the North Korean invasion had closed the subway a few hours early, except for possible use as an emergency underground shelter. Now, though, it was late enough that the system was closed to the commuting public anyway, and there were only the usual two men on duty in the Seoul Metropolitan Subway system headquarters office. It was a shift that often fell to whoever had most recently displeased their superiors, and ordinarily little of importance took place.

In theory, both were supposed to monitor the screens that covered most of one of the walls with views of the 21 different lines that made up the system. In practice, unless an alarm sounded indicating that one of the closed stations had actually been broken into neither man would pay any attention to them. Since there was nothing to steal in any of the stations, neither had ever heard of a break in.

A temporary camera system had been set up to monitor work northward on Line Number 7, but it was operated by the construction company. One screen provided the feed from that setup, placed all the way to the right in the only open space left. Because the contract provided a bonus for on time completion and another bonus for early completion, work continued at a lower staffing level even when the subway system was closed. Sim had heard that today's crew was boxing equipment and preparing to shut down the work site because of the invasion.

Neither man was looking when the feed cut off, although it had been the only screen at that point showing activity of any kind, and neither had noticed before the phone rang.

The supervisor answered, "Seoul Metro Operations Center, Sim speaking."

"Sim, this is Yon speaking. You know my company?"

Sim groaned inwardly. He knew Yon was president of the company building the extension of Line No. 7. His eyes moved automatically towards the screen showing construction, and widened as he saw it was dark.

"Yes, sir," he said carefully.

"So, then, you know why I'm calling," Yon said.

"Yes, sir. You have lost the camera feed to the construction site," Sim said.

"Yes. So, what are you doing about it?"

If Sim had been a genius, he wouldn't have ended up in this deserted office at 3AM. But he had made it to supervisor, so he wasn't an idiot either.

"Sir, I was just about to request that some of our security staff check in with your crew, to see if they need assistance."

There was a long pause. "Just about to, eh?"

Sim winced.

"All right. I can't see anything else to do at this hour. Get back to me once they report to you."

"Yes, sir," Sim said, breaking the connection and immediately keying in the extension for security. He knew they only had a few people working at this hour, and that none would be thrilled to made the long trek to an underground construction site. But, Sim saw no way around it.

He didn't envy the poor bastard who got the job.

CHAPTER ONE HUNDRED FORTY ONE

Subway Line No. 7, South Korea

Lee Ho Suk swept the flashlight he had found in one of the South Korean's tool chests back and forth over the tunnel walls and ceiling. Though a string of temporary lights had been attached to one of the walls, the explosion had cut whatever powered them. It made even a cursory check of the tunnel's stability slow going, and for reasons Lee could not explain he actually cared whether the tunnel would collapse as the North Korean subway car passed through it. Maybe it was the human desire to put off death until the last possible instant. Or maybe, he thought wryly, he was just curious to see what Yoon thought was worth all this effort. Lee shook his head as he asked himself what difference Yoon's handful of men could possibly make against the entire Southern enemy.

One of the guard's, though, misinterpreted Lee's shaking head.

"Problem?" he asked in a hissed whisper.

Lee wanted to ask who he thought could possibly hear him. Instead he said the truth in a low voice. "I'm not worried about anything I've seen. I'm worried about the many things I could have missed with just one flashlight. And now we've run out of time. We have to return now if we're to get back within an hour."

The guard just grunted and gestured with his rifle for Lee to turn around. Apparently he'd missed Lee's veiled criticism of the guards' unwillingness to pick up flashlights and help. More likely the guards both knew that Lee would have taken advantage of any distraction to attempt escape.

Lee trudged back towards Yoon and the subway car at a pace that would get them back within the hour almost exactly. The two guards fell in behind him being careful to stay just out of reach, as they had the entire time. Lee's mind raced as he tried to think of some way out, but nothing came as he looked down at one foot moving in front of the other.

Camp Mobile, South Korea

What made no sense to Captain Hong Sang Ook was that the missile that blew off their reactive armor came out of nowhere. Cha swore he hadn't missed an infantryman with an AT-4, and Hong believed him. There were no tanks or APCs in sight. That left...something he couldn't see...

"Cha! Get up on the turret and sweep the skies with the Igla! The Americans may be hitting us with one of their armed drones!"

Cha said nothing, just scrambling up the crew ladder to the turret with a speed that made it clear he thought Hong could be on to something.

The Igla, or SA-16 Gimlet as it was called by NATO, had been replaced in Russia by the SA-25 Verba. The Igla wasn't much of a threat to a fast moving combat jet, but a drone would be an easy mark. While it was probably flying out of eyesight, the Igla's infrared sensors had an excellent chance of spotting it.

Just a few minutes after Cha had climbed up to the turret, Hong was rewarded with Cha's exultant "Found it!", followed by a growling tone that announced the Igla's lock onto the drone as a target.

The tank rocked slightly as the backblast from the Igla's launch washed over the back of the M-2002. "Look at it go!" Cha exclaimed. "That's one American devil machine that won't be bothering us anymore!"

Hong would never admit to anyone, least of all the members of his crew, that he was deeply superstitious. In particular, he never did what in the West they would call "counting chickens before they hatched."

Still, he had faith in Cha, and in the equipment they had from the Russians. After all, the Russians had beaten the Nazis, and who came tougher than that?

CHAPTER ONE HUNDRED FORTY TWO

Camp Mobile, South Korea

At first Sgt. Josh Pettigrew had been delighted with his success in his first combat use of a drone. After launching hundreds of autonomous drones designed to jam and confuse North Korean air defenses, as well as dozens of combat drones operated by others from as far away as the U.S., it was more than satisfying to finally land a blow on the enemy. Even better, an enemy that was doing his best to kill him.

Until the smoke from the hit cleared and Pettigrew could see that the Pokpung-ho tank was still moving. In fact, moving really fast. Right at his building.

Pettigrew's training in operating a combat drone had focused on launching it, since most were flown by pilots when actually used in attack. One reason for this was that pilots did not need to be taught the importance of follow through when attacking. That meant planning an attack so that if the first hit did not destroy the target, a second attack could quickly mop up.

Without training in actually using a combat drone to attack a target, Pettigrew had made a rookie mistake. After firing the Hellfire, he had focused the drone's sensors on the target and followed the missile in, though at a much slower speed. By the time the smoke cleared, though, he had overflown the M-2002.

Combat drones, or drones of any type, are not designed to turn on a dime. Pettigrew also quickly discovered that turning a drone 180 degrees with a 45 kilogram Hellfire on one wing and nothing on the other while still keeping balanced control meant moving....slowly.

Finally, Pettigrew had the Predator lined up to launch the second Hellfire missile. As he pressed the fire button, he noticed that someone appeared to be on the M-2002 tank, and seemed to be pointing something straight at the drone. He just had time to wonder what it was, when the screen suddenly went dark.

Osan Air Force Base, South Korea

First Lieutenant Dave Fitzpatrick and Lieutenant Herb Dremer stood next to their F-16s as crews swarmed over them to arm and fuel them for their next mission. Both were being loaded with AGM-65 Maverick missiles, which gave them the ability to target North Korean tanks well out of the range of most of their mobile antiaircraft defenses. Most...

"Still no word on Chuck?'" Dremer asked. Fitzpatrick shook his head. "No, and we're not likely to get any soon. Even if he ejected and survived, it'll take time to get him back to us. I hope he made it too, but we have to stay focused on the mission."

Dremer nodded. "I can't believe how many tanks they've got. From altitude they look like a swarm of ants. We squish some every time we go up, but how are we going to keep some of them from getting to Seoul?".

Fitzpatrick had already had the same thought, but he certainly wasn't going to say so to Dremer, who clearly needed some encouragement. "Remember that we're only part of this fight. The South Koreans are throwing everything they've got at this."

Dremer cocked his head and looked intently at Fitzpatrick. "I know. As soon as we clear the target area, KF-16s are on their way in. Each time we hit them, though, they're further south."

Fitzpatrick nodded. The KF-16s were Block 52 F-16 fighters built by Korean Aerospace Industries in the 1990s under license from Lockheed Martin. Upgraded to the F-16V standard starting in 2015, they were nearly as good as the F-16s the Americans flew.

"Nobody expects the tanks to be stopped by air power alone. We're just thinning them out so that by the time we and the South Koreans hit them with our own tanks, we'll finish them off."

Dremer shrugged. "I hope you're right. Too bad we can't hope they'll run out of gas before they get to Seoul. I can look at a map like anyone else, but I still have trouble wrapping my head around how close Seoul is to the DMZ."

Fitzpatrick pulled on his flight helmet as he saw the crew chief give him the thumbs up for ready aircraft, and gestured for Dremer to do the same. In a few seconds, they were both trotting towards their fighters.

"Remember that closeness cuts both ways. In a distance that short there's no place to hide, and no way to bob and weave. And we're going to make sure they know they've been in a fight every step of the way."

Dremer slung his foot onto the first rung of the ladder, and then turned and gave Fitzpatrick his own thumbs up. "Roger that, sir."

Minutes later they were approaching their targets. As they were arming their Mavericks both Dremer and Fitzpatrick heard their radios crackle to life. "Zulu flight, Zulu flight, break off your attack, acknowledge."

Though they were surprised, they were also well trained. In a maneuver they had practiced in a dozen exercises, they both smoothly banked to the left in a direction that would return them to base.

"Zulu flight, say weapons state."

Both reported that they had not fired their Mavericks.

"New way points are being uploaded, as well as your new target. Be advised that this target is approximately 80 feet below the surface, and within Republic of Korea. Command is aware that you are carrying Mavericks, not designed for such a target. Flight with appropriate ordinance will follow. Your discretion as to best approach."

Both Dremer and Fitzpatrick acknowledged. In a few minutes both had made the course correction needed to follow the new way points, and were flying in formation to the new target.

Dremer radioed Fitzpatrick first. "So, how should we do this?"

Fitzpatrick's voice in response was thoughtful. "We both know that if we do this as a normal standoff attack whatever's eighty feet down will barely notice."

Dremer's head nodded inside his helmet, even though he knew Fitzpatrick couldn't see him. "Agreed. So, how can we get their attention?"

Fitzpatrick's voice was still thoughtful. "We need more energy directed to the target. We can boost the Maverick's velocity and increase its penetration if we're flying straight down at the objective."

Dremer's voice captured his doubt of that plan quite well, he thought. "That will mean we have to climb to an altitude high enough that we can be targeted by everything between here and Pyongyang, and break out from the dive late enough that we'll be pulling enough Gs to make us black out."

Now Fitzpatrick's voice sounded amused. "Don't forget that the airframe could fail. I'm pretty sure yours is older than you are."

Dremer laughed. "I'm pretty sure you're right. So, who goes first?"

CHAPTER ONE HUNDRED FORTY THREE

Camp Mobile, South Korea

Captain Hong Sang Ook could barely hear the "whoomp" of the drone's explosion over Sergeant Cha's cheer. Hong had no sooner thought he'd been wrong to doubt Cha's confidence than Hong heard a sound like the end of the world, and everything went black.

En Route to Attack Subway Tunnel No. 7, South Korea

"Say ready, wingman." A quiet voice in the back of Lieutenant Herb Dremer's mind wanted to respond, "Nope, this plan is crazy!"

Instead he heard a voice that sounded remarkably like his respond to his commander, "Ready, sir."

First Lieutenant Dave Fitzpatrick's F-16 accelerated smoothly as it gained altitude, up to and passing the ceiling for normal combat operations, followed at a much greater than usual distance by Dremer's Falcon. The reason for staying low was immediately driven home by lights and buzzers warning them that they were being detected by North Korean long range missile batteries.

Both Fitzpatrick and Dremer had the same thought simultaneously. North Korean missiles were the least of their worries.

Having passed the combat ceiling, both pilots lit their afterburners to minimize their time exposed to missile fire as they gained altitude. If this attack worked as planned, they would both be on the deck before a missile could lock on and reach them.

Fitzpatrick wasted no time after reaching attack altitude. With a terse "targeting objective" Fitzpatrick's F-16 dipped its nose at a ridiculously acute angle and dove nearly straight down.

One Maverick after another lept from the Falcon's wings, aimed at the target about 20 seconds apart. Fitzpatrick's theory was that each Maverick's explosion would act as a drill, tossing up earth and rock and allowing the next one to do the same another five to ten feet lower. To have any chance of working, each impact had to be focused straight down. That meant beginning to pull out only after firing his last Maverick.

Fitzpatrick immediately thought this time he'd been too smart for his own good. As he fired his last Maverick and pulled back on the stick, he knew it would be close. The Falcon's trajectory remained stubbornly earthward, but Fitzpatrick resisted panic. Flaps, vary thrust, attitude...Fitzpatrick had plenty of time in F-16s, and he knew this one well.

The ground rushed up to meet him, but Fitzpatrick still believed in his plane. And in fact, it didn't let him down. As Dremer watched with horrified fascination, Fitzpatrick's Falcon pulled out from its dive at an angle that appeared to defy physics.

Gouts of earth from the target rose with each Maverick impact. Of course, there was no way to know how deep each had gone.

Fitzpatrick's voice was deep and rasping, but still amazingly calm, Dremer thought.

"Recommend you fire each Maverick as soon as possible rather than leaving an interval. Initial attack plan left insufficient time for egress."

Well, yes, Dremer thought to himself. Aloud, he said "Acknowledged," and began his attack run.

Dremer was certain he would have time to pull out once he'd fired his last Maverick. And he should have.

Unfortunately, once he pulled back on the stick, nothing happened. He tried the same inputs Fitzpatrick had, and then something did happen. Multiple red warning lights appeared.

It's not fair, Dremer thought furiously. I did everything right!

And it was true. He had.

The fault was actually with a maintenance technician who had failed to perform a check that would have detected a faulty component. He could have swapped it out in about ten minutes. When he worked on Dremer's plane, he had slept three hours out of the previous 48.

Dremer would never know this.

Ironically, it was only his death that allowed their mission to be even partly successful. The plane's frozen controls sent it straight to where the Mavericks had been pointed. The mass of the F-16 and its hundreds of pounds of jet fuel combined with an explosive force greater than all the Mavericks they had fired.

Even so, ordinarily the subway tunnel terminus that they had unknowingly been ordered to target would have been unaffected by their attack. If the tunnel had its normal concrete reinforcing shell. Of course, the South Korean construction crew had not even begun that phase of construction before they were killed.

If their ghosts were present in the tunnel, they would surely have smiled.

CHAPTER ONE HUNDRED FORTY FOUR

Camp Mobile, South Korea

"Nice shooting, sir! I'm amazed we made it through this with only two soldiers wounded." Corporal Martz stood next to the smoking hulk of the M-2002 tank, which laid on its side with a large hole in its armor. Sgt. Pettigrew was looking in the other direction, at one of the buildings the Pokpung-ho had destroyed before it was stopped.

"From what I can see, it looks like we've lost our reserve fuel stores and some of the ammo we use for the combat drones. Am I missing anything?"

Martz shook his head. "No, I think that's it. We should ask HQ for replacement supplies, but we can keep up operations without any problems for at least the next two days. Assuming we don't get any more visitors."

Pettigrew nodded. "I really hope this is as far as they get."

Subway Line No. 7, South Korea

Lee Ho Suk's head snapped upward as though pulled by a string. What was that vibration? He had never felt anything like it. Again, and a little stronger. And again! What was happening?

Lee looked around, but no one else seemed to have noticed. And indeed, the vibrations seemed to have stopped.

But no, they're back, and even stronger! Now even Colonel Yoon had noticed, Lee saw. Yoon was standing next to the open door of the subway car, looking at the blinking electronic display in the front of. ..whatever it was...that occupied nearly half of the available space. Yoon gestured for Lee to come towards him.

"What is this?," Yoon scowled, gesturing towards the ceiling, from which clumps of earth were beginning to fall.

Lee opened his mouth to answer, but was unable to say the words "I have no idea."

Because he was jerked forward, and everything went black.

Lee slowly opened his eyes, hoping that he wouldn't be buried in earth. Not only wasn't he buried, he was lying on the floor of the subway car without a bit of dirt visible. But his head! He'd hit it many times before, but never like this!

As Lee slowly drew himself to a sitting position, he heard Yoon's voice behind him.

"Ah, I see you are still with us. You have me both to thank and to blame. To thank because you weren't buried like my men out there. To blame because when I pulled you inside I hit your head on the door's edge. On balance, though, I'm sure you're fine with the outcome."

Lee nodded. His head still hurt, but the pain was already starting to subside.

"I do thank you," Lee said, meaning every word. He could see outside the subway car window, and was glad indeed not to be part of the carnage he saw.

Lee added as carefully as he could, "How many of us survived the accident?"

Yoon grinned sardonically. "Don't you mean 'How many guards are left?' It's just you and me. And I don't think this was an accident. Do you?" Yoon asked, clearly curious to see what Lee thought.

Lee looked more carefully outside the window. Much of the ceiling had fallen in this section, but only the end of the tunnel where the break-through had happened was completely buried. Yoon had promised the men trapped on the other side that they could follow once he and his men moved forward. Now it looked like their only hope would be rescue from the North Korean side.

Yoon's men had managed to use jacks, pry bars and brute force to place the subway car on the South Korean tracks while Lee and his guards had been exploring the way ahead. They had also cleared the tracks about a hundred meters ahead of the breakthrough from the earth and debris thrown by the explosion, and the car had inched forward as they did.

The more Lee looked, the more he thought Yoon was right. Earth and rock had been dislodged from the ceiling, but the walls were intact. In fact, Lee saw that many of Yoon's men weren't actually buried, but had been killed by rocks that had fallen from the ceiling.

He was so puzzled, Lee's thoughts came out of his mouth without conscious thought. "It's like someone was hammering the ceiling from the other side."

Yoon laughed, and nodded thoughtfully. "Yes, just so. I'm afraid the Southern devils, or more likely the cursed Americans, have figured out we're here. Those bombs were their way of letting us know we're not welcome. I think we can expect company sooner rather than later."

"Bombs," Lee repeated numbly. So "company" meant enemy soldiers.

Peering through the front window Lee saw there wasn't too much dirt on the tracks. Yoon followed his gaze approvingly. "Yes, if we hurry up and clear these tracks maybe we can move out before the enemy gets here."

Lee got up slowly, expecting the motion to start the throbbing in his head again. He wasn't disappointed. But, after he stood still for a moment, the pain and dizziness began to recede.

"Good man," Yoon said, gesturing for Lee to exit. "I'll be right behind you. Two things to keep in mind. The people who just tried to kill you with bombs are up that tunnel and won't hesitate to try again with bullets. You've got a much better chance of surviving inside this steel subway car than stumbling through a foreign tunnel."

Then Yoon's expression blanked, and his voice softened. "You should also know," he said, patting his holster, "that I'm a really good shot."

CHAPTER ONE HUNDRED
FORTY FIVE

Seoul, South Korea

Gwak Seung Hyun didn't plan to be working as a security guard long for the Seoul Metropolitan Subway system. He had taken the exam for the Seoul Metropolitan Police Agency (SMPA) as soon as turned 21, and come close to passing. Gwak was hoping that the time he was putting in as a security guard would help him stand out among the other new recruits once he did pass. Of course, that would only be true if he had an outstanding record as a security guard.

Much to the annoyance of many of the other guards, this meant that Gwak had a gung ho, can do attitude each and every day. Gwak always volunteered for extra shifts, and when the call came to check out the construction crew going silent at the end of Line No. 7 his hand went up immediately. Nobody else was interested, and for that matter no one believed it was worth worrying about.

North Korean tanks headed towards Seoul? That was a big deal, and all most people were thinking about was heading south with their families while they still could. Everyone had to wait, though, for the military and police to organize the evacuation, which was to get underway the next day with transportation and security provided.

Gwak studied the system map, but it was really unnecessary. He had it practically memorized. The closest access point to the construction crew was an emergency access and exit hatch, accessible only by authorized system employees. It would still be a hike to get to the crew, but Gwak was in excellent physical condition, since that was also a requirement to get into the SMPA. In fact, Gwak's unusually trim and athletic build had attracted the favorable attention of some of his female colleagues, but he regarded any relationship at this point as an unwelcome distraction.

He spent much of the limited free time he had left after volunteering for extra shifts at the shooting range. Security guards were some of the few people in Korea authorized to have firearms, and this was one of the main reasons he had joined. Gwak was now highly proficient with the Daewoo K5 9mm pistol. Produced by Daewoo starting in 1989, it had been used by the South Korean police and military since 1989. Compact and lightweight, it held fifteen rounds in its magazine, and had a good reputation for accuracy.

Gwak had never heard of a security guard actually using his weapon, and in the short time he planned to remain a guard certainly did not expect to be the first.

Subway Line No. 7, South Korea

"Slow down for a second," Lee Ho Suk said quietly. "I think I see movement ahead of us."

Colonel Yoon grimaced. "We haven't even gone a kilometer yet. Maybe we should speed up and take our chances."

Lee shrugged. "Of course, the choice is yours. However, our chances of success may be better if we wait to see what is ahead. It might be a minor obstacle, easily and quickly cleared. We can always speed up later once we know for sure."

Yoon stared at Lee for a second, and then let out a bark of laughter that made Lee jump.

"Lost bet, cautious to the end! And why not, it's kept you alive this long. Fine, I'll slow it down until we can get a better look. Tell me as soon as you know what's ahead."

Gwak Seung Hyun had climbed down to Tunnel No. 7 through the access hatch and a bare metal ladder, neither of which looked like they had ever been used. He was well past the last station, and estimated he had well over a kilometer to walk before reaching the construction crew. This was the part of the tunnel that had been extended by the crew, and it had no lights. He pulled out his flashlight to help him make his way through the pitch darkness.

Gwak had trouble believing his eyes when two lights began moving toward him from the direction where he had been told the construction crew was working. It was certainly not a standard subway car's lights. After almost a year working in the subway system, he knew exactly what those looked like. These were both fainter and pushed closer together.

He almost reached for the radio on his belt, but stopped the motion before his hand reached it. At the rate the car was moving, it would reach him before he could make the call. Time enough once he knew what was going on. Maybe the construction company had a special car they used to move their crew and equipment that nobody had bothered to tell him about? He turned on his flashlight's highest setting, and started to wave it at the oncoming car.

Lee Ho Suk's eyes widened as his excellent eyesight made sense of the motion ahead. It was a man waving a flashlight. Before he could say anything, he could feel the subway car slowing, and then stopping. Evidently Colonel Yoon had seen him too.

"Do you see how many there are?" Yoon asked, in a near whisper.

"I can only see one," Lee said, truthfully.

"Very well," Yoon said, and his hand reached for the throttle.

"Not a good idea," Lee said. "His body might get caught under the rails. We might even be derailed."

At first Yoon looked annoyed, but finally he nodded sharply. He then shut off all the lights both inside and outside the car, and quickly cracked open the car doors just wide enough to allow him to exit.

In the sudden darkness, all Lee could see was that the man was no longer waving the flashlight.

A moment later, three flashes of light were followed by the sound of Yoon's pistol discharging, and with each flash Lee could see Yoon kneeling and taking careful aim by the side of the train.

The man dropped immediately, and his flashlight fell onto the tracks. Once again, the tunnel was pitch black.

Yoon reentered the car, and sat back down in the driver's seat. "Keep an eye out for any other obstructions," he growled. "I'm going to go slowly for the next hundred meters. If that man's body is on the tracks, I'll need you to clear them."

Lee suppressed a shiver and nodded. That's all the man he'd just killed was to him, an obstruction.

Lee had absolutely no doubt about what was waiting for him the instant he was no longer useful to Yoon.

CHAPTER ONE HUNDRED FORTY SIX

Subway Line No. 7, South Korea

Gwak wasn't dead, but he had been shot. It was only a flesh wound in his lower leg, and it didn't hurt much yet.

He had never experienced the incandescent rage that possessed him right now, as he laid on the side of the tunnel. It made him almost light headed, but after a moment he was able to regain his self control.

Gwak knew just one thing. That car was going no further down the track if he had anything to say about it.

He could see its lights come on again, and pressed himself even more firmly against the wall of the tunnel. It was moving slowly, but soon he could see inside the car.

There were two men, one pressed against the front window, and another in the driver's seat. The man at the window was the skinniest person Gwak had ever seen. Gwak had trouble getting a good look at the driver, but his bearing and haircut immediately said "military."

Why would the military be shooting at him?

Gwak shook his head. Why didn't matter. Stopping these lunatics did.

He had never thought about it, but now realized that his black security guard uniform served as almost perfect camouflage. He was sure, though, that it wouldn't be good enough to stop them from spotting him before he got into pistol range. Maybe he could at least take out the skinny man at the window before they finished him off, he thought bitterly.

Sure enough, he could see the skinny man's eyes widen as he saw him at the tunnel's edge. Just as he was taking aim, though, he saw the man shake his head and say something to the other man. The car kept moving.

As it moved beside him, Gwak jumped up and immediately saw the driver, and the pistol lying beside him. Without conscious thought Gwak fired the entire fifteen clip magazine through the window.

The car kept moving. Gwak was sure at least some of his rounds had hit, but could see the man was still moving.

In fact the flesh wound in his leg had not been very serious, but it had been bleeding freely. Before he could reach his radio, consciousness fled and his limp body fell to the floor of the tunnel.

"Lee, come here," Yoon rasped, his voice steady but unable to completely disguise his pain.

Lee quickly came to Yoon's side, seeing that he was bleeding from at least one wound. He was clutching his pistol in his right hand.

"Help me up," Yoon said thickly. Lee put his arms around his chest, and with some difficulty was able to help Yoon stand. Once he was standing, Lee could see he had at least two more wounds, and all were bleeding.

"You should let me bandage your wounds," Lee said, not out of any real concern for Yoon, but because he knew Yoon expected him to say it.

From his smile Yoon understood why Lee had made the offer, but shook his head.

"No," he said, "It's too late for that now. Help me over to that side of the case," Yoon said, pointing at the metal object that filled more than half of the car.

Lee did as he was told, and in a few moments both were leaning against the metal side of the case.

"Now, help me remove the top panel," Yoon said. Now that he was against it, Lee could see that there was indeed a metal panel set flush against the top of the case.

It came off easily, and revealed a series of lights glowing green, and a digital screen with a row of seven red numbers all reading zero.

Yoon's eyes were beginning to look glassy, but Lee could see that his grip on the pistol was still firm.

"Reach into my right pocket for a key. Be careful," Yoon said, gesturing with his pistol.

Lee reached carefully into Yoon's pocket. Yoon gripped the metal case with both hands, and looked unnaturally pale. Lee pulled out the key, and placed it carefully on the case in front of Yoon.

Yoon's left hand stretched forward, and clumsily started to insert the key into a matching keyhole near the digital display. After his first attempt failed, Yoon cursed and picked up the key again, moving it more carefully towards the keyhole.

Yoon and Lee both heard the sound outside the car at the same moment, but neither was sure what it was. It sounded like a voice, but there was also a crackle that made it hard to be certain.

CHAPTER ONE HUNDRED FORTY SEVEN

Subway Line No. 7, South Korea

The blood flow from Gwak's wound had slowed and then stopped once he fell down, and his uniform's fabric pressed against it and gave it a chance to congeal. Lying prone had also helped to improve blood flow to his head, so that combined with his excellent physical condition Gwak regained consciousness remarkably quickly.

The first thing Gwak noticed was that the subway car had only moved a short distance down the tracks. The second was that he had no clip to reload his pistol. Gwak doubted that any security guard in the entire country bothered to carry one. How likely was it that a guard would fire his gun, let alone empty the entire magazine?

As his eyes regained focus, Gwak realized his top priority had to be to call for help. While an ordinary radio handset would have no chance of reaching outside the tunnel, there were signal repeaters in the Seoul Metro tunnels specifically designed to let subway workers and guards communicate with headquarters. Gwak's problem was that he was still in the newly excavated section of Tunnel No. 7, and so some distance from the nearest repeater.

Gwak knew all this. He also knew that he had nothing to lose by trying.

Dropping the key on top of the case, Yoon turned clumsily to Lee and said, "Help me get to the car doors."

Seeing Lee's dubious look, Yoon barked out a short, mirthless laugh. "I'm not quite dead yet, Lee. I have to make sure that man doesn't call for help. We're almost finished with our mission, and we can't allow any interference now."

Lee helped him to the car doors, and then to open them. Yoon squinted into the darkness, and when he thought he saw the man near the tracks took shaky aim.

Lee looked at one of the shovels he had used to clear the tracks lying between him and Yoon. Without conscious thought, he grabbed the shovel and swung it at Yoon. He stumbled as he took the swing, so instead of hitting Yoon in the head he connected with his right leg.

Quickly as a snake, Yoon shifted his aim to Lee, almost as if he had been expecting the attack. However, Lee's stumble threw off his aim as well, so he only grazed Lee's left shoulder.

Yoon would certainly have shrugged off the shovel's impact if he hadn't been seriously wounded. As it was, though, he lost his balance and fell through the open doors of the subway car. As he grit his teeth and pulled himself back up, Yoon roared with frustration as the car doors were slammed in his face.

"Lee!" Yoon screamed as he tried unsuccessfully to open the doors. He guessed correctly that Lee had wedged a tool between the door handles, making them physically impossible to open. Yoon realized immediately that the windows offered the only way in. Since the windows were sealed and locked from the inside, that meant breaking one thoroughly enough that he could squeeze his body through without ripping it to shreds.

And that was a problem. The North Korean order for the subway train had asked that the windows be bulletproof. Though the manufacturer had said that bulletproof windows would be too thick to fit within the existing window frames, they did say the windows would be "bullet resistant." They explained that meant depending on the bullet's caliber, velocity and angle of impact it might bounce off, and at worst would leave only a small hole.

So at best, Yoon's remaining pistol rounds would only leave a few holes in the window. At worst, at this short range they might bounce off and hit him.

Yoon's eyes lit up as he felt the answer to his problem near his feet. The shovel Lee had struck him with had followed him out the door.

After Gwak made his call for help, he lost consciousness again before hearing a reply. He briefly wondered what had roused him, at first hoping that help had arrived. Repetition of the sound that had started him awake quickly made it clear he was not so lucky. About ten meters down the track he could see the man who had shot him swinging a shovel at one of the windows of the subway car.

With each swing he could hear a distinct "crunch", but from his angle couldn't see what impact the shovel was having. The whole scene made no sense. Why was the man outside the subway car? Who was inside keeping him out?

Gwak finally decided that if the man who had shot him wanted to get inside the car, he should do whatever he could to keep him out. Slowly, Gwak began to crawl down the tunnel towards him.

CHAPTER ONE HUNDRED FORTY EIGHT

Subway Line No. 7, South Korea

Lee could see from the look in Yoon's eyes that as soon as he made it inside every round left in his pistol would be fired at him, and it wasn't as though he had any place to hide. To Lee's surprise, though, the window was holding up quite well to Yoon's assault. In part this was certainly due to Yoon's weakened condition, but the glass was also much tougher than Lee would have guessed.

Obviously, Yoon wanted to get back to finish whatever he was going to do with what was inside the metal case. Lee had always suspected it might be a bomb, but couldn't see the point of exploding one inside a tunnel. Was damaging one tunnel inside the South really worth all this effort?

Lee had seen news reports on state TV before his arrest describing their progress with nuclear weapons, but that had been many years ago. Besides, his hazy mental picture of a device capable of producing a gigantic city-killing mushroom cloud was of one far larger than the metal case in front of him.

Frowning, Lee gave up on solving the puzzle. It was enough that Yoon wanted to do...something... with the case. Lee knew in his bones that whatever that something was, it wouldn't be good.

And at the rate the cracks in the window were widening, it would be just a matter of minutes before Yoon made it back inside.

Lee looked around the car, and quickly settled on a pick as the best tool. Yoon screamed curses at Lee as he raised the pick high, but Lee paid no attention as he brought the sharp end down on the top of the case.

The result was anticlimactic, to say the least. The pick's tip skipped off the surface of the case, without causing a bit of damage that Lee could see. Lee looked at the results of his efforts with dismay, while he could hear that Yoon was actually laughing.

Lee lifted the pick to his shoulder again, and regarded the case more carefully. The only part that was any different than the rest was the digital display, so with a shrug Lee took careful aim at it and swung as hard as he could.

Yoon stopped laughing.

Sparks flew from the display, and the part that remained intact immediately went dark. Encouraged by Yoon's renewed curses, Lee swung again at the display, and this time was rewarded by wisps of smoke beginning to rise from its remains.

Lee had thought Yoon was angry before. Now he swung at the window like a man possessed, his injuries seemingly forgotten. Lee took what he expected to be his final swing.

Now small flames danced over the ruins of the display.

At the same moment, Yoon was able to thrust his pistol through a gap he had created in the window with his shovel, and fired twice. One round caught Lee high in the back, throwing him to the ground, where he twitched once and was then still.

Yoon ignored Lee's prostrate form as a problem now solved, and reversed the shovel as he saw a way to solve another. Frowning with concentration, he worked the handle back and forth until he was able to get it to the other side of the car's window, where it was horizontal. Then, he leaned against the shovel's blade and shaft with the full weight of his body, using the handle as a lever against the window.

At first, nothing happened. Then, Yoon saw a hairline crack appear across the entire top half of the window. Next, he rotated the handle until it was vertical, and leaned his back and shoulders against the shovel's blade and shaft. Deeper cracks now appeared on the left hand side of the window. Yoon repeated the process on the window's opposite side, and was finally rewarded with a deep crack that dislodged a piece of the window, which fell onto the car's floor.

With the window's structural integrity now compromised, it only took a few minutes for Yoon to clear away enough of the remaining glass to safely pull himself through. Forgotten, the shovel fell onto the tracks behind him with a loud clang.

After at first making good progress as Gwak crawled down the tunnel towards Yoon, blood loss once again caused him to lose consciousness. A loud clang roused him, and he opened his eyes just in time to see a shovel bounce off the tracks a few meters away.

At the same time, Gwak noticed that the man who had shot him had managed to get back in the subway car, where he was leaning against a metal case. He then bent down, and seemed to be looking for something.

Gwak had resumed crawling while he watched the man, who still clutched a pistol in one hand. As quietly as he could, he picked up the shovel from the tracks.

The man had found what he was looking for, a metal key of some kind with a black fabric cord running through it. He moved the pistol to his left hand, while with his right he leaned forward with his back to Gwak to insert the key into a keyhole set in the metal case.

Awkwardly thrusting the shovel through the window, Gwak swung its blade against Yoon's head. Yoon fell down with a curse, and both his pistol and the key went flying. Blood streaming from the fresh cut in his head, Yoon got back up and lunged towards Gwak.

Yoon was too close for Gwak to hit him again with the blade, but he still had a firm grip and was able to hit his body with the wooden shaft. Purely by chance, he hit one of Yoon's bullet wounds. The pain of the impact sent Yoon to the floor, barely conscious.

As a result, Yoon felt nothing when Gwak hit him again in the head, and everything went black.

CHAPTER ONE HUNDRED FORTY NINE

Seoul, South Korea

Lee opened his eyes slowly, and looked around what was obviously a hospital room. This one, though, was different than the one he had been in after the tunnel collapse that felt like a lifetime ago. The room was full of beeping machines with digital displays, and he had clear plastic tubes attached to his body, carrying liquids of some sort.

Lee was puzzled by the lack of pain. When he woken in the hospital before, it had been there for days, and though it had eased it had never left entirely. Of course, to work in the tunnels meant learning to live with many kinds of pain, above all the dull pain of constant exhaustion.

Now, though, he was entirely comfortable. It was such an odd sensation that it was almost disorienting.

Before he could think about it further, though, he heard the man in the bed next to him move.

"Still with us, then? Glad to see it! Anybody who had the sense to hit that bastard with the pistol is one of the good guys in my book. By the way, my name's Gwak."

Lee slowly nodded. "Mine is Lee. Is the man with the pistol still alive?"

Gwak shook his head. "Nope. They tried really hard to keep him alive, and they did get answers to some of their questions before he died, mostly about you. I like the 'Lost Bet' story. Is it true?"

Before Lee could answer, two nurses entered the room. Both immediately descended on Lee, exclaiming as they saw he was conscious. One began checking displays and examining his bandages, while the other washed and shaved him.

As he felt the razor rasp against his skin, Lee asked "How long was I out?"

The two nurses just giggled, with their hands over their mouths.

Another nurse came in and started to wash and shave Gwak, who laughed. "Yeah, you'd have no idea, would you? You've been unconscious for almost two weeks. The war's over. Your surgery for the bullet wound wasn't too tough, but there were internal injuries from some earlier trauma. Did you really survive more than one tunnel collapse?"

"Enough questions!" the nurse washing Gwak exclaimed, slapping his waist with her washcloth for emphasis.

Gwak winked at Lee and said in a low voice, "I think I'm going to marry this one."

Gwak's nurse blushed and said something too fast for Lee to follow, but it made Gwak laugh and Lee's nurses giggle.

"You see, we're national heroes, Lee. You know what you were taking your pickax to in that tunnel? A nuclear bomb, that's what!"

Lee grunted. "I thought it was probably a bomb of some kind. I'm just glad it didn't go off."

Gwak nodded gravely. "You, my friend, prevented the death of thousands. There were several apartment buildings directly over that tunnel that would have certainly collapsed if that bomb had gone off, and many others that may have been damaged as well. The war caused remarkably few civilian casualties, but if not for you that could have been very different."

Before Lee could protest that Gwak had done at least as much, all three nurses nodded and bowed. The two nurses on either side of Lee bent down and, to his astonishment, each gently kissed him on the cheek.

Gwak winked at Lee and said "Lucky man! I wonder if my nurse will think I'm worth a kiss."

Lee thought Gwak's nurse had blushed before, but now she seemed to turn crimson to the roots of her hair. Then to Lee's amazement the nurse grabbed Gwak's head with both hands and kissed him on the lips. She then slapped him forcefully enough to rock his head in his pillow, and marched out of the room.

"Wow, that settles it! I'm definitely marrying that woman!"

Gwak's pronouncement was met with renewed giggles from Lee's nurses, and even Lee couldn't help laughing.

Gwak then looked at Lee seriously. "The truth is, we all know a lot about you. The man who shot us both had a smartphone on him with many digital files. One of them was on you. All of that file was made public over the past week, and played repeatedly on TV and social media. Everyone agrees, you deserve the nation's gratitude, and I think you're going to see it very soon."

Lee was surprised by the nurses' reaction. They both became very upset, and told Gwak in no uncertain terms to shut up.

Rather than being chastened, Gwak just grinned and shook his head. "Hey, he still has no idea!"

Before Lee could ask what he was talking about, a doctor wearing a white uniform entered the room, walking directly to Lee's bed.

"So, awake at last! You have made a remarkable recovery. Still, I need to examine you, now that I see these young ladies are finished with you. My name, by the way, is Dr. Park."

Giggling, Lee's two nurses quickly left the room.

Frowning, Dr. Park examined the readouts from the equipment hooked up to Lee, poked and prodded him, and asked him question after question which were all versions of the same one - "Are you really sure you're feeling OK?"

The truth was, Lee felt fine. He did wonder how he would feel if the medicine flowing into him through the clear plastic tube stopped.

Park was an experienced doctor, so Lee didn't even have to ask the question.

"You may be wondering how much of your comfort is due to your medication. The truth is I have had the dosage reduced progressively over the past three days, which is why you finally woke up. Like many pain medications, for this one drowsiness is a principle side effect. If you're really comfortable at your current dosage, then I think you're ready to see visitors."

With that, Dr. Park strode out of the room.

Lee's heart sank, though he worked hard to keep it from his expression. If Gwak was right that people thought of them as heroes that was nice, but he really wasn't interested in hearing repeated thanks. There were only three people Lee really wanted to see, but he had known for years he would never see them again.

Seeing Lee's expression as the doctor left, Gwak said "Hey, I wasn't kidding! I think you're going to be impressed at the trouble people are going to for us. After all the death and destruction of the past few weeks, everyone wants something to be happy about. My big dream was to become a policeman in Seoul, but I just missed the passing score on the exam. They announced on national TV that stopping that crazy guy in the tunnel was worth 'extra credit' and that I'd passed after all! I can't tell you what a relief that is to me. And we're both getting houses in Seoul! Real houses! There are millionaires in this city living in apartments, Lee!"

Lee wanted to care about what Gwak was telling him, but all he could manage was a tired nod and a mumbled, "That's good."

His eyes were just beginning to close when there was a tapping at the door. It was Dr. Park again, this time wearing a broad smile.

"Mr. Lee, I am here with some visitors I think you will like to see."

Dr. Park then stepped aside, and ushered in a woman and two teenage boys, all painfully thin.

At first Lee could not believe his eyes, and thought maybe he had fallen asleep. But no, his dream would not have that fool Gwak laughing and clapping his hands and chortling "See, I told you so!"

His wife leaned down and touched his right cheek gently. "I had never dreamed I would see you again." Lee's eyes were filled with tears, and for several moments he could not speak.

Finally, he was able to say "I am so happy to see you and the boys again. Are you all well?"

She nodded and Dr. Park, who had been waiting just outside, said "We have given all of them a thorough examination, and there's nothing wrong with them a few good meals won't cure."

She smiled gently and said, "They have already been feeding us like all the food in the world is ours for the taking! I think I've doubled in size, and they've given us all new clothes!"

Lee nodded, again for a moment unable to speak. His wife was nearly skeletal, and the boys not much better. How thin has they been before they started getting proper food? Lee realized that the improved diet workers on Tunnel No. 1 had received must have been better than the food available to ordinary civilians. The irony was breathtaking, but he forced himself to speak.

"They tell me that I will soon be able to leave this hospital. Then we can all live together again, at last," Lee said, looking at Dr. Park for confirmation.

"Yes, yes, absolutely! I just heard the end of what your friend Gwak was telling you, but it's true. You and he will each receive a home as a personal gift from the President. Citizens nationwide have contributed millions to both of you to reward you for your heroism. Your actions saved thousands of lives, and nearly cost your own. Koreans would never allow such a feat to pass without the recognition it deserves."

Lee's wife and boys were all smiling, but clearly even more confused than Lee himself. "So," Lee said carefully, "I understand we will all be allowed to live here together. But what will we do?"

Dr. Park laughed. "Whatever you like! I expect you'll want your boys to finish school. Dozens of schools and private tutors are clamoring for the honor of educating the children of a national hero. As for you and your wife, men from the government will be here as soon as I allow them to discuss what you and your family will do next. I will hold them off as long as I can. In the meantime, talk with your wife about what you want to do. First, though, you all need food, privacy, and rest. I will do everything I can to make sure you get it."

CHAPTER ONE HUNDRED
FIFTY

Washington, DC

"Mr. President, it's the Chinese Ambassador," the Chief of Staff announced.

"Thanks, Chuck. Please show him in," President Hernandez replied. This would be a one on one session with no note takers.

After being ushered into the Oval Office and the door closed behind him, the Chinese Ambassador was left standing in front of a sitting President Hernandez. After several uncomfortable moments, Hernandez looked up and coldly gestured for the Ambassador to sit.

Hernandez looked at the Ambassador directly. "I will come straight to the point. We hold your government responsible for the attack on our aircraft carrier. Any other aggressive move on our forces will be considered an act of war."

The Ambassador looked uncomfortable, but was clearly prepared for the President's statement. "We regret the attack on your ship, which was carried out without the authorization of my government. It was the action of criminal elements who have been brought to justice."

"Next I will bring to your attention the attack at Dulles Airport, and the attempt to shoot down a Trans Pacific Airlines flight en route to that airport. Both were unacceptable terrorist acts for which we hold your government accountable," the President said.

"We learned of these incidents after they occurred, and discovered they were perpetrated by the same criminal elements that were responsible for the attack on your carrier. Rest assured that none of those responsible will be repeating their actions. We are also prepared to offer restitution for the costs your government has incurred in responding to these attacks. We will leave it up to your government to determine a reasonable amount."

Hernandez was silent for several moments. Then he said, "You could dismiss the attackers at Dulles as criminals, even though one had a sophisticated contact poison that my experts tell me would have required the resources of a government to produce. But the attack on the Trans Pacific flight and the one on our carrier required the use of fighter jets. Do Chinese criminals have access to those?"

Now the Ambassador looked distinctly uncomfortable. "Mr. President, my government is not shirking its responsibility in any of these matters. I will repeat that we can guarantee that all of the criminals involved have been brought to justice, and we stand ready to provide just compensation."

Hernandez allowed the silence that followed to stretch until finally he nodded. "Let us now discuss the matter of Taiwan. The policy of the United States is unchanged with regard to Taiwan, and I understand that there has been no change by the government of China. Is my understanding correct?"

The Ambassador nodded immediately. "Quite correct, Mr. President."

"Good, then that brings us to Korea. As you know, President Pak has announced the reunification of Korea following the death of Marshal Ko and the surrender of the armed forces of the former North Korea. We have recognized the new Republic of Korea, and hope the Chinese government will join us in approving the UN Security Council resolution we will introduce later today calling on all Council members to both recognize the new ROK and to eliminate all sanctions affecting the now defunct North Korean regime."

The Ambassador's lips tightened, but there was no other reaction.

Hernandez continued, "ROK armed forces are currently disarming the remaining troops of the former North Korea, and have so far encountered little resistance. I will now explain the continued role of the United States in this conflict."

Now the Ambassador nodded and leaned forward. Clearly this was what he most wanted to hear.

"U.S. forces will not advance north of the former DMZ. Unarmed U.S. citizens engaged in providing humanitarian aid will not be barred from the territory north of the former DMZ, and for that matter the ROK government will shortly be issuing a call for assistance to all friendly governments. President Pak has authorized me to tell you that one of those to be contacted later today will be the Chinese government. I will add that if your government's response is positive, you will be able to see for yourself that there are no US forces north of the former DMZ."

The Ambassador nodded. "I will immediately convey this news to my government. I believe their response will be positive."

For the first time Hernandez allowed a small smile to show, and the Ambassador visibly relaxed.

"As far as US military bases in the ROK are concerned, I can offer you assurances that we will establish none north of the former DMZ. It is too early to determine whether our existing bases will be reduced in size, but they will certainly not be increased. For now, the focus of US military forces in Korea will be on assisting recovery efforts south of the former DMZ."

The Ambassador nodded again. "This news will be very welcome to my government as well." He hesitated, and then added, "My government's primary goal is stability. I sincerely hope that with this conflict behind us, we can work towards a peace that serves all our interests."

Hernandez nodded and rose. "A worthy goal, Mr. Ambassador."

The Ambassador rose and bowed, correctly taking this as his cue to depart.

As the door closed behind him, Hernandez scratched his chin absently. Would the Chinese see the folly of repeating their intervention in the first Korean War? It looked hopeful, but only because the Chinese were too busy dealing with their "criminal elements" to stop Korean unification on the South's terms. Hopefully he had given them enough reassurance to convince them war wasn't worth it.

Who would have believed just a month ago that North Korea would have disappeared as quickly as East Germany?

The Chief of Staff, Chuck Commons, stuck his head in the door. "Any follow up from the meeting, sir?"

Hernandez nodded. "Yes, Chuck, come in. Reading about the high speed rail line construction going from Nakhon Ratchasima in Thailand to China in the briefing papers for the meeting reminded me that we need to name a new Ambassador to Thailand."

"Yes, sir. We were thinking about an important donor from your last campaign, Tim Grefe," Commons said.

"Let's make it that Martinovsky fellow that helped arrange the two defections. I want someone competent keeping an eye on what the Chinese are up to in Thailand. Tim will just have to wait."

CHAPTER ONE HUNDRED FIFTY ONE

Moscow, Russia

Grishkov and Vasilyev were still exhausted, but at least they were full. They had thought Smyslov's spread of food and drink had been extensive on their last visit to Moscow. This time there had been at least twice as much, in fact so much Grishkov was sure the table was bigger.

Now Smyslov lifted his glass and said, "So, now that you've been fed and congratulated, all that's left is for me to ask whether you know the reward for good work."

Grishkov immediately said, "More work."

Smyslov roared with laughter, and pointed at Vasilyev. "See, I told you I like him!"

Vasilyev smiled and nodded. "But, first we need to get home."

Smyslov cocked one eyebrow. "Home? But my dear friend, you are home. You both are."

Seeing that silence and confusion followed his announcement, Smyslov quickly added, "You didn't imagine your success in averting war with the Americans would be worth only a good meal, did you? You have both been transferred to new jobs in Moscow."

Pointing at Grishkov, he said "Your wife and children and all your belongings are already in your new apartment, just a short walk from your new office. Very convenient!", Smyslov beamed.

Gesturing towards Vasilyev, he added "Your move presented far less of a challenge. I made the call to abandon what you might have charitably called 'furniture'. You will find your clothes in the apartment that my wife selected and furnished. You are welcome to take up any issues directly with her."

Vasilyev's eyebrows flew up. "With Natasha? I am sure I will speak to her only to convey my thanks. She knows me well, and as a lifelong bachelor I guarantee she did better at apartment furnishing than I ever could."

Grishkov coughed, and then said, "I don't want to seem ungrateful, but there are a few loose ends we need to tie up in Vladivostok."

Smyslov nodded. "For example, a certain Lieutenant Anton Fedorov? You were right to suspect him. And he was right to take the precaution of paying a clerk at the cell phone service he used to make the call that led to such trouble for you in Khabarovsk. That protected him from a local police check of phone records. Of course, it didn't protect him from us."

Grishkov was hardly surprised. Like all Russians, he had assumed since childhood that the FSB knew all about every phone call.

"So, is he in custody?" Grishkov asked.

"Sadly, no." Seeing Grishkov's expression, Smyslov once again roared with laughter. "My dear Grishkov, don't be so quick to think the worst! Though I know it's just the Russian in you. No, Federov isn't in custody because he resisted arrest. He made the mistake of reaching for his service weapon when my men identified themselves. They are trained not to take chances," Smyslov said with a shrug.

"And what about the North Korean so-called 'diplomats' that were in Russia. Have they been expelled?", Grishkov asked.

Now Smyslov looked uncomfortable. "That was not handled by the FSB. I can tell you that both the President and the Foreign Minister were furious at the news that a police detective's family had been targeted by the same criminals who had made off with one of our nuclear weapons. Once the North Koreans were conclusively identified as responsible by our interrogation of their agent, the decision was made to expel all of them back to North Korea on a single flight departing from Moscow and stopping in Khabarovsk en route to Pyongyang."

Grishkov frowned. "So, now that the country has been reunified, will they be tried by the Koreans?"

Smyslov shook his head. "No. The flight never reached Pyongyang after leaving Khabarovsk, and its wreckage has not yet been discovered."

Into the silence that followed Smyslov said, "I know what you're thinking, but it's very possible that the crash was due to the poor quality and maintenance of the aircraft. It belonged to the North Korean embassy in Moscow, and was over thirty years old. In any case, there will be no repetition of their crimes."

Grishkov shrugged. "I, for one, think they got exactly what they deserved."

Smyslov clapped his hands and said, "Now that we have settled that, let me get back to your new jobs. You, Grishkov, are now assigned to the Moscow metropolitan police with the rank of captain. You are on indefinite special assignment. Vasilyev, you now have the rank of Assistant Director, and report directly to me. Neither of you will receive official recognition of your achievements in this matter, which our government is even more eager to pretend never happened than the Americans. Each of you are receiving one million cash in U.S. dollars from a special fund administered directly by the President, who has asked me to convey his personal thanks for a job well done."

Smyslov paused. "If it were up to me, you would both be on leave for at least a month. However, as you see your performance in America has attracted notice at the highest level. Another matter has arisen that is believed to fit the skills you displayed in your last mission. I successfully argued that the agents who discovered the problem need to finish preliminary work on identifying those responsible before you two take over. That will take about a week."

Grishkov nodded. "So, I will at least have time to say hello to Arisha and the children. Where are we going?"

Smyslov just smiled and looked at Vasilyev. "Your file says you speak Arabic and Farsi. How much do you remember?"

Made in the USA
Middletown, DE
19 June 2020